TEARS OF CORAL

A QUINT AND DAWSON BOOK

FRANK WILEM

DeepBlue Press
Gulfport, MS
Copyright © 2014 Frank Wilem
First Edition
ISBN # ISBN: 978-1-941369-01-2
Printed in the
United States of America

Cover Design and Interior format by The Killion Group
http://thekilliongroupinc.com

The Keys

Ever considered just getting into your car and heading to parts unknown? Most people have—few actually do. Quint not only considers ditching his cheating wife and dead-end job for a tropical escape, he does it—and heads for the Keys.

After finishing two tours of duty as a Navy SEAL, Quint had longed for an ordinary life away from death and brutality. However, his post-service American dream—a loveless marriage and a mind-numbingly boring job—becomes nothing more than a deep sleep, and he finds himself longing for a sense of purpose, a mission. He begins his new life tamely enough as a charter boat captain in the Florida Keys, but soon events converge to thrust Quint into a race to find the world's most valuable treasure. While diving an old Spanish shipwreck, he faces rogue naval forces and a vile cadre of pirates and thieves who are also committed to snatching the treasure from the grasp of ancient history or from anyone who gets in their way.

The Pass

Fact: A live nuclear bomb lies in shallow water off the U.S. coast—one of dozens lost around the world!

The year is 1958. A B-47 bomber carrying a live nuclear weapon is returning from a simulated attack on the Soviet Union when it collides with an F-86 Sabre jet fighter plane. In a desperate attempt to land safely, the crew jettisoned the bomb. But instead of being over deep water as they believe, they are just off the coast of the southern United States when they drop the bomb in less than twenty feet of water.

Based on this true event, *The Pass* takes you inside the cockpit of the bomber for this harrowing experience before joining Quint and Dawson over fifty years later in this sequel to *The Keys*. They are on a mission to locate and recover the lost bomb—a mission that quickly becomes a wild race against a group of terrorists bent on detonating the bomb in their twisted jihad against the U.S. With one of the worst hurricanes in history bearing down on them, Quint's team is pushed to the limit as they struggle against overwhelming odds and a well-armed enemy that will stop at nothing to get the bomb.

The Aral

A fleet of fishing boats sits in the middle of a desert where the waters of the Aral Sea once stood. No more fish; no more lush vegetation. Just massive dust storms spreading chemical pollutants from the lake sediments, sickening the few locals who remain.

Not only did the Soviets cause the worst manmade ecological disaster in the history of the world, they made matters worse by building the world's largest bioweapons lab in the middle of this wasteland.

With the sea shrunk to a mere fourth of its former size, a band of criminals now has easy access to a cache of anthrax, VX nerve agent, and—most terrifying—a genetically altered strain of small pox for which there is no prevention and no cure.

When Quint learns that terrorists are bent on using these bioweapons to wreak havoc and further their twisted jihad, he knows his plans for fishing in the Florida Keys are about to be placed on hold. He and his buddy Dawson find themselves facing death at every turn as they race from Key West to Uzbekistan to the frozen Arctic, determined to prevent a terrorist attack.

Refusing to give up, they face obstacles including dust storms, armed mercenaries, old enemies, and even traitors within their own ranks. As they navigate the frigid expanse of northern Russia, not everyone will make it out unscathed.

The real-life ecological disaster of *The Aral* serves as a perfect backdrop for this fast-paced adventure novel. The quirky characters on Quint's team make it a fun ride.

ACKNOWLEDGEMENTS

I would like to acknowledge the encouragement and support of my wife, DeeDee. Katherine Hart and Eliza Dee of Clio Editing worked tirelessly editing the manuscript. Also thanks to Mary Page, Mary Perkins, Nel Ducomb, Pat Coggins, Judith Ann Bates Pique, and my father for their contributions during the novel's development. Thanks to the Killion Group for the cover design and formatting the manuscript for publishing.

A special thanks is due to Don Gaddy for his medical advice and to Dianna Love, who has been most generous in sharing her experience and advice.

PROLOGUE

Near the End of WW II

Under cover of darkness, the battered German submarine slowly limped into the shallow water, listing to starboard. The hum of the engine was barely audible above the sound of rain beating on the hull and waves crashing on the deck below.

With the port engine disabled and a bent propeller on the other side, it was barely making headway. Captain Klaus knew that they had been lucky to survive the Allies' depth charge attack.

Despite the cold stream of water running down his neck, he was glad to be above decks. He even welcomed the sheets of rain and the cover the miserable weather provided. He pulled his collar tighter and then inhaled deeply on his cigarette one last time before tossing the soggy butt overboard.

Above him, the Third Reich Naval Ensign flew proudly, its bold red background and white accents contrasting sharply with the grayish black of the sub's hull. In the upper corner above the swastika, the flag bore the Knight's Cross awarded to him just before they'd left port several weeks before. A second Cross had been hurriedly added to the conning tower alongside the Berlin coat of arms, the paint still wet when they'd set sail.

Two senior officers joined him, choosing the open wetness above decks over their dry but confining quarters below. He heard them breathe deeply, savoring the salty smell of the ocean laced with the scent of land and that of the diesel exhaust.

His men, sick of the rotten food and weary from being sleep-deprived, were eager to escape the cramped below-decks area. He could hear the sailors gathered below the open hatch greedily filling their lungs and knew they envied the officers, privileged to be outside.

The occasional whiff of fresh air made it all the more noxious below decks. The air inside the sub was fouled by stale sweat, tobacco smoke, and chlorine from salt water leaking into the battery compartment. The pervasive dampness from the multitude of leaks that seemed to sprout from everywhere added to their misery.

Fearing that his radio transmissions might be intercepted by nearby enemy forces, the captain ordered a coded message sent via signal light to the sub base ahead. After repeating it for nearly thirty minutes without a response, he ordered the inflatable tender brought on deck.

A few minutes later, Horst and Reinhart were headed toward the island, moving as quickly as their small paddles would propel them through the driving rain. It would be dawn shortly. If the U.S. Air Force or Navy were to spot them surfaced in shallow water, the damaged sub would be defenseless and would almost certainly be sunk.

The two men pulled the dinghy up to a low concrete dock and tied off to a cleat. They went in search of a guard to open the door to the wolfpack's lair but soon concluded that they were alone.

"This is supposed to be a manned base. Where is everyone?" Reinhart asked, swinging the beam of his flashlight back and forth.

"Captured, deserted, dead—who knows?" Horst wiped the moisture from his forehead with his sleeve and fastened the top button of his jacket against the driving rain.

The two sailors looked nervously at the sky. The first rays of dawn would come over the horizon in the next hour. They knew they had damned sure better find a way to open the doors to the concealed harbor in time to get the sub inside before then.

The men continued along the base of the cliff across from the channel entrance into the lagoon for another ten minutes when Reinhart yelled, "I think I've found it." Horst broke into a run and joined him at the small side door. Together they entered the concealed harbor and a few minutes later had opened the massive entrance doors. Horst sprinted back to the water's edge to signal their captain.

Klaus gripped the edge of the conning tower white-knuckled, while shouting orders to his crew. Slowly, the battered submarine crept through the narrow channel dotted with a row of massive coral heads on either side. There were not many sub crews and even fewer captains that could pull off such a desperate move. With only one engine, their maneuverability was severely reduced. The slightest mistake would send them onto the coral, slicing open the bottom of his beloved sub like a tin of food.

The decks were barely above the surface. One ballast tank was ruptured so they were unable to blow all of the water out of it, increasing their draft by nearly a foot. Klaus held his breath twice as he felt the keel scrape over the coral bottom.

Finally, the sub reached the lagoon, crossed to the harbor, and disappeared inside. The massive steel doors immediately swung closed and the captain clutched the coaming of the tower to support his rubbery knees.

The exhausted crew, awake for most of the past forty-eight hours, were granted permission to come on deck with their blankets. The men filed from the ship onto the concrete dock where they sprawled out, enjoying the simple pleasure of breathing the fresh, briny air in the cavernous harbor. The engine crew was the last to disembark after securing the sub. In minutes, half the crew was asleep while the rest lounged, smoking and quietly chatting.

The ship's cook explored the abandoned base and found a storeroom carved into the rock, brimming with provisions. After half-rations of tainted meat and moldy bread, the sub's crew could now feast on their first decent food in weeks.

The powdered egg and canned ham breakfast was heavenly, and Reinhart ate until he could hold no more. "What do you think is in all those crates below decks?" he asked while downing the last bite of his breakfast.

"What the hell do you think? Treasure smuggled out of Germany so our fearless leaders can flee in style if they think we've lost the war." Horst reached for a cigarette and tossed the pack to his buddy.

"I hear we're heading for South America next," Reinhart said as he lit his own cigarette off of Horst's match.

"I hope you're right." Horst exhaled a lungful of smoke. "I'm told the women there are beautiful and the booze is cheap."

Reinhart laughed. "As long as I can be free of that miserable steel can long enough to get drunk, the women can look like dogs for all I care."

The captain and executive officer remained standing atop the badly dented conning tower, enjoying their own heaping plates of breakfast. From this vantage point they could observe the welding torches sparking as the crew repaired damage from the depth charge explosions which had nearly sunk them. Down below, the metallic cacophony of hammers beating out the dented prop made speech impossible, and the smell of burning metal tainted the air.

Opening the jammed conning tower hatch when they'd surfaced had been no easy task. The sub's gun mount railing aft of the conning tower was mostly ripped away and the entire 37mm flak gun mount was destroyed. But the 105mm forward deck cannon appeared unscathed.

Despite all of the damage, Klaus was proud of the sub. Its twin rudders improved maneuverability, and with its rear torpedo tubes located inside the pressure hull, they could reload at sea. With its 23,700 nautical mile surface range and speed of over nineteen knots, it truly was a ship to be feared. The Type IXD2 was the best in its class, and many even claimed it was the best submarine ever built.

"Sir, what are we to do next?" the XO asked. Their original mission had been to transport their valuable cargo on to Patagonia, Argentina.

"Await our orders like good German sailors. What else?" the captain said, the sarcasm thick in his voice. During the past months, their orders had become increasingly more ill-advised, and he believed that the SS was now running the show.

The XO nodded. "Our last orders got us shot to hell and nearly sunk—and for what?"

The captain swallowed a mouthful of thick coffee. "In any event, we won't remain here long. I suspect we'll be ordered to re-enter the battle."

"We're nearly out of torpedoes and in no condition to fight. It would be suicide."

"Perhaps—but if that is our destiny, we will face it like the loyal German sailors we are."

"Indeed, such a shame to have all this gold—"

"You mean cargo; we are not to say that word."

"Sorry, our *cargo* would end up at the bottom of the sea. Running on one engine and with only two torpedoes and a couple of cases of shells for the deck gun, we are no longer the formidable threat we once were."

"We can still ram the enemy." The captain laughed.

"If that is to be our fate, we would be wise to pick a small target." The XO hesitated for a moment before continuing. "There is another alternative. The war will soon be over and all will be lost. Perhaps before then, we could take the cargo and get lost ourselves."

The captain gave a weak smile. "Appealing as that thought might be, we must follow orders. To do otherwise would be traitorous and we are not traitors, are we?" the captain asked, unwilling to admit that the thought had also crossed his mind. The XO shook his head. "As regards our cargo, I'm sure if we are to rejoin the fight, they will order it be left here. Of that you can be certain. While we may be expendable, our... cargo... isn't."

The XO remained silent for a moment. "It will take us quite a while to off-load it once we do get our orders."

"Good point," the captain agreed. "Starting with the next shift, have the men off-load half our cargo. Find a secure area, preferably hidden, in which to store it. If we do manage to live and it comes up missing, it will be our asses."

His XO smiled. "Good idea; it'll keep the men busy and we'll be well ahead if we are ordered to leave the cargo here. Given our damaged tanks, I hope that is the case. But if not, we can re-ballast the ship when we reload it to compensate for the ballast problem and the torpedoes we've already fired."

"Yes, and if we're ordered back into the fight, we'll have a long trip home on one engine once we've fired our remaining torpedoes. So take on fresh water and all the food and medical supplies we can cram aboard from the stocks here. As you pointed out, we can't repair our damaged ballast tank, so off-load all of the weight you possibly can. Dump our extra uniforms and those damned field rations; I doubt we'll be needing them. Also, get rid of the light weapons and ammunition except for the deck cannon. With our limited maneuverability I don't plan on doing any surface fighting, but who knows—we may need it."

Two hours later, the XO called the crew to attention and ordered them to assemble into teams to off-load the cargo. One by one they passed the heavy wooden crates off the boat and stacked them at the end of the dock. Each crate was stamped with a swastika and a unique number.

Reinhart was on his second trip when he stumbled. The crate slipped from his grasp and smashed onto the rock floor with a resounding crash. The wooden crate splintered and gold bars tumbled out onto the dock, each bearing the imprint of the German government eagle and "Deutsche Reichsbank," followed by the weight and a serial number.

Though they had all heard the rumors and suspected their cargo was gold, the men gaped in awe at actually seeing the fortune stacked in the pile of crates before them. The sound of approaching footsteps broke the spell, and they hastily tossed the bars behind the stack of crates and the wooden pieces into the harbor before heading back to the sub.

By the time the crew had a mound of crates stacked at the end of the dock, the XO had found the perfect place to hide the cache. Near the far corner of the main warehouse, a section of wall appeared rotted. When he poked at it, he found that a barely accessible narrow opening no more than three feet tall led to a small natural cave beyond.

"You and you," the XO said, pointing at two of the crewmen, "enlarge this opening. Make it big enough for a man to walk through. Then find some scrap material to patch it in case we're ordered to leave our *cargo* here." He deferred to the captain's wishes by not referring to it as gold. "We'll make it appear as if it is part of the original wall by camouflaging it with scuff marks."

The captain had made it clear that if they were to end up leaving the gold here, they had to do everything possible to prevent the discovery of the crates should anyone else arrive before they returned.

"As soon as they have the opening enlarged, the rest of you start moving that stack of crates inside the cavern." The XO then returned to the sub while the men attacked the rock passage with pickaxes.

An hour later, they had moved the majority of the crates into the small cavern. Horst set his crate beside an existing stack to start a new row and then walked toward the end of the natural cavern room. The ceiling sloped downward as he neared the end, where the rock floor gave way to a still pool of water. Klaus squatted and dipped his hand to taste it. "Salt water. Must be connected to the sea," he muttered to himself.

Much of the sub's damage was beyond their ability to repair in the field. But they did what they could using the few spare parts they'd scrounged from the warehouse at the base. Soon, they were as ready as they would ever be. In his quarters below, Klaus held the decoded message that the radioman had just brought. He poured two fingers of brandy in each of two glasses, handing one to his XO before reading their new orders.

The captain rubbed his eyes with the palms of his hands and took a deep breath. "Okay, proceed with unloading the rest of our cargo. But first assemble the men above decks."

Thirty minutes later, Klaus studied his men gathered into a double row. He was proud to command a sub with such a loyal and capable crew. He envied their naivety in believing that Germany still had a chance to win the war for the Führer. It pained him greatly that his latest orders were certain to send them all to their deaths.

For a moment, he had considered disobeying his inane orders as earlier suggested by his XO. But following orders, no matter how ludicrous they seemed, was his duty.

From the time of the Light Brigade and even before, men in battle had died trying to carry out ill-advised orders. All the while, they hoped that some bit of knowledge beyond their pay grade made orders make sense that seemingly otherwise didn't.

"Men, we've just received orders to rejoin the wolfpack and engage the enemy until we are out of torpedoes, which shouldn't take us long. I promise to do everything possible to keep us alive in hopes that we can all return home. Try to get some rest. We leave tonight under cover of darkness."

An hour after sunset, the crew opened the massive harbor doors and the sub limped through the opening. After sealing the doors, Horst and Reinhart paddled their inflatable back out to the sub, where they came aboard and stowed the deflated tender. All night and the next day, they proceeded at a painfully slow pace on course to join the wolfpack. The following night, they had just surfaced to run the engines and recharge the batteries when their luck ran out.

An American destroyer spotted them on radar and came roaring down on the barely submerged sub. They were so shallow that the first volley of depth charges exploded far below them; however, the next salvo was right on target. Two exploding in quick succession disabled their already damaged running gear and dive planes.

The captain ordered their ballast tanks emptied, choosing to surface and fight rather than die in the depths. But it soon became clear that a second tank had ruptured and they were in a slow descent toward the bottom, over two thousand feet below.

With a hull crush depth of only seven hundred feet, they all knew the sub was no match for the pressures where they were headed. The creaking, groaning hull told Horst that it would soon rupture.

"It would have been nice to see my family one last time," Reinhart said quietly as he lit a last cigarette, took a drag, and passed it to his buddy.

Horst nodded as he inhaled. "What do you suppose will become of the gold?"

Before Reinhart could reply, a cracking sound announced the hull's rupturing. The image of gold bars was the last to go through Horst's mind as a laser-thin stream of high-pressure water cut him in two.

CHAPTER 1

Present Day

Quint lay sleeping, blissfully unaware of the creature stalking him. The beast's mouth hung open, saliva dripping from the points of its sharp, gleaming teeth. Once in position, the reptile launched itself through the air, landing squarely on top of his victim.

Quint's eyes flew open, as did his mouth. As he lay there gasping for air with the breath knocked out of him, he looked up into the eyes of a giant lizard staring him in the face.

"Damn, Barney! What are you doing?" Quint yelled, shoving the green reptile off of his chest.

Drawn by the commotion, Evie appeared in the doorway holding a spatula, a block of morning sun highlighting her fine features and flawless complexion. "Boys, no fighting."

"Fighting? Your psycho, nutjob lizard just attacked me in my sleep. That's low—even for a lizard."

"Oh, Barney." Evie walked over to stroke the iguana's head. "He's just playing with you."

"No, he's not. The lizard hates me."

"You're being ridiculous."

Quint's arm brushed against his chest and he realized his t-shirt was wet. "Gross! He peed on me too. Now I have to take a shower."

"You needed to get up anyhow; breakfast is nearly ready and we've got a full day ahead."

"Oh, joy," Quint muttered, less than enthused about spending the day helping Evie with one of her never-ending house projects. Though he loved her quaint Florida Keys cottage, the modest wood-frame structure demanded constant maintenance.

He swung his legs off the side of the bed and rubbed his shoulder while working his arm in a circle. Having skipped his daily workouts for the past few days, he felt the stiffness in his body as he rose from the bed. While the angry red scar from his recent knife wound was fading, his shoulder still throbbed.

Quint raised the blinds and groaned as the sun burst in from the cloudless sky. *A picture-perfect day made for diving and fishing, not chores.* Resigned to his fate, he turned from the window and plodded into the bathroom.

After a quick shower, he ran his fingers through his shaggy blond hair, worn long to conceal an array of wounds, souvenirs from his SEAL days. His bright green eyes tracked the safety razor across his lathered face in the mirror. He cursed when he nicked the scar on his left cheek. Finished shaving, he wiped his face with a cool washcloth and slapped a piece of toilet paper on the cut.

Quint's mouth watered from the smell of bacon frying as he entered the kitchen barefoot to find Evie removing several strips from the frying pan. "Just in time. I'm about to put the eggs on to cook." She emptied the egg mixture into the skillet and placed the empty glass bowl into the sink.

While she busily worked the scrambled eggs with a spatula, Quint enveloped her in his arms and held her. He gently kissed the top of her head and leaned down to nuzzle her neck, the brown ponytail brushing his forehead. "Stop! I can't concentrate on cooking with you doing that," she said, playfully swatting at him with the spatula.

Her girl-next-door ways and unpretentious manner stood in stark contrast to the many shallow, model-like women he had met these past few years. But it was her sharp wit and big heart that he found most compelling.

Evie had come to the Keys on a whim and, after a short stint working in a bar, she'd begun working as a freelance software developer for a number of clients around the world. The ability to work her own hours and upload her work product when she finished a job gave her the freedom upon which she thrived.

He was ecstatic that she finally seemed to be moving past the nightmare of her kidnapping and brutal rape by terrorists a few months earlier. It gave him little satisfaction that he had helped send those involved to their graves—except for Rashid. That score remained to be settled.

Quint had finished breakfast and was adding a heaping spoon of vanilla creamer to his second cup of coffee when the phone rang. "Rogers, did you forget it's Saturday?"

"I thought you'd want to hear the good news right away, but if you're too busy—"

"Never too busy for good news."

"It looks like the Cuba deal is finally wrapped up— you've got your base." Through his company, Vector, Rogers had recently hired Quint's team on the government's behalf. In lieu of a bonus earned during the team's recent search for a lost nuclear weapon, they had requested Rogers' assistance in securing a base from which the team could operate outside of the U.S.

"Hot dog! You can interrupt my weekend anytime with that sort of news."

"It took rattling a few cages but we got lucky," Rogers said. "It seems both sides were able to get several key concessions they had been wanting, your project among them.

"You'll still need to go to Cuba to complete the paperwork. If you're available tomorrow, I'm making a trip on my company's jet and can arrange to drop you off along the way. Then you can meet with them on Monday."

"Hell yeah, I'll make myself available," he replied, secretly happy for the excuse to escape part of Evie's weekend project.

"See you tomorrow morning," Rogers said. Quint thanked him before hanging up.

"Good news?" Evie asked.

"No... great news. Our island operations base deal finally got approved and I need to go down there to finalize the paperwork."

"That's great. I can hardly wait for you to up and leave me wondering if I'll ever see you again," Evie replied.

Ignoring her sarcasm, Quint continued. "Rogers is flying me down tomorrow. Oh, and I need to call Dawson." Quint raised his phone to call.

"Wait a minute, big boy." Evie grasped his hand. "You can call him on our way to the hardware store. With you planning your escape for tomorrow, we'll just have to work harder today to get everything done." Evie ignored the face he made in response.

"Congratulations, I can't believe you pulled it off," Dawson yelled upon hearing Quint's news. The two men had been buddies since their final days of high school. Their bond had solidified while serving together in the SEALs. A couple of years after getting out of the service, Quint invited Dawson to help run his charter boat on a fishing trip to Venezuela.

The innocent fishing trip turned into a search for a sunken Spanish galleon and then a life-or-death race to find a lost Incan temple in the jungles of South America. The two men, along with the team they'd built for their South American escapade, ended up with enough money to form a company chartered to take on one-of-a-kind projects. So far these projects had ranged from finding lost nuclear weapons to thwarting terrorists intent on getting their hands on lethal bioweapons.

"So when do we leave?" Dawson asked.

"*I'm* leaving tomorrow. *You're* staying here to start gathering supplies. And to lease a boat for our initial trip down there."

"How come you get to go to Havana and I have to work?" Dawson asked.

"Because Rogers promised the Cubans he'd send the smart, handsome one to meet with them." Before Dawson could reply, he continued. "Okay, to be fair, pick a number between one and ten to see who goes."

"Three," Dawson replied without hesitation.

"Nope, it was six. You lose."

"Wait a minute, that's not—" Quint hung up before he could finish.

While growing up, Quint had studied Cuba's history in the years before Fidel seized power and turned the thriving paradise into a land of squalor with his grand communist experiment. Since then, he had always wanted to visit. A trip to the island country was one big item about to be crossed off of his bucket list.

CHAPTER 2

After breakfast the next morning, Evie drove Quint to the airport. She followed the signs to the FBO, the fixed base operator facility which handled the private plane traffic.

"Please be careful," Evie said.

"Yes, Mom."

"I'm serious." Evie punched his arm as he leaned over to kiss her. "It's not like I don't have any reason to be worried after your last... adventure. You know, the one where you came back with a knife wound in your chest and Dawson sporting multiple bullet holes and minus one eye. Remember?"

"You have my word." He grabbed his luggage from the back seat and waved goodbye as Evie pulled away. A dark sedan pulled up beside the chain link fence as he stepped inside the FBO's small lobby.

As always, Rogers' plane arrived precisely on time. The person in the sedan sat quietly waiting until Quint emerged from the building and headed toward the small jet. The man pulled his cell phone from his breast pocket and speed-dialed a number. "November eight-one-eight tango kilo," he said, repeating the plane's tail number before ending the call and driving off.

Quint bounded up the plane's steps. "Good to see you. Thanks for the ride," he said, shaking hands with his host as he entered the plush leather and walnut cocoon.

Rogers looked to be in his midfifties but kept himself in great shape. Had it not been for his thick gray hair, which he wore combed straight back from his forehead, he might have been mistaken for ten years younger.

He handed Quint an envelope. "Here's the papers you'll need to wrap up the deal. There's also a very large check inside, so don't lose it."

Quint pressed the envelope to his heart. "I'll guard it with my very life." Rogers rolled his eyes, laughing despite himself.

"Be very careful who you do business with in Cuba. I've arranged for a man named Santiago to pick you up at the airport. He's a taxi driver who knows everyone. Just look for the biggest Buick you've ever seen. He can be trusted, so feel free to take him into your confidence." A short time later, they were landing in Cuba.

"My plans have changed and we'll be heading back tomorrow. I can pick you up early evening if you can finish your business by then."

"I should be able to," Quint replied, "unless Cuba's bureaucrats are a whole lot slower than ours."

"You can reach me on my satphone to confirm tomorrow afternoon." Quint nodded and left the comfort of the buttery soft leather seat to enter the sweltering Cuban heat.

After clearing customs and immigration, Quint exited the terminal and found a man lovingly polishing an enormous 1956 Buick taxi. He looked up as Quint approached and tucked the rag into his pocket. From the lined face and salt-and-pepper hair, Quint judged the man to be in his midfifties.

"You Santiago?" The man nodded and shook hands before slinging Quint's bag into the car's mammoth-sized trunk. Quint slid into the back seat and laid his briefcase beside him.

Though the worn vinyl upholstery revealed the car's age, it was otherwise spotless. The carpet had obviously been replaced with what looked like some indoor-outdoor variety. A tire iron lay on the rear floorboard within reach of the driver. As they pulled away from the curb, Quint paid scant attention to the hulking green Plymouth a few car lengths back, which followed suit.

Driving through the streets of Havana, filled with cars from the fifties, made Quint feel as if he had gone back in time.

"Where can I take you, señor?" The driver adjusted the rearview mirror so that he could see Quint without turning around.

"Hotel Ambos Mundos, please." Santiago nodded. "Like your car."

"Thanks." Santiago beamed, clearly proud. "I was just a boy when my father bought it new. Our fearless leader say, 'The Cuban people refuse to be forced into consumerism, and for that we are the most democratic nation on the planet.'

"My father always wished we had less of Castro's democracy and a new car instead," he finished in a low voice. Then changing subjects, he spoke louder. "But this Buick, she has served me well. GM built them damn good back then."

Santiago laid on the horn as another lumbering sedan swerved in front of them, forcing him to slam on the brakes. He grabbed the steering wheel knob and spun the wheel, sending the heavy sedan into an abrupt right turn. Quint hung on to keep from being flung across the seat. With tires squealing and pedestrians scattering, they roared off down the side street.

"I can't talk about most of it, but me and your Rogers have a long history," Santiago said calmly, while effortlessly maneuvering the car down the narrow street at breakneck speed. "He's a good man."

"He says the same about you, and also that you could help me with my business with your government."

"I can try, but you have to watch those lazy bastards; they're all crooks."

Quint laughed. "Nothing special about that. It's the same everywhere."

"True. Politicians are like a young man courting a pretty girl. Promise anything until they have what they want."

"True. Say, my meeting is not until tomorrow. Any suggestions on how I might spend my day?"

"You should have daiquiris at the El Floridita bar, and then go to Doña Eutimia for dinner. Visitors say it is the best, though I have not eaten there. I cannot afford. Try the costillitas; if they're not on the menu, ask for them."

"Costillitas?"

"Sí. How you say, baby back ribs. The best," Santiago said, as they pulled up in front of the hotel. Quint fumbled through his wallet and withdrew double the fare.

He paused as he handed over the bills, which Santiago accepted with a broad smile. "Join me for dinner. We can talk a little business. I hate eating alone." Though partly true, Quint's offer was driven more by Santiago's comment that he could not afford to eat at the very restaurant he had recommended.

"I would be honored. I'll tell my wife not to expect me this evening."

"Bring her along."

"No, she does not speak English and would be uncomfortable. But thank you."

Quint spotted the same ancient Plymouth he had seen earlier pulling into a parking place near the end of the block as Santiago handed his bag to the bellman. His train of thought was interrupted when Santiago spoke. "I'll come in with you. The hotels often double-book. I can help."

The two men approached the front desk, where Santiago engaged the clerk in a rapid-fire exchange in Spanish. "There was problem, but I fix. They wanted to keep your passport but I refused. It is good now; they agreed to just make a copy. You need to fill this out." He handed Quint the registration card and a pen. "I got you a room on the second floor. The view is not so good, but many tourists come to see Hemingway's old room on fifth floor, so the elevator is very busy. This way, not many stairs to climb and you don't have to wait."

A minute later the clerk handed back Quint's passport, along with a room key.

"Make sure to keep your passport with you," Santiago said quietly. "So, can I take you somewhere else?"

"I think I'll take your advice and visit El Floridita. Can you pick me up there around seven?" Santiago nodded. Quint watched him return to his car and hand a coin to the small boy washing his windshield.

Quint let the bellman carry his bag, not because he needed the service but because he deemed it rude to do otherwise. He followed the man to a modest room, where the bellman set his bag on a low table and turned on the air conditioner. The bellman droned on and on, pointing out the obvious features of the room, instructing Quint on the restaurant and bar hours, and offering whatever assistance he might need. Then, clutching his large tip, the man left with a smile.

Quint freshened up in the tiny bathroom and twenty minutes later was headed back down to the lobby. He stepped outside and looked up and down the street. The green Plymouth was nowhere to be seen.

Deciding to stretch his legs, he walked the short distance to the harbor, where he took a deep breath of the salt air. He bought an empanada in a small street-side café and ate it while continuing on his journey.

Quint popped the last bite of meat-filled pastry into his mouth and was looking for a trashcan to deposit the greasy wrapper into when he spotted the green Plymouth again. It was a few cars back, creeping up the street with two men in the front seat, both wearing dark glasses and baseball caps.

Okay, this is no longer a coincidence. Unsure who would be following him or why, Quint decided it best to avoid finding out.

On a lark, he joined a group entering the Castillo de la Real Fuerza and paid the modest admission fee to tour the fort. He glanced back as he entered to see the Plymouth creep slowly by before vanishing amidst the heavy traffic.

Quint spent the next hour studying artifacts recovered from numerous wrecks. He was particularly impressed with the enormous model of the *Santisima Trinidad* launched in 1769 as one of over two hundred ships built in Cuba for the Spanish crown. Featuring a hundred and forty cannons on its four gun decks, it was once touted as the most heavily armed ship in the world.

When he emerged, he scanned the street. For a moment, he thought he caught a glimpse of a man wearing sunglasses and a baseball hat. But after failing to spot the old Plymouth, he opted to take a taxi to El Floridita.

Quint entered the room, outfitted in 1930s Hollywood Regency-style décor, and found a seat at the end of the bar. He ordered a drink from one of the small army of red-aproned bartenders, all of whom were working feverishly to turn out a steady stream of the bar's signature daiquiris. On the far end of the bar, a full-sized bronze statue of Hemingway suffered the indignity of an endless stream of tourists posing alongside it for photos.

Having finished his third or fourth daiquiri, but not entirely sure which, Quint declined yet another drink. Santiago's arrival saved him from the bartender's glare, which he felt sure was for remaining too long at the busy bar without ordering another drink.

Quint left a sizeable tip as a peace offering. The bartender's smiling nod as he scooped up the cash suggested that all was forgiven. Quint slid into the big Buick and enjoyed watching the city coming alive during the short ride to the restaurant, back near his hotel.

"You like El Floridita?"

"Perhaps a little too much," Quint said, glad he had refused another daiquiri.

Santiago gave a hearty laugh. "They make damn good drinks. Many call our country the Isle of Rum. We have good cane, good climate, good soil, and the best rum makers."

"Well, today I proved my loyalty to the Bacardis. By the way, what's with the bat image on their labels?"

"Ha, many ask that." Santiago paused while manhandling the big sedan alongside the curb a half block from the restaurant. He then got out and opened the door for Quint before replying.

"Before coming to Cuba, Don Facundo Bacardi was a wine merchant from Spain. His rum, filtered with charcoal and then aged in oak barrels, was very popular. His wife gave credit for his good luck and success to the fruit bats that lived in the roof of his distillery. So she insisted on adding the bat to his logo."

As they approached the restaurant, an impeccably dressed man held the door open. Quint followed Santiago inside, where they were seated at a prime table. Santiago fired off an order to the waiter in Spanish before turning to Quint. "You tried our daiquiris; now you must try a mojito."

Though the buzz from his earlier daiquiris had not yet subsided, Quint begrudgingly agreed to avoid a cultural slight. "Okay, but then I'm quitting."

Santiago laughed and Quint's pledge was quickly forgotten when their continued discussion of Cuban rum resulted in Santiago ordering a sampler tray of small glasses, each filled with a different color and flavor of rum. While they sampled the rum, Santiago ordered dinner for them both and then began relating the history of Cuba. Following a lengthy discussion of his own family's background, he asked, "So, how can I help you with your business?"

Quint hesitated for a moment but since Rogers had vouched for the man, he decided to trust him. "We are interested in an island off the coast of your country." He briefly explained the deal he was there to close, without divulging their intended use of the property.

"You must have many important friends to do such a deal. Since the Russians quit funding Castro's great experiment, I know the government has been cash-strapped. But even though you already have approval, with our bureaucracy you may not find it quite so easy to complete the transaction.

"My nephew, Luis, works in the government. He's one of the few honest men there and could guide you. Maybe save you much time and frustration. I'm sure he would do this for his favorite uncle. I will tell you how to find him. You can use him or not as you wish."

The waiter arrived bearing a huge tray and began covering the table with plates, easily enough food for a large family. The conversation lagged as the two men dug into their meal for the next twenty minutes. Quint finally tossed a rib bone onto his plate and pushed it away. Santiago ordered each of them a glass of seven-year-old Havana Club straight up.

"So, if you don't mind me asking, this place you intend to buy, where is it?"

"Several miles off the southern coast of Cuba. It was used as a base by the Russians during the Cold War."

Santiago's eyes widened. "I know of this place." Now it was Quint's turn to show surprise. They paused as the waiter delivered the drinks. Santiago took a sip of the dark rum. "Damn good stuff, no?" Quint nodded.

As the waiter walked away, Santiago continued. "My taxi driver friend, Renaldo, worked there during the construction."

Quint considered it for a moment before replying. "Could you arrange for me to meet him?"

"No problem. He speaks English well and would be happy to talk with you. We can meet him for coffee after I pick you up tomorrow morning."

They finished their rum and Quint settled the check. Feeling the full effects of the rum and mojitos combined with his earlier daiquiris, he weaved his way back to the taxi. Santiago, seemingly unaffected by the liquor, drove slowly back to the hotel where he stopped and got out to open Quint's door. "Thank you for the best meal I've had in many years. I will be here at your service early tomorrow to take you anywhere, anytime."

Quint climbed out and, after checking for the green Plymouth but not spotting it, headed for his room.

CHAPTER 3

The next morning, Quint awoke feeling like he'd had too little time in Cuba and too much rum. He downed three aspirins and headed for the hotel's rooftop restaurant. After a big breakfast washed down with three cups of coffee, he was feeling much better. He stepped out of the hotel to find Santiago leaned against the front fender of his old Buick across the street, talking to two men.

"I am ready to take you for your business," he yelled when he saw Quint.

Though Quint checked traffic both ways, he was still almost run over by the familiar green Plymouth careening around the corner with two men wearing caps and sunglasses. "Hijo de puta!" Santiago yelled at the driver, who continued on without a backward glance. "You must be very careful. Drivers here, they do not give one shit."

"It seems I must agree," Quint said, as he ducked into the backseat of the mammoth four-door hardtop.

"Thank you very much for the dinner last night. It was every bit as good as I had imagined," Santiago said.

"My pleasure."

Santiago lit a cigarette and threw the match out the window. After exhaling a lungful of smoke, he continued. "I arranged for us to join my old friend, Renaldo, for coffee."

Santiago drove to a tiny café a few blocks away where he guided Quint toward an older man who sat alone at a small table in the back corner. Santiago made the introductions and they chatted while the waitress brought their coffee. "So, Santiago tells me you are familiar with the island we plan to purchase."

"Purchase? I didn't know that was possible," Renaldo said.

"I'm sorry, you're right. It's a twenty-five-year lease."

Renaldo emptied his cup and motioned to the waitress for a refill. "Yes, I am more than familiar with the island. I worked at Tears of Coral for over a year helping the Russians."

"Tears of Coral—is that the name of the island?"

Renaldo nodded. "Many years ago, a channel was dredged there. During the process, large chunks of coral were piled on either side of the cut. A Cuban pilot who later flew over thought it looked like two rows of tears and so he called it 'Tears of Coral.' The name stuck and we still call it that today, though I presume you will have the choice to rename it."

"That name's fine." Quint finished his coffee and set the tiny cup back on the saucer. "We could certainly use someone with your knowledge."

"I know her secrets as well as any man still alive in Cuba today. Of course, there are no longer so many."

"Would you go there and help us for a few days? Of course, we'd pay you for your time."

"It would be my pleasure." Renaldo replied, with a bow of his head. He suggested meeting again when Quint returned to visit the island. "Here is a number where you can reach me to let me know when you wish to meet." Renaldo scrawled a row of numbers and then handed over a crumpled piece of paper, which Quint thrust into his pocket.

They men shook hands and Quint followed Santiago back out to his taxi. Halfway down the block, the green Plymouth stood waiting.

"There's that damned careless fool car that nearly ran you down."

"Santiago, I'm not sure it was an accident."

"What do you mean?"

"I spotted that very same car following us yesterday. It was parked near the hotel and shadowed me when I was walking alone. Any idea who it might be?"

Santiago shook his head. "Could be one of Castro's thugs. Could be some crazy person. Or maybe a thief looking to rob you."

"With Cuba being a police state, I thought crime was rare here." Quint grabbed the door handle to keep from sliding across the seat as Santiago made a hard left turn without slowing.

"Used to be. But these days, criminals are becoming bolder. That is why I carry that tire iron on the back floorboard. While you can see that there is no shortage of policemen, with one on nearly every street corner, their response to crimes, even those involving foreigners, is slow."

Santiago glanced in his rear view mirror and saw the big Plymouth round the corner and swing in behind him. "Damn, you're right. He's following us.

"I'll stop at the office building where you need to go in just a minute. When I do, please jump out and enter quickly." He expalined where Quint should go once he was inside. A few minutes later, they arrived.

"I wait for you here. Now, hurry."

Quint grabbed the briefcase with his papers and without a backward glance, sprinted toward the main entrance. Once inside, he looked back to see the Plymouth cruise by slowly and then speed off.

He followed Santiago's instructions and found the right department, where he asked for Luis. A minute later a handsome young man appeared, dressed in worn but immaculately laundered slacks and a crisp white shirt. "I am Luis. My uncle told me to expect you. Please," he said, motioning with his hand for Quint to follow.

They entered an expansive room. While neat and orderly, it appeared that the walls had last seen a fresh coat of paint some years before Fidel took power. Luis led Quint past throngs of workers stationed at endless rows of plain wooden desks.

They finally stopped at a row near the back of the cavernous beehive of activity. After muttering something in Spanish, Luis's coworker rose from his desk carrying an empty coffee cup, a sour look on his face. Luis quickly rolled over the man's chair and made a show of dusting off the cracked vinyl cushion with his hand.

"Please, have a seat," Luis said, and plopped down in his own chair. The scarred surface of his ancient desk was immaculately clean. A row of neatly stacked files lay across the top with a single pen on the right hand side. A photo of his family in a cheap brass frame was the only personal item on display.

Unsure of the chair's stability, Quint eased into it, wincing as it groaned and wobbled, nearly dumping him over when he leaned back. Perched back upright, Quint faced Luis, who sat with eager anticipation, his hands folded on the desk in front of him.

"I'm surprised not to find everyone puffing away on a Cohiba."

Luis laughed. "The government has imposed a no-smoking policy in government offices and many other areas. And with our salaries averaging twenty dollars per month, few people can afford to smoke. Sadly, the cigar factory workers cannot buy the very product they make."

"I guess that image of Castro puffing away gives the impression that everyone does the same."

"I think even he gave it up many years ago. But it is said that he once smoked six a day. After the CIA tried blowing him up with a loaded cigar, one of over six hundred assassination attempts, he began having his private stock produced exclusively by four of the country's finest cigar makers in the palace of a former sugar cane baron.

"Now we mainly destroy the health of others in the world with our exported cigars." Luis finished with his eyes cast down. He leaned back with his legs crossed, revealing a hole worn in the sole of his heavily polished left shoe. Perhaps to draw attention away, he softly clapped his hands together and looked up. "So, how can I be of service to you, Mr. Quint?"

"It's just Quint. Your uncle said you might help guide me through the paperwork process." He explained about the island and the arrangements which had been made. Wide-eyed and sitting with both feet back on the floor, Luis focused on every word. When Quint finished, he gave a soft whistle.

"You must have very powerful friends."

"Yes, but Santiago felt that you might help me avoid any... problems."

Luis smiled, then hurried off, returning a minute later.

"Follow me." As Quint rose to follow, Luis' office mate, who had been standing just inside their break room, drinking coffee and looking anxious, dashed back to reclaim his chair and return to work at his desk.

"You may find the man I'm taking you to see somewhat... rigid, but he's honest." After climbing the stairs to the floor above, they continued down a long hallway to a modest-sized office.

Like Luis, the clerk wore a nearly threadbare shirt and pants that were freshly laundered and starched. His slick, jet-black hair and thin, neatly trimmed mustache gave him an air of formal professionalism.

Quint pegged him as a prissy bureaucrat at first, but quickly came to realize the man was simply trying to appear professional and probably felt somewhat intimidated.

Luis explained the nature of his business. Though it was clear the clerk judged Quint a fool for his intended purchase, he filled out a long form and presented it to Quint for his signature. Afterwards, he instructed him on where he would need to go next. "When you have all of the necessary approvals on this form, come back to see me."

With Quint trailing close behind Luis, they moved from office to office for several hours while Luis encouraged, begged, flattered, threatened, and at one point bribed a succession of bureaucrats. Finally, they were back at the first clerk's desk with a stack of fully executed forms, which Quint handed over along with the certified check from the U.S. Government to cover the balance due. By the time the clerk finished reviewing the documents, his tone had changed considerably.

"I am not certain how you arranged to lease this island, but everything appears to be in order. Permit me to outline the procedures for entering and departing Cuba. With these documents you need only radio customs when entering Cuban waters by boat and you are assured a cursory customs inspection. Just make sure whatever you bring in remains on your island. Otherwise there would be unpleasantness.

"You are also permitted to fly to and from your island without being required to clear through Havana, provided you remain within this air corridor," he said, pointing to a map sketched on one of the documents.

Quint accepted the completed ownership documents and followed Luis back to his desk. As they approached, Quint saw Luis's office mate look up anxiously. "I think he's afraid you're going to take his chair again," Quint said.

Luis waved and after muttering a few words of assurance in Spanish, the man relaxed and returned to work on the stack of paperwork towering before him.

"I want to thank you, Luis." Quint realized that without the help of Santiago's nephew, it would have taken days to complete the process. As they shook hands, he pressed two one-hundred-dollar bills into Luis's palm.

Luis glanced down, taking care to keep the cash concealed. His eyes widened when he saw the amount. "Thank you, but I cannot accept this for doing my job. I have little, but I prize my honor." He shook hands again, this time leaving the bills in Quint's hand.

"But if there is anything I can ever do for you, Mr. Quint, just call me. Here is my number." He jotted down a number on a scrap of paper. "Do you have a card with your number?" Quint shook his head. "If you don't mind, please write it down for me." Quint wrote down his satphone number on another paper scrap.

"I have many friends with connections... to get things done. From time to time, I may learn things that could be of interest to you... things that you might find of value," he said, hinting that he could accept payment for that type of service. "Things that are not a part of my job are different. I am honest, but not stupid," he said with a laugh, while escorting Quint back to the building's entrance.

A minute later Quint left, wearing a broad smile on his face and tightly clutching the large brown envelope filled with papers that declared the team to be the island's rightful new lessor. Now they would get to see just what their millions had bought. He hoped they would not be disappointed.

CHAPTER 4

Quint emerged into the late afternoon sun and donned his sunglasses. He spotted Santiago's Buick parked across the street and scanned the block for their tail without spotting them. A few broad steps and he was across the street and into the safety of the big car's backseat.

"You were successful?"

"Yes, thanks to Luis. I appreciate you hooking me up with him."

Santiago nodded. "Where to now?"

"Good question," Quint replied, as he withdrew a satphone from his briefcase. A moment later, he heard Rogers answer. "You still good to give me a ride home?"

"Sure am. In fact, we're running ahead of schedule. We'll be there in about ninety minutes. See you then."

Quint looked up at Santiago, who was waiting for directions. "I need to be back at the airport in an hour and a half, so we've got some time to kill. Ideas?"

"After I take you back to the hotel to get your luggage, we can stop at a little bar I know by the ocean. I think you'll like it." Santiago pulled away from the curb and merged with traffic amidst a chorus of horns. They had gone only a block when they entered a busy intersection, and Quint saw the familiar green Plymouth out of the corner of his eye.

He heard the familiar crack of gunfire just as the driver's side window shattered and Santiago slumped over the steering wheel.

The Buick continued forward through the intersection, veering toward a solidly built concrete building. Seeing that they were about to wreck, Quint threw himself onto the floorboard. The impact tossed him into the back of the driver's seat hard enough to knock the breath out of him.

Even as he was struggling to regain his senses, he knew that in mere seconds the two men from the Plymouth would be upon him. He climbed back onto the seat just in time to see the green vehicle pull up alongside and the passenger leap out.

Steam spewing from beneath the hood of Santiago's ruined Buick shrouded the car as Quint cracked open the back door on the driver's side opposite the Plymouth. With the tire iron in his right hand, he feigned unconsciousness. When the man approached the door, Quint drew his legs back and kicked it open with all of his might.

Quint heard the man gasping for air as he jumped out of the taxi, briefcase in hand. He struck the man hard on the side of his head with the tire iron and then bolted for the driver of the Plymouth. Seeing Quint running toward him, waving the tire iron like a wild man, he gunned the engine and shot down a side street.

Quint went back to the Buick and opened the driver's door. He felt for a pulse and found Santiago still alive, though bleeding heavily from a gunshot wound in his shoulder. Quint lifted him out the door and dragged him beside the building, where he laid him on the sidewalk. He then retrieved his satphone and called Luis.

"I will get help on the way and be there myself in a few minutes. But you should go. You do not want to face the Cuban police; you could be here far longer than you planned. Thank you for helping him."

By the time Quint hung up, Santiago was coming around and Quint explained what had happened.

"I'll be okay, but you must go."

"I'm so sorry about the car. I know how much it—"

"It's a car. There are more. Now go, before it's too late," Santiago insisted as a crowd gathered and a policeman sprinted toward him from down the block. Quint turned and walked quickly down a side street away from the wreck. Halfway down the block he ducked into a small restaurant.

Without slowing he continued through to the kitchen and out the back. Cautiously, he opened the door and, seeing no threats, emerged to jog down the alley to the end opposite the wrecked Buick.

As he exited the alley, he spotted a taxi stuck in traffic and sprinted toward it. He had just opened the door and was sliding into the back seat when he saw the driver of the Plymouth talking to two menacing-looking men at the next corner. He happened to be looking Quint's way and stared him right in the face. The man yelled and started running toward Quint, with the other men right behind him. One was reaching inside his coat for what Quint assumed was a gun.

"Oh, shit," Quint yelled. With the taxi jammed in traffic unable to move, Quint jumped back out and leaped over the trunk of the taxi. He bolted down a side street where traffic was flowing and leaped into the back of a passing stake bed truck. The driver of the Plymouth stopped and stood frustrated as the truck continued away. He then headed back toward his own car.

Knowing his pursuers would be looking for the truck, Quint jumped off and ran across the median where he flagged down another taxi. He barked instructions for the driver to take him to the airport and they made a loop past the wrecked Buick. Quint saw the green Plymouth rounding the corner ahead. As they approached the airport, they passed the stake bed truck. It was stopped in traffic with the driver of the Plymouth approaching it from the back with his gun drawn.

Quint slid down in the back seat until they had passed. With time to catch his breath, he began to replay the episode in his mind. It was clear that whoever had been following them wanted Quint—alive. And they wanted him bad enough to kill and risk being caught by the Cuban police. Since he wasn't carrying much cash, it had to be about kidnapping him. Either for ransom or perhaps a reward from one of Quint's adversaries looking to settle an old score.

Could it be my old nemesis Syndy? Or maybe Rashid?

He felt horrible that Santiago had been shot and his beloved car wrecked. But there really had been no reason to suspect such a thing might happen. He was relieved it didn't appear fatal and that Luis had help on the way. But he would need to make good on replacing the Buick.

While the taxi continued toward the airport, Quint reconsidered his plan. Since he still had his passport, it made no sense to return to the hotel and risk being caught to pick up his bag with a few clothes and toiletries. But he still had nearly an hour before Rogers' scheduled arrival.

Whoever was after him had to suspect that the airport would be his most likely destination. "Driver, on second thought, take me to El Floridita." It was unlikely they would expect him to go to a tourist bar under these circumstances. Plus the thought of hiding out in a crowded bar held a certain appeal.

The driver pulled to the curb and Quint tossed him a handful of bills. "Please wait. I'll be back in thirty minutes." After a quick scan both ways, he hurried inside the bar carrying his briefcase. Though it was already crowded, Quint scored a seat at the bar when a customer rose to stumble out. He ordered a daiquiri and sat quietly trying to puzzle out what had just happened, but with little luck.

He finished his drink, glanced at his watch, and after settling his tab, headed outside to his waiting taxi. By the time they reached the airport, Rogers was waiting. Tossing another handful of cash at the driver, Quint grabbed his briefcase and sprinted for the terminal. A few minutes later, they were in the air headed home.

CHAPTER 5

The woman behind the porcelain mask pressed the button on her wheelchair, triggering a small pump to deliver a lungful of smoke through a yellowed plastic tube that held her lit cigarette. She exhaled before answering the call on her cell phone.

"Preston, so nice to hear from you. Why, I was beginning to think you had forgotten me. And you know how upsetting that would be," the woman said in her eerie, robotic voice.

"N-n-never would I f-forget you, S-syndy."

"I'm very glad to hear. So tell me, how did things go in Cuba? Do you have Quint?"

"Uh...er...well...not exactly."

"Not exactly? What does 'not exactly' mean?"

"Well, after I got the tail numbers of the plane Quint boarded, I arranged with your contact to have him followed in Cuba. I was clear, actually quite clear, that they were to follow and capture Quint. But they blew it. He got away."

There was a pause long enough that their connection might have been dropped. "Syndy...you still there?"

She exhaled before speaking. "Yes, I'm still here. The real question is, 'Will you continue to be?'"

"Look, Syndy, it wasn't my fault. I used the contact *you* gave me. He's the one you should be angry with, not me. I was just following your orders."

"Just following my orders, you say? Well, not really. If you had followed my orders, then Quint would be standing before me right now, wouldn't he?"

"But—"

"Don't I pay you quite well to deal with such... minor obstacles? Or am I mistaken?"

"No, it's just that I—"

"Good. Having missed a golden chance to capture Quint, I can't stress how important it is to locate their little hidey-hole. It's high time we dealt with them once and for all. And I prefer we do it outside the U.S., where we're much less likely to suffer any consequences. Keep in touch. I suggest you not disappoint me again anytime soon. Do I make myself clear?" Before Preston could reply, she hung up.

Using her joystick, Syndy propelled her wheelchair over to the floor-to-ceiling windows in her massive stateroom aboard her yacht, *Syntillate*. The tinted wrap-around windows sat atop an unusual conning-tower superstructure on the 240-foot science-fiction-like yacht, lending it a submarine-like appearance.

Two massive diesel engines delivered 16,500 horsepower, capable of propelling her at an astonishing maximum speed of fifty knots. Given the nature of her business, the option to move quickly whenever the need arose was critical. At a more modest twenty-five knots, the yacht had a cruising range of nearly four thousand nautical miles.

She gazed out at the low clouds, which threatened rain. She had banned all mirrors here save one concealed behind a wooden panel, which her remote unit controlled. But nothing could prevent the occasional glimpse of her reflection in the yacht's window.

She swept the ceramic mask from her face, allowing it to shatter on the floor. Later, her assistant would bring another from the drawerfuls in her closet.

Without the mask, Syndy saw the charred and blackened skin clinging to a skull where hair no longer grew. The flawless white skin which had once covered the perfect features of a face framed in silky-thick burnt sienna hair was now gone. The face that had once turned men's and women's heads alike to admire her stunning image whenever she strode through a room was no more.

A glass eye lacking an eyelid stared unblinking, while her remaining one blinked rapidly from the smoke, the damaged tear duct struggling to keep it damp. Her gums and a few remaining teeth on one side of her ruined mouth lay exposed, no skin or flesh to conceal them, while the other side of her face held a frozen sneer. Smoke drifted from two holes in the front of her face where a perfectly formed nose had once sat.

The elbow of her right arm rested on the stump of her left wrist holding the cigarette tube between the bones of her first and second fingers in her clawlike right hand. The remainder of her scarred body lay concealed behind a silk robe as she sat leaned to one side of the chair. Her thoughts drifted to the two men she blamed for her ruined body—Quint and Dawson. For the next hour, she sat imagining the most gruesome ways to end their lives.

CHAPTER 6

After a hectic two-week period spent making arrangements, Quint and Dawson set out for the south coast of Cuba in a charted trawler loaded with an assortment of supplies. "It's hard to believe you actually pulled this off," Dawson said.

"Actually, as I recall, this was originally your idea, and a fine one at that." Dawson glanced at Quint with his remaining blue eye while adjusting the eye patch, which seemed to be irritating him more than usual this morning.

"Eye bothering you?"

"Technically, it's the eye I lost that's the problem, but yes, it's giving me fits. The worst part is my limited field of vision. I'm constantly running into things or misjudging distance. I suppose I'll eventually get used to it, provided I don't kill myself first."

Dawson had recently lost an eye when he was shot while trying to prevent a truckload of stolen bioweapons from falling into the hands of terrorists. Though it had been several weeks since the injury, the adjustment was proving much harder than he'd ever imagined.

"Give up on the glass eye?"

"Yeah. Maybe I'll try again later, but it's uncomfortable and seems to freaks people out trying to decide which eye to look at. Wearing sunglasses makes me feel like Stevie Wonder. So for the time being, I'm going with the pirate look and getting used to the patch." Dawson ran his hand over the side of his head, pushing the few grey rebels in his otherwise brown hair behind his ears. The eye patch heightened his no-nonsense looks, caused by his almost total lack of body fat and an array of scars including an often-broken nose.

They had just entered Cuban waters when a ship popped up on radar, approaching at flank speed. "We're about to see how well our fancy new papers work," Quint muttered as a voice burst from the radio speaking Spanish. While the men's fluency in the language was lacking, the tone of voice conveyed the message. Quint slowed while Dawson retrieved the radio mic from the panel.

"No hablo español."

Immediately, the voice switched to crisp English. "Slow to idle and prepare to be boarded."

"We are in possession of documents authorizing—" Dawson began before the voice stepped on his transmission.

"Follow our instructions. We will discuss any other matters after boarding your vessel." A few minutes later, the Cuban gunboat maneuvered neatly alongside in the light chop and a squad of men leaped onto the trawler.

"Reminiscent of our last encounter with the Cuban Navy," Dawson muttered.

"Let's just hope it doesn't go downhill like last time." While working a Spanish wreck on the Cay Sal Banks, they had engaged the Cuban Navy in an unpleasant encounter that had ended poorly for the Cubans.

"What is your purpose?" the Cuban officer demanded as he approached. Quint explained while handing him the sheaf of papers with their authorization. "I have never heard of such a thing. These documents must be forged."

"We have a satphone. Let's call the number listed below the Commandant's signature at the bottom of that first page." Though appearing uncomfortable with the idea, the officer offered no easy alternative, so he watched Quint dial the number and then hand over the phone. The officer's entire demeanor had improved by the time he gave the phone back to Quint.

"It is as you say. You are free to proceed. I will forward the information along so perhaps you might avoid any future inconvenience. Have a safe passage." He then led his men back off the trawler and a minute later was gone.

An hour later, they arrived at a point just off the west end of Cuba where they had arranged to meet Santiago's friend, Renaldo. As they slowed and turned toward shore, Quint spotted an ancient wooden skiff heading toward them through the low swell.

A man in his late seventies waved as he stood in a low crouch at the front of the skiff. The man in the rear expertly swung the skiff alongside and with careful timing, Renaldo jumped onto the trawler with the grace of a man half his age.

"Good to see you again, meester Quint."

"Glad to see you as well, but it's just plain Quint. Grab a beer from the cooler and make yourself comfortable."

Renaldo withdrew a beer from the compartment, popped the top off the dark brown bottle, and took a deep pull.

"How is Santiago after our... incident?" Quint asked.

Renaldo swallowed before replying. "He's fine, though he mourns the loss of that damned old Buick. I think he might have chosen to die rather than have that car wrecked."

"I hate that. I've been trying to find a way to make that right, though I'm sure there's not another car like his baby."

Renaldo laughed. "That is very true, but he will certainly appreciate your kindness."

"I think it's the least I can do given that it happened while he was helping me. Speaking of which, I guess I need to pay you." Quint reached into his pocket to pull out a wad of cash.

"No, I must earn it first. Besides, there is no place to spend it now. Let me start by telling you more about Tears of Coral." As they continued toward the island for the next two hours, Renaldo shared a wealth of information.

"The Germans were the first to use it but abandoned it at the end of World War II. The base sat vacant until Castro offered it to the Soviets when the Cold War heated up in the late 1950s. The Russians spent millions of dollars and I was part of an army of men sent to refurbish it with modern equipment.

"When the Soviet Union collapsed in the 1980s, it was once again mothballed. Few people remember much about it today. With few beaches and little flat land, its remote location and unfavorable terrain make it of little value for commercial development. So it's just sat there vacant all this time."

They arrived two hours before dark. Renaldo gave directions as they approached. "This narrow inlet on the southwest side opens into a small lagoon surrounded by a nearly vertical mountainside. That is where the base is hidden."

In the waning light they made their way through the inlet into the island's lagoon, where Quint came to a slow idle a hundred feet from the rock wall of a sheer cliff face. He eased slowly forward and docked alongside a crumbling concrete jetty. Dawson threw over a fender, then hopped out to secure the bow line to a heavily rusted cleat.

Quint bumped the starboard engine into reverse once to swing the stern in, and Renaldo tossed Dawson a second line. After deploying another fender Quint stepped off the boat, armed with a shoulder bag containing Dawson's special tool assortment and flashlights.

With Renaldo leading the way, the three men approached what appeared to be solid rock. Quint and Dawson watched while Renaldo searched each small nook and cranny. Finally, he removed a loose rock from the wall which concealed a handle.

After Renaldo failed to budge it using all his strength, Dawson hosed it down with WD-40 from his tool bag. Renaldo then tapped on it using a small rock before trying again with the same result. Finally, on the third try, the handle broke free and a fissure widened into a small doorway revealing an enormous cavern within.

Quint handed a flashlight to Renaldo and the three men stepped through the open doorway. The moist, salty air inside was laced with the smell of seaweed.

With a broad smile on his face, Renaldo played the light along the walls as Quint and Dawson looked on in amazement. To their right lay the entrance channel. On the inside wall, a system of cables and counterweights were connected to another lever.

At Renaldo's suggestion, Dawson proceeded to spray the rusty lever with more WD-40 and work it repeatedly until it finally broke free. He then swung it all the way to the up position. Immediately, a set of counter weights descended and, with a horrific shriek of metal against metal, the enormous camouflaged doors slowly opened out into the channel.

The doors were halfway open when they began to slow, Quint imagined due to the accumulation of rust. A loud crack was followed by a sound like a discordant note on a piano, after which the doors stopped moving.

"Damn!" Quint saw where a cable had snapped; it would have to be repaired before the doors could be opened farther.

Renaldo eyed the gap between the partially opened doors. "It is no problem. That opening is wide enough for your boat to enter. We will need the generator to close the doors in any case."

It was nearly dark by the time Quint returned to the boat, untied the lines, and fired up the engines. He bumped the throttles forward and carefully idled through the narrow opening. Once inside, he switched on the bridge spotlight.

He eased the boat up to the dock on the left side of the cavern where Dawson grabbed the line Quint had hung on the bow rail and secured the boat to the ancient wooden dock. Once Quint killed the engines, the echo of the deep-throated diesels faded and the cave was silent save for the slap of wavelets against the hull and the muffled hum of the boat's generator below.

The dock faded into the darkness ahead and the sheer rock wall to his left vanished into the glare of the trawler's lights above. Other than the reflection of the lights on the shiny water's surface, Quint could see nothing.

Quint and Dawson stepped onto the dock, where the two men set the fenders back in place before following Renaldo, who was already headed off to explore the facility. Once away from the glare of the trawler's lights, Quint could see that the docks formed a "U" with a large crane located midway on each of the two legs.

"This was once a natural cave. The Germans enlarged it when they set up their base here. Later, the Russians beefed up the docks and turned what was an 'L' dock into the 'U' that you now see before you.

[Include sketch]

"It seems that your new fleet has been waiting a long time for you to arrive," Renaldo said. Two boats sat on chocks at the far end of the dock. Two more, tied against the bulkhead, rode low in the water, Quint imagined from heavy marine growth on their hulls. A fifth was sunk, with only its superstructure visible.

Overhead ran a system of scaffolding and catwalks extending from stairs at the base of the "U" dock to the front, where each catwalk ended at a door above.

"The warehouse is there." Renaldo pointed to a large roll up door built into the wall on the side opposite the harbor entrance. Their footsteps echoed loudly on the concrete dock as they made their way across the harbor. A small door to the right of the roll up one was unlocked, so they stepped inside. A mountain of crates filled the left side of the huge warehouse before them, and a long row of floor-to-ceiling shelves ran along the right. As they walked down the length of the warehouse, they noted a few useful items.

"Other than needing of a good coat of paint, this place is in surprisingly good condition," Quint commented.

Dawson nodded. "Except for that area." He walked over to a dark rectangular stain on the west wall of the warehouse and scraped at the surface of the wall. "Looks like mold, but only in this one spot. That's odd—what's the deal?" he asked Renaldo, who simply shrugged.

Quint laughed. "If that's the worst of it, we can count ourselves lucky." Returning to the front of the warehouse, they exited and followed Renaldo to the far side of the harbor area. A rusty door led to a much smaller room with a desk, filing cabinets, and other doors leading to what appeared to be a couple of small offices and one larger room. Cyrillic writing labeled each door and many of the crates, a holdover from the earlier Russian occupation.

"This way." Renaldo climbed the staircase immediately to their left up to the second floor. "These were the living quarters... for our Russian bosses, that is. We slept on straw pallets down in that warehouse. Beyond these are more offices, two conference rooms, and at the end of the hall, a large dining room.

"This was their main meeting room," he said, pointing on a room to their left. A glass wall on the back side of this large room overlooked the harbor below. The opposite side had an elevated area separated by a long glass wall, behind which sat numerous heavily damaged computer workstations. Several large displays and an enormous map of the world hung in the middle.

On the floor below, a number of seats formed an auditorium facing the elevated area. While Quint was pretty sure what to expect, he was nonetheless in awe. Dawson, seldom given to emotional displays, was almost giddy—more talkative than Quint had ever seen him.

"Damn! Is this perfect or what? Quint, you've pulled off some pretty incredible shit in the past, but this takes the cake! I mean, Superman's Fortress of Solitude had nothing on this. Plus, his place was way up in Popsicle Land."

"It's hard to believe this was originally developed by the Nazis during World War II. From the looks of that old electronics gear, I'd guess it was in full use during the Cuban missile crisis. Shoot, Khrushchev himself might have pounded his shoe on one of these very tables." Quint chuckled. "Why did the Russians leave?"

Renaldo rubbed his chin and looked off for a long moment. "As you can see, the technology became outdated and when budgets got tight, the Soviets chose to mothball the place."

Dawson nodded. "Yeah, I'm guessing it would have cost a fortune to upgrade these old electronics systems. But the mechanical structure still looks sound. In typical German fashion, I imagine that it's seriously overengineered. It'll probably still be here when we ain't."

Renaldo snorted. "That is for damn sure."

"They must have had some sort of maintenance engineering department. Let's see if we can find it and dig up a set of facility blueprints," Quint said and followed Renaldo as he set off down the hall.

He led them to the last office at the foot of the stairs, which appeared to be Maintenance and Engineering. A faded drawing depicting the facility layout hung on the wall. A further search netted them an extensive set of blueprints, which they took back to the boat. After throwing a frozen lasagna in the convection oven, they each opened a beer and sat down at the trawler's dinette to examine the drawings.

[NOTE: Insert sketch]

"So what are we going to call this place?" Dawson asked as he scanned over the blueprints.

"The island? I figured we'd stick with Tears of Coral."

"No, I mean the facility."

"Shoot, I don't know. I'm not so good at coming up with names. You compared it to Superman's hideout; why don't we just call it the Fortress for now and let the team come up with a permanent name?" Dawson nodded.

They continued studying the drawings until their eyes were bleary before stopping for dinner. While Quint threw together a salad, Dawson spooned huge helpings of lasagna onto each of three plates.

"I hope we got lucky and entered between satellite passes. A huge benefit of this place is the stealth aspect and it'd be a shame to blow it," he said through a mouthful.

Quint nodded. "Yeah, we'll need to be cautious if we're to continue to enjoy the full advantage of our little lair. A sat image of our boogying in or out would not be a good thing. The U.S. Government obviously knows about the island, but they may no longer be aware of this little feature." Quint made a wide gesture with his tomato-sauce-covered fork at the facility hidden outside the salon.

"I'll see about getting a schedule from Rogers so that we can time our future approaches and departures between satellite passes." He finished with a yawn. "What say we turn in for the night? Tomorrow we'll explore further and begin to make this our new 'home-away-from-home.'"

Quint fetched a set of sheets and a pillow from below decks and helped Renaldo make the couch up as his bed. After bidding him goodnight, Quint headed for his stateroom and, after a quick shower, climbed into his own bed.

Normally quick to sleep, Quint was pumped up, his mind racing with excitement. He lay awake in his stateroom until well past midnight jotting down action items before finally drifting off.

CHAPTER 7

The creak of the bulkhead from Dawson's movement in the forward stateroom woke Quint the next morning. He heard the shower running as he slipped on the previous day's wrinkled khaki shorts and a fresh t-shirt and entered the galley to fix a quick breakfast.

"Damn!" Quint cursed as he stained the front of his clean t-shirt with a red glob from his strawberry-jelly-slathered biscuit. He had just finished wiping up the mess when Dawson appeared.

Armed with a thick mug full of coffee, he glanced at the red stains. "I like the use of jelly to accent your ensemble and the blueprint," he said, pointing at the facility blueprints Quint had been poring over. Renaldo's face broke into a wide grin as he carefully took a bite of his own biscuit.

"Let's get to work," Quint said, ignoring the comment.

While Renaldo took on the project of getting the generator fired up, Dawson repaired the broken cable on the door-operating mechanism and Quint methodically explored the facility. He was just returning when he saw Dawson round the corner of the base's workshop, on a collision course with an open cabinet door which his missing eye prevented him from seeing. Before Quint could shout a warning, Dawson struck his head.

A string of expletives broke forth. Dawson grabbed a wooden two-by-four lying against the wall and proceeded to engage the offending cabinet door. Three blows later, the door was clearly getting the bad end of the stick when an errant splinter struck his face. drawing blood.

"Are we done now?" Quint quietly asked once Dawson's anger seemed to have played itself out.

"Pretty much." Dawson tossed the wood aside and stomped off in search of a bandage, leaving the cabinet door hanging by one hinge.

Most of the machinery seemed to be in good working order. Renaldo located spare belts and hoses for the generator plant. After changing those parts and the oil, he had the generator fired up by lunchtime. With the cable repaired, they were finally able to shut the massive doors leading into the harbor.

Other than a number of light bulbs in need of replacement and a few thrown breakers, everything seemed amazingly functional. The computers were another story. Apparently, the Russians had taken an axe to them.

The two boats resting on the dock against the far wall looked much like they must have the last time the facility had been occupied. The two steel-hulled boats in the harbor would need a great deal of work to remove the heavy marine growth from their hulls. The one sunk at the far end had either sprung a leak or been dragged completely under from the heavy accumulation of growth. It would need to be refloated and then taken offshore and permanently sunk. A great deal of effort would be required to ready their new "fleet."

After lunch, they followed Renaldo up a staircase which led to a steel door at the top of the facility. They stepped from the relative cool of the damp cavern into

the midday heat of a large concrete airplane hangar.
Its perimeter was lined with workbenches laden with
worn parts and ancient tools. The building was
recessed into a rock outcropping, hidden from above,
and it sat at the end of a small runway in need of
considerable maintenance.

Across the airstrip, a stand of palms partially
concealed an antenna array. Of the three antenna
masts, one lay crumpled, the result of time or maybe
severe weather during the years since the facility had
been abandoned. The second appeared to be solid,
while the third would need at least two of its guy wires
replaced but otherwise appeared to be sound. While
the rusted antennas were of little value, they could use
the towers to mount their own communications
antennas. Heavy growth camouflaged a radar dome
which seemed to be more or less intact, though the
outdated radars were certain to be obsolete.

"High on the list for our new base is a new radar
with a full security and electronic surveillance suite.
The harbor entrance, including the inlet, and every
door should be covered. We need wide-angle cameras
covering pretty much the entire island as well as the
facility interior. If it has two legs and breathes, I want
to know about it as soon as it enters a one-klick radius.
I also want a full defensive weapons suite, including
an underwater RCV and a couple of drones launchable
from that concealed hangar," Dawson finally
concluded.

"Any ICBMs or tactical nuclear weapons?" Quint
replied sarcastically.

"Hmm. I hadn't thought of it, but now that you
bring it up..."

Quint took Rogers' satphone call the next morning.
"How'd it go?"

"We had the chance to test our Cuban papers."

"And?"

"Not a problem. I have to admit I was skeptical, but the Cubans were polite and after a pleasant five-minute conversation, we were on our way."

"So, how's your new operations base?" Rogers asked.

"If anything, it's better than I had hoped. It'll take a while to get everything set up, but I think it's perfect. Tomorrow we'll drop off Renaldo and then it's back to the States, where we'll make the necessary preparations to bring the facility online."

"Hope it doesn't take too long. I've got a feeling you're going to be needing it shortly."

CHAPTER 8

The first hint of sun appeared over the flat sea
horizon as the captain of the *Donegal* leaned against
the starboard railing outside the ship's bridge. He was
savoring the early morning hours and the perfume‑
sweet aroma of his favorite blend of tea wafting off the
chipped mug he clutched in his hand.

While a year ago being this close to the coast of
Somalia would have made him a basketcase, Raoul
was at least somewhat relaxed. According to the latest
news media reports, piracy had been eliminated
during the recent UN‑led housecleaning. Besides, with
their cargo of scrap steel, they hardly presented a rich
target. Even so, he had scheduled himself to be on
duty when they were close enough to be attacked.

"Radar clear?" he yelled to his first mate stationed
inside at the helm.

The mate glanced at the screen on the port side of
the console. "Yes, Captain."

They continued on for the next fifteen minutes while
the captain finished his tea. "You can take a break.
I've got the bridge," he said. From force of habit, he
glanced at the radar screen in passing and came to an
abrupt halt at what he saw.

"What the hell have you done?" The range had been
zoomed in so that the display showed only the nearest
quarter mile. Savagely, he pressed the button to
increase the range and sucked in a deep breath as two

small blips appeared on the radar, less than half a mile off their port bow.

The mate leaned over to study the screen. "J-just a c-couple of fishing b-boats. Nothing to worry about."

"They're moving far too fast to be fishing boats." The captain smelled liquor on the man's breath. "You're drunk again, you fool! Sound general quarters."

As he picked up the intercom handset to ring the radio room, a stream of tracers from a heavy machine gun arched over the bow. "Radio room, radio room."

"Radio room," the radio operator answered in a sleepy voice, after the second attempt to rouse him.

"We're being attacked by pirates. Send a Mayday with our position. Keep sending it until I tell you to stop." Another stream of tracers flew over the bridge, striking the superstructure above.

"Yes sir," the startled radio man replied.

A few minutes later, the radio on the bridge burst alive. "Captain, I can't raise anyone; all I get is static. We are either being jammed or our antenna has been disabled ...Captain?"

The captain did not respond; a Somalian pirate had a gun to his head. The *Donegal* had been captured.

CHAPTER 9

Being a pirate had never been Jamal's dream; rather, he'd dreamed of being a musician. He often imagined himself seated at a grand piano in a concert hall, dressed in formal attire, pounding the ivories while the crowd listened in awe. Just like in that movie he'd once seen as a child. Yet the only real piano he had ever seen was at the home of a wealthy customer of his father's.

Jamal had spotted the magnificent musical instrument in a small room off to the right of the foyer upon entering the mansion where his father was working. Drawn to it as if by a tractor beam, his hand had shot out to touch the pure white ivory keys. His moment of elation had ended abruptly when his father had hauled him by the shirt collar into the bathroom where he was repairing a leaky toilet.

It wasn't ivory that his fingers softly stroked in the first light of morning, but the cool barrel of an AK-47 rifle. He waited along with the others for their leader, Ghedi, to finish "entertaining" a recently kidnapped young woman. His previous conquest had been bequeathed to his lieutenant, who had in turn passed his conquest down to the next lowest man in the pecking order as perks of their positions.

Such women never lasted long enough to make it down to Jamal's level. But as a virgin with idealistic visions of love, he was okay with that. Particularly since he was not certain he could perform the expected duties with an unwilling victim. He hoped his first time would be with Desta, the girl of his dreams, though sometimes he wondered if she even knew he was alive.

The sun was well up now, savaging the cool of morning, scorching the earth, and sucking the moisture from the living. A ragged wisp of cloud hung in the faded blue sky as if it were all this destitute land could afford. Jamal gnawed on his fingernails while he anxiously waited.

Finally Ghedi appeared, buttoning his shirt, sweat coursing from his shaved head to form dark spots on the collar of his freshly laundered khaki shirt and legs of his shorts. Jamal found him less dashing than back when he'd worn the traditional ma'awis, a sarong-like robe, and an imaamad, a decorative shawl, slung over his shoulder as their revered pirate leader.

But then, no longer did bodyguards and throngs of beautiful women surround Ghedi at the extravagant parties he'd once hosted as a reward for his hard-working men. And the days of fancy clothes and blaring music until dawn were long gone, along with the free-flowing, top-shelf liquor which they openly drank in defiance of Islam.

One of his men handed Ghedi a wicked looking M-16 with a grenade launcher he inspected closely as if his life might later depend on it—which might very well be the case. He nodded to his lieutenant before climbing into a battered pickup truck without even noticing Jamal.

A year ago, Ghedi would have made the trip down to the beach in a new Mercedes, waving at those along the way like some rock star while throwing whatever cash he happened to have left in his wallet. But a month earlier the Mercedes had gone to settle a debt with one of his backers, leaving him with only this wreck and barely enough fuel to make it to the beach.

Jamal, still desperately hoping to be chosen to go with Ghedi, reached down to remove his broken sandal and then set off at a brisk pace toward the beach, where Ghedi and the other pirates would gather before leaving on their next foray. Now that they worked from a mother ship and came back into port only when successful, there were not many opportunities to be picked.

While thirteen-year-old boys were sometimes selected, they were seldom as small as Jamal. His friend Ayan assured him that soon he would have a growth spurt and become even bigger than his friends. He prayed she was right—being the smallest pirate was not easy.

While he was grateful to have a job on the hostage ship anchored in the harbor, he hated working for Korfa and most everything else about being a guard, except for the food. The meals were far better fare than the pirates had while searching for ships to plunder in the waters far offshore. He heard that all they had to eat out there were rice, onions, and crushed dates, all stored in roach-infested holds.

Even so, Jamal longed to be a real pirate, not just a guard. He wanted to fire his rifle rather than threaten cowed hostages, most of whom were either too scared or too weak to fight. The higher pay would also be nice and he often imagined buying gifts to repay Ayan for her many kindnesses.

Ahead, Ghedi's rusted truck passed a group of men, leaving them behind in an enormous cloud of dust. "Look at Mr. Big Man," Jamal heard as he covered his mouth and nose with his shirttail until the dust settled. "He makes all the money. He eats the best food and gets the best whores."

"That is because he is Ghedi and you're not," Jamal yelled back and then ducked as the man flung a rock toward him.

"I work for months cooking for that stinking hostage ship and what do I get?" the man continued. "Maybe five dollars an hour. With the high cost of nearly everything these days and every friend and relative coming to me with their hand out, I can barely live on that pay and sure can't afford a decent whore. I'm lucky these days to afford Ayan," he said with a raucous laugh.

Jamal winced at the harsh words directed at his friend. "The only reason you can afford her is because she takes pity on men with small—" Jamal was cut short as he ducked another rock.

"Still it's better here than in that village we left," said one of the other men. "The only big bellies there were those swollen from hunger."

"True," Jamal heard him say before he neared the beach and was out of earshot.

Half the money always went to the men who captured the ships and a third to the investors. The rest was then split among everyone else, including the guards, cooks, suppliers, and translators. With things being so slow, these days the poor and handicapped were seldom included.

Overturned skiffs dotted the water's edge, cast aside like the starving poor in the small nearby town. The shore beside the dock was littered with empty whiskey bottles. While most of Somalia strictly followed the Islamic edict forbidding alcohol, in the pirate enclave it was ignored.

By the time Jamal reached the dock, Ghedi had already parked his truck. He was standing beside the mother ship arguing with an older white man with dark, slicked-back hair.

"What's this?" Ghedi demanded, pointing at a rusted drum of fuel that sat on the back deck of the weathered fishing trawler. A hose ran to an ancient engine which periodically coughed but continued to run. "Ethan, there's not enough fuel to go where we must and return."

"It's all you're getting," Ethan replied. It had been more than a month since Ghedi had captured the *Donegal* with its disappointing plunder of hostages, for which the company would not pay any ransom, and a load of scrap steel that they were having a hard time selling. "If you don't like it, find another backer."

"You know there are none," Ghedi replied with disgust.

"My point. It costs a great deal to finance your trips. I'm still paying to feed and guard your last bunch of unloved hostages. I doubt anyone will ever pay their ransom."

"So kill them if we can't get our price."

"I'm sure not paying to keep them alive until next season. I'll wait a few more days but after that, I'll sell the women. The unransomed men... well, they'll have a *big* problem." Ethan gave a low chuckle. Jamal wondered if he actually meant to kill them.

"Problem solved." Ghedi removed several leaves of khat from a bag in his pocket, placed them into his mouth, and began to chew the stimulant. "Haven't you made a fortune off the cargo I've brought you these past few years?"

"I have, but this is today. If you don't like it, don't go. There are others," Ethan said over his back as he walked away.

Ghedi raised the rifle which hung from his shoulder, his hand easing toward the trigger. Then, appearing to think better of it, he instead sent a stream of green spit into the water. He chewed in silence while watching his crew finish preparing to depart. Finally, he marched up the sagging wooden plank onto the ratty mother ship and yelled, "Time to go."

Jamal stood on his tiptoes, trying to make himself appear taller as he saw Ghedi's lieutenant scan over the group of young boys standing along the shore. He motioned at three of them, all barely a year older than Jamal.

Jamal's spirits sagged and he eased back off his toes as he jealously watched the lucky boys run to board the ancient trawler. He stood watching the boat as it left the Somalian harbor towing a string of skiffs in its wake.

When it was out of sight, he slid his foot back into the broken sandal. Scrunching his toes to keep it on, he slowly headed toward a graffiti-covered building in search of Ayan. Perhaps she might have something to ease his stomach, grumbling from missing dinner the night before.

"You didn't get picked."

Jamal was deep in thought and the voice startled him. He looked up to see Ayan in the cool shadows of the decrepit concrete hut, the former storage building a far cry from the lavish quarters where she'd once lived. The cloud of smoke she exhaled contrasted with her smooth dark skin.

"No. Maybe next time. Soon, I'll be fourteen." But with monsoon season only a few weeks away, he knew this might be the last chance this year.

"Well, I like having you around here. I know you dream of being a swashbuckling pirate, striking fear into the hearts of your victims with that AK-47 you so proudly carry. But with your job here, you're not so likely to be killed."

Jamal scowled while chewing on the index fingernail of his left hand.

"Stop that!" Ayan barked.

"Stop what?" he asked, wiping the sweat from his dark forehead with his shirtsleeve.

"Chewing your fingernails. I've told you a million times to quit. That's a nasty habit." Jamal blushed and removed his finger from his mouth. "Hungry?"

He nodded.

"Come, I'll fix you something." She pushed aside the ragged fabric which served as her door and Jamal followed her inside.

During the past year, most of the younger prostitutes had left in search of greener pastures but Ayan had remained. Though she was older than the others, her delicate features and full figure, coupled with her quick wit and knowledge of how to make a man feel like a king, kept her regulars coming back.

Ayan seemed to have a soft spot for Jamal and had taken to mothering the small boy, orphaned when his parents were killed in one of the bloody skirmishes that racked the country. Despite the taunts of the other boys, he was happy to have someone who cared.

He followed her into the cool, dark space. The scent of her perfume hung in the air, reminding him of the flowers his mother used to grow. Here he felt safe.

"Maybe they'll be back in a few days with a big fat prize," Jamal said and then caught himself chewing his nail. He quickly put his arm back down by his side before Ayan noticed and scolded him again.

"Maybe. We can hope, can't we? Once I might have prayed, but those days are long gone." Ayan lit a cigarette and used the same match to fire up the one-burner stove in the corner of the tiny room. Jamal wrinkled his nose at the smell of sulfur from the burning match.

"What?" she asked.

"That smells nasty. Plus you shouldn't smoke, it's bad for you."

Ayan gave him one of her stern looks. "Thank you, but *I'm* the one who gives such advice. *You* are the one who takes it." Jamal nodded and dropped the subject. "I hear when you're not working on the hostage ship, you've been helping Nasir with the boats. He says you're good. None of the boats you work on ever have problems."

Jamal beamed with pride. "Someone has to maintain them, and it's more fun than working for that asshole Korfa." Ayan shot him another look. "Sorry for the bad word. Anyhow, I figure once I'm a real pirate, it will come in handy to know how to fix things when we're offshore."

"Staying here as a boat mechanic would be better." He gave her a sour look. "Besides, Desta would miss you."

"Desta?"

"I've seen how you look at her."

"What?" Jamal protested.

"I think you have a crush on her." With a broad smile, she reached for a jar of ghee on the rickety shelf. She opened it and spread a thin coating on the canjeero. She offered it to Jamal, releasing it only after he thanked her.

He rolled up the pancake-bread and eagerly took a bite, nearly finishing before the tea was ready.

"At least chai is once again affordable," she said and added a dollop of sugar and a single mint leaf to the cup of steaming tea before handing it to Jamal. "I miss the days when Ghedi and the others would radio us with news of their latest prize. What fun it was to meet them on the dock dressed in our finest clothes and gush over the latest ship they had captured. And the parties." Jamal saw her look out the door wistfully before continuing. "I've been thinking that I might leave. If I do, I want you to come with me."

"Where would we go?" For the first time he noticed the crow's feet at the corners of her eyes. From all those parties and all that whiskey, he imagined.

"If I knew, I wouldn't still be here." Her laugh was punctuated by a cough and a cloud of smoke.

"Your cough is getting worse; you need a doctor."

"Sure, maybe I'll just go to that new two-hundred-room hospital just down the road. Then afterward, I'll check into a spa for a few days."

"Sorry, but I can't help worrying."

Ayan reached out to stroke Jamal's hair as he rose to wash his cup. The ringing of her cell phone interrupted them, and she gave Jamal a kiss on his forehead before taking the call.

As he was leaving her hovel to go work with Nasir on the boats, he heard Ayan's voice.

"Credit? Ha! Korfa, you come pay me what you owe from last time, then we talk. Until then, you don't call and waste my time."

It made Jamal sad. *I wish we could leave here. I wish I could take her to someplace nice... without those men.*

Ayan hung up the phone and watched Jamal as he walked away. Though he wasn't her son, it was the closest thing to a child she would ever have. Her ability to have babies had been taken along with her virginity—and her dignity—in a rape those many years before. After that, her chosen profession seemed almost natural. *What more can they take from me?*

CHAPTER 10

"Where's Colin?" Quint heard Dawson ask as he entered the team's rented conference room in their usual shabby hotel meeting place.

"Who gives a shit?" Kira replied while awkwardly maneuvering away from the coffee pot on her artificial leg.

Dawson grinned. "So much for marital bliss." Colin and Kira, recently married and expecting a baby, were famous for their volatile relationship.

"Heard from Preston?" Kira asked.

"Who gives a shit?" Dawson shot back before adding, "I prefer to let sleeping sociopaths lie."

From the expression on Kira's face, Quint could tell she wasn't sure if Dawson was serious. Dawson's brother, Preston, had shown up in the Keys a few months earlier and struck up a relationship with Mimi, another team member.

After borrowing money from most everyone on the team, his credibility was somewhat tarnished. Even after paying it back, most still viewed him with suspicion, though they tolerated him out of respect for Dawson.

Quint made his way over to the coffee service and poured a cup from the beat-up urn. What the meeting room lacked in ambience, it made up for with its convenient location and low cost.

He had called the meeting to discuss plans for setting up their new base, and as he looked over the assembled group, he was proud. In the first two missions since forming their LLC, they had become quite a capable team.

Each member of the team had originally been hired for some specific skill when Quint and Dawson were staffing to search for a Spanish shipwreck. But they had proven to blend well and function effectively together. So when Quint had decided to set up a corporation to pursue subsequent projects, he'd offered each of them the chance to be both shareholders and actively involved team members.

"Let's get started," Quint said to the group. "The purpose of this meeting is to develop a plan for setting up our new base on the island we've leased off the coast of Cuba. One thing to keep in mind: once we're there, we'll be on our own. There'll be no Walmart down the block, so we need to carefully think through what's important to take along. We have a seaplane scheduled to fly in on a biweekly basis to bring fresh food, parts, and so forth. But it's not intended as a solution for failing to bring in things that we should have thought of beforehand, particularly heavy or bulky items.

"That's why I asked each of you to provide Kira with a list of the items you feel will be essential for our new operations base. Kira's in charge of merging these lists, eliminating duplication, and assigning responsibility for procuring what we need."

A stunning, well-educated woman who could pass for a somewhat older college cheerleader, Kira had a down-to-earth manner that made it clear she did not rely on her looks nor expect any special entitlements. Her model-like face was framed by long, thick, naturally blonde hair. She had originally been chosen to join the team because of her experience in ocean surveying as well as her ability to handle herself in tough situations.

Kira's recent marriage seemed to be helping her cope with the twin challenges of being pregnant and the loss of a leg in a motorcycle mishap after the team's most recent mission.

"Leo, $11,000 for a coffee maker, really?" she asked, as she rifled through the stack of handwritten lists submitted by the team members.

Not only was Leo large, everything he did was on an XXL scale. His full head of curly hair and his bushy beard made him appear bear-like. He took enormous pleasure in celebrating his considerable appetites, be they exotic foods, drinking, fishing, sex, or, in his younger days, even drugs.

Leo had originally been recruited for the team because of his experience in finding old ship wrecks and his ability to navigate the Spanish archives. Now that he was a full-fledged member of the team, Quint had little choice but to tolerate his many annoying quirks. But he was very bright and dependable—for the most part.

"Hey, it makes really great coffee," Leo replied. "It has a computer to precisely control the water temperature, the dosage, the attraction time, and pretty much everything you can imagine to recreate a perfect cup every time customized to the individual. Shoot, they've got one that costs nearly twice as much, but you've got to be some sort of coffee ninja to operate it. And I figured it was waaay too expensive."

"Like eleven grand isn't?" Dawson asked.

"Not everyone shares your plebian tastes. Some of us appreciate the finer things in life," Leo said indignantly.

"That's nuts. I'll bet you've got some high end kitchen appliances in there too," Dawson fired back.

"As a matter of fact, he does," Kira said. "$100,000 for a range and stovetop and a walk-in beer fridge that holds 30 cases and 4 kegs."

"It's a handmade range with solid walnut drawers, and the beer fridge—" Leo protested.

"We're not spending $11,000 on a coffee maker." Quint ended the bickering. "We'll splurge for one of those K-cup machines, and Kira will pick out the appliances. Next item."

"Leo's list aside, most of the rest of it looks reasonable. Mimi and I will tackle the appliances and bedding; I don't want to sleep on mattresses that any of you guys would buy. Dawson, you take weapons and systems. Leo can handle provisioning," Kira said, and then paused. "But Quint and I will review the shopping list before ordering, so we don't end up with a pantry full of snails and bugs," she added, with a smirk directed at Leo.

Leo started to reply but was distracted by Nigora's entrance into the room. Her fine features and figure usually commanded male attention. She and Marcia had arrived late from a meeting in Miami to secure Nigora's U.S. citizenship. After her father was killed while helping the team in Uzbekistan, Quint had insisted that they bring her to the "Amelica" she had always longed to visit.

Quint had asked Marcia to mentor the young woman. One of her first struggles was to quell Nigora's desire for the breast enhancement surgery she understood to be common in the States. With a great deal of effort, Marcia had talked Nigora out of having actual surgery and into wearing a prosthesis in hopes that she would eventually lose interest. But so far, Nigora seemed to enjoy inflating her super-sized models to the max and flaunting her enhanced figure at every opportunity.

"Marcia and Nigora will help you with the provisioning." Kira added and looked up as someone else entered the room. "Colin, so nice of you to join us."

"So nice to be here," Colin replied with an exaggerated bow. A Brit whom Dawson had hired to oversee operations, Colin was in his midforties and in good physical condition. Right under six feet tall, he weighed in at two hundred pounds and was ordinary in appearance, except for piercing grey-blue eyes and a square jaw which looked like it could crush nails.

Kira shot daggers back at him and, ignoring his performance, continued. "If Colin takes electronics and communications, that leaves Dakota to focus on transportation, tools, and mechanical systems. With Marcia's help, Quint has volunteered to take everything else, which includes special equipment for things like diving and rappelling. I've also made Nigora responsible for assigning pods."

"Pods?" Dawson asked. "I think you mean rooms; why can't we just call them that?"

Kira laughed. "Relax. These pods won't be strapped beneath a drone like the one you recently rode in Russia. They're called pods because from what I understand, they're quite small, and pod sounds better than cell."

"I have one quick item," Dawson said. "I've arranged for Nigora and anyone else who can make it to undergo some weapons and defense training. See me after the meeting for details."

"Anything else before we adjourn?" Quint asked.

"What about security? How far will our base be from Guantanamo?" Mimi asked. From a poor family in which higher education was a fanciful dream, Kira had taken her under her wing, grooming her to be a critical part of the technical team. Despite losing her left index finger to pirates and nearly dying from a gunshot wound a short time later in the Venezuelan jungles, Mimi maintained that joining the team was the highlight of her entire life.

"Both are on the south side of Cuba, but at opposite ends some distance apart," Quint replied. "We can't count on any support from the navy. Rogers made it

very clear that with all of the ill will over
Guantanamo, they don't want to risk stirring up the
Cuban regime."

"Speaking of security, how about drones?" Leo
asked. "I've been thinking we might consider getting a
couple to help patrol the base. I think they might also
prove valuable in the future."

"For what?" Dawson asked.

"Unless we plan to add a bunch more folks, we'll
need to use the ones we have efficiently. I believe they
call it force multiplication. Given our remoteness, we
could also use them to fly in cargo." Leo paused for a
moment. "Maybe on our next project we can hit Rogers
up for a Predator and a Global Hawk with all the
whistles and bells. Maybe even include a weapons
package."

"Don't know if he'll go for it; those things are
pricey," Quint replied, "but I'll broach the subject with
him." Quint noticed Dakota seemed agitated and
nodded for him to speak.

Though Dakota's legal name was Jimmy
Chattopadhyay, everyone just called him Dakota.
"What about Nigora? She's not going down there with
us, is she?" he asked, ignoring Nigora's glare.

"Yes, she is," Quint snapped defensively.

"Might I ask why?" Dakota asked.

"For starters, her father died helping us during our
Aral Sea episode, and I... I mean we have an
obligation to look out for her. My first thought was
that she would remain in the Keys, but she
successfully argued that we'll need domestic help.
She's willing to serve as a maid, cook, or whatever we
need in order to earn a place at the Fortress. So I
agreed," Quint said.

"Chicken. You weren't man enough to deal with
her," Dawson said in a low voice that only Quint could
hear.

"And there's that," Quint muttered with a grin.

Mimi raised her hand. Short and more than a few pounds overweight, she had bobbed black hair that did little to complement her plain features. She had been hired as the most junior member of the team but had proven to be fiercely loyal and surprisingly brave in the face of being shot and maimed. Her distinctive snort when she laughed was the source of constant ribbing. "Uh, I had a question... sort of... I mean, I—" Mimi said.

"Spit it out, girl," Dawson said with a laugh.

She took a deep breath and then cautiously began. "We're going to have a lot of work to do when we get down to our new base. And"—she paused as she saw the look on Dawson's face, realizing he had already guessed where this was headed—"since Nigora's going, I wanted to mention that Preston has volunteered to go."

"No! Absolutely, positively, oh hell no!" Dawson yelled, the veins on his neck standing out.

"Hear me out," Mimi shot back defensively. She and Preston had started seeing each other when he'd shown up a few weeks earlier claiming he wanted to patch things up with his brother before terminal cancer took his life. "He offered to work for free and we're just going to be spending a couple of weeks setting up. It's not like we're going down there on a job. He's your brother and he's trying to make amends. In fact, he's been the only one to make any effort at a reconciliation. I don't think it's fair for you to let your own selfish interests trump those of the team. We could certainly use free help. And then there's the fact that he's dying of cancer—"

"Well, I think—"

"Wait, you already spoke," Mimi interrupted Dawson. "Let Quint have a say."

Quint hated being put in this position—forced to weigh his best friend Dawson's interests against those of the team—but saw no other option. "Dawson, she makes a good point."

"Yeah, what's your problem?" Mimi asked.

"You know very well what the *problem* is. But for the sake of the team, I'll recuse myself. Do what you want," he said, as he stomped away.

Mimi watched him leave before continuing. "Again, Nigora's going, and Preston is Dawson's brother, for goodness' sake. He's family. And it's not like we're involved in some big-time secret stuff. All we'll be doing is setting up shop."

"Dawson has been a member of this team since the very beginning, and I don't think any of us have sacrificed any more than him," Quint said rubbing his left eye. "You're right; he is Dawson's brother. But in this case, I think we owe it to Dawson to honor his wishes. Preston is not going." This time it was Mimi's turn to stomp off, but only as far as the coffee pot.

CHAPTER 11

"Have time for lunch at El Siboney?" Dawson asked as he noticed Marcia approaching him in the parking lot a few minutes later.

"I'll find time," Marcia replied eagerly, pushing her thick dark brown hair behind her right ear.

"You know, Quint is still singing your praises for rescuing his butt before Syndy could make a eunuch out of him... or worse." Dawson paused when he noticed her blush.

Marcia had been a waitress in New York. After reaching the end of her patience with a particularly irksome customer, she'd quit abruptly. With no other immediate job prospects, fortune had smiled upon her when she'd gotten hired as a trainee by a firm specializing in undercover security for retail merchants. This had led to work in the Middle East for a private firm contracted to provide security for the military.

Recruiting her had proven to be an exceptionally wise choice after Quint was taken hostage by an old nemesis. Marcia's training and experience had paid dividends when she'd rescued him from being tortured and killed.

"I just do my job like the rest of the team," Marcia replied.

Dawson nodded. "Hey, I'm in the mood for Cuban food. What do you say—" Dawson stopped when he spotted his brother, presumably there to meet Mimi.

Before Dawson could react, Preston saw him and yelled from across the parking lot.

"Dawson, please give me a minute. You've been avoiding me," Preston said as he smoothed a wrinkle out of his silk shirt.

"Oh, looks like you need to speak with Preston. We can do lunch some other time... if you like," Marcia said, looking down at her shoes.

Dawson let out a deep sigh and turned to Marcia. "No, you go on ahead and I'll catch up with you. This won't take long," he said, bringing an instant smile back to her face. She turned to walk away but abruptly stopped to stare at Preston. "Problem?" he quietly asked.

"That tattoo on Preston's neck."

"The 'S-203'?"

"Yeah. I've seen a tattoo like that before, but I can't think where. Maybe it'll come to me," she said with a shrug. "I'll see you at the restaurant. But don't be long or I'll start without you." Dawson laughed as he continued on toward Preston.

"Look, I can't undo a lot of the stupid, selfish things I've done in the past. Wish I could, but I can't. But I'm trying, really. I've changed."

Dawson rubbed the back of his neck with his hand. "Then how do you explain all that shit you told the team a few weeks ago? You know, about owning an imaginary mansion, divorcing a nonexistent wife, selling fictitious oil wells, and—"

"I stand guilty as charged of... embellishing the truth."

"Now there's an understatement. I doubt you'd know the truth if it bit you on the ass. Looks to me like more of your old conman tricks."

"But this is different. I was desperate to borrow money. I fully intended to pay everyone back as soon as I got that job I was working on, and indeed I did. I've changed, I promise."

"What kind of job was that? I mean, I didn't know what job skills—"

"For which someone would actually pay Preston?" Preston interrupted, referring to himself in the third person as he commonly did. "You've really never had much faith in me." He paused for a moment to look Dawson in the eye. "It was a consulting gig. They were insistent I not disclose anything. In fact, they made me promise to keep completely quiet." Dawson laughed.

"I guess they put more stock in my word than you," Preston said, ignoring Dawson's reaction.

"They'd have to. Tell you what, the day I'm convinced you're out of the con business, we'll talk about fence-mending over a beer. Until then, you're just the same old scumbag," Dawson replied. Preston stood silent as Dawson walked away, still shaking his head and chuckling to himself.

For a moment, Dawson almost regretted being a hard-ass, but then he remembered all the pain Preston had caused all those people over all those years. *I hope he really is coming around and if he does, I'll work hard to fix things. But he needs to go first this time.*

CHAPTER 12

After the meeting, the team milled around chatting. Quint was still talking to Kira when Preston stormed through the door.

"I guess that's why Mimi hasn't left," Kira said, pointing at Preston, who was headed toward Mimi. "She didn't take your refusal to let him come too well."

"No, she didn't," Quint agreed.

"Well, it didn't hurt my feelings. That man's a manipulative user."

"You seem to have broken him of hitting on you."

Kira laughed. "Took a while, but luckily I got through to him before Colin got involved. You know, he looks amazingly healthy for someone supposedly dying of cancer. I thought he only had a few weeks to live?"

"That's what he claimed," Quint replied. "You really don't like him much, do you?"

"You have to ask? Look, I really tried to like him, but he's an asshole. I'll be glad when he leaves. Dawson's been right about him all along." She looked over as the two headed for the door. With his arm around Mimi, Preston nodded slightly without speaking.

Most of the team had left when Dakota finished a call on his cell phone and caught Quint's eye. "So do you have a plan for us to get all of this stuff down there?" Dakota stroked the long braided pigtail which sprung from a round spot in the back of his otherwise shaved head as he sat down. An American Indian with the broad shoulders, general physique, and complexion to match, he'd captained oilfield boats for years. When Quint had initially interviewed him to be the team's boat captain, Dakota assured him that if it had propellers, he could run it.

"Good question," Quint replied. "I've leased another offshore supply ship from my old buddy, Tex. He's the same guy who sold us *Searcher.*"

"She served us well until Katrina sent her to Davy Jones' Locker."

CHAPTER 13

"So is Preston about to set sail for Cuba with you?" Preston asked as he and Mimi headed for a bar down the street.

Mimi shook her head, overlooking his annoying habit of referring to himself in the third person. "No, unfortunately. I tried again, but your *beloved brother* vetoed the idea, same as last time."

Before Mimi looked up at the waitress to order her drink, she caught the flash of rage on Preston's face, gone in an instant. Without commenting, she ordered a gin and tonic.

"I'll have the same. And bring us both a shooter of Patron," Preston added.

Mimi took Preston's hand and looked into his eyes. "I'm sorry. The team could definitely have used your help, and I was looking forward to spending time together," she said earnestly as the waitress returned to set their drinks on the table.

"I understand; don't give it another second's thought. Perhaps one day Dawson will warm up to me, but I have to earn that after all the mistakes of our youth," Preston replied, staring out across the harbor. Although he was saying the right words, Mimi saw a steely look in his eyes rather than the wistful expression of a brother desperate to reconnect with his wronged sibling.

Preston shot his tequila to calm him and then downed Mimi's when she deferred. He then excused himself to go to the restroom.

As soon as Preston turned the corner, he slipped outside to call Syndy. Though he hated calling her, after downing the shots of liquid courage, he was able to force himself to dial her number.

"There just hasn't been much to report. The team has been more closed-mouthed since Quint's capture in Murmansk," Preston said. "I've been trying to get the location of the base out of that woman I've been seeing. I want you to know the sacrifice I've had to make courting her. I've managed to cultivate her as a source, though she's become quite tight-lipped of late. She did mention that she might have to leave soon for a couple of weeks. My guess is that's where she'll be heading."

"Excellent!"

"I've been trying to talk her into letting me go with her, but that's proven a tough sell—even for me."

"In case Mimi isn't cooperative this time, I've sent you a tracking transponder. You should have it by tomorrow. Perhaps you could slip it into her bag before she departs."

"That shouldn't be a problem."

"I suppose it was fortunate that Quint never saw you during that fiasco aboard my ship a few weeks ago. We just finished the repairs on *Syntillate*, and she's as good as new. Has Quint's team given any indication they suspect you were involved in the death of that man from his team...Willy, I believe it was?"

"Not in the slightest. I believe Preston has proved that you can, indeed, fool some of the people all of the time. They're gullible and I've found it easy to pull the wool over their eyes. None of them suspect a thing." Preston hung up, breathed a sigh of relief at having that conversation behind him, and re-entered the bar.

CHAPTER 14

"Dakota, why don't you brief us on the status of the ship we've leased," Quint began, having gathered the team back in the ratty hotel conference room for a final meeting before their departure for the Fortress. He smiled at Dakota's t-shirt du jour: *Beer: So much more than a breakfast drink.*

"The ship is out of dry dock and ready to go. Most of the supplies have arrived and are packed into shipping containers to be loaded."

When he finished, Quint thanked him. "You and Colin will finish getting the cargo loaded, after which you'll head down to the Fortress to join us.

"While the Cubans shouldn't give you any problems, with a shipment this large, they might. Here's an envelope with enough cash to cover any bribes and to pay Luis should you need his help. He's a clerk I met in Havana who might prove to be quite... resourceful if you have problems. His contact information is in the envelope as well."

"When are you and Dawson leaving to go to the Fortress?" Dakota asked.

"Tomorrow. We're taking the trawler back down with a load of essentials to prepare for the rest of the team's arrival a day or so later. Everyone should already be down there by the time you guys arrive," Quint replied. After covering a few more details, he ended the meeting. As Dakota headed for the door, he noticed Colin and Kira in a serious conversation on the far side of the room.

"Am I intruding?" Quint asked.

"No, not at all," Colin said. "Just baby talk."

"My due date is still a ways off, so I'm going to ask the doctor tomorrow about taking a quick trip to the Fortress for a few days," Kira said. "I'd hate to miss it, but after our... er... my motorcycle accident, I'm not about to do anything else to put our baby at risk."

Quint nodded, impressed with the new, more conservative Kira. He imagined her mother-to-be hormones had a lot to do with it. "You don't have to tell him the exact location, but make sure to mention the fact that it's a remote island, in Cuban waters, with no medical facilities."

"Of course," she snapped. "Why don't I tell him the docks have splinters and the water is teeming with flesh-eating barracuda, while I'm at it?"

Quint ignored her response as he refilled his coffee cup. "I enjoyed meeting your sister, Jenny, at your wedding. I believe she was about to leave on a sailing adventure. How's she doing?"

Before she could answer, Colin jumped in. "That's the reason *someone*"—he cut his eyes toward Kira— "has been crabby."

"The problem is I haven't heard from her. Though she checked in with me on their satphone for the first few weeks as promised, I haven't heard a peep from her since they actually set sail from the Seychelles."

"Well, maybe the phone broke or fell overboard, and she couldn't call from offshore. Perhaps she'll call when they reach their next port."

Kira replied softly. "That's what I thought, but it's been two weeks. I keep trying her satphone but can't reach her."

"Oh," Quint said. *She's right to worry. I would.* "Do you want me to see if Rogers can find out anything about her status?"

"Please. I think it's time we hit the panic button."

CHAPTER 15

The next morning, Kira had been waiting on the exam table for nearly an hour when the doctor finally entered. "Sorry I'm late; we had an early delivery. These babies show little regard for my schedule." The doctor laughed as she reviewed Kira's test results.

"You and the baby seem to be doing great. But I guess we'll need to start seeing you on a weekly basis." She proceeded with the routine exam and then as she washed her hands asked, "Anything else?"

"Actually, there is. I need to take a short trip and wanted to get your opinion about whether it's safe for me to travel."

"How far?" she asked Kira.

"It would be a short flight," Kira replied, neglecting to mention that it was to a remote island off of Cuba.

"Are there nearby medical facilities?"

"Uh... well, not really. But I would be leaving next week, and it's only for a few days. They're about to set up a clinic there," she added, referring to a closet-sized room with the elaborate first aid kit another doctor friend had helped her assemble.

The doctor smiled. "I can tell this is something you really want to do. In answer to your question, most doctors urge pregnant women not to travel starting sometime between weeks thirty-two and thirty-five. I tend to be a little more liberal than most; after all, you can't quit living your life. And unless you were to take to bed for the last trimester, there is always risk.

"You appear to be quite healthy, your recent mishap aside." She glanced quickly at Kira's artificial leg. "At week thirty-three, I would have to go on the record advising against it. I don't have to tell you that you do not want to be having this baby in the air or in some remote location."

"I'm with you on that. While you're right that I don't want to quit living my life, the health and safety of the baby has to take precedence. I just want to strive for a happy medium."

"Will you have telephone access?" Kira nodded. "Okay, if you plan to leave in the next day or so and will be back within two weeks, I feel that the risk should be minor. I'll have the nurse put together a little kit for you to take. In the unlikely event that anything were to happen, you could call me and we could handle it."

CHAPTER 16

The day after Quint and Dawson returned to the base in the trawler, the generator was back up and running and all of the supplies were unloaded.

Quint heard the sound of a plane's engines in the distance just as the satphone rang. "We've just landed and are taxiing toward the harbor entrance," Kira said. Quint and Dawson opened the main doors to the concealed harbor and were waiting when the big seaplane arrived a minute later.

The plane lined up on the harbor and eased in. Quint and Dawson turned their heads and closed their eyes to protect them from the fusillade of dust and debris stirred up by the plane's powerful engines. When the plane had come to a stop, the pilot killed the engines and stepped down onto the pontoon, where he secured the plane alongside the dock.

Kira eased down from the plane into the expansive concealed harbor, taking care not to stumble on her prosthetic leg. "I'm still a klutz with this thing. I had hoped to be handling it better by the time the baby came, but I don't know if I'll ever get used to it," she said, one hand resting on her swollen belly.

"You choose a name yet?" Quint asked.

"No, Colin's recused himself from the process, but I still haven't picked from my short list."

"When's the due date?" Quint asked for the tenth time.

"June seventeenth. You want me to stencil it on your forearm so you can remember?" Kira laughed.

"Guys can't remember that sort of stuff. But I promise to try harder this time. July twentieth, right?" Kira started to glare but couldn't help laughing.

"Wow!" Mimi said as she climbed from the plane to stand in awe of the facility.

When the team had all disembarked, Quint stopped to chat with the pilot, an old buddy from his Special Forces days whom Quint had chosen as much for his trustworthiness as for his aviation skills. A moment later, Quint cast off his lines and the seaplane taxied back out for takeoff.

"What do you think?" Dawson asked.

"If anything, you undersold it," Kira replied. "This is way cool."

"Come on, we'll show you around." Quint said proudly and set off with the group in tow.

When they finished the tour, Quint took them to their quarters. Kira wrinkled her nose. "Can't say much regarding the accommodations. I'm not sleeping on that nasty mattress," she said, tossing it onto the floor as Quint chuckled. "I'll need an extra blanket to soften those iron springs until they get here with the down-filled replacements I bought."

They followed Quint to the small dining room where fresh-brewed coffee awaited. "When are our supplies supposed to arrive?" Kira asked as she poured herself a cup, ignoring the stale biscuits left over from breakfast.

"The last of the shipping containers were to be loaded onto the ship, and the guys were supposed to leave the port of Miami yesterday. Per our agreement negotiated with the Cuban authorities, customs inspection and duty are supposed to be waived. So,

Dakota and Colin ought to have cleared customs and should be headed our way by now."

"I just spoke with him on the satphone," Leo said as he made a beeline for the coffee pot and snatched up the remaining biscuits. "I confirmed the weather window is holding. Assuming they don't run into problems, they plan to arrive just after dark during a gap in satellite coverage."

"Did you notice I made sure to bring your beloved vanilla creamer?" Kira asked when she saw Quint pouring a cup. He barely nodded in response. "Well... aren't you going to thank me?"

"Kira, I'll spend the rest of my life in your debt."

"You don't have to be sarcastic."

The team spent the rest of the day making the facility operational. That evening, they all gathered at the dock to watch Dakota guide the ship into the cavern where the team secured it.

"Everything go okay?" Quint asked.

"We had a little hassle with Cuban customs, so we called your boy Luis. He made the problem go away, for a wad of U.S. greenbacks, of course. That, and we bumped bottom coming in on a bar outside the inlet channel. According to the tide charts, it's unusually low. I'll be more careful making the turn into the lagoon in the future. But it seemed like a sand bottom, and I had already backed off on the throttle, so we were idling."

"Still a good idea to make sure we didn't bend a prop. I'll take a look-see tomorrow," Dawson said.

"Are you really that concerned, or mainly itching to get wet?" Quint asked with a laugh.

Dawson shrugged. "A bit of both."

While the team off-loaded the ship the next morning, Dawson donned a scuba tank to inspect the ship's running gear and hull. With the doors to the harbor closed, he switched on his underwater light as he entered the still waters inside the Fortress's hidden harbor and descended into the dark waters. Beginning his inspection at the stern, he noticed a tiny ding in the starboard prop. As he worked his way forward, he found a fresh scrape on the keel with one deep gouge where Dakota must have bumped bottom.

Satisfied that the damage was cosmetic and the running gear was intact, he swung the light's beam around the enclosed harbor. A large school of baitfish skittered back and forth, keeping their distance from a lone barracuda. The antennae of numerous lobsters waved from beneath the dock ledge and the rock wall lining the harbor on all three sides.

An assortment of debris lay along the harbor bottom, most of it dating back to the German or Russian occupation of the facility. As he swung the beam back towards the ship's bottom, Dawson noticed a dark area at the far end of the dock. It appeared to be an opening near the bottom, beneath a rock overhang concealed from above, and he swam over to check it out.

As he neared the end of the dock, he could tell there was found a narrow cave. He tentatively swam in a few feet and saw it was actually more of a tunnel, continuing as far as he could see with the beam of his light. Lacking cave-diving gear and a buddy, he decided to wait until later to explore farther.

He was about to leave when he spotted a pocket of air above him and ascended. He took a breath of air and examined the space with his light. The only feature was a shallow ledge with something wedged in a crevice near the back. He reached in and with a little effort worked it loose. It was a piece of an old wooden crate with German writing on it and an insignia of some sort.

It appeared to have floated in at low tide and become wedged during an abnormally high one. On a whim, he carried it with him as he swam back out to end his dive.

An hour later, Dawson had showered and changed into a pair of cargo shorts and a Marty Wilson t-shirt bearing the image of a billfish, a tuna, and a wahoo. He was drinking a Coke in the lounge area while studying the piece of wood he had found when Leo came walking past.

"What you got there?"

Dawson looked up. "Not sure. Looks like a piece from an old wooden crate."

"How exciting," Leo replied sarcastically.

"It's not the wood I find interesting, Mr. Smartass, but the German markings."

Leo's interest was immediately heightened. "Let me see." Leo studied it for a moment and then looked at Dawson with genuine excitement. "The marking on this edge appears to be one wing of a Nazi symbol. See this cross on what appears to be the chest of an eagle? And this lettering." Leo paused for a moment, and when he continued, he did so in a low voice. "Dawson, this looks like the insignia used on crates carrying World War II Nazi bullion."

CHAPTER 17

Jenny awoke and noticed the gentle roll of the boat as she stretched. It appeared that the storm had made its way through during the night; no complaints from her on that count. She slid on her previous day's shorts and a fresh t-shirt. Opting to ignore her hair and makeup, she entered the galley and felt something sandlike on her bare feet.

"Damn!" she yelled. During the night, a can of coffee had fallen off the shelf in rough seas and now lay open on the floor, most of its contents spilled out. Carefully, she scooped some off the top of the pile, glancing over her shoulder to make sure that Brad was still above decks.

What he doesn't know won't hurt him. He's lucky I'm even making his coffee. A few minutes later, she emerged into the sailboat's cockpit carrying two spill-proof mugs of steaming java.

Brad was busy checking their heading but glanced up with a broad smile. "Morning. Just confirmed the autopilot is good as new after yesterday's repair job. Am I good or what?"

She nodded without commenting and eased into the seat across rather than alongside him. As she handed him his coffee, he leaned over to give her a quick kiss. She found herself struggling not to pull away and then was afraid he might have noticed when he continued to look at her. Thoughts of the previous night flooded back and her stomach knotted. *I hope he doesn't sense anything; I'm not ready to go there right now.*

"What?" she asked, unnerved by his unbroken stare.

"I love how the early morning sun catches the highlights in your blond hair, and the I-just-got-out-of-bed look the wind gives it."

"Thanks, but that's because I did just get out of bed," she replied, quickly changing the subject. She hoped to avoid another heated conversation about why she was insisting they sleep in separate beds. "Where are we?"

"Right on course. With these favorable winds, we're actually making better time than I had planned, so I pulled her back. Don't want to be getting close to land before nightfall. Coffee's good," he said after gulping a mouthful.

"We still had some of those high-priced grounds, so I splurged," Jenny said, choosing not to mention that she had scraped them off the galley floor.

He nodded as he took a sip. "Mmm. I have to admit, it's worth the ridiculous price you paid for it." They continued to sail in the gentle breeze for a few minutes before Brad spoke again. "After all those months of planning, I still have a hard time believing we're boat owners sailing around the world. I'm torn between being excited about living our dream and being terrified at the prospect of having to get jobs and go back to work again when our first leg is over."

"I'd prefer not to think about that... at least until we have to," she said, dreading the inevitable conversation about... them. "I'm scared about the pirates off Somalia."

"Look, I know you're worried, but they prefer big, fat freighters or tankers; not little sailboats like ours. It'll be okay. We'll hang back until dark and then stay well offshore. You'll feel better once we clear Somalia.

"Speaking of that, do you mind taking over for a bit? I'm going below to break out our guns just in case, and then try to get some shuteye. I want to be rested before tonight. I'll keep you safe. Promise," he said and kissed the top of her head before heading down below.

It was early afternoon when Brad reappeared with a plate of dinner in his hand. As she took the food, there was no smile or joking. "I loaded the guns and prepared for our night sail off Somalia then managed to snag a couple of hours sleep."

Jenny nodded but remained silent.

"Still worried about pirates, aren't you?"

"Is it that obvious?" she asked.

"Afraid so."

"Why do they do it?"

"I guess for the same reason they've been doing it since the time of Julius Caesar."

"Piracy goes back that far?" she asked.

"When he was twenty-five years old, pirates captured Caesar and held him for twenty talents of silver in ransom. Evidently, his sizeable ego was injured at the puny demand so after he escaped, he saw to it that the pirates were captured and crucified."

She finished her meal and headed below without hugging him as she might once have. Hoping to take a quick nap before dark, she lay there quietly, but her thoughts once again turned to Brad.

Months before, it had become clear that the spark was gone from their marriage. Not just gone, but dead cold. When she had discussed her misgivings about taking the sailing trip, her sister, Kira, had encouraged her to give it a shot, suggesting, "Maybe the time alone on the trip will change your feelings." But it hadn't.

The first two weeks they had spent in the Seychelles getting the boat ready had gone okay. But by the time they were ready to set sail, it was clear the trip was a mistake. *I owe him honesty, but I hate to ruin the rest of the trip. I'll wait until we get back home. Then we'll talk*, she told herself to ease her conscience.

After dozing off for an hour, she awoke to find it was not yet dusk. Immediately, she thought of her failing marriage. *This is driving me crazy. I've got to tell him; there's no point in putting it off longer. I'll do it after it gets dark. At least that way, I won't have to see his face when I break his heart.*

She thought about it for only a minute before changing her mind. *No, I'll wait. Broaching the subject now will just make us both even more miserable.*

Jenny took a seat with her back against the cabin, rather than sitting beside Brad to watch the sunset as she normally did, hoping he wouldn't notice. She needed this separation to have a prayer of avoiding the unpleasant subject.

She watched their wake and the reflection of the setting sun in his sunglasses. Neither spoke as they enjoyed the gentle sound of water passing the hull and the wind in the rigging.

It was an hour after sunset when Brad finally broke the quiet. "Is something wrong? You just haven't seemed yourself since we left the Seychelles."

"I'm fine," she snapped, biting her tongue.

"Look, I've known you for a long time, and I can tell when something's bothering you. Is it about us?"

"Not really, I've just been thinking about our future... I mean, I've been thinking—"

"Spit it out, woman."

Jenny took a deep breath. "We've been married a long time, and I—"

"Jenny, I love you."

He's not making this easy. But I just need to wait.

"Well...?"

"Well, what?"

"I said 'I love you.' Isn't there something you usually say in response?"

Her mind screamed, *Don't say anything. If you do, you'll regret it. Now is not the time.* But unable to control herself any longer she heard her voice blurt out, "The problem is, Brad, I don't love you anymore." *Crap! You've done it now, you stupid, stupid woman.*

Brad jerked as if he had been shot. He looked at her with such sorrow in his eyes that she nearly lacked the courage to continue.

She paused to take a deep breath before forcing herself to finish. "You must have noticed things have been different these past few months even before we left on our trip. You must have."

"You've been a little more withdrawn, but I figured it was hormones or whatever."

"Brad, I wish it were. I really wish it were. But I'm afraid that it's—"

"Shh," Brad said, holding up his hand. She stopped talking and caught the sound of an engine in the distance. Both of them strained their eyes in the direction of the sound but could see nothing. For a while the sound seemed to remain the same, but it soon became obvious that it was getting louder.

"A powerboat, probably just a fishing trawler," he said to comfort her, knowing full well that there were no fishermen in these waters, particularly at night. "With this heavy overcast and no moon, I doubt anyone can see us. But just the same, take the wheel; I'll be right back." A minute later, Brad reappeared in the cockpit carrying the loaded pump-action 12 gauge shotgun and the big .357 revolver, which he handed to her, tossing a bag filled with extra shells on the deck.

He stood leaning against the cabin while scanning the seas in front of them, the shotgun lying on top of the cabin. Eyes straining against the curtain of black, he was looking for the source of the sound when a spotlight shattered the dark. It probed for only an instant before coming to a stop shining directly in his face. Before he could raise the shotgun, the sound of automatic weapons fire had him dropping behind the cabin wall.

"Pirates! Jenny, get down, dammit!" She collapsed to the cockpit floor beside him. He reached up for the stock of the shotgun still hanging over the cabin when a stream of bullets sent him sprawling backwards amidst a shower of fiberglass from where the cabin hatch had sat an instant before. He eyed the shotgun now lying on the cockpit floor beside him but made no effort to pick it up. Instead, he jammed the pistol into his shorts pocket.

The engine sound grew louder and he heard the boat's hull strike his own hard enough to splinter the fiberglass toe rail and a section of the hull. Immediately, three men leaped aboard brandishing AK-47s. One dropped down beside him and snatched up the shotgun, striking Brad's head with the stock of it. Without speaking, they jerked the couple to their feet.

One of the pirates patted Jenny down, deliberately running his hands over her breasts, a leering smile on his face. The larger burly man withdrew the pistol from Brad's pocket and whipped the barrel across his face, knocking Brad to his knees. He then struck him again with the butt of the gun and Brad collapsed to the cockpit floor.

Jenny was forced into the pirates' skiff, and a moment later, two men tossed Brad after her. Blood poured from his face as he lay there groaning. Throughout the entire episode, one man stood watching with an M-16 slung across his chest, his shaved head gleaming in the spotlight.

"Welcome! I am Ghedi. And you would be...?"

"I'm Jenny, and this is Brad."

"We will have plenty of time to get to know each other, but for now, you must remain quiet. If you resist in any way, you will be beaten... severely... until you learn to behave. Clear?" Jenny nodded.

Ghedi's men removed the cap from the boat's fuel tank and fed a hose into it. While they pumped out fuel, others searched the sailboat, returning to the pirate skiff a few minutes later with an armload of food, supplies, and a few valuables.

Jenny could smell gasoline, and gasped as she saw them pumping the remaining raw fuel into the sailboat's cockpit. One of the pirates untied the boat while another shot a flare, igniting the fuel inside the cockpit of the sailboat. As they pulled away, a column of flames erupted, heavy black smoke obscuring the sails and mast. A few moments later, the entire boat was engulfed in a billowing curtain of orange. The pirate skiff was well away by the time the raging fire found the sailboat's fuel tank and an impressive fireball erupted.

Jenny watched their burning boat until it slipped beneath the waves, plunging them into complete darkness. They were captured.

CHAPTER 18

It was late when Dawson left the Fortress to walk along the narrow strip of sand lining the harbor's edge. He could hear waves crashing offshore on the distant reef and the more gentle sound of waves lapping the protected beach. The scent of seaweed mixed with salt was carried on the soft breeze

He was perched on a rock enjoying the solitude when Kira appeared—walking back from a late night stroll—and startled him.

"Sorry, didn't mean to sneak up on you," she said.

"You didn't. You were just on my blind side. Man, I really miss having both eyes. What's the matter? Can't sleep?"

"No, so I figured I'd put some time in working out with my new prosthesis. Whenever I sit for too long, like on the flight down here, my... uh... stump gets stiff and sore the next day. Damn, I hate that word— stump. After that accident I wish I'd never seen a motorcycle."

"I've been wanting to tell you how great I think you're coping with... everything. Not many women could do so well, particularly being pregnant at the same time."

"Thanks. I won't lie; it's been a bitch. I just decided my family has to come first. How're you doing with one eye?"

"Like you said, it's a bitch but I'm managing," Dawson replied. "You've seemed troubled. Something bothering you?"

"I've been worried about my sister, Jenny. I still haven't heard from her, and I'm afraid something's happened. Women's intuition, you know," she said, with a sad grin.

"I can understand your worrying, but she's probably just having a good time and forgot to touch base. Did you mention it to Quint?"

"Yeah. He called Rogers, who promised to look into it and get back with us."

"Maybe it's time we give Rogers a jingle and see what he's found out."

Kira nodded and they sat for a minute in silence. "So, you can't sleep either?"

"Not really, I enjoy *la madrugada*."

"Huh?"

Dawson laughed. "A Cuban expression, appropriate considering where we are. It means the lost time or the empty hours before dawn. Supposedly, that's when the weirdos get restless on land. At sea, it's known as the death watch. But not by me. Whenever I'm offshore at night, I volunteer for it."

"Well, since you're awake on land, does that make you one of the weirdos?"

"Probably."

"Don't let me intrude on your solitude." Kira started to walk away.

"You're not. Have a rock, and make yourself comfortable."

"How's married life?" Dawson avoided looking her in the face with his good eye.

"It's all good, but it takes some getting used to," she said with a pat on his arm. Dawson struggled to ignore the nearly electrical effect of her touch.

"You're a valuable part of the team, and our occasional head-butting aside, I'm glad to still be working together," he said, a little louder than necessary.

"As am I with you." Kira hesitated before continuing. "Are you okay... with... things?"

"You mean your being married and an expectant mother?" Kira nodded. "Kira, the time we spent together is a good memory. But it's just that—a good memory."

They sat for a moment before she broke the quiet. "You and Preston getting along any better now?"

Dawson laughed. "Not really, though we don't see each other too much. I've tried, but I think things are just too far... off track with us."

Kira paused for a moment before continuing. "I...uh... probably shouldn't say this, but I have to tell you he bothers me. He didn't at first, but after being around him, there's just something creepy about him."

Dawson nodded, feeling that no comment was necessary given his clear position on the matter. He had spent years trying to find the good in someone where there just wasn't any to be found. He was glad Kira was coming around.

"So... am I wrong?"

"No, you're definitely not wrong," Dawson replied. "I know the team wants to help the two of us patch things up, particularly if he really is dying of cancer as he claims."

"You don't believe that?"

Dawson laughed. "Well, let's just say that most everything he says is a lie, so draw your own conclusions. Though I got little credit for it, when he first showed up, I kept my mouth shut, but he's screwed me over time and time again. Me and everyone else he comes in contact with." He was surprised to hear himself telling Kira more than he had shared in the past about his black sheep brother.

When he finished, they sat in silence, enjoying the gentle breeze and the sound of the ocean beyond the small harbor, before Kira finally spoke. "You know, we've been pushing it hard. We ought to have a clambake out here on the beach this weekend."

"That's a misnomer."

"Beg pardon?" Kira asked.

"Clambakes. Nothing is really baked; it's actually all steamed."

Kira rolled her eyes, "I guess we could call it a clam steam, but that sounds stupid. So I prefer we be less than precise and have a freakin' clambake."

The next morning at breakfast, Kira found Quint. "As we approach the end of our first week, our operations base is beginning to take shape. I think it's time to celebrate with a clambake, or to be precise, a lobster-and-conch steam," she said, grinning at Dawson, "since clams appear to be in short supply." The team jumped at Kira's suggestion, and the event was set for the coming Friday night.

CHAPTER 19

The pirates' skiff slipped alongside the dhow serving as their mother ship. "You will be held here until we can transport you to shore," Ghedi said after motioning for the couple to board the dhow.

"How long will that be?" Brad's speech was thick from his swollen tongue, and his face was covered with dried blood from the pistol whipping.

"It will take as long as it takes."

"Why are you doing this? We've done nothing to you. This is monstrous," Jenny yelled in the big man's face, rage overcoming her better judgment.

"Monstrous? I'll tell you about monstrous!" Ghedi screamed back. "Monstrous is watching hundreds of your people get sick and die from the filth dumped off of our shores by the Europeans. *That* is monstrous. Monstrous is having the U.S. and European navies seize our boats under the pretext of a police action."

"But they only seize your ships because you're pirates—"

"Don't interrupt me! You Americans are so naïve. When we exercise our sovereignty and take your ships in retaliation, we are called pirates. Is our poor country not entitled to the same rights as your richer ones?"

"That's not the same. You're mixing—"

"I am mixing nothing. You are the one who is mixed up, not I. You people come and takes our natural resources, kill our people, yet when we say, 'Enough,' it is we who are wrong. We are warriors, defending our country from you imperialists. It's now personal. We intend to tweak the nose of the Great Satan, kill westerners, take your wealth, make you miserable, and force you to pay." Ghedi finished his tirade and then went silent, his expression daring her to speak further.

The smell of the filth-covered mother ship took Jenny's breath away. A small man, armed with a wicked-looking machine gun, herded them with rifle barrel pokes to their backs toward the stern of the ship. Ahead of them, a second man opened a deck hatch. As they approached, their guard spoke.

"Down inside." He forced them into the cramped space below decks, where the odor from diesel fuel, waste, and rotting food was overwhelming. Jenny clung to Brad; neither spoke while they tried to breathe through their mouths. A rat darted through a small opening in the bulkhead, and Jenny began to wretch as Brad tried unsuccessfully to comfort her. They both sought refuge against the side of the boat, trying to stay out of the oily bilge water and keep away from the rat.

"Brad, I'm scared. What's going to happen to us?"

"We'll be okay. Obviously, they didn't want our boat, which means they plan to hold us hostage for ransom."

"Oh, my God!"

"But that's a good thing."

"Good thing?" she echoed.

"Yes, that means they want to keep us alive. Dead hostages aren't worth much, though I think he was serious about the beatings. We need to keep in good shape until we can escape. So it's best if we just cooperate, at least for now."

Jenny was unconvinced but nodded without replying. With neither money nor the slightest clue as to the location where they would be held, it wasn't clear what chance they would have if they did manage to break free. "Let me look at your face."

The cut across Brad's cheek was deep, but the bleeding had stopped. Without clean water and a bandage, there was little she could do. "Does it still hurt where he hit you with the pistol?"

"Yeah, my head is throbbing. But it'll be all right. At least we're together... right?"

Jenny gave a weak smile and desperately wished she hadn't broached the problems with their relationship. That earlier conversation now loomed like a huge elephant in the room.

Hours later, the hatch was lifted and a bucket with a foul mixture of cooked rice, onions, and what appeared to be table scraps mixed in was lowered. A second bucket, half-filled with stagnant water, appeared next. "Please, let us out. My husband is hurt and we need to use the bathroom."

"You're in it." She heard the man laugh as the hatch slammed closed.

Once a day, the hatch was opened to retrieve the old buckets and lower new ones. They both became violently ill with dysentery from the food or water or both. Their attempt to confine their own waste to the far end of the compartment helped only slightly. But eventually they became accustomed to the stench.

They were nearly delirious and had lost track of how long they had been held prisoner when they heard shouting from above and the sound of the boat docking. An hour later, the hatch opened and a man appeared above. The couple shielded their eyes from the blinding midday light as Ghedi spoke. "Whoa! What an odor you guys have made. Ready to come out, or would you prefer to remain in your current quarters?"

In partial disbelief that this part of their nightmare was at an end, Jenny stood slowly and was helped out of the compartment and onto the deck above. Brad followed close behind. They were in a port filled with derelict looking vessels of all descriptions. On shore, a series of dilapidated concrete buildings were surrounded by wooden huts built from scrap.

The couple was herded off the dhow and into a skiff, which immediately set out for a larger ship anchored in the center of the harbor. When the skiff pulled alongside the rusted hull, Jenny followed Brad up the ladder to the deck above. Several men brandishing automatic weapons glared at them. She now realized that many of the gunmen were really teenagers, most of whom chewed khat and constantly spat green over the side of the ship.

CHAPTER 20

Over the next two days, the team unpacked, assembled, tested, and stored thousands of dollars' worth of equipment.

"Unloading these crates is sort of like the 'mother of all Christmases,'" Leo exclaimed.

Quint smiled. "Okay, time to take on the more serious tasks to prepare our base. Dakota, we need to get our communications and Internet up and running. Can you and Colin oversee getting the towers repaired and installing the antennas?" Quint asked.

"You got it, boss," Dakota said and headed for the tool room with Colin following close behind. "Grab a tool belt and that second coil of line. We'll need to do some climbing." Ignoring Colin's sour look, Dakota buckled the web belt around his waist, adding a few more tools to those already loaded. The two men ascended the stairs to the top of the Fortress and then climbed to the hilltop above.

Dakota surveyed the three antenna towers. They needed two—a primary and a backup.

"That one is junk," Dakota said, pointing to the first tower. "Maybe later we'll dismantle the rest of it to cannibalize for parts. This second tower looks pretty much intact. But we'll still need to climb it to conduct a proper inspection."

Glancing up at the third tower, Dakota grimaced. Halfway up, one of the three guy wires supporting the tower was clearly badly damaged. "We'll definitely need to repair this one. Which tower you want to climb?"

"Uh... actually, none. I don't mind helping, but I've got a serious issue with heights."

"No problem, we all have our fears. I'm not much on snakes. And big dogs scare the crap out of me. Though I don't fear heights, I do have a problem with falling. We'll use this rope if we need to hoist any parts." He finished tying the coil of rope around his waist and then began climbing the second tower with the rope trailing behind.

A short way up, he spotted a damaged strut and stopped to replace it. Retrieving a socket wrench from his tool pouch, he began to remove the bolts from the bent brace. He had one bolt out and was working on the second when the rusted bolt broke and the wrench slipped from his hand and fell, nearly striking Colin before careening off the rocks below. "Damn," Dakota cursed, nursing his skinned knuckles.

"You missed me," Colin joked.

"I promise to do better next time," Dakota replied with a laugh.

"I know the wrench landed in these rocks, but I can't find it."

"That's okay, I'll repair this brace later. Just hang tight while I finish the inspection." Dakota continued to climb. A few feet up, he spotted another weak brace and made a mental note to replace it, too. Though the tower had seemed in good shape from below, it was clearly in worse condition than he had first thought. As he continued to climb higher, it began to sway. Two-thirds of the way up, a sudden gust of wind hammered the tower, stressing the corroded cables on the far side. Dakota's weight coupled with the wind gust caused one of the guy wires to snap with a loud "thwang."

Now free to move with the wind, the tower leaned dangerously toward the side where Dakota was perched. For an instant, it seemed as if the tower might hold. But then the steel buckled and bent far enough to leave him leaning dangerously far out—just barely able to hold on. Though the remaining support wires had prevented the tower from collapsing completely, it was not clear how long they would hold.

Dakota was concerned that the tower might not withstand another wind gust, but the angle was too steep for him to climb down. If he attempted to shift to the tower's opposite side, he feared the force might collapse the tower.

Using his right hand, he slowly untied the rope from his waist and looped the end over the brace above him, tying a bowline knot. He then rigged a simple rappelling harness by feeding the line around his back and back up between his legs.

He took a deep breath and let go with his left hand to rappel down the side of the tower. As he approached the ground, he tightened the line to slow his descent, placing a shock load on the tower just as an ill-timed gust of wind hit. Unable to withstand the combined load, the tower began collapsing with a high-pitched squeal.

Twenty feet from the ground, Dakota let go and rolled as he hit the ground, coming to rest on his back. He looked up in horror to see the tower falling toward him in slow motion and rolled quickly to the side, barely clearing the base of the tower as it came crashing down a scant two feet from his head.

The metal structure slammed into the ground with an enormous thud amidst a shower of broken tree branches, raising a huge cloud of dust. He completed a silent prayer of thanks before opening his eyes to see Colin staring down at him. "You okay?"

"Sure. I could have rolled one less time and still cleared the tower," Dakota said, with a grin.

Colin just rubbed his face with both hands. "You almost had *me* peeing in *my* pants. You're one lucky man."

Dakota lay there for a few minutes while his pulse returned to normal and he caught his breath before remarking, "Well, one down—literally. One to go. Looks like Quint is going to have to make do with a single tower, whether he likes it or not. And that's assuming the remaining tower doesn't fall in a heap, too. Guess we'll know in a few minutes"

"You can't be serious after what just happened. You should wait and try again later," Colin said.

"Nope. As they say, 'It's best to get right back on the tower that threw you.'"

"Uh, I believe that's 'horse.'"

"What? There are no horses; don't be stupid." Colin just sighed. "Anyhow, we need to get our Internet link up. So, I'm going to get the remaining tower working, assuming I can do so without riding it to the ground as well."

"At least take a break to catch your breath while I go get another wrench. Be right back." Colin headed back down the hill while Dakota splayed out on a rock, recovering from his near-death experience.

A few minutes later, Marcia came walking up. "What the hell are you doing?" she asked, seeing the crumpled tower and Dakota on the flat rock sunning, bare-chested, his skin glistening with sweat in the wicked heat.

"Working on my tan," he said, with a big grin. "We had a little mishap, so I decided to take a break."

"*Little* mishap?" Marcia exclaimed, pointing at the bent and broken tower lying a few feet away. Dakota just grinned. As she handed him a bottle of water, she noticed Dakota's left bicep. "What possessed you to tattoo your own name on your arm?"

"Don't want to forget who I am," he replied with a smile, contrasting with Marcia's sour expression. "No,

I want to make sure it gets spelled right in my obituary. Don't know why that's important to me, but it is."

"Maybe it's your shot at immortality," Marcia said.

"Immorality is probably closer to the truth. Where's Colin?" Dakota asked.

"Dawson needed him, and I felt like stretching my legs, so I volunteered to bring you this," she replied, handing him a wrench. "You need me to stick around?"

"Actually, Colin wasn't much help. But I would appreciate it if you could hang around in case I have another problem."

"Sure. I'm not afraid of heights."

"Just stick around to catch me when I fall." Dakota drained his bottle of water and then coiled the rope back around his waist. "When I get up there, would you tie the end of the rope to that duffle bag with the antennas?"

Thirty minutes later, he had climbed the tower as far as it appeared safe. After bolting the antennas in place, he dropped the end of the cables for each antenna down to the ground. He then worked his way back down, securing the cables in place with plastic ties as he went.

"Finished. We can tackle the major repairs later. Now I think it's beer o'clock," Dakota said, gathering his tools before heading below.

CHAPTER 21

Leo and Mimi spent much of the day preparing for Kira's lobster-and-conch feast. Several tables and a bar were set up on the beach near a roaring fire built to cook their dinner. The sun had set, and the moonless night was illuminated only by light from the homemade tiki torches which lined the periphery, lending a primal feel to the event.

After finishing his conch salad, Quint dove into Leo's cracked conch. The next course consisted of succulent lobster, plucked fresh from the adjoining reefs by the team during their rest breaks. When everyone had finished and armed themselves with after-dinner drinks, a chant begin to arise. "Speech. Speech. Speech."

"Okay, okay." Quint arose from his table near the fire, where the dancing flames cast long shadows. "First of all, thanks to everyone for all your hard work in readying the facility. Particularly to Dakota for his bungee-less jumping episode."

"As you're aware, the secure location of our new offshore home offers us the ability to do many things which might give the U.S. government, or any government for that matter, major heartburn, even though the mission itself might actually be sanctioned by them.

"Our business agreement with the Cuban government requires that we pay an annual service fee and absolve them of any responsibility or liability for our actions. In return, we gain an unprecedented degree of freedom, as well as unique capabilities we could have only dreamed of before.

"I look forward to our future adventures together in our new island Fortress."

"You've been calling this the Fortress, but shouldn't we go through the process of formally choosing the name?" Marcia asked.

"Good point. Any suggestions?" In machine-gun fashion, numerous possibilities were volunteered, ranging from humorous to ridiculous. The stream of corny suggestions soon dwindled and with no serious suggestions under consideration, Dakota finally spoke up. "What's wrong with Fortress? It's simple and seems to aptly describe it."

"But that implies that it's a stronghold from which to carry on a battle. I see it more as a retreat where we go to plan for battle elsewhere," Kira said. "How about 'Sanctuary?' The dictionary defines that as a hideout, oasis, or harbor, which I think fits quite well."

"I second that," Colin agreed. Quint guessed his support came more from wanting to suck up to Kira after their most recent tiff than from any sincere enthusiasm. But the general response to the suggestion caused Quint to take the name seriously.

With no opposing candidates, Kira's suggested name was put to a vote and affirmed. "'Sanctuary' it is," Quint announced, to which thunderous applause and a chorus of "hear, hears" erupted.

Quint finished speaking and was about to open a fresh beer when Mimi called his name. "It's Rogers," she said, handing him the phone. She had anointed herself guardian of the portable satphone. Quint imagined it had to do with her keen interest in keeping in touch with Preston after Quint had refused her request to allow him to come along with the team.

Before answering, he walked down the beach, where he could hear over the noise of the team's celebration and also speak in private.

"How are things going?" Rogers asked.

"Making progress, but we've got a ways to go. We took a break tonight for a little clambake—without the clams." Quint laughed. "Any leads on Jenny's whereabouts? Kira's worried sick."

"We just got a call from the American embassy in Nairobi. Actually, the contact was from a special envoy in Somalia."

"And..."

"Both Jenny and her husband have been captured and are being held for ransom by Somali pirates."

Quint's stomach knotted. "Damn, I was afraid of that."

"Do you know what Kira's sister was doing there?"

"She and her husband had this grand dream to sail around the world in stages. This leg required sailing near Somalia on the way back to England from the Seychelles. Sounds like the pirates screwed up their plan."

"Big time."

Quint thought for a moment. "How did Somalia's special envoy end up in the middle of this?"

"They claim the pirates contacted them with the ransom demands. Of course with the Federal Government of Somalia being so new, who knows? Given the country's history, it's not out of the question that their government officials may be getting a piece of the pirates' action."

Quint digested the information. "So what can we do?"

"At this point, neither the U.S. government nor my company, Vector, is authorized to do anything. The U.S. is involved on a limited basis in trying to discourage pirate attacks, both diplomatically and militarily. They also urge private companies to adopt something they call 'best management practices,' such as proceeding at flank speed through high-risk areas and using razor wire to help prevent boarding. If pirates are captured, the U.S. supports their prosecution and—"

Quint interrupted. "But what about the victims?"

"I'm afraid they're out of luck."

Quint kicked a piece of driftwood and sent it sailing across the sand. "Then what can we do?"

"Not much. As you know, our country discourages the payment of ransom. Most European nations do as well, though some are notorious for publicly condemning such payments while secretly making them when it involves their own citizens."

Dawson approached carrying fresh beers. Quint stuck his empty bottle in the pocket of his cargo shorts and popped the top on the fresh one. He mouthed Rogers' name in response to Dawson's questioning look. "So you're suggesting that we pay the ransom?"

"Not really. In fact, there's no guarantee they would be released even if we paid. Personally, I'm opposed to extortion; it simply kicks the can down the road for the next poor soul to become a victim. If I was going to spend money on their behalf, I'd rather it go toward the pirates' demise. Just saying."

Quint smiled. "So, what exactly is the U.S.'s position on private efforts to free such victims?"

"The use of onboard armed security is an accepted practice these days, especially outside of territorial sea limits. But as far as a military-style engagement once hostages have been captured, I don't know. I'm guessing it would be discouraged—strongly discouraged."

"Discouraged, but not prevented?"

Rogers hesitated for a moment. "Let me be clear. For the record, I do not and cannot authorize your team to become involved in freeing these people."

"And off the record?"

"Off the record, I don't think anybody will give a shit if you blow away a bunch of pirates, provided you're somewhat subtle. But if you were to go into their base with guns blazing, incurring significant collateral damage—by which I mean dead civilians — in the process, there'd be a major shit storm.

"These guys have the ear of the civil rights zealots, particularly in Europe. Of course, many of them are on the pirates' payroll. Anytime they get wind of a pirate being killed or even dealt with in a harsh manner, they go nuts. So you'd have to be careful. But if you do decide to try something crazy, call me first—off the record," Rogers said before hanging up.

"Somebody been kidnapped?" Dawson asked.

Quint nodded. "Kira's sister."

"That sucks."

"Yes, it does."

"You going to go tell Kira and the team?"

"Not tonight. Let them enjoy their break. We'll deal with it first thing tomorrow."

CHAPTER 22

Brad and Jenny were shoved inside a small room some twenty feet square with a dozen other forlorn-looking people, also imprisoned on the rusty ship. The familiar odor of raw sewage filling the small compartment took her breath away.

"Oh, my gosh!" she gasped, struggling to keep from heaving.

"The shitter gave up the ghost a week or so ago," said a man with a thick British accent. He had dark, greasy hair, his face was streaked with dirt, and his shirt was stained with what appeared to be bits of food. He sat on the gray linoleum floor leaned against the opposite wall.

"Welcome to hell. Please have a seat." He motioned to the empty spot beside him. "My name's Ethan."

Jenny caught a glimpse of what appeared to be fear wash over the face of a woman nearby, but it vanished so quickly she decided it had been imagined. "I'm Jenny and this is my husband, Brad." She inspected the painted green wall and floor before choosing a spot to sit, with Brad sliding down beside her. "How long have you been held here?"

"Me? I've been here over two years. Can't exactly say for sure with such a full schedule and being busy all the time with shipboard activities," he said with a crooked grin. "With the economy these days, it's hard for the pirates to get anyone to pay the ransom. Plus, many attacks on the larger ships are unsuccessful, so they're going for smaller targets. They're treating hostages more harshly and holding them longer in hopes of extracting higher ransoms."

"W-what do they... I mean, how much would they—"

"You want to know how much your freedom will cost? The answer is every last cent your family and friends have. Plus as much as they can borrow. These days, I'm told the going price is anywhere from two hundred and fifty thousand dollars to over one and a half million."

"Oh," Jenny said, her face turning pale.

"The sooner the ransom is paid, the quicker hostages are set free."

"What about escape?" Brad asked, and noticed that one of the men in a group on the far side of the room glanced up quickly.

Ethan gave a loud laugh. "Don't even think about that. As you saw, they chain the doors closed with heavy locks and take turns guarding us. Anytime they let us out, which isn't that often these days, they always have a machine gun aimed at us.

"One guy tried to get friendly with them and then made a break for it. He leaped over the side of the ship and started swimming. Before he made it very far, one of their boats came speeding up to block him from reaching land and circled around him to make waves. When he finally became exhausted and surrendered, they hauled him into the boat and smashed a rifle butt into the back of his head. Once he was back on the ship, they beat him with sticks and then hung him from the mast for hours in the middle of the day. He lived a while longer, but he was never the same."

Jenny felt queasy.

"They said the next time it happens, everyone will be severely punished. No, you don't want to be thinking about doing something stupid," Ethan said firmly.

"Every once in a while, they'll take one of us out for a random beating," an older man added. "You can hear the screams. I guess it's sort of a deterrent." Brad nodded and then crossed the room to introduce himself.

"I'm Raoul," the man replied. "I am, or at least I was"—he looked at the man beside him, who quickly looked off—"captain of the *Donegal,* rather than a prisoner aboard my own ship. This is the rest of my crew." He gestured at the men sitting to his left. "Now that you have joined us, we are no longer the newest of the unfortunate." Brad chatted with the man for a few minutes before re-joining Jenny.

The couple slept most of the day, waking only when one of the other hostages accidentally bumped them or made a noise. It was late afternoon when the opening of the door finally roused them. A young boy, barely a teenager, brought in two buckets of slop, and a second lad set two more buckets of putrid water alongside. If anything, it looked worse than what they had endured while on the mother ship.

"Well, I see the food is no better here. We've been starving from the little bit of lousy food, and we're both sick from the water."

"Get used to it. They want us alive; a dead hostage isn't worth much. But they don't seem overly concerned about keeping us healthy. They feed us just enough to keep us alive, and we're always sick. Bobby over there can't see anymore, and they finally hauled one guy out in a coma. Do you have family or friends who might be able to spring you?"

"My grandfather is a man of means," Brad replied. "But we haven't spoken in years and I would never ask him." In the waning light, Jenny noticed the same woman across the room slowly shake her head. She wondered what she was trying to signal but thought it best not to bluntly ask. "The only other way we could—" Brad started to continue when Jenny squeezed his hand hard. He gave her a puzzled look but said nothing further.

Ethan broached the subject of their paying ransom a few more times during the evening before the door opened once again and two men appeared. They motioned to Ethan, and without speaking, he followed them from the room. Once he was gone, the woman from across the room scooted over to sit on the floor beside Brad and Jenny.

"I'm Lisa," she said in a low voice. "I tried to warn you earlier; Ethan is with the pirates. He sometimes joins us just before a new hostage is brought in. The more information he gains, the stronger their hand."

Jenny touched her arm. "Thanks for trying to warn us. You took quite a risk. Though Mr. Blabbermouth here," she motioned toward her husband with her chin, "gave them more information than he should have, at least you helped me shut him up before he went too far."

"For all the good it'll do. They have a long list of tricks ranging from torture, to separating the two of you, and even pitting one against the other. They'll eventually get the information they want, but no point in making it easy. I'm guessing the game will begin tomorrow."

"Game?" Jenny asked.

"You'll see. It's best for all of us if you don't appear to be too well-informed."

Raoul walked over near Brad. "You mentioned escape. Are you interested in trying?"

"Not so much after what Ethan had to say on the subject. Was that true or a scare tactic?"

Before Raoul could comment, the woman spoke up. "Oh, it's true all right. Raoul's interest in escaping is because of what happened to another ship's captain last week."

"Which was...?" Jenny asked.

Raoul glanced at Lisa. "When ransom negotiations broke down over a freighter's crew, the pirates cut the arm off of the Vietnamese captain and then had his crew members call their relatives begging for help so they wouldn't be next."

"Oh, my God." Wide-eyed, Jenny bit her fist. "Did it work?"

"Unfortunately... for me," Raoul said and went back to take his seat.

CHAPTER 23

Kira began sobbing when Quint relayed the news about her sister. He had dreaded telling her since the previous evening and she was every bit as upset as he had feared.

"When she didn't call, I just knew something was wrong."

"I thought the whole Somalia problem had been solved," Colin said, holding her in his arms to comfort her.

"On the larger ships it has, to some extent," Quint replied. "But that's made the pirates more desperate."

"Can't the navy get her back?" Kira asked.

"Unfortunately, I'm afraid not."

"Well, then, we've got to do something. We have to, Quint," Kira sobbed. "We have to."

"I agree, but I'm just not sure what. I've called a team meeting to discuss it. Join us when you feel up to it." After offering her a few more lame words of sympathy, he left Colin to console her and went to meet with the team.

"With our work here at the Fortress ... excuse me, Sanctuary, nearing completion, it's time we discuss what comes next," Quint said. "I'd like to get our business meeting started. But before Leo, our self-appointed parliamentarian, can take me to task, in accordance with our by-laws—"

"Paragraph Eleven," Leo interrupted.

Quint shot Leo a dirty look. He then began reading from a sheet of paper. "It's specifically required that we review the purpose of our limited liability corporation before partners' meetings. Leo, would you please do me the honor of reading our mission statement?"

Leo stood with a wide grin, cleared his throat, and began reading in an authoritative voice.

"The three purposes of the LLC are the pursuit and acquisition of objects with intrinsic, historical, or other value; the neutralization of special threats for which conventional remedies are inappropriate or otherwise impractical; and missions involving the rescue of key personnel assets or execution of other programs deemed worthy for humanitarian, scientific, or other such purposes.

"The Company will be operated as a for-profit business entity under the control of the board, comprised of all shareholders. Unless otherwise agreed, the LLC's board will select projects with an acceptable risk–reward ratio, preferably those offering significant economic upside. Projects may have multiple objectives, with some deemed to have a higher purpose than financial gain."

"Now, if there are no further such items requiring our attention," Quint said, looking directly at Leo, "I'll proceed. Rogers called last night."

"What mess does the government want us to clean up for them now?" Dakota asked.

"This one's not about the government. It's about one of our own. Kira's sister, Jenny, was captured by pirates and is being held for ransom." Quint paused as the room fell silent.

"How did that happen?" Marcia was the first to speak.

"Jenny and her husband were sailing from the Seychelles to Aden, Yemen. While their plan was to stay well off of the coast of Tanzania and Somalia, they were attacked by pirates nonetheless."

"I'm sure most of you are already familiar with the piracy problem off Somalia," Leo began lecturing. "With no effective government, and with its coastline in close proximity to major shipping routes, it's pirate heaven."

"After the UN finally passed a resolution authorizing international cooperation to combat piracy, I thought the pirate problem off Somalia had been solved," Marcia interrupted.

"The UN did take action," Leo continued, "though it took forever because several member nations lobbied against it under the pretext of concern for innocent Somalis who might be injured in reprisals. Of course, most of the opposition was paid for by the pirates themselves, in an effort to thwart the UN's actions. But after the hijacking of a super tanker valued at over a hundred million dollars, the opposition was no longer successful, and a very watered-down resolution was passed. It limited the amount of force that could be used, and while it did permit pirates to be pursued on Somali soil, it tied the peacekeeping forces' hands to the point it was nearly useless.

"After the insurance companies tired of paying an average ransom of five million dollars per ship, they began hiring mercenaries to protect the vessels. This has been a key factor in slowing piracy. But the pirates haven't given up. As Quint mentioned, they've now turned their focus to low-profile targets in order to stay alive while biding their time."

"Why doesn't the U.S. just fly a drone over their camp and take out their boats with a few missiles?" Colin asked.

"For one thing, they want to get the pirates, too. Otherwise they'll just steal more boats and keep doing their thing. Also, when the boats are back home, innocents in the area use them for legitimate purposes," Quint replied.

"Then why not do the same thing when they're at sea, clearly intent on committing acts of piracy?" Mimi asked.

"It's a big ocean and they're small boats. The cost of maintaining such a reconnaissance effort would be considerable," Quint answered.

"While stopping the pirates in the long run is certainly an important issue, I believe the more pressing matter is freeing Kira's sister and her husband," Dawson added. "If no one pays the ransom, they're not going to be set free. Even if the ransom were to be paid, they still might not be released. And from what I understand, their chance of escaping is zilch. Bottom line, unless somebody goes in and rescues them, they're screwed."

Quint nodded. "He's right and we don't have a lot of time. With monsoon season approaching, the high seas will soon make their operations impossible, so they'll go dormant for a while."

"So?" Leo asked.

"So, the longer they remain there, the higher the risk that they... uh... " Quint glanced up as Colin entered the room alongside Kira, her eyes red and makeup streaked from crying.

Kira cleared her throat and then finished the sentence. "... the higher the chance they'll be killed."

Quint hesitated for a moment before continuing. "And there's one other thing. Kira, I don't mean to upset you but I think everyone needs to know what we're facing. The pirates have learned that the more horrific and gruesome the story, the higher the odds of collecting on the ransom.

"Though there's been no proof of life, assuming that Jenny and her husband are still alive, I'm afraid they may not be for much longer. It seems the pirates are not holding hostages as long as they once did before they kill them—or sell the women into white slavery."

The room fell silent until Mimi spoke up. "So, what do we do?"

"That's the question we're here to answer," Quint replied.

"At the risk of being blunt," Leo said, "this is not a project for which we'd be paid and it's not even one of our team that's been captured. Plus, we're talking about going up against a bunch, a very big bunch, of ruthless, well-armed maniacs."

"That's true," Quint conceded. "What do the rest of you folks think?" A long silence followed while the team struggled with the issue.

"I realize that I'm the newbie"—Marcia had joined the team just before their last mission—"but I don't see how there's much to think about. Even if it's not one of the team, imagine if it were one of us and not Kira's sister being held. What then?"

Dakota rose and cleared his throat, looking toward Leo. "Please allow me to remind you of the last phrase in the first paragraph of our charter which you just finished reading. I believe rescuing pirate hostages fits well within our charter."

"Dakota's right," Kira added. "But it's more than that. We're talking about a much broader issue here than the fate of my sister and her husband."

Marcia added, "If Rogers had called and proposed that we rescue hostages for pay, wouldn't it be the sort of thing we'd do? So the real issue here is money. I can't answer for the rest of you, but family is family and I'd go in to rescue anyone in this room. And the same goes for their close relatives. If not, then our mission statement is just a lot of bullshit."

"Well said," Dawson said. "We've got most of what we need left over from our previous missions, and I'm betting we can call on Rogers to help with logistics support. I move that we take on this project and call for a vote."

"Anyone else care to add anything?" Quint asked and saw Nigora meekly raise her hand. Nigora had become an honorary part of the team but sought to become a valued member instead of continuing to play the role of mascot.

"I not real member of team, but see your team do great good," she began in her broken English. "For this you should be proud. Hostages you save from this sad fate would be much grateful."

After a brief silence Quint spoke. "Thanks. If there is no one else who cares to speak, let us conduct a secret ballot. I'll grant Nigora the honor of overseeing the vote."

A few minutes later, the ballots had been tallied. "Is easy count, no? Everyone want kill pirates," Nigora said and then looked toward the back of the room. "Even Leo want help these poor people. You good man! You all good people," she added and started the applause.

"Dawson, you and Colin work up a plan to rescue Jenny and the others," Quint said, clearly moved by the team's unanimous support.

"Jenny is a good sister, but she's also a great person. We're her only hope. Thanks so much, I—" Unable to continue speaking, Kira left with tears streaming down her face.

CHAPTER 24

It was midmorning the next day when the door opened and Brad and Jenny were led to a cabin. "Wash up in here. You have thirty minutes," the guard said, locking the door behind him.

On the wall just down from the door they had entered was a small porthole. Jenny looked through the salt-streaked glass, but all she could see was the vast ocean beyond and desolate land on the far side of the small bay.

The walls were painted the same pale green as the room where they were being imprisoned, though their new quarters were not nearly as filthy. In the corner was a small bed with a cabinet serving as a nightstand bolted to the wall. She tried the drawers, finding them unlocked but empty. A door at the opposite end of the room led to a tiny compartment with a toilet and sink.

"Boy, it feels good to get some of this grime off," Brad said a few minutes later, as he scrubbed his face with a washcloth to remove the remaining dried blood.

"A shower and clean clothes would be better," Jenny replied.

They had just finished when they heard the door being unlocked. The same man led them up a flight of stairs to the captain's cabin adjacent to the ship's bridge. A painting of a tall ship adorned the wall above a leather couch, flanked by mahogany bookcases filled with volumes of books. Two inches above each shelf ran a brass rod, Jenny imagined to keep the books in place in heavy seas. It appeared that Raoul was quite the avid reader.

But what quickly caught Jenny's attention was the heavenly smell of bacon and fresh coffee. At the far side of the room, a table was draped in a spotless white tablecloth. Atop it were three place settings of glistening white china trimmed in gold with the ship's name, *Donegal*, written in matching gold script. On the buffet which ran the length of the end wall, a carafe of coffee sat beside a pitcher of orange juice and another filled with ice water, condensation dripping from both. To the right sat a lavish spread of breakfast foods, including fresh muffins, fruit, and bacon. The couple stood, eyes transfixed on the feast before them, ignoring the incongruity of their surroundings.

A man appeared from the next room, and Jenny gasped in astonishment—it was Ethan, the filthy hostage they had met when they first arrived. But now he was dressed in a crisply pressed white shirt with a matching linen suit.

"Welcome, please help yourself," he said, with a broad smile and a sweeping gesture toward the breakfast buffet. "I know you must be famished after being so deprived these past few days." The couple hesitated, unsure whether all of this was some kind of cruel trick.

"Go ahead; nothing is poisoned. What would be the point in that? But if it puts your minds at ease, I'll join you."

Brad gingerly picked up a plate and handed it to Jenny before taking one for himself. Struggling to exercise restraint, she politely heaped a plate with twice what she would normally have taken, but only half of what she wanted, before taking a seat at the table. The couple waited politely until Ethan was seated, at which time they both attacked their breakfasts.

"I'm not a hostage, as the two of you have no doubt concluded, or as I'm sure the others have told you by now." He smiled at the tense look on Jenny's face. "Relax, I know they talk, but so long as they don't... how should I say... spill the beans too early, I take no issue."

He said nothing more for the next few minutes while the three of them ate in silence. Finally, he pushed his plate away and rose to refill his coffee. "Please, don't be bashful; get some more. Eat as much as you like." The couple needed no further encouragement and loaded their plates again, taking even more this time.

"Permit me to explain the situation," Ethan said after downing a mouthful of coffee. "Piracy here has its roots in the people's effort to defend their fishing rights. But what really kicked things up a notch was the toxic waste dumping."

Jenny swallowed a bite of toast and cleared her throat. "Toxic waste dumping?"

Ethan smiled. "I'm not surprised that you're unaware. While they will vehemently deny it, European nations have been dumping their toxic wastes off the coast of Somalia for years. Tuna taken from our waters often contain high traces of heavy metals, which is puzzling given that Somalia lacks any industrial base which might use such chemicals.

"Proof positive came with the tsunami which struck our coast back in 2004." Brad and Jenny had stopped eating and were now listening intently, empty forks resting on their plates. "You may recall it."

"Yes, I do. It was horrible," Jenny replied.

"When the waters receded, metal barrels littered the beaches, some smashed open while others remained sealed. The locals began combing through the debris in hopes of finding something of value to sell. Instead, they found the barrels filled with the same dirt, rocks, and assorted plastic and glass which littered the beach.

"In the weeks after the storm, the locals began to suffer skin rashes, diarrhea, bleeding gums, and hair loss. Over three hundred people died. The UN finally confirmed that Somalia had, indeed, been the dumping ground for radioactive, industrial, chemical, and even hospital wastes. Some claim that Somali officials signed agreements authorizing the disposal, which they, of course, deny. Others claim it's the work of the mafia.

"In any case, it's food for thought." Ethan paused as an orderly entered to clean the table. "You can take mine, but leave theirs. They might want some more." Jenny glanced at the pile of fruit on the buffet and rose to place a few pieces on her plate. When she had returned to her seat, Ethan continued.

"You may have heard reports that the U.N. had dealt with piracy in these waters. After those bumbling idiots finished their speeches, they sent a small force over to threaten us. We gave up one of our weaker competitors; they declared the war won and ceased operations, ostensibly victorious. But once piracy fell off the front page of the newspapers, we were back to business as usual.

"The ironic part is that for a small portion of what those fools spent grandstanding, they could have negotiated a real end to piracy here." Ethan rose to fill his coffee cup and then changed the subject.

"Allow me to explain how this is going to work. Before I came here, these crude savages immediately set about beating, raping, and starving new hostages as soon as they were captured. It seemed they enjoyed indulging their sadistic urges nearly as much as getting paid. But I showed them a better way, certainly for you, that is.

"I convinced them that this is a business, and it's infinitely easier, faster, and far more profitable to have everyone's interests aligned. Over time, I graduated from being merely a translator to earning a piece of the pie. They made more money and I became rich to the point that I am one of their few remaining... bankers.

"This may prove difficult at first, but think of us as a football team with the motley crew of pirates you've met as the opposition. I'm your coach and we've got the ball, so to speak, but don't have long to score.

"Working together, we've got to establish a reasonable ransom goal and then deliver it to them while we still have the ball. If it becomes clear that we've set the target too low, they'll take the field—not so good for you. But if it appears we've set a realistic goal and are making steady progress toward getting paid, then we'll continue to have possession—good for you."

Jenny found it hard to grasp the analogy between a sporting event and their being taken hostage by murderous pirates. "So, how long should we expect to have... uh... possession?"

"That's the spirit," Ethan said with a smile. "There's no set time. It could be a matter of a few days, or perhaps a few weeks. Maybe even a month. It all depends on how honest you are with me and how... enthusiastic you are about playing along. Of course their patience is limited, especially these days. If they decide our approach is not bearing fruit, then the gloves come off and I can no longer help you. Those people you met yesterday have not performed so well while others were gone in a matter of a couple of weeks.

"The first step is to develop our game plan. For that I need your full cooperation." He retrieved a pad of paper and a pen from the next room and handed them to Jenny. "After you finish your breakfast, make an estimate of your net worth. List all of your assets— homes, buildings, land, and any other real estate you own, along with the estimated mortgages. Then summarize the value of all available bank accounts, stock portfolios, etc. List any pieces of art or other valuables. Finally, make a list of all of your close friends and family members and your best estimate of their net worth.

"I know that you are clever folks and will be tempted to lowball much of this. But you should know that their network of contacts is quite good at confirming such things. Should they find any discrepancies, any at all, then I'm afraid the game will be over, and the opposition will take the field—permanently."

"But Ethan, I don't know how much anyone is worth and even if I did, they aren't going to cash in and pay it all to save us."

"Maybe, but through experience, I have gained a rather uncanny ability to estimate what percentage they might give. So don't you worry about that part. You just focus on this first, actually quite simple, step. I'll be back in a bit, so get to work. And please, continue to eat as much as you like."

He rose and started toward the door but then paused. "By the way, do you prefer roasted quail or lobster? Oh, never mind. I'll see to it that they serve both for lunch."

"What do we do?" Jenny whispered once Ethan had left.

"I don't see that we have a lot of choice; we do as he said."

"You trust him?"

"Of course not," Brad replied. "But I'm convinced things will get real ugly real quick if we don't cooperate. Maybe we can buy some time to find a way to escape, or maybe even get rescued."

Jenny nodded. "And if not, giving up everything we own still beats dying."

An hour later Ethan returned. "So, how we doing, team?" he asked, snatching the pad of paper from Jenny without asking. "Hmm, not bad, not bad at all. But I see we've still got quite a ways to go. What about coins, antiques, that sort of thing? And don't forget any retirement accounts. I'll see you two at lunch. Keep up the good work.

"Wait a minute, I almost forgot," Ethan said as he unlocked the door to a second room. "You'll find fresh clothes and a shower right in there. Leave your old clothes in the bathroom. I'll have them bagged—just in case we need them later." He then left the room, locking the main door to the captain's cabin behind him.

As soon as the door closed, Jenny leaped to her feet and stripped off her filthy shorts and t-shirt as she ran into the second room. She noticed two sets of freshly laundered clothes on the bed, though it was clear they had originally belonged to someone else.

Jenny returned a few minutes later toweling her wet hair. "I don't think a shower has ever felt that good."

Brad, who had continued working on the list, smiled and rose to take his turn. Once they were finished showering, they continued to work on the list and had just about finished when they heard the door being unlocked.

"Who's ready for lunch?" Two young boys followed Ethan, each carrying a massive tray heaped with food. Though it had been only three hours since breakfast, they greedily eyed the feast.

Ethan joined them, playing the role of polite host while they ate the lavish meal, which included both lobster and quail as promised. When they were finished, he turned to Brad. "You're done with the list?" Brad nodded, handing him the pad. "And it's both accurate and complete?"

"That's everything, at least everything we could think of."

"Remember what I told you earlier; we're a team, and you have to be straight with me to make this work."

Brad nodded.

"Very well." Ethan stood up and placed the folded list in his shirt pocket. "Go ahead and make yourselves comfortable. Feel free to use the bed, for sleeping or... whatever."

Jenny heard him snicker as he headed out the door. She stole a glance out the open doorway and could see two armed guards standing on the bridge outside the captain's cabin and a third man who approached Ethan carrying a camera. The two men spoke briefly after which Ethan stepped to one side and allowed the man to enter their new quarters.

"He wants to take your picture," Ethan explained. The couple rose and stood together. "Not you," he said, pointing to Brad, "just your wife." Brad looked puzzled but Jenny nodded and he moved away.

The man with the camera approached. "My, my, don't look so glum. Smile for the camera," Ethan said. Afraid to do otherwise, Jenny complied. After taking pictures from three different angles, the man left with Ethan.

Brad and Jenny remained in the captain's quarters for the next couple of days. While the food was not nearly as exotic, it was far better than what they had been forced to eat a few days earlier. Though they were eager to be released, at least they were comfortable in their new quarters. Unfortunately, Ethan returned late on the third day with bad news.

CHAPTER 25

"I did a little research on Somalia after our last meeting," Leo began once the team was gathered in the Sanctuary conference room to discuss the pirate mission. "I learned that Somalia has the longest coast of any African nation. But of far more interest was something else I found.

"Permit me to read you advice from one of the travel guides. 'Somalia is a war zone and is considered the most dangerous country in the world to visit.' Not just Africa, mind you, but the whole freakin' world. Do we really want to go there? I mean—"

"No, we don't, Leo," Dawson interrupted. "But then we're not talking about where to take this year's vacation, now are we?" Leo didn't reply. "And as I recall you did vote for us to take on this mission."

"Leo's not denying that he voted for the mission," Kira replied. "But perhaps he's having second thoughts after conducting his due diligence, which is, of course, his right."

"Is that it, Leo? You want to change your vote?" Quint asked, and saw him shrug. "Anyone else having second thoughts?" Seeing no raised hands, he continued.

"Look, Somalia is a shithole, no doubt about it. And I don't want Leo or anyone else to feel pressured into being part of this mission. So we'll finish our discussion, listen to the plan that Colin and Dawson have come up with, and then we'll have another vote.

Fair enough?" Leo nodded as did Kira and a number of others. He then turned to Dawson. "Okay, the floor is yours."

Dawson downed the rest of his coffee, wiped his mouth with his sleeve, and cleared his throat before he spoke. "As requested at our last meeting by our fearful leader," Dawson began, pausing until the team's laughter subsided. "Colin and I have been trying to better understand what we're up against.

"Over the past several decades, drought, famine, and a dysfunctional, corrupt government have left the country in shambles. The country is embroiled in war and plagued by anarchy with no one actually in control."

"Sort of like the U.S.?" Dakota grinned.

"Yeah, but with even more widespread corruption," Colin added.

"I don't know much about Somalia, but I've heard Mogadishu is not such a nice place," Mimi said with a frown.

"That it's not," Dawson replied. "But Mogadishu is far to the south of where we plan to be. Compared to U.S. standards, the entire continent of Africa is poor, but Somalia is considered the poorest of the poor. People there live in huts built out of trash and are desperate to survive. Some will kill you for the price of a loaf of bread.

"Vessels crossing the Arabian Sea headed for the Mediterranean must enter the Gulf of Aden to pass through the Red Sea and on through the Suez Canal," Dawson said, pointing to a large map that hung on the wall. "Somalia is located here on the Horn of Africa. And on the north coast of the Gulf of Aden is Yemen, which is equally dangerous. So transiting this area is tricky under the best of circumstances.

"It appears that rescuing Jenny may be no easy deal." Dawson looked directly at Leo. "The pirates are mostly thugs lacking formal training, but there are a whole bunch of them. To make matters worse, one of their defenses when back on land is to embed themselves with the civilians. So a lot of innocents would die if we were to try a direct assault, even if we had the people to do that, which we don't.

"Based on the reconnaissance data Rogers was able to get for us, the pirates are operating out of a well-established base located here," he said gesturing at the map.

"The leader of the pirate group holding our hostages is believed to be a man by the name of Ghedi. He would just as soon put a knife in your stomach as chat about the weather. He got his start as some sort of Robin Hood, capturing foreign fishing boats which were illegally raiding fish stocks in Somali waters.

"His group became Somalia's home grown coast guard, called badaadinta badah or 'saviors of the sea.' But once they got a taste of easy money, it was a short step to becoming full-fledged pirates." Dawson paused to take a drink of water and rifle through his notes.

"Pirate teams generally have three types of members: fishermen with knowledge of the sea, militia who are experienced warriors, and techies who operate electronics and run the ships they capture. Often times their attack force is less than a dozen men. But these are the real badasses we'd rather not deal with.

"They station a mother ship offshore and use small boats to search a broad area. When they find a target vessel, they call in the rest of the boats by radio and attack from all directions in fast skiffs, firing their weapons to strike fear in the ship's crew. They board using crude ladders or ropes with grappling hooks. Crews seldom fight back.

"Once a vessel is hijacked, they bring on their second force, usually poorly trained men, to operate the ship, guard hostages, and defend against rescuers. On land, a third group, believed to be part of a former military group, serves as a defense force against any retaliatory strikes. We should avoid giving them the chance to earn their pay.

"We propose a somewhat radical plan that involves eliminating the *real* pirates before going after the hostages."

"Why not just go after the hostages when the pirates are offshore searching for fresh victims?" Mimi asked.

"We could, but then they'll simply continue to spread misery on new hostages," Dawson replied. The team debated the point in a heated discussion, during which it became clear that everyone except Leo was supportive of taking out the pirates.

"You refer to the hostages as if we're rescuing a large group. I thought this was about Kira's sister and brother-in-law—period," Leo said.

"What are we supposed to do with the rest? Just leave them there because they don't have the right friends?" Marcia asked.

Ignoring her question, Leo continued. "So how do you propose to deal with the pirates?"

"Divide and conquer." Dawson paused while he took a drink of water. "First we sink their mother ship. It's a fairly easy target to identify and sinking it will disrupt their operations, forcing the remaining boats to operate from their shore-base, where they'll be more susceptible to a covert force such as ours."

"Oh, so after we take out their mother ship by some unknown means, we then shoot it out with their smaller boats? That sounds like a good way to never collect Social Security," Leo said sarcastically. Quint was finding Leo's smug expression more and more irritating.

"We don't shoot it out. We use limpet mines to sink them once they're offshore." Dawson said. "While we're busy whittling down the pirate force, our overwatch team will be spying on the village to pinpoint the most likely locations for holding hostages."

"I thought you said that they would be held on a ship anchored in the harbor?" Kira asked.

"And well they may be," Dawson agreed. "But we don't know that for sure, and nothing is to say they don't have hostages at more than one location."

"Or they may have relocated them at some point," Quint added.

Dawson nodded. "After locating the hostages, we go in at night to rescue them, hopefully without a shootout."

"So how do we take down the mother ship?" Mimi asked

"I suggest we make that Rogers' problem," Dawson replied.

"And we're doing this out of pocket, pro bono, so to speak?" Leo asked.

Quint shook his head. "Not necessarily. I asked Rogers to discreetly contact some of the vulnerable shipping firms who have been forced to hire security forces. After discussing the concept of using private resources to deal with the problem permanently, the group agreed to ante up fifteen million dollars. Compared to the losses they might otherwise suffer and the cost of continuing private security, they view this as a bargain."

"I'm not stupid, Rogers. I realize you don't have a fighter jet and a couple of choppers just sitting around, but then, neither do we. Look, if we're going to do this, we'll need you to provide at least some support," Quint said. "The centerpiece of our plan requires taking out the mother ship, and that's beyond our current capabilities."

"Okay, but there are ways to take it out besides using fighter jets."

"Such as?"

"Give me time to see what I can come up with," Rogers said as he hung up.

"Okay, I think I may have something," Rogers said when he called Quint the next day. "A single covert drone flight and a couple of air-to-sea missiles— problem solved. I have a good friend whose company builds electronic systems for unmanned combat air vehicles and I've arranged to borrow a couple of his older drones."

"Oh, we know about UCAVs." Quint said, referring to the transportation solution Rogers' people had recently employed for him and Dawson while chasing stolen bioweapons in Russia. "Thanks to you, I had all the experience I ever care to have riding beneath one in your prototype pod."

Rogers laughed. "Anyhow, he has several UCAVs that he uses as test platforms. One is an earlier version of the Reaper that he no longer uses."

"And how do we take out the mother ship with it?"

"He has another buddy with a vested interest in putting a stop to the whole Somali pirate thing. He can pull some strings and have a couple of AGM-114 Hellfire missiles or maybe a GBU-12 Paveway II smart bomb added to a shipment bound for Israel. Once we get them out of the country, he can arrange to have them shipped wherever we need them. We'll have to pay for them, but at least that solves the problem."

"Well, partly. Who's going to fly it?"

"I thought I would make it a gift to you guys, and I'll also provide someone to train your folks."

"That'll work. I'll pass on the good news. We'll owe you big time if you pull this off."

"Yes, you will," Rogers replied before hanging up.

Dawson and Colin walked up just as Quint hung up, so he quickly related the gist of his conversation. "A UCAV? Maybe you've forgotten our last experience

with them," Dawson said, rubbing the patch on his left
eye.

"The important difference is this time neither of us
will be catching a ride beneath it."

CHAPTER 26

"I'm afraid they're not happy and we've lost the ball, so to speak. Your vacation here is over." Ethan said.

Jenny's stomach knotted and she felt her lunch rising. "But we've done everything you asked. We've been straight with you the whole time."

"I know, but they still don't have the money."

"We need more time. They can't do this, they just can't!" she pleaded.

"I'm all too afraid that they can … and they will. They've become very impatient and I'm afraid it's now out of my hands. Here are your old clothes," he said with the bag held at arm's length.

"At least they could have washed them," Jenny said, gagging from the smell.

"I'm afraid they're savages."

"So they're putting us back with the others?" Brad asked.

"They're putting you back there but I'm afraid they're pretty mad about not getting paid after all the time I bought us. So they're putting Jenny down in the ship's bilge… with the more hardcore male hostages."

"You can't do that. Put me in the bilge. Let her go back with the others."

"Sorry. Once they've cooled off, I'll keep trying to reason with them. But it'll take some time."

"Being the banker, I thought you were in charge."

"I am the banker but they run their own operation. I never interfere. Think of it as a balance of power."

After the hatch slammed shut, Jenny had never felt more scared and alone. In the dim light, she could barely make out the dark forms of the other prisoners being held in the bilge. After the relative luxury of the captain's quarters, it was like being back in the dhow only worse. Her eyes adjusted after several minutes and she could see nearly a dozen men seated or lying helter-skelter about the dank place. It smelled of sewage mixed with diesel fuel.

An older, scarecrow-looking man dressed in stained, ragged shorts and t-shirt approached her slowly, stopping several feet away when she withdrew in horror. "Don't be afraid, no one will hurt you here. We're not savages like our captors. What's your name?"

"Jenny."

"I'm Walter. Pick yourself out a spot and make yourself at home," he laughed.

"I hope not to be here long. Ethan is still trying to talk them into moving me out of here and back with my husband." The man began a cackle which soon turned into a belly laugh. "What's so funny?"

It took a minute before the man could stop laughing enough to speak. "He's the one who put you here, not 'them'—whoever 'them' is supposed to be. They gain leverage by separating the hostages to create fear." Jenny felt like the air had been let out of her.

She sat in silence, wiping away a steady stream of tears until sleep overtook her to momentarily ease her agony.

Though the ship's bilge was dark and depressing, at least it wasn't as cramped as the hold on the mother ship. After Jenny's exchange with Walter upon her arrival, the men had left her alone. It seemed they were simply fellow victims relegated to the brutal conditions of the bilge. Several attempted to be chivalrous and even offered her some of their own meager food which she politely refused.

Her mind drifted back to when she was a child. Whenever she had a bad day, she would run to greet her father as soon as he returned home from work. She would bury her face in his chest and breathe his scent mixed with the smell of tobacco in his starched shirt. She now longed for that same feeling of security she always felt with her father. The same security she had felt with Brad when they first married.

She dozed off and when she awoke decided to chat with Walter. She learned that the men were from two different fishing boats, the owners of which lacked either the money or desire to pay the ransom. "So how long you been here?" Jenny asked.

"Don't rightly know, seem to have misplaced my calendar." Walter and the others laughed. "Best guess is me and my crew been here about fifteen months. The rest a couple of months after we arrived."

"Well, I sure hope that my husband and I aren't still here fifteen months from now."

"Don't worry, that's not going to happen," Walter said.

"You think we'll be free well before then?" she shot back excitedly.

"Only if someone pays your ransom," he said with a sad laugh. "Things have gotten much worse these past three months. The crappy food has gotten crappier. The threats are more frequent and desperate." Jenny gasped. "In any case, I'm guessing that none of us have long here. Don't mean to scare you, just being honest."

"What do you mean?"

"I don't suppose anyone has explained the 'sifting' process to you, have they?"

"What's that?" Jenny asked.

"Your husband will remain here as long as they have reasonable expectations that ransom may still be possible. These days, attractive women like yourself are sold into white slavery after a few months. Those that aren't considered to be still marketable are given to the pirates."

"Oh my God."

Walter hesitated. "But that's not as bad as what happens to us men once it becomes clear we're no longer serious ransom prospects."

"What happens?"

"We're tagged as O.D."

"Huh?"

Walter hesitated for a moment. "Organ Donors."

The blood rushed from her head and she collapsed onto the floor, not bothering to avoid a puddle of oily water.

CHAPTER 27

"Sorry for being late. Leo cornered me," Quint said as he entered the small conference room where Kira and Mimi were waiting. Kira rolled her eyes and smiled as he set his coffee cup on the table. "Rogers will be providing us with some drones the military considers to be obsolete. Assuming you're interested," he said, looking each of them in the eye, "I'd like for you both to go to Redstone Arsenal in Huntsville, Alabama to get trained to fly them."

"I'm in," Mimi squealed with excitement and then quieted as Kira spoke.

"How long will the training take?"

"Two days, maybe three at most."

Kira, excited to finally have the chance to be involved in helping to rescue Jenny, thought for a moment. "I had planned to head back to the States soon anyhow to be close to medical facilities with my pregnancy, so I don't see a problem. And if there were to be one, I'll have convenient access to plenty of skilled medical care there. I'll discuss it with Colin but that won't be a problem. You can count on me."

"Okay, but it needs to be quick. You'll be leaving tomorrow."

"With Jenny being held prisoner by those savage pirates, it can't be soon enough," Kira replied.

"Speaking of which, it's not going to be just training. After you've had a chance to get familiar with each of the drones, the plan is to launch the Reaper to attack the pirates' mother ship."

"While we're still there training?" Kira asked.

"Yeah, we don't want to delay a single day in rescuing Jenny. Plus, with you guys just getting up to speed, we need some more experienced drone pilots involved. The problem is, they have to have plausible deniability. They'll treat it as a long-distance training exercise. They'll train you on what to do regarding firing a live missile.

"From what I've been told, it's much like a video game controller. All you do is point, shoot, and then let the system take care of it. Your training instructor will know what's going on, but the actual attack is not to be discussed with him openly. Rogers is arranging to have the drone armed once it's out of U.S. airspace. Just before the actual attack, the instructor will leave the room so as not to be present during the actual... 'event.'"

Quint paused for a moment and drained the last of his coffee. "While flying the drone will be much like playing a video game, the results sure won't. Kira, do you think you're up for doing th—"

"I'll do whatever it takes to save Jenny from those animals," Kira interrupted, making it clear that it would not be a problem. The two women then left, planning their trip.

As Dawson left the armory, Marcia happened by. "What's that?" she asked, admiring the fearsome-looking weapon he was carrying.

"An AA-12." She looked puzzled. "It's a badass shotgun. You can choose a thirty-two-round drum magazine loaded with conventional rounds or one with fragmentation grenades. You point this baby in the general direction of the bad guys and start wreaking havoc."

She listened intently as Dawson explained. "I want to learn how to handle it!" she exclaimed.

"With your experience, no problem. Come on, I'll check you out on it," Dawson said as he continued toward the stairs.

A few minutes later, they were standing at an improvised shooting range that Dawson had set up on the far side of the landing strip. After showing Marcia how to use and maintain the weapon, Dawson blew giant holes in the targets and disintegrated a couple of bottles that they had brought along. "With the combined weight of the gun and the loads, it's heavy, but being recoilless makes it easy to handle."

Next, Marcia emptied a few magazines to get the feel for using it and then practiced loading it. "Yeah, this is definitely way cool. I love it," Marcia said.

Kira and Mimi were finished packing and Colin was helping them with their bags when Nigora happened along. "Where you go?"

"We're headed to Alabama."

"Why you go there?"

"We're learning how to fly drones." Nigora looked puzzled. "Oh, that's right—you were in the kitchen cooking when we talked about the whole drone thing."

"Drone?"

"Small, unmanned airplanes."

"Oh, I go too."

"Nigora, we're leaving in less than an hour and you don't have approval—"

"No problem. I see Quint, then pack and put on my breasts. Be right back. Don't leave me."

Mimi shook her head and laughed as Nigora hurried off. "Like that's going to happen." Kira smiled without replying.

Quint was talking to Dawson as Nigora rushed up. "I want fly drone too."

"Fly drones?" Quint remarked with surprise. "Nigora, I don't know about that."

"I tired of just cleaning and cooking. This I can do. Make me more part of team."

"What do you think?" Quint asked Dawson who just shrugged his shoulders.

"Please, please," she replied.

"What does she want?" Marcia asked as she walked up.

"Nigora just volunteered for UCAV training," Quint replied.

"I know she's young but she's bright. I think it's good that she wants to serve a more important role on the team. I'd let her do it... I mean, if you approve, that is," Marcia added, seeming concerned about overstepping her bounds. "I mean, what's the harm?"

Quint stood considering it while Nigora's pleading eyes remained locked onto his. He knew that Mimi had been just a "fish tech" when Kira took her under her wing. And Nigora did seem to be a quick study much like Mimi.

Actually, it would get her out of my hair for a few days. And it wouldn't hurt to have another skilled drone pilot to fly surveillance. Really, I don't think there's much harm in giving her a chance. Then we'll see if she has the hand-eye coordination. But she's damned sure not going to be firing weapons at anything. Quint looked at Marcia, who had been assigned the job of mothering Nigora. Then she and Quint glanced at Dawson who mouthed, "Why not?"

"Very well. Nigora, you are now a member of the team's air force," Quint said. Nigora squealed in excitement before running off to grab her things.

Kira was standing on the dock waiting for the seaplane to arrive and noticed that Mimi seemed preoccupied. "Something on your mind?"

Mimi fidgeted with the strap on her carry-on bag for a moment before replying. "Yeah, I've been trying to decide how to tell you."

"Tell me what? Spit it out."

"Well...uh... Preston's going to be meeting me."

Kira laughed. "And that's what was bothering you?"

"Yeah...I... know that Dawson doesn't like him, maybe Quint, too. So when I called Preston on the satphone to tell him where I was going, he asked if he could meet me. I hated to say no but—"

"Mimi, you're giving up a lot of your free time to develop skills that will help the team. Provided Preston doesn't interfere with your training, I think that's your own business."

"So I shouldn't worry about it?"

"Absolutely not."

The seaplane had just landed and was taxiing toward them. "Looks like Nigora and her stupid blow-up tits won't be coming with us," Mimi commented with a grin. Though she seemed to like Nigora and was well aware of the sacrifice Nigora's father had made when he died helping the team in Uzbekistan, enough was enough. Both she and Kira had discussed being irked at how the cute young woman often seemed to be granted favored treatment.

"I'm not so sure," Kira replied, nodding toward Nigora who was bouncing along toward them, her strap-on breasts inflated to maximum size, with Leo dutifully carrying her bag.

"Quint say I go with you to Amelica! I learn to fly and maybe we go shop, no?" The sound of the approaching plane drowned out Mimi's response.

CHAPTER 28

With nothing else to do while imprisoned in the bilge, Jenny spent most of her time thinking. In the harsh reality of her current situation, her marital concerns seemed silly. She now wished she hadn't blurted out her feelings about Brad and had stuck to her original decision to wait until they got back home. She longed to be back on their sailboat and the comfort of having him beside her.

Without a watch and no windows in the bilge, Jenny lost track of time. She guessed a week had passed in the hold when the hatch opened and a man descended from above.

"You, come," a gruff voice commanded. She looked up to see him pointing at her. Unsure whether she was being freed or summoned to her execution, she hesitantly approached the open door. "Come on, come on. Move, damn it."

Walter's worried face was the last thing Jenny saw before she was jerked out of the compartment. She followed the two raggedly dressed pirates up the stairs she had descended a lifetime earlier, emerging into blinding sunlight where she took a deep breath of clean air.

With her arm held before her face and her eyes squinted, she stumbled forward until she was directed back inside the ship.

"Jenny!" Brad rushed forward and hugged her, seeming oblivious to the stench of her filthy clothes and unwashed hair. "I've been sick worrying about you. Over and over I begged them to take me instead."

She clutched him tightly, tears streaming down her face. "I thought I'd never get out of there. The filth and all those pitiful men. It was horrible."

"What did they do to you?" Brad said alarmed.

"Nothing, they mostly just left me alone. What happened? Why did they let me back out?"

"I'm not sure. Every other day, Ethan asked me the same questions over and over. He said that if I ever wanted to see you again I'd better tell him how we could get them more money. I would have told him anything to have you back but saw little point in lying. I knew he'd quickly figure it out and then there'd be hell to pay. Maybe after I kept repeating the same answers, he finally believed me." Jenny smiled and took his hand in hers.

They sat together in silence for a long while before Jenny pressed her face to his ear. "Brad, I'm sorry, I don't want to leave you. I've been stupid. Can you ever forgive me?"

Brad pulled away and smiled back at her. "I forgave you the minute you said it. I'll be happy to stay with you, for however long we may have." His last words brought the reality of their predicament crashing down on both of them.

Jamal rose and stretched, his body aching from having spent the night lying on the concrete floor. Despite being tempted those many times when Ayan implored him to stay with her, he always refused. For one thing, he felt that it was inappropriate given her profession. So he slept in a one-room abandoned building with a slew of other orphan boys.

Once he'd had a fine blanket that Ayan had bought him. It had his name embroidered at the top and he'd carried it with him everywhere. But after being teased by the older boys, he'd begun to leave it rolled up in the corner of the building. One day he'd returned to find one of the older boys urinating on it. He'd flown at the boy in a fit of rage and been badly beaten for his efforts. The smelly remains of the defiled blanket still lay rotting in the far corner.

Jamaal entered Ayan's home, chewing a mouthful of khat and carrying a spit bottle. She took one look, grabbed him by the ear, and marched him outside. She snatched the bottle from his hand and slung it across the street.

"Spit it out! Now." She stood twisting his ear until he obeyed. "Don't you ever enter my house chewing that filth again."

She was caught by surprise when Jamal thrust her hand away and yelled, "I'm a man now. You can't tell me what to do. You're not my mother—"

Ayan recoiled as if slapped. "You're right." She ducked back inside, leaving him standing alone.

He was right—she wasn't his mother and if he wasn't quite a man, he certainly lived in a man's world. It was just that she wanted to protect him... from everything.

She thought of the other little orphan boy she had failed to protect. Though he wasn't her own, she had raised him most of his seven years after his mother was stabbed during a drunken spat with one of her "regular customers." She could still see him lying in the corner in his little bed as he gasped his last breath after the filth in those barrels the tsunami had thrust upon their shores sucked the life from his tiny body.

An hour later, a shadow crossed the doorway and she looked up to see Jamal. "I'm sorry," he said sheepishly.

She stifled a grin at his hangdog look and changed the subject. "So how did work go today?"

CHAPTER 29

Over the next few days, Jenny settled back into her earlier routine. After spending time in the ship's bilge, she felt reborn.

The only contact with the pirates was the occasional visits to bring food and water or the walks around the deck. With little to occupy her mind, Jenny recalled a reality television show in which a missionary group was coached on how to handle a kidnap situation. They were taught that hostages should always put their captors at ease, maintain their dignity, and try to develop a rapport with the kidnappers.

Jenny had noticed a skinny young boy who delivered their food each day. He had a kind face and always lingered for a moment, seemingly interested in talking. Jenny decided she would try to befriend him.

When the boy appeared the next morning, Jenny rose and, in as nonthreatening manner as possible, eased toward him and asked, "What's your name?"

The boy had just set his pail of food on the floor and was startled. For a moment, he looked back at her without speaking before replying, "Jamal."

"That's a nice name. Where are you from?"

Before he could answer, a gravelly voice bellowed from outside, "No talking. Put the food down and get out of there." Jamal glanced up at Jenny, appearing a little flustered, but said nothing further before rejoining his companion back outside.

A few days later, Jenny was glad to be paired with Jamal for a walk out on deck. "Jamal, it's so nice out today. What a lovely morning." Her comments earned only a stony silence and stern stare. But once they were out on the foredeck, away from the others, he whispered a reply.

"Hostages are not permitted to speak while on their walk."

"Oh, I'm sorry. Oops, there I go again, speaking to apologize for speaking." Jamal laughed despite himself. "If I speak quietly, then I suppose it's not as bad, right?" Jamal shrugged. Deciding to take that as permission and seeing no one within earshot, she continued. "I'm from England. Lived there all my life. That is, up until we set out to explore the world. Is this your home?"

Jamal glanced back toward the ship's stern before replying. "No, I was born in Mogadishu. When I was eight, my parents were killed in the fighting between the government and the Islamists. In our country, someone is always fighting someone else and we get caught in the middle."

"I think it's not so different in many other places. The Protestants and Catholics in Ireland have been fighting for years," Jenny replied. "What made you leave?"

"Mogadishu was not such a good place for a poor orphan. I heard about the pirates here and decided to come."

"But with no money, how did you get here?"

"I'm small and fast. It's easy to sneak inside a large truck or on the back of a bus to hitch a ride. It took many days but finally, I arrived—hungry and tired."

"How did you survive after you got here?"

"In my country, if you can't find work you either steal or starve. I stole scraps and did odd jobs for the pirates. I worked cheap so they hired me to help guard the hostages and gave me this rifle," he said proudly rubbing the pitted barrel.

"You go to school?"

"I used to but here there is no school." Jamal placed his finger to his lips and began chewing on his nail.

"You really shouldn't do that," Jenny said.

Jamal quickly moved his hand away. "You sound like Ayan. She's always telling me that."

"Who is Ayan?"

"A friend. She helps me sometimes."

After a short pause, Jenny asked, "What do you want to be?" Jamal seemed startled by the question. With his focus on surviving, it was something she imagined he seldom considered.

"I-I... would like to play the piano," he finally blurted out.

"Well... that's... very admirable." Not wishing to offend him, Jenny struggled to contain her surprise. "I love the piano, too. I've been playing since I was your age. Have you had lessons?"

"Hardly." Jamal laughed. "But I saw a real one once. And the bands which used to play here had keyboards."

"Perhaps I could teach you."

"Sure," he scoffed. "And then maybe we could rent a concert hall where I could perform."

"No, I mean, I could teach you the keyboard layout. Maybe even how to read music. If you could bring some paper and a pen, then next time you come—"

"Jamal! What are you doing? Get back here," Korfa's angry voice bellowed from the ship's bridge above.

"We must go. I have stayed too long." Jenny quickly described the size and layout of the keyboard before Jamal prodded her back toward the rear of the ship in silence.

"You have been gone a long time," said Korfa. "Does somebody have a girlfriend?" the big man added with a broad smile.

"Shut up. I just do my job, you should too," Jamal spat back and then ducked when Korfa lashed out at him with an open hand.

"We have work to do." Korfa motioned for him to follow. "Come with me... if you can leave your woman." Jenny could see Jamal was embarrassed and knew that to survive in his brutal world, it was important to look tough. She would have to be careful not to put him at risk.

"Do you have paper and maybe some glue?" Jamal asked Ayan when he got off work that afternoon.

"I think so." After rummaging around in a cardboard box which served as her night stand and storage, Auan scrounged up several dog-eared sheets of paper and a half-dried-out bottle of glue.

"Oh, and I need a pencil."

She continued to search and found the stub of a pencil. "Use a knife from the kitchen to sharpen it." She lit a cigarette and watched as Jamal carefully pieced together an actual-sized keyboard by gluing sheets of paper together. Using the pencil, he then sketched out a crude set of keys and then left it to dry overnight.

The next morning, Jamal was back at Ayan's home to examine his finished paper keyboard, which he carefully folded.

"Canjeero for breakfast okay?" she asked.

Jamal nodded, certain that the simple pancakes were all she really had to offer. "They were great yesterday, but could I have two more? I'm really starving."

She hesitated for an instant before replying, "Why, sure. You're a growing boy." A few minutes later she placed the stack in front of him on a coarse napkin.

"Thanks," he quickly replied lest she lecture him on his manners. When he thought she wasn't looking, he wrapped the extra two in a napkin and slid them into his shirt, ignoring the slight smile on her face.

After finishing his breakfast, he placed the folded paper piano keyboard in his pocket and headed for the boat that would take him out for his shift on the hostage ship. He looked forward to spending time with Jenny learning about piano scales.

He walked with more swagger than usual and cursed at every opportunity, desperate to restore his image as tough and insensitive after Korfa's comments about having a "girlfriend." When the boat reached the ship, he struggled not to show his eagerness as he bounded up the stairs to the hostage holding area. He joined the guard stationed outside the door.

"I hate walking the stupid hostages, but today is my turn," the guard said.

"I don't mind the exercise," Jamal replied as the guard opened the hostage cell. "If you like, I'll do it for you. But you'll owe me one," he quickly added.

The guard looked at him with a knowing grin. "You just want to see your girlfriend. You're not getting soft, are you?"

"You keep it up and I'll show you soft," Jamal said, stretching tall and puffing out his chest.

"Hey, it's okay. You can have her, especially if it means that I don't have to walk her big ass around." Jamal winced before realizing that she could not understand his native tongue and was blissfully unaware of the insult.

On the far side of the room, Jenny crouched against the wall, appearing weary. "You, come with me for your outside time. Make one move, and I'll bust your head with this rifle butt," Jamal said, poking the barrel into her kidneys for show.

Once they were out on the open foredeck, away from the others, Jamal stopped. After a quick glance over his shoulder, he withdrew the napkins and removed a pancake. "Here. Eat. Face toward the bow and be quick. Don't let them see you."

Jenny greedily snatched the pancake and actually moaned as she took the first bite. "Thank you so much. It tastes wonderful, what is it?"

"We call it canjeero. I like mine with ghee, but I didn't have any to bring. I do have this," Jamal said as he carefully removed a beer bottle filled with clean water from the pocket of his cargo shorts.

"I'll just drink half. The rest will be for Brad along with half of this pancake too," she said.

"No, you eat that. I have another for him."

While Jenny ate, Jamal removed the keyboard from his pocket and spread it out furtively. "I brought this."

Jenny looked at his work. The sheets were somewhat crooked with gaps where the crude glue had not stuck, and the sketched keys were crudely drawn. "Jamal, you did great." His face beamed with pride. "Okay, piano lesson number one," she said and began teaching him the scales..

That afternoon, as soon as the launch touched the dock, Jamal leaped from the boat and ran to see Ayan. Without thinking, he barged into her place to find her asleep on her mat.

"Oh, sorry," he apologized while noting that she appeared ill. "Are you okay?"

"Just a bad headache," she replied groggily. "Probably from not eating... I·I mean... maybe it's the heat." Ayan rose from her bed and lit a cigarette, exhaling a cloud of blue smoke which Jamal fanned away from his face.

"Well, if it's hunger, I will make you dinner." Jamal entered the small cooking area. Before Ayan could stop him, he lifted the large jar from the shelf and was surprised at how light it seemed before realizing that it was empty.

She's hungry because she had nothing to eat. Those extra pancakes this morning... He realized why she had not eaten. All this time, Jamal had never considered that someone had to pay for the food. And since she wasn't working very often, she had little money.

How stupid and selfish I have been. But I will fix this, he vowed and then set out for the tiny market.

CHAPTER 30

Though the people in Jamal's village of Hafun no longer dressed in their finest to meet the pirates, on Fridays they held a modest party. Each person brought a dish and—in defiance of Islam—whatever alcohol they could afford, hoping to forget their miserable existence for a few hours. It was a far cry from the old days when a famous band would play while they feasted on roasted goat and drank all the top-shelf liquor they could hold.

Every other Friday, Jamal had the evening off and always looked forward to the party. He had tried drinking once but it had made him very sick. So now after making a great show of taking a drink, he would discreetly pour the rest of it out after a few sips and then proceed to act goofy. Though he didn't like the drinking, it was nice seeing everyone have fun.

He particularly enjoyed watching Ayan, always the life of the party, tell her funny stories and jokes. Everyone liked her and he was proud she had taken an interest in mothering him.

He stepped from the skiff and headed off to change clothes before walking Ayan to the party.

Ayan was excited. After spending the previous evening with a rare paying customer, she'd splurged on a pint of harsh rum from the old man who ran the village liquor store. At one time, she had traded her favors for the fine whiskey he stocked but that was a long time ago.

Now he was too old and she would not stoop to trade for the cheap liquor or recycled bottles of sour beer which lined a single lonely shelf in his store. He could be trusted not to sell the bad homemade brew like that which had been laced with methane and killed nearly a hundred people in Mogadishu a few years back.

Fine liquor was another casualty of the pirates' decreased success. Once, they'd managed to seize a ship loaded with a cargo of liquor and the whole village had stayed drunk for most of a month. Usually, their victims had at least some liquor stores which the pirates would share with those in the village. But these days, with few victims there was little liquor to be shared.

Ayan bought a small pack of goat cheese to make a dip for the bread she was baking. Jamal would be here shortly and they would leave once the bread was done. She wondered if he might take Desta to the party. *It would be good for his ego to have a girlfriend.*

Wearing her remaining fine dress with several tears crudely mended, Ayan scrounged mascara from the nearly empty tube and used the last of her lipstick. She looked in the mirror, finding it hard to believe she had gotten so old.

It wasn't the years so much as the alcohol, the smoking, the drugs, and living hard during better times that had taken its toll. She longed for the fine house in which she had once lived along with several other prostitutes. Back then she had had a closet filled with fine dresses, booty from captured ships brought by flush customers.

Ayan finished touching up her makeup and went to the kitchen. She lit a cigarette and was making tea when she saw the shadow of someone entering her doorway and was surprised to see that instead of

Jamal, it was his scumbag boss, who was also her least favorite customer.

"What are you doing here, Korfa?" He lurched forward and she caught a whiff of cheap rum on his breath that meant trouble. "Did you come to pay me? I told you no more credit when you called the other day," she yelled at the burly man, who had entered uninvited.

"Credit? I don't need no damn credit. I can take what I want for free." Before she could react, the hulking man bounded across the room in two steps and was upon her. She struggled, bit, and kicked at him with all of her strength, to no avail. He ripped the dress from her and tossed it to one side, knocking the cigarette from her mouth to fall onto the dress, where it lay smoldering.

Jamal entered in the midst of the struggle. He smelled the stench of burning cloth and saw Korfa raping Ayan. Without pause, he ran toward them and began beating on the man's back with his small fists. With one blow of his massive fist, the giant sent Jamal reeling backward over a table smashing a rickety chair and knocking him unconscious.

An hour later, Jamal awoke to the sound of Ayan crying and he struggled to his feet.

"Don't look, I'm not decent. Wait," she yelled.

Jamal obeyed and after picking up the broken pieces of her best chair, sat down at the table. He held his aching head in his hands while waiting for her to pin her torn and scorched dress back in place as best she could

"Are you okay, Jamal?" she asked as she entered the room and saw his swollen eye.

He nodded. "What about you? What did that beast do to you?"

"It's okay, it's not the first time. When he's been drinking, Korfa gets like that and there's no reasoning with him."

"I will find him and make him pay." Jamal rubbed the knot on the back of his head.

"You'll do no such thing. Thanks for your concern, but that killer is best left alone." Jamal said nothing further as he pressed his head to hers to comfort them both.

CHAPTER 31

First off the small commuter plane, Mimi was greeted by a handsome uniformed man awaiting them on the tarmac. "Hi, I'm Lt. Lewis. I wasn't expecting such lovely trainees," he said.

"Why, thank you," Mimi replied blushing, "but I wouldn't really—"

"Amelica! I love Amelica," Nigora announced as she exited the plane in movie-star fashion with her back bowed to highlight her massive inflatable chest. Kira saw the lieutenant's eyes nearly bulge from their sockets at the spectacle. He rushed over to greet her, leaving Mimi standing alone.

"You Hollywood actor, no? You teach me to fly?" Nigora asked, flashing Mimi a sly grin. With no assistance from the smitten young air corpsman, Kira descended the steps, taking care not to fall with her artificial leg.

As he drove them to their hotel, Nigora continued to dominate the conversation while Kira exchanged eye rolls with Mimi. After dropping off their bags and freshening up, they loaded back into the van to continue on to the training center. Once the three women were seated in a classroom capable of accommodating thirty, the lieutenant began.

"Okay, ladies, we've got a lot of ground to cover, or I guess I should say air." He gave an awkward chuckle as he checked for Nigora's smile. "So let's get started. We're not really supposed to be training civilians like you. But your friend Rogers seems to have a lot of stroke and apparently called in some favors.

"I've spent the past couple of days familiarizing myself with the UCAVs Rogers managed to dig up for you. He got you early versions of the Predator, Global Hawk, and Reaper, the latter of which we'll be sending to Somalia for your... exercise. Though they're pretty old, they fly just fine.

"In your training, we'll cover how to fly each of the drones, how to use their weapon systems, and how to perform basic maintenance, though I'm certain you'll have no problem finding someone else to do that for you," he said, exchanging smiles with Nigora . "You'll also need to have someone... like me, for instance... come in every hundred and fifty to two hundred hours of flight time to perform a detailed inspection." He gave a nervous laugh and once again cut his eyes at her.

"Unmanned Combat Air Vehicles, or UCAVs, were developed for missions considered too 'dull, dirty, or dangerous' for manned aircraft. The Predator is the cheapest and smallest. It's used to get close in. The Global Hawk, is the most expensive and flies the highest and the furthest. The Reaper is somewhere in between and is designed to carry the most extensive weapons suite." He then launched off into his training lecture.

During a break, Kira approached the lieutenant. "I understand that as part of the training we'll be making a long distance flight with one of the drones and I was wondering—"

"When that would be?" the lieutenant finished. "Soon. I understand the reason for your... shall we say... eagerness and we will make it happen as soon as you're ready."

Before ending class for the day, it was agreed that they would meet for dinner. Lt. Lewis pulled up sharply at seven o'clock. He stepped from the car to open the rear door. "Good evening, ladies, your chariot awai—"

"Ever been to Maison's?" Preston interrupted the young lieutenant as he, Mimi, and Nigora piled into the large government sedan, leaving Kira to the front passenger seat. Preston had arrived late in the afternoon and was waiting at the hotel when the team finished class.

"No... uh... it's not exactly a place that I can... uh... I heard it's really nice."

"Preston thinks we should treat these lovely ladies to a place worthy of such beauty. Preston hears that the food there is like a gift from God, or at least the French. Driver, take us there." Preston gave a great laugh while Mimi and Nigora tittered. "Preston has already made reservations, but please hurry lest we be late," he said, referring to himself in third person as usual.

Mimi spoke up to introduce the two men. "Oh, sorry. Lieutenant, this is my... uh... fian—"

"I'm Preston."

"I gathered," he muttered low enough that only Kira caught it.

Preston then continued to dominate the conversation. After listening to the first of Preston's self-aggrandizing stories, Kira was already wishing she had stayed behind. For the rest of their brief ride, she tried to focus her thoughts on what her soon-to-be-born baby would be like.

Lt. Lewis pulled up in front of a building that looked like it might have actually been built by French nobility. A valet sprung forward as if launched and opened the passenger side doors before making his way around to the driver's side.

"Uh... I'm afraid I need to park my own car. It's government issue and... uh... it's policy." Lt. Lewis finished and then noted the expectant look on the valet's face. It appeared that not availing himself of the service did not eliminate the necessity to tip. He fumbled for his wallet and handed the man a twenty. Before he could ask about change, the valet had vanished.

The rest of the group had already been seated when Lewis made his way through the garish foyer, decorated in formal French fashion. "Please join us." Preston pointed to a seat on the opposite end of the table.

Kira noticed that Preston had manipulated the seating to place himself at one end of the table with Mimi and Nigora seated on either side of him, leaving Lewis to sit at the far end beside her and an empty chair on Mimi's side.

Seeing Nigora sandwiched between Kira and Preston, Lewis hesitated before sitting down.

"Here, you don't want to be seated by the married pregnant woman." Kira struggled to conceal a smile as she insisted Nigora swap seats, placing her beside Lewis and earning her an angry glare from Preston. At that moment, the waiter appeared offering the wine menu, which Preston snatched from his hand.

After distributing menus, the waiter heard Preston's wine selection and laughed, much to Preston's chagrin. "Sir, I would strongly recommend against that wine," he said with a condescending smirk. "I don't know why they even keep it on the list. No one who knows wine ever orders it and the few that do always send it back."

Once again, Kira covered her mouth with her hand to conceal her smile as the blushing Preston quickly changed his selection to the highest-priced choice on the list. The waiter nodded, gushing over his second choice before disappearing.

The group made small talk while becoming absorbed in the array of entrée choices listed on the parchment paper held inside thick tooled leather portfolios.

A short time later, the waiter reappeared to cork and pour the wine. After reciting the evening's specials, he left to wait on another table. Preston tapped the side of his glass with a spoon to gain everyone's attention to the apparent irritation of their neighboring diners and then said in a booming voice, "I would like to make a toast." He rose to his feet, glass held in exaggeration fashion above his head and proceeded to recite a few words.

Red-faced, Kira looked down self-consciously from the open stares of nearby diners. She let out a sigh when Preston finally took his seat when the waiter reappeared. Each of the women opted for one of the evening's specials.

"I'll take the lobster," Preston said.

"And what size would you pref—"

"Big, the largest you have."

The waiter's eyes widened as he noted the order. "And you, sir?" he asked Lewis.

"I'll just have a ribeye, the ten-ounce one will be fine."

"Nonsense," Preston interrupted. "You'll do nothing of the sort. Bring him a twenty-four-ounce cowboy ribeye. If you don't have one, find one." The waiter nodded without commenting. Preston then went on to order an array of side dishes which included one of nearly everything on the menu. "Now if you'll excuse me for a moment, I shall retire to the boys' room. Back in a jiffy."

Preston returned a few minutes later, a hint of white powder on his left nostril. He stopped beside the empty seat between Mimi and Lewis and across from Nigora. "I think I'll join you down here. We men have to stick together," he said and slapped Lewis on the back, jolting him enough to spill his water. Kira caught the hint of a frown on Mimi's face, quickly disguised by a forced smile at Preston's next joke.

During the meal, Preston continued to "treat" the group along with his captive audience of diners within earshot to a barrage of off-color jokes and fabricated stories from his youth.

With the arrival of each course, Preston flipped through the wine list and ordered another pricey bottle, working his way from light to heavy. As their designated driver, Lewis declined to imbibe and Kira did the same due to her pregnancy.

This left an army of half-empty, high-dollar bottles of wine remaining beside plates still filled with uneaten food and at least half of the exorbitantly priced lobster. Yet Preston ordered several flaming desserts for the table and after-dinner cordials for any takers. By the time the group had surrendered their dessert forks and were rubbing their full bellies, the restaurant host appeared.

"I trust your dinner met your expectations," the host said.

"Absolutely, everything was fabulous, simply fabulous," Preston replied as the waiter was heading their way with the check. "When I booked our reservation, I was told you offer a tour of the kitchen and what I understand is quite a wine cellar. Would it be possible to arrange one for us?"

"Certainly sir, I will have—"

"Splendid. Ladies," Preston said offering an arm to both Mimi and Nigora. "Kira, while Lewis takes care of business, care to join us?" Kira shook her head. "No problem, what with that belly and your peg-leg, Preston understands."

It wasn't clear to Kira whether he was intentionally being rude as payback for her seating changes or just clueless.

"Well, then, lead on," Preston said to the host, who immediately pawned them off on one of the staff to lead the tour.

Kira saw Lewis' eyes widen as he scanned the bill. He thumbed through a few bills in his wallet before removing a credit card which he held in his hand hesitantly. The waiter plucked it from his hand and scurried away before Kira could react.

Lewis appeared nervous and was fidgeting as Kira discreetly reached into her purse to remove her wallet, just as the waiter reappeared holding the plastic card. "Sir, I'm sorry but—"

"How rude of us, I guess I just wasn't thinking. Here, put this on my card, it's the least we can do after all you've done for us," Kira said, handing the waiter her card. An awkward silence followed with Lewis sitting red-faced, and Kira unable to think of anything to say to ease the uncomfortable situation.

By the time Kira had settled the bill and followed Lewis to the foyer, the trio led by Preston staggered up having completed their tour. Obviously drunk, all three were laughing far too loud. "What a magnificent wine cellar. Not as large as some I've seen, but an exquisite selection. Lewis, please fetch our carriage?"

Lewis left to get the car while the host held the door and Kira heard him breathe a sigh of relief as they filed outside to wait beneath the porte cochere.

CHAPTER 32

The next morning Kira woke up thinking about Jenny. They had been quite close growing up. Though these days they didn't see each other as often as she wished, they still kept in touch via email and social media. Kira found it hard not to dwell on what Jenny must be facing but knew that her efforts were best spent in doing whatever she could to rescue her.

Kira tapped on Mimi's door on her way to breakfast and grinned at the half-open, bloodshot eyes in the face that answered. "Have a good time after I left last night?" Kira asked.

"I...uh... guess so," Mimi said softly before placing her hand over her mouth to run toward the bathroom.

"I'll see you in class," Kira said as she closed the door and headed for Nigora's room.

"Come in. Door not locked," came a voice from within. Kira opened the door to find her sitting on the edge of her bed looking no better.

"You okay?"

"I never drink again. I can hold my vodka but not the stuff these Amelican men drink. What they call, tequika?"

Kira laughed. "Tequila, yeah, it's bad stuff. Look, I'm going on to breakfast. You can either meet me there or back at class." Nigora nodded and then lunged toward the bathroom.

After a light breakfast, Kira poured a cup of coffee in the conference room where Lt. Lewis was already waiting for them, looking surprisingly chipper. A short time later, the other two women came in favoring their aching heads and he began lecturing.

"This morning, we'll wrap up the lecture and then go to the vehicle control center to start your hands-on training. Yesterday we covered the basics of drone theory and operation. Now let's talk about the three UCAVs that you'll actually be operating." The lieutenant went on for the next hour covering a seemingly endless list of specifications for each type of drone.

"As far as weapons systems go, both the Predator and the Hawk have none. Not to say that they can't be added. The Reaper is capable of carrying missiles, which we, of course, will not be providing, and is equipped with a thirty caliber machine gun which, in accordance with U.S. law, will not be operational when we transfer the drones to you. In order to be fully operational, they require the parts which I have had removed and which are in this small box... here on my desk... totally unsecure and unguarded..." He paused with a wide grin on his face.

When they took a break a few minutes later, Kira smiled as Nigora snatched the box off the desk as soon as the lieutenant had left the room. A few minutes later, she had replaced the empty box and its pilfered contents were tucked away in her purse.

"Okay, let's get started with the fun part of your training." He took a drink of coffee and then set the cup back down on his desk, nudging the box, which appeared lighter. He looked up with a smile as he continued to speak. "We've received the go-ahead to launch a UCAV and I figured we'd start with the Predator. Since it's the cheapest, if you have to crash one of your toys, make it this one. Please follow me to the drone command center."

They entered a small prefabricated building near a runway which appeared to be dedicated to drone operations. "That new building across the runway is now our main ops center. This was the original one, which is now our backup. And we use it for 'special' projects, such as training unauthorized private civilian groups with well-placed friends," he said with a nervous laugh.

They spent the rest of the morning practicing takeoffs and landings with the Predator, each of the three women taking a turn. After lunch, they continued their training with the other drones.

"All of the drones are easy to fly, it just takes some hours behind the stick to develop a feel for it. Mimi, you continue flying the Predator while I get Kira started on the Reaper." With Nigora watching, Kira practiced flying the Reaper, quickly getting the hang of it. "Okay, keep it up while I get Nigora started with the Global Hawk. You guys can cross-train yourselves when you get back home."

By the end of the afternoon, all three women had made significant progress toward becoming skilled drone pilots but were exhausted from the tension of flying the drones. "You guys are doing great. After we landed the Reaper earlier, they fueled and serviced it so it's ready to be loaded aboard a C-141 and be flown overseas for your... Somalia training mission which Rogers has arranged and which I can formally know nothing about." He stopped and looked each of them in the eye. Kira understood and nodded.

"Now, ready to go out to dinner and do a little partying again?" Lewis chuckled.

"No!" came the three women's chorused response.

He laughed. "I thought that might be the case. I'll drop you off at your hotel. You can take the hotel shuttle tomorrow morning and we'll meet at six sharp back here in the drone control center. Have a good night."

As they entered the hotel, Preston was there to greet them. "What a beautiful trio," he said. Kira noticed him leering briefly at her before shifting his gaze to Nigora, whom he proceeded to undress with his eyes. "Preston is honored to welcome you," he said in his typical weird third-person fashion. "Will you permit me to take all of you to dinner?"

"I appreciate it, but we're just going to eat a light dinner here in the hotel restaurant and then head to our rooms. Nigora needs to finish getting over her hangover. The baby and I need to get rest as well as. You two go have yourselves a blast."

Kira led Nigora toward the restaurant while Mimi pulled the leering Preston toward the front door.

After a quick meal, the two women headed to their rooms, where Kira called the Sanctuary. "Hey, Quint," she said as soon as he answered the team's satphone.

"Good timing, I just got off the phone with Rogers. He got us a position fix on the mother ship. I understand that the Reaper is on its way via cargo plane. He's arranged to have it fueled and weaponized. Since they're nine hours ahead of us, the plan is to confirm the mother ship's position shortly after sunrise tomorrow and then to attack an hour later. That means you'll need to be standing by around eight p.m. tomorrow evening to fly the drone. Your guy Lewis has been briefed off the record but help him maintain his plausible deniability, understand?"

"Got it."

"Want to chat with your hubby?"

"You have to ask?"

Quint laughed. "He's right here. Good luck and break a leg, or sink a pirate, or whatever," Quint said and relinquished the phone to Colin.

"We're coming down the homestretch. Today, you're going to start flying the Predator and Hawk back to your base. This will give you a chance to get more experience and land a time or two for servicing. My guys will take them from wherever we end up today and fly them the rest of the way back to your base tomorrow. Tonight, we're going to have our long-awaited... training exercise... with the Reaper."

It was late afternoon when they finished and broke for dinner. Lewis asked Kira to remain behind. "You understand my position regarding the plans for tonight?"

"I do," Kira replied.

"Good. It's important that I remain at arm's length. When you return tonight, the Reaper will be in position, refueled, and ready for your 'exercise.' I'll take a few minutes now and show you how you would fire missiles—that is, if the Reaper were to be armed with them, which it isn't, of course, because that would be illegal, right?" Kira replied with a smile.

A half hour later, they had finished and Kira joined the others for dinner. Her stomach was unsettled from worrying about Jenny, and found she had little appetite. She also failed in her attempt to take a short nap in hopes of making the time pass faster. But finally it was time to return to the drone control center.

They launched the Reaper from a base in eastern Africa and flew it away from the Horn of Africa at a high altitude where it was virtually invisible from the sea surface below. Kira flew the drone for the next hour. She was still at the controls when she spotted the pirates' mother ship and made a pass to confirm the vessel's identity. She banked the UCAV in a wide circle and then approached from the east with the sun behind the drone. She locked the target designator into position and glanced at the Lieutenant, getting the thumbs up in response.

"Please continue. I'm going for a cup of coffee," Lt. Lewis said and left the room. As soon as the door closed, Kira pressed the fire button, unleashing a pair of hellfire missiles.

The pirates aboard the ratty mother ship below had no warning as the two missiles came screaming out of nowhere to tear into the ship. The first missile hit squarely on the bridge while the next struck the fuel tank causing a massive secondary explosion. An instant later, the ship had vanished from sight.

Several thousand miles away, a cheer went up from the three women watching the UCAV's camera image of the pirates' mother ship bursting into flames before sinking a short time later. In their excitement, the women hugged each other.

The lieutenant re-entered the room at the sound of the women's celebration. "Your exercise go well?"

"Perfect," Kira replied with a grin as Nigora gave him a big hug.

"So, that's it?" Kira said amazed. Lewis nodded. "It truly is like a video game."

"Unless you happen to be on that pirate mother ship... err, I mean if you're the target," he said with a laugh. Kira then excused herself and headed back to the hotel along with Mimi, who planned to meet Preston, while Nigora accepted the lieutenant's offer to go out for drinks.

CHAPTER 33

The pirate leader, Ghedi, had the good fortune to be on the foredeck directing the maintenance efforts of three low-level workers when the missiles hit. The force blew all four men clear of the ship. One was knocked unconscious and quickly drowned, but Ghedi and the other two survived.

When the pounding in his head stopped, Ghedi swam to a small boat tied to the stern of their mother ship and cast off lines just before the larger ship sank. A minute later, the other two men arrived, with one towing the second, who had a broken arm.

Ghedi's men, heavily armed to engage security guards on any ships they might chance upon, wore vests filled with grenades and extra ammo. So when the mother ship sank, they followed close behind, leaving only floating debris to mark where they had been a few moments before.

The three men sat silently in the small skiff amidst the mass of debris, stunned over the rapid turn of events.

"What happened?" one finally asked.

"Our ship blew up, stupid," Ghedi answered venting his frustration on the worker.

"I meant, how did it happen?"

Ghedi shook his head. "I haven't the slightest idea. But we best come up with some explanation before we face Ethan." Though Ghedi hated being forced to deal with the man as his banker, he feared his power.

Finally, somewhat recovered from the shock, Ghedi started the engine and pointed the small boat toward shore, many miles away.

Jamal sat on the dock enjoying the evening breeze while practicing on his imaginary piano.

"Hello, Jamal." He jumped at the sound of a female voice when Desta suddenly appeared from the dark. "What you doing?"

"Uh... nothing... just enjoying the night breeze." Jamal replied as he folded up the paper keyboard. He was glad it was night so that she couldn't see him blush.

"You were doing something, I saw you moving your hands on that paper."

Jamal rose to his feet. "Let's take a walk," he replied, changing the subject. As they walked toward the mouth of the bay in silence, Desta reach over and took his hand. Jamal could hardly think for the blood rushing to his head.

He was still struggling to think of what to say when a boat rounded the corner from the sea. "Look." Jamal pointed at the boat and, with Desta in tow, headed back toward the dock at a fast pace.

He had just reached the end of the pier when he saw it was Ghedi who was running the boat. A man in the bow tossed Jamal a line, which he quickly tied-off to a rusted cleat on the dock. "What happened? Where is the mother ship?"

Ghedi ignored him as he killed the engine and leapt from the boat. Without a word, he left his two men and the young couple behind. Jamal helped the man with the broken arm out of the boat. As the last man stepped onto the dock, he looked at Jamal.

"Gone."

"The mother ship is... gone?" Jamal asked, unbelieving.

"Yes, gone. But tell a soul and Ghedi will cut out your tongue." With that, he followed the injured man up the dock, leaving Jamal alone with Desta once again.

"The mother ship is gone. Can you believe it?" he asked her. Unsure what to say, she just shook her head. They sat on the dock for a while longer before Desta headed home.

Jamal sat alone for a while longer thinking. *What about all of those men? What will Ghedi do now? Maybe this misfortune will be my chance.*

"What sank my ship?" Ethan asked, making no attempt to conceal his disbelief.

"You mean that ratty old death trap of yours we were forced to use? I have no idea. One minute I was working on the foredeck and the next I was being thrown from the ship."

"And there were no other ships in the area?"

"None that we saw."

"So you would have me believe that the ship exploded for no apparent reason and sank, taking everyone along with it except for the three of you?"

"Yes, and the other small boats which I assume are still out on patrol."

"Damn it all!" Ethan yelled. "You lost the mother ship and have nothing to show for it. What do you plan to do now?"

"I don't know," Ghedi replied.

"Well, you best come up with something before the other backers of the mother ship learn about your fiasco. I doubt that they'll be as understanding as me," Ethan said as he walked away.

Ghedi suspected that if there were indeed other backers, Ethan pulled the strings.

Ghedi and the other two men from the mother ship stood on the dock most of the next day chewing khat and watching the six skiffs return one at a time. The last towed another which had run out of fuel.

"When we realized that the mother ship was gone, I saw no choice but to return here," his second in command told Ghedi, who then repeated his own story.

"Even if I could raise the money to buy and outfit another mother ship, with monsoon season only a couple of weeks away, we don't have time." Ghedi filled his mouth with a fresh batch of khat leaves and chewed while racking his brain. He was all too aware that he was in big trouble.

"In the old days, we never even had mother ships," one of his older men remarked quietly a few feet away.

"What did you say?" Ghedi asked. The man looked startled and was trying to repeat himself when Ghedi continued without waiting for the man's reply. "You're a genius. We'll do it old school. I'll assemble the largest force ever, an armada of skiffs, and we'll swarm over our next prize with little boats. It'll be grueling to stay out there that long, but we'll be able to cover more area and have more firepower when we attack."

He continued, the excitement obvious in his voice. "That's exactly what we'll do. I'll line up two more backers so we'll have enough money to ready the boats and launch the operation. I'll talk Ethan into splurging on information about ships due to sail in the near term." He knew he would be betting everything on a single attack in a risky move. He preferred not to think about what would happen should his attempt fail. *Sometimes desperate men must do desperate things.*

CHAPTER 34

Having finally taken the first step toward freeing Jenny, Kira awoke the next morning feeling rested. With their primary mission complete, the women continued training on the remaining UCAVs, under the watchful eye of the more experienced pilots. Confident that they understood the basics after several more hours, the women packed up the UCAV control units which they would set up back at the Sanctuary.

"You ladies ready to head home?" Lewis asked as he drove them to their plane.

"I'll say," Kira replied, noting Nigora's lack of excitement at the prospect.

"Here's a little gift from the folks here at the UCAV training center." Lewis handed Nigora a long cylindrical bag with a shoulder strap as they unloaded in front of the terminal. He laughed at her puzzled look.

"It's a new low-cost prototype version of the Switchblade miniature drone you thought was so cute. Since we've finished our testing, it's really just surplus, so I figured you might like it. I threw in the manual, which should answer all your questions. But don't break it, there's no spares."

"Oh, you nice man. Thank you very much," She threw her arms around him and planted a firm kiss. When she finished, it was clear he felt that it had been a fair trade.

The women boarded the plane and took their seats as the door closed behind them. Mimi and Kira eyed Nigora's gift. She gave them a sly smile. "We must all do our part for the team, no?" The women joined her in a laugh.

"What are you two up to?" Kira asked as she entered the hangar a short while after they had returned to the Sanctuary.

Colin looked up, wiping grease from his hands on a stained rag, and laid his socket wrench on the workbench. "Just showing Quint my little surprise."

"Which would be?" Kira asked.

"Since the Predator and Hawk lack armament, Dawson and I are adapting modified fifty caliber weapons so that we can use them as belt-fed sniper platforms. But I figure when it's too gusty to use in sniper mode, it can be used as a more conventional weapon.

"Best case, it works and we end up with a couple of flying sniper platform. Worst case, we end up with the ability to rain down serious lead. I'm guessing at some point it's going to come in handy. I also added some hard points on the Hawk's wings so we can fit them with the same missiles as the Reaper."

"Cool," Kira said.

"Yes, very cool," Dawson echoed. "Hopefully we'll not need it anytime soon, but it'll certainly come in handy when we do."

CHAPTER 35

Ethan leaned back in his office chair with his feet propped up on a massive mahogany desk. The large space, which made the statement that he was a man of means to be respected, was cluttered by mounds of spoils from the ships of their many victims. While some of it had value, like jewelry and shipboard electronics, much of it was simply junk.

"I understand that, after losing the last mother ship, you don't intend to use one. Instead your plan is simply to use a bunch of small boats." Ethan seemed oblivious to the squeaking sound of the unbalanced overhead fan that grated on Ghedi's nerves.

"Yes, Ethan, I did lose your rusty piece of shit that cost us over thirty percent of our haul. But the plan I've put together will put way more money in both of our pockets."

"Using the old approach with a fleet of much smaller rusty pieces of shit sounds more like the act of a desperate man than a brilliant new plan to me. I don't like it. You should have discussed it with me before now."

"Why, because you're afraid I'll succeed?" Ghedi asked.

"Don't be stupid. None of us gets paid if you don't succeed. But it bothers me putting all of your eggs in one basket."

Without commenting, Ghedi eased to one side of the overstuffed chair and reached into his pocket to withdraw a small bag. He retrieved a couple of khat leaves, placed them in his mouth, and began to chew. "Don't worry, I know what I'm doing. My plan will work."

"How will you get all of the boats you'll need? Are you expecting me to loan you yet more money? And who will run them?"

"I've already got the boats—and the captains." Ghedi smiled at the shocked look of surprise on Ethan's face. "It was easy. I even convinced the boat owners to wait until after we returned to be paid. But we'll need heavy weapons... that and information."

"What type of information?"

"I need a fat juicy target. You have a contact that can get such information for us... what's his name?"

"Asad?"

"Yes, that's who I've heard you mention," Ghedi replied.

Ethan shook his head. "He's good but expensive. With the cost of buying your information and the heavy weapons you'll need, our usual split will have to be re-negotiated."

Ghedi nodded without enthusiasm. Ethan was getting greedy. If he could capture a rich prize it might be time to consider eliminating his banker altogether. "But don't forget, if the sailboat woman's ransom isn't paid, we'll still get paid for selling her."

"Ah, but that is part of our last deal, not this one." Ethan grinned.

Ghedi's reply was to launch a wad of green spit which splattered on the floor between the chair he was sitting in and Ethan's desk. "I'm moving the hostages."

"Moving them where?"

"Into the old salt factory building."

"Might I ask why?"

"Moving the hostages on shore will simplify the logistics of guarding and feeding everyone and free up more men for our next job. I'll be needing everyone I can get."

"Taking all of the trained men leaves only a small security force along with a few armed children to guard the hostages." Ethan picked up a wooden-handled letter opener from his desk and toyed with it as he spoke. "Have you forgotten why I've insisted that we hold the prisoners on the freighter?"

"I'm not stupid. But even if they were to escape, where would they go?"

Ethan's feet came off the desk. "I don't like it."

"Well, I really don't give a shit." Ghedi slammed his fist down on the desk "I run my end of things. You're just my banker. That is, unless you mean to challenge me. Is that it?" He emphasized his point by lifting the automatic rifle that lay across his lap.

Ghedi stared him down until Ethan finally shook his head.

"Good." Ghedi launched another wad of spit onto the floor. "You just worry about getting me what I need," he added as he walked away

Jenny was anxious. Raoul had been hauled off over an hour earlier. She looked up as the door opened and saw Raoul returning white-faced.

"What happened?" she asked. Without answering, he walked to the far side of the room where he collapsed against the wall, nearly catatonic. She waited for several minutes before repeating her question. "What happened?"

Raoul wiped the sweat from his forehead on his salt-encrusted shirtsleeve. "Right or left; high or low," he finally replied in a flat voice.

"Huh?"

"If the owners of my ship don't meet the ransom demands, the pirates are going to cut off one of my arms. They've given me until tomorrow to choose my right or left one. Then they asked me high or low, meaning above or below my elbow."

"Oh my God!" Jenny bit her fist in horror. She was still struggling to cope with the specter of Raoul losing an arm when her thoughts were interrupted by the door opening once again. It was too soon to be dinner, so she feared it spelled trouble. She was right.

"You." The man pointed directly at her. She looked around with a puzzled look on her face. "Yes, you! Come with me." She rose on shaky legs and stumbled toward the door.

"No, take me." Brad rushed forward. In response, the man raised his rifle and pointed it in Brad's face.

Knowing that resistance was futile, Jenny gently pushed Brad aside. She followed the guard down the stairs to the waiting boat. A few minutes later, they reached the dock and she was led past several shanties to what she imagined was some sort of warehouse. Inside, piles of ship's cargo from countless victims were stacked everywhere. She followed along to the far side, where the man paused to knock on the door. They both entered when summoned.

Ethan sat behind a desk amidst more piles of clutter which she imagined were the crème of the remaining junk. The warehouse building served both as a storage facility for their ill-gotten gains and as Ethan's office.

In an overstuffed chair on the far side sat the same huge man who had seized them. The ebony skin of his shaved head was beaded with sweat. The overhead fan seemed to create more noise than breeze and barely moved the humid air.

"Please, join us." Ethan extended his hand in a broad gesture at a chair on the opposite side of his desk. "I have a problem. Unfortunately, that means you, too, have a problem. Ghedi and I have been very patient but your friends and family have failed to meet our ransom demands."

"So what am I supposed to do?"

He raised the fine china cup and saucer off his desk and took a sip of tea before continuing. "I want you to call your family and convince them to pay the ransom we are asking. Because in one week, if you are still unsuccessful, I intend to sell you."

"Sell me?"

"You are an attractive woman for whom we already have a buyer. And at a much higher price than I had hoped."

"How can that be? No one would agree to pay for someone they haven't even seen."

"Oh, but they have." Ethan smiled at Jenny's puzzled expression. "Do you remember that day the man came to photograph you?" Jenny's stomach cramped as she nodded. "Well, suffice to say the photos came out good and I have a buyer who is eager to make the purchase... and make your acquaintance," he finished with an evil snicker.

"What about Brad?"

"Your husband, will become an organ donor. However, being the reasonable man I am, I was able to get Ghedi here to agree to give you one last chance to raise the money. Who do you wish to call?"

Jenny thought for a moment. "My sister." She went on to recite the phone number. Ethan dialed the number and then handed over the satphone. Jenny was surprised that he was not insistent on listening to both sides of the conversation though she suspected he probably had some way of monitoring the conversation.

Jenny listened to the sound of the phone ringing at the other end, silently praying. "Kira?"

"Jenny! You okay? Where are you?"

"I'm being held for ransom by pirates."

"We heard that much and I've been trying to... raise some *help*... I mean the money." Jenny noticed her emphasis on the word *help* and hoped it meant what she thought.

"Well...uh... we don't have much more time. If they don't have the money within a week ... they...uh..." Her voice began to break. "They plan to sell me into white slavery and kill Brad to sell his organs." Actually saying it caused her to start sobbing.

"Jenny... Jenny... it's going to be okay. I'm working on it. I'll find some way to *help* you before it's too late." *There it was again*, Jenny noted, *the emphasis on help. Not raise the money but find some way to help. Is Kira planning to rescue us?*

Her further thoughts were interrupted when Ethan gestured for her to end the conversation by drawing a finger across his throat. "Thanks, Kira. I'll pass it on. Hopefully, I'll see you soon. Goodbye." Jenny quietly sobbed as she was led back to rejoin Brad and the others.

"What happened? What happened? Are you all right?" Brad asked as soon as the door closed behind Jenny.

She knew he was afraid they might be planning to cut off her arm as well. "The good news is that I didn't get asked the right or left question." She glanced at Raoul to convey her sympathy. "But...but..." Her voice began to break.

"What? What?"

"If the ransom isn't paid within the next week, they're going to sell me."

Brad's mouth dropped open. "Sell you... to who?"

"Does it matter?" she asked sobbing. He took her into his arms and they sat together without speaking.

"What about me?" Brad asked quietly.

"They plan on selling your organs." This time, it was Brad who broke down.

That evening, when the rest of the captives were sleeping, Jenny shook Brad awake. He looked at her while rubbing his eyes. "Kira said she would find some way to help within the next week."

"You mean raise the money?"

"That's not what she said. She emphasized the word 'help' twice." Jenny lowered her voice even further. "She would know that the pirates would be listening in and would have to be subtle. I think she was trying to tell me that someone is coming to rescue us. We have to be ready."

CHAPTER 36

"We leave tomorrow morning." Quint announced.

"So soon?" Marcia asked.

"Yeah, Kira got a call from Jenny. They're threatening to sell her into white slavery if she can't raise the ransom in one week," Quint replied.

After a short pause, Dawson spoke up. "We've got to get there, get things set up, find out where the hostages are being held, and plan our rescue. We don't have much time."

"We leaving here by boat?" Marcia asked.

"Boat? Why not a plane?" Leo complained.

"Because the seaplane's not large enough and our airstrip is in bad shape. We'll need to fix the runway before we can land a plane on the island," Marcia replied.

"How did you land the drones?" Leo asked.

"Landing a drone is a lot different than landing a multiton charter plane," Marcia said with a slight eye roll.

"While Marcia's right, we are going by plane," Quint said.

Marcia looked up in surprise. "But how?"

"Repairing our airstrip will be at the top of our list when we get back. But given the condition of our strip, Rogers scrounged us up an Osprey," Quint said with a flourish.

"Wow," Dakota replied.

"The Osprey was scheduled for a training flight and he managed to direct it our way. They'll drop us off in Miami and then Rogers has arranged for us to hitch a ride to Africa on a military transport plane. Though it's not a direct flight—we'll have a couple of stops along the way—it's the fastest way."

Quint dreaded what he was about to say next, knowing the likely reaction it would have. "I've arranged to drop off the rest of the team not involved in this mission in the States when we leave for Africa."

"No," Kira replied firmly.

"What do you mean no? In case you haven't noticed you're nearly due," Colin replied.

"I'm not stupid. I made it clear after our Aral Sea venture, even before the bike wreck, that I'd pull back when I got further along with the pregnancy. In case you haven't noticed, I've been getting plenty of bed rest just as the doctor recommended.

"Mimi, Nigora, and I want to... look, the team needs to get their stuff together. Quint, finish the meeting and we can talk after everyone is dismissed," Kira said, ignoring Colin's confused look.

Quint covered a few details and recapped the basic plan. "Now, if there are no more questions, I think we're done. We'll meet up top, outside the hangar tomorrow morning at eight a.m. sharp. Meeting adjourned." Once the room was empty except for the women, Dawson, and Colin, Quint turned to Kira. "Okay, I'm all ears."

"We want to stay here," Kira repeated.

"Just the three of you?" Quint asked, eyeing her swollen belly. Though he wisely chose not to comment on her being pregnant and having only one leg, the fact of her being left with Nigora, who had no training, and Mimi, who was capable but certainly no Kira, left him unsettled.

"I told her it was a bad idea and—" Colin exclaimed.

"Hey, the three of us can hold things down for the short time you'll be gone," Kira said, glancing at Nigora, who nodded then piped up.

"Yes. We do good—you no worry."

"I don't know, Kira, I just hate leaving you three here alone," Quint protested.

"As far as worrying about me getting close to delivering, I'm already scheduled to catch the weekly supply run seaplane back to the States. I plan to stay there until the baby is born. But I want to stay to help finish getting the drones fully operational. The training was really helpful, but we could all use some more hands-on practice. And I need to help Mimi tweak the software based on what they taught us," Kira said.

"Are the UCAV control stations even active?" Quint asked.

"Yeah, they're totally self-contained and—"

"I thought you needed to have the antennas mounted on the towers?" Quint asked.

"We do," Kira said, glaring at Colin. "We've been bugging the guys but—"

"I know, I know," Colin interrupted. "But we ran the cables yesterday and set up the antennas beside the hangar temporarily. They appear to be working just fine, don't they?" Kira nodded reluctantly. "When we get back from Somalia, I promise we'll get them mounted permanently."

Quint smiled. "Kira, I'm impressed with your initiative and trust your judgment, but we're barely settled in our new base and have no idea what type of problems might pop up."

Kira looked offended. "Is it leaving only three of us here or is it about us being 'just' women?"

Quint felt the blood rush to his face. "You know damned well I trust you. And it has nothing to do with your sex. It has to do with your being pregnant and their lack of experience," he said, thrusting his finger in the direction of Mimi and Nigora.

"Look, it's only for a few days and I'll feel much better about leaving once you've rescued Jenny. I can always schedule the seaplane to pick me up on short notice if I need to. Besides, what could possibly go wrong that we can't handle?" Kira asked.

"I prefer not to find out the answer to that question the hard way," Quint said firmly.

Dawson grinned. "Quint, I suggest you concede defeat."

"Okay, I know when I'm beat," Quint replied, shaking his head.

"Who's beat?" Leo strolled up near the end of the conversation. Quint explained.

"You know, there's really not a role for me on this mission. Perhaps I should stay here to protect the women." Kira rolled her eyes, then thanked Quint before leaving with the other women, all three talking excitedly.

Quint considered Leo's offer for a moment. Despite the fact that it was certainly self-serving, Quint would feel better having at least one more person remain, even if it was Leo. "Good idea," Quint finally said.

"Really?" Leo made it clear he had not expected for his idea to actually fly. "Great. Hey, do me one favor. Bring me back some Arabica coffee. Oh, and some cardamom to spice it... and a bag of fresh dates."

"Sure, I plan to take a week or so for a shopping spree while we're there. Anything else you need me to bring you back?" Quint asked sarcastically.

"Nope," Leo replied and then quickly left without giving Quint time to reconsider his decision.

CHAPTER 37

Quint was packed and ready by seven o'clock the next morning. He set his bag down on the airstrip and walked to the edge of the cliff, which overlooked the lagoon and the sea beyond. Two black inflatables were rounding the west end of the island.

Cuban military? They had never shown their presence here. In fact, it was rare to see any boats at their remote outpost save the occasional freighter or fishing boat in the distance.

He watched as the inflatables cruised along the south side of the island. He tensed while waiting to see what they would do but then relaxed when he saw them throttle back up after clearing the channel. *That was odd.*

"I always wanted to see an Osprey in operation," Dawson said as the bizarre-looking aircraft swooped in at two hundred and fifty miles per hour. It quickly slowed, then hovered and landed like a helicopter. "Man, we need one of these," he said as the flight engineer swung the side door open.

"Hope you've got a spare seventy million dollars," the man replied as Quint, Dawson, and the others boarded.

The three women and Leo had come to see the team off. Nigora handed a long plastic tube to Marcia. "Here, you take bird. You may need."

"Thanks," Marcia said and, ignoring Quint's puzzled look, handed it up to the crewman before boarding.

A few seconds later, the pilot revved up the engines and the plane lifted vertically. By the time the engine nacelles had rotated horizontal, they were past the end of the runway, headed north.

The aircraft provided plenty of room for the team to stretch out. Quint took a seat while Dawson laid down on the floor of the fuselage. With his head resting on a backpack, in moments he was fast asleep.

After the short flight to south Florida, the team exited the Osprey to transfer to a military C-47. "Well, I guess this is where we take our leave," Quint said and shook hands with the pilot.

"Good luck," the pilot said and turned to leave.

"Oh my God," Marcia quietly gasped, staring at the tattoo of an eagle on the back of the pilot's neck.

"What?" Quint asked.

"That tattoo on the pilot's neck. It just hit me. Now I remember where I saw a tattoo like the 'S-203' tattooed on Preston's neck. It was on that yacht, *Syntillate,* while I was trying to rescue you. Most of the staff had the entire ship's name tattooed on their neck along with a three digit number, but a few of the officers had the letter 'S' followed by a unique number. Maybe it's a coincidence, but it's odd."

"More like incriminating. I don't believe in coincidences," Dawson replied.

"When we get back, we'll see if we can get to the bottom of that," Quint said as he led the group toward their waiting military transport plane.

CHAPTER 38

"Preston, I've been tracking the transponder I gave you. It would appear that you successfully slipped it into Mimi's luggage," Syndy said.

The sound of her unnatural mechanical voice over the telephone always caused Preston to shudder. "Yes, it wasn't easy but I was able to slit the lining of her suitcase and slide it inside just before she left."

"We now have the location of their base, just as we had hoped. You've done well."

"A roaring success, if Preston must say so himself," Preston replied shamelessly in third person as was his quirk.

"Is your research ready?"

"I can wrap it up by tomorrow."

"Excellent." Syndy set a meeting time before they hung up.

Two days later, Preston walked into the salon aboard Syndy's ship, *Syntillate*, to find a group of serious-looking men waiting. Their muscled bodies and the way they carried themselves screamed mercenaries. A minute later, Syndy rolled into the room, a plume of smoke trailing in her wake. She quickly scanned the assembled group and then nodded to Preston. "Begin."

"Quint's base is on an island off the south side of Cuba. To avoid an unpleasant encounter with the Cuban Navy, we will use the cover of a tourist scuba diving expedition. The plan is to learn more about their base while we are in Havana.

"I've obtained some satellite images which will enable us to at least infer some information." Preston made a few key strokes on his laptop and switched on the attached projector. An overhead satellite photo appeared projected on the forward wall.

"As you can see, the island appears mostly devoid of manmade structures. Based on the locator transponder I was able to plant on our behalf, their facilities are located here," he pointed with a red laser dot to a sheer cliff on the edge of a small lagoon. "You will note that it appears to be simply a wall of rock.

"My research indicates that this was once a base for the Soviets. Thus, it is reasonable to assume that a facility exists, most certainly constructed underground, perhaps in what once was a natural cave. If so, the entrances are exceptionally well camouflaged.

"An old airstrip is located along this ridgeline, though it appears to be in bad repair. The rectangular shape shown on this thermal imaging shot is believed to be a camouflaged hangar. Given its existence along with the airstrip, it is likely that access to the hidden facilities also exists in or near the hangar. Their communications antennas are most likely situated on one of these two towers.

"This inlet"—he motioned with the red dot of the laser pointer—"is located on the south side and provides deep water access into the lagoon. The west end of the lagoon has cliffs falling to the water except for the derelict dock located here." Again he motioned with the pointer. "While it could be feasible to attempt to land on the airstrip, given its state of disrepair, an approach by water is preferable along this wide beach area on the eastern side of the lagoon.

"As soon as we arrive in Cuban waters, we'll dispatch a team to conduct reconnaissance and set up a jammer which will temporarily disrupt their communications prior to our attack. Once we've established our cover in Havana, we'll launch the attack force in inflatables while *Syntillate* continues to maintain the illusion of a sport diving trip until we meet back up with the attack force.

"The inflatables will land near dawn on this section of beach. After establishing a foothold, a three-man team will head for this high ridge area to sever Quint's communications links. They will continue their attack through the hangar while the main group sweeps along the shore to locate the lower entrance and attack their facility in a pincer movement."

Syndy's face, hidden by the porcelain mask, was incapable of conveying any emotions, so until the briefing was finished there was no feedback. Preston found this unnerving.

"An hour after the initial attack force has been launched, I will accompany a second wave to help mop up, secure the priority prisoners, and deal with the rest."

After a lengthy silence Syndy finally responded, "Excellent job. I approve your plan. Please understand, you are to kill all of them, except for Quint and Dawson." She spit out the names of the two men whom she blamed for her horrible disfigurement. "It's worth a considerable bonus for them to be taken prisoner. But every other living soul is to be left dead. Clear?" The heads of those gathered before her nodded in unison.

"Perhaps it is stating the obvious, but we'll be attacking their home base. It would be a mistake to underestimate their resistance. I would favor the U.S. military's shock and awe strategy by employing the use of overwhelming force."

"Yes ma'am, that's our intent. Our attack is scheduled to occur while they are distracted by their efforts to bring the facility operational."

Syndy paused for a moment before continuing. "But what happens if your attack is unsuccessful? What happens if Quint and Dawson somehow manage to overcome your force?"

Preston smiled. "In that case, we have a little surprise in store for them. As soon as our men breach their facility, they will plant a little present with a delayed fuse." He went on to explain his plan. "You have waited a very long time for vengeance. One way or another, after tomorrow, you will wait no more." Preston had learned to play up to Syndy to curry favor. Those that didn't...

Syndy nodded, then, using the joystick in her lap, spun the wheelchair about and left the room.

CHAPTER 39

When the C-47 landed in Africa, Quint turned his satphone back on and it immediately began to ring. "Load the gear and the inflatable boat into the helicopter while I catch this call."

"Meester Quint?"

"Yes."

"This is Luis Perez," a man's voice said in a thick Spanish accent. Quint was silent as his mind raced to recall who the man was. "You remember, I helped with the paperwork when you were in Cuba."

"Ah, yes, Luis. Good to hear from you though I imagine you didn't call to chat."

Luis replied with a nervous laugh and then resumed speaking in a low voice. "No, I'm calling because a few days ago, someone was here to gain entrance to our country. They seemed to have an interest in you and your island."

"Really? They asked about me by name?"

"It appears so. Though I did not speak with the people myself, I am told that they asked about the island—where it is; how many people are there; whatever they could learn. They dealt with someone else in our office. I only found out a few hours ago. Since our landlines are closely monitored, I paid a friend to use his secure satphone. I thought this might be important for you to know."

"You did well, thank you. Did they happen to mention why they were asking?"

"No sir, I have told you all that I know."

"Thanks, Luis. I'll reimburse for your cost and trouble," Quint said as he hung up. *I can't imagine any reason for someone poking around that doesn't spell trouble.* He dialed the Sanctuary satphone number and let it ring until someone picked up, but heavy static made it impossible to communicate. A few minutes later, he tried again with the same result and left a message before giving up to finish loading their gear. It was nearly dark by the time they had everything loaded in the helicopter and were underway.

Quint instructed the pilot to make a wide sweeping approach for reconnaissance when they approached the landing site. He motioned for the others to put on their headsets, then began his briefing. "Since Leo's not here to be our travel guide, I'll be his stand-in.

"We're just south of the point of the Horn of Africa. That's Hurdiyo, on the north side of this bay." He pointed to the left. "On the south side of that sand spit," he said, pointing to what appeared to be a glorified sandbar, "is the town of Hafun, where roughly five thousand villagers live. It can only be reached by that damaged section of road which now supports only a single lane of traffic.

[NOTE: Sketch]

"That small walled compound near the ruins of the larger building, the old salt factory, is believed to be the pirate headquarters. The hostages are most likely being held on one of those ships anchored just offshore. That collection of huts near the town was built after the area was savaged by a tsunami in 2004.

"From what Rogers was able to learn, the pirates frequently move back and forth between Hafun and the compound. Their boats are staged right there off the beach, just as we had hoped." The pilot banked before they approached close enough to be identified and swung east.

"You'll notice there's nothing much but scrub bush.
That lack of cover makes it a difficult place to attack
covertly. But we have some luck: it will be a moonless
night." Quint paused for a moment as they flew away
from Hafun and then thought of one more thing.

"The salt factory was built by the Italians in the
early 1900s. The Italians continued to operate the
factory until World War II, when the British shelled
the crap out of it and then looted the scrap steel to
meet their wartime needs. Those factory remains will
be our only cover."

As they continued back to the east, the land sloped
up steadily to form an area with low cliffs where the
land met the sea. They rounded the end of the
peninsula and then flew a short distance to the north
until they spotted a small cape. At the south end of it
lay the area they had flagged on the satellite photos. A
narrow sandy strip beneath the low cliffs was pierced
by a tidal creek that would provide cover for the
inflatable. The chopper approached and flared before
landing on the beach.

"This will be our base site," Quint said before
stepping out of the front seat. Thirty minutes later,
they had unloaded their gear and the chopper lifted
off.

"Colin, you and Marcia set up the camouflaged tents
over there." Quint pointed to a flat sandy area at the
base of the cliff concealed in a small niche. "I'll give
Dawson and Dakota a hand assembling the RIB."

"RIB?" Marcia asked with a puzzled look.

"Sorry. It's an acronym. RIB simply means rigid
inflatable boat," Quint said, pointing to the impressive
craft already unloaded and being assembled. Heavy
metal tubes provided a protective cradle for the engine
and also lined the console. Along the inflatable tubes,
large loops served as hand holds for passengers
perched atop the tubes while the boat was running in
rough seas, not likely to be encountered for this

mission. Its oversized outboard would give them all the speed they could possibly handle.

The team reviewed their plans over a dinner of freeze-dried entrees. "As we discussed, we're banking that with the loss of their mother ship, the pirates will launch another foray before monsoon season using small boats," Quint began. "Dawson, Colin, and I will attach our camouflaged limpet mines to each boat.

"Marcia, you and Colin will plant a transceiver high up on the lighthouse. As long as the pirates remain in the harbor, no problem. But when they head back out, we'll arm the mines using the transceiver. It will continue to transmit a signal which will prevent the charges from detonating. This will serve as a failsafe backup, keeping the charges 'safed' until the boats are well offshore and out of range of our lighthouse transmitter, at which time the detonation timers start. As a backup, we can also blow the boats remotely.

"Assuming things go according to plan, when the timers complete their countdown, the boats will be destroyed and sink several miles offshore. No one will know what happened; the pirates simply won't return. We'll have cut off the head of the snake, eliminating the worst of them."

"Then we go in and rescue the hostages," Marcia added and Quint nodded. They continued to chat for a while and at 8 p.m. they all took an Ambien, knowing that with the adrenaline still flowing from the pending mission, they were unlikely to get much sleep otherwise.

CHAPTER 40

Two in the morning came much sooner than Quint had hoped. He splashed water from his canteen on his face and joined the team. After downing another MRE for breakfast along with some foul-tasting coffee that Colin had made, he was ready.

They assembled their gear and Marcia steadied the inflatable boat while they loaded up. A few minutes later, the team was headed down the coast of Somalia toward the Hafun lighthouse located near the pirate base. Their arrival was timed for 3 a.m.

They skimmed over the glassy-smooth waters at nearly fifty miles per hour. The silenced engine could not be heard over two hundred feet away and with no moonlight, the black hull of the boat was nearly invisible against the dark waters.

As they approached shore, Dakota lined up on the barely visible lighthouse ahead. It had fallen victim to the turmoil within Somalia and the wishes of the pirates, who preferred it not remain operational.

While Dakota approached the beach at idle, they scanned the area with night vision goggles. Seeing no threats, Marcia and Colin eased over the side once they reached shallow water and moved stealthily toward shore. Dakota spun the boat around and a few minutes later was headed west down the beach to the secluded bay.

When they approached the bay, Dakota once again slowed and made for shore while Quint and Dawson scanned for threats. The two men waded ashore as Dakota backed the boat out and returned to the lighthouse, where he stood by.

With her AA-12 shotgun cradled in her arms, Marcia followed Colin to the brush line along the first sand dune. They peeked over the top and, seeing movement in the distance, dropped to the ground. After listening and scanning the area for several minutes, it appeared there was no threat, just a couple walking down the lone road. The two rose and quietly continued their trek toward the lighthouse.

By the time Dakota returned to begin waiting just off shore, Colin and Marcia had reached the base of the lighthouse. Though the fence surrounding the lighthouse was beaten down on the far side, they decided it best to break through on the closest side to minimize any chance of being spotted.

Using a set of heavy bolt cutters, Colin cut a hole in the chain link fence surrounding the lighthouse. He held it open while Marcia wormed her way through the opening and scampered in a low crouch toward the base. Colin then faded back to the cover of some scrub bushes at the edge of the clearing.

Marcia set the big shotgun against the side of the lighthouse, then cinched the straps on her backpack. Sweat streamed down her face and back in the stifling heat as she worked to jimmy the lock. She was about to give up and risk using her pistol when she pushed on the door and found that the latch was broken. *What a dummy I am.*

A quick scan with her flashlight confirmed that no one was inside and she edged forward to ascend the stairs. Once she reached the top, she caught her breath while removing the small transceiver from a zippered pocket in her backpack.

Using several cable ties, she attached the unit to a rusted mounting bracket and switched it on. With no other alternative, she coated the entire unit with a thick layer of camouflage grease, hoping to make it appear less visible.

Marcia then ran a cable to the outer walkway, where she fastened the antenna to the railing using its mounting bracket. She tightened the screws down as far as she could and noticed that while the clamp seemed to be gripping, it wasn't as tight as she would have preferred.

A few minutes later she climbed back through the fence, bent the cut section back in place, and rejoined Colin. They jogged back to the beach and used their infrared light to signal Dakota for a pick up.

"The transceiver signal is coming through strong," Dakota said. "Everything go okay?"

"Like clockwork," Marcia replied. "We saw a couple of locals in the distance but they didn't see us. Otherwise, it was routine."

CHAPTER 41

After the Osprey carrying the team had flown out of sight, Kira, Nigora, and Mimi returned to the Sanctuary to find Leo hard at work in the kitchen. The smell of garlic hung heavy in the air.

"What's cooking?" Mimi asked.

"A surprise," Leo replied without looking up from the cutting board where he was intently focused on chopping an enormous mound of vegetables. The floor surrounding him was dotted with bits of vegetable that had fallen during his slice-and-dice frenzy.

Kira screwed up her face. "Yeah, I've had some of your surprises. Like your cow-brain tacos."

"Sesos."

"What?" Nigora asked.

"She was referring to my sesos, but I promise that you will love tonight's dinner. It won't be exotic... or 'weird,' as you insist on referring to my tastes."

"I hope not. Call me when it's ready, I think I'll go lie down. My hands, feet, and face are swollen and I feel like a blimp. Call me for dinner."

When Nigora came to wake her two hours later, Kira was still sleeping soundly. Between her advanced pregnancy and the effort involved in getting around with a missing leg, she was exhausted.

"I noticed you haven't been wearing your boobs," Kira said referring to the huge strap-on contraption Nigora wore on occasion.

"Yes, Marcia smart to talk me into trying that before have surgery. It helped me to... how you say... get it out of my process."

"System."

"What?"

"Helped you to get it out of your system."

"Exactly. If man not like me like I am, screw him... I not mean really."

Kira splashed water on her face and joined the others in the dining area a few minutes later. "Leo, your dinner smells wonderful. But before I'm taking a single bite, I want to know what's in it."

Leo smiled as he finished setting bowls on the table. "It's ciopinno, a seafood stew. Back in the 1800s, Italian fishermen gathered at the end of the day, each bringing along something for the communal supper pot. This is a San Francisco version made with onions, celery, tomatoes, and local seafood including tenderized conch, fresh fish, and lobster. I mix it with a bunch of spices, a little white wine, and presto, a meal worthy of Italian royalty."

Kira gave Leo a suspicious look. "That's it, nothing weird? No monkey brains, snails, insects—"

"Nope."

"No animal organs or roadkill?"

"Nope," Leo replied, appearing only slightly offended.

"So help me, Leo, if you're lying I'll neuter you with a rusty can opener and then feed your man-parts to the sharks."

Leo shivered. "I swear."

"Mmm, it very good. You try," Nigora said, dunking a chunk of bread into the broth, with Mimi following suit.

Kira tentatively took a bite and her face lit up. "Excellent. Leo, I've never taken issue with your culinary talent, just your choice of ingredients." The room fell silent save for the clinking of spoons on the ceramic bowls. After they had finished their second helping, the group adjourned to the lounge area to relax.

"Leo, that was one of the best meals ever," Mimi said as Leo beamed. She glanced at Kira who had her hand resting on her upper stomach. "Baby acting up?"

"No, heartburn. Guess it's the spicy food. I need to take some antacid," she said, struggling to rise from her chair.

"I'll get it for you." Mimi disappeared into the clinic area and returned a moment later with a bottle of pills.

"I appreciate that, it hurts to walk on my swollen feet," Kira said.

"Happy to help our favorite mother-to-be." Mimi laughed.

"I'm ready to get back to the States and have this baby." They continued to chat for the next hour before turning in for the night.

At breakfast the next morning, Kira pushed her plate away with the remains of a crab-and-Swiss omelet.

"You didn't like it?" Leo asked appearing hurt.

"Leo, it was great. I'm just... feeling out of sorts. So what's your plan for today?" she said to change the subject.

"With no real work to do other than cooking for you ladies... and serving as your protector," he said, grinning at Kira's eye roll, "I'm looking forward to a vacation of sorts. Today I begin my 'get Leo in shape' regimen. I'm turning over a new leaf and seeing how far I can hike. My plan is to go a little farther each day. Eventually I hope to make it all the way around the island. I figured I'd take my snorkel gear and scope out some new areas for lobster diving, too."

"Good for you, I'm proud," Kira replied.

"Care to join me?"

"Love to, but walking distances is tough for me these days." She laughed while motioning at her prosthesis and swollen belly.

"Oh, uh... sorry," he said in a low voice.

"Plus, I've been really tired these past couple of days."

Leo was still busy in the kitchen when the women headed for the hangar to service the drones. They went through the preflight procedure on all three UCAVs as they had been taught during their recent training class. Kira spent most of her time observing and was impressed with the meticulous care that Nigora seemed to take. She patiently, almost lovingly, pored over every aspect of the drone prep. By late afternoon, all of the UCAVs were serviced, fueled, and ready for training exercises.

The next morning they focused on touch-and-go take-off and landing practice with the drones. Mimi and Kira began while Nigora remained asleep in her pod, after the two women failed in their efforts to rouse her. They had been practicing for over an hour when they heard Nigora's sleepy voice.

"Why you no wake me?" Nigora walked in holding a cup of coffee while rubbing her eyes.

"We tried! You were dead to the world," Kira replied.

"Come join us," Mimi said, motioning for Nigora to take the seat beside her.

The three women continued practicing. Thirty minutes later, Kira excused herself to go lie down after completing her training flight. It was unlike her as she generally insisted on being present whenever a drone was in the air.

By late afternoon, Mimi and Nigora were worn out from the focused concentration and headed off to take a shower.

CHAPTER 42

"How'd it go?" Mimi asked as she joined Leo in the kitchen, where Kira was up from her nap.

He looked up with a smile. "Made it almost to that beach area east of us. Tomorrow I plan to hike all the way there... that is, if I'm not too sore. I saw the drones buzzing around overhead while I was walking. How about the drone training?"

"Very good." Munching on a piece of celery from the tray Leo had set out, Kira continued. "Though we'll need to continue practicing, I'm officially declaring our training completed. The Sanctuary drone team is now fully operational."

"Great!" Leo popped opened a bottle of champagne. "In honor of this notable event, I'll treat our entire air force to grilled steaks with my famous mushroom risotto and a caesar salad made with my special dressing. And in the interests of full disclosure, Kira, it does include anchovies, which you might consider to be weird."

Kira, who was looking a little ill, gave a half laugh and then shook her head as he made a half-hearted gesture offering her a glass of bubbly. Mimi and Nigora eagerly accepted theirs while Leo downed his as well as the one declined by Kira.

"Has anyone heard from Quint and the team?" Kira asked.

"We had a couple calls on the satphone," Mimi replied, "but when I answered, there was too much static to hear who it was. Could have been them. I tried to call them back but had the same problem."

"Maybe I'll try again later," Kira said wearily.

"You okay? You not look so good." Nigora asked.

"I woke up fine but now I'm feeling bad. I need to use the satphone to make my weekly check-in with the doctor."

"I get for you," Nigora said.

"Would you please bring the blood pressure monitor also?" Nigora nodded and then disappeared, heading for the clinic. A minute later she returned and handed the items to Kira, who proceeded to take her blood pressure and then, appearing too tired to leave the room, made the call. While Kira dialed her doctor, Leo began building their salad.

"So how we doing?" the doctor asked when she came on the line.

"Not so great. Everything is swollen and I can't seem to shake the heartburn."

"Hmm. Have you been taking your blood pressure regularly?"

"Uh... well, I..."

"Kira! If you recall, part of our deal was your promise to be diligent about monitoring it."

"I know, I know. I just forget sometimes. But I did just take it—one forty-three over eighty-nine."

"Hmm, your blood pressure is borderline. Though your symptoms may mean nothing, they could also signal the onset of pre-eclampsia. Do you feel tired?"

"Yeah, like I have no energy and I've been nauseated."

"First thing tomorrow morning, do a urine dipstick analysis on your protein level. The strips are in that kit I gave you," the doctor said. "Then take your blood pressure again and call me with the results. I have to be up before five, so call my cell early, particularly if the results are elevated. In the meantime, take it easy. Nothing strenuous and get plenty of bed rest."

"What did the doctor say?" Leo asked.

"She's worried about pre-eclampsia. I need to take some tests in the morning and call her back." Leo nodded as he set a heaping bowl of salad on the table.

After they had finished their salad course, Leo handed each of the women a plate with an enormous steak nestled atop a mound of mushroom risotto. The group chatted while gorging themselves on Leo's feast.

"Leo, you're going to have to stop feeding us like this or I'll be so fat I'll never lose all of my baby weight." Kira chuckled. But halfway through the meal, her nausea returned and she pushed the plate away.

"Kira, since the UCAVs are already prepped, Nigora and I were talking about getting started a couple of hours before sunrise while it's still dark so that we can practice nighttime flying," Mimi said as she pushed the remains of her grilled steak aside and poured a second glass of wine.

"Works for me," Kira replied.

"I thought you were done training," Leo said.

"For the most part we are but you can never practice too much. Besides, we haven't tried nighttime operations and we need gunnery practice."

Before sunrise the next morning, Kira strolled into the small kitchen, where Mimi and Nigora were in the process of having breakfast.

"You feel more better?" Nigora asked.

"Not really. I just wanted to check on you guys before doing the tests and calling the doc," Kira replied.

"I fix you breakfast, no?"

"I appreciate it, but I'm so queasy I couldn't possibly eat. That, and I've got a major-league headache."

"The Predator still has two hours' fuel remaining. Think I should fill it up?" Mimi asked.

"Nah. The sun will be up by then and you'll be ready to take a break anyhow," Kira replied.

Mimi nodded, seeming not to agree but not arguing. When Kira returned to her pod, Mimi and Nigora headed for the hangar above. Under the glare of the hangar lights, Nigora and Mimi loaded the .50 caliber to test the stability of the Predator's platform.

Kira took her blood pressure and then the urine test. She shook her head as she saw the results. Glancing at the clock, she noticed it was 5:05 and immediately dialed the doctor.

"I hope I didn't call too early."

"Hello, Kira. No, I just stepped out of the shower. Calling this early I assume is not good news."

"Afraid not. The urine dipstick test showed that my protein is elevated and my blood pressure is up to one fifty-five over one-oh-six."

"You're right, that's not good. You need to come in right now."

"Uh... well that's going to be tough. As I mentioned, this place is remote and it will take a while to arrange transportation."

"Kira, I don't want to scare you but this can be serious for you and the baby and you must treat it as such."

"I understand. I'll arrange to get back there just as soon as I possibly can."

"Make it within twenty-four hours."

"I'll try," Kira replied and then scheduled an emergency seaplane pickup as soon as they could arrange it.

In the UCAV operations center, Mimi sat at her console with Nigora watching as she taxied the Predator into position. After a short run, the plane lifted off into the star-filled skies.

CHAPTER 43

Quint and Dawson worked their way up the far side of the narrow bay to a position across from the pirates' boats, where Dawson studied the shore with one side of a set of night vision binoculars held to his good eye. He counted three sentries. Two hadn't budged in the past ten minutes and appeared to be asleep. More worrisome was the erratic appearance of locals headed to the latrine at the edge of the beach near the boats.

"Damn! How many boats were we planning to rig?" Dawson asked.

"We got charges for eight—that's the most we thought they'd ever use. Why?" Quint replied.

"I count fifteen."

"Maybe the extras aren't all pirate boats. Let me see those glasses." Quint focused the glasses and immediately saw they had a problem. "Nope, they all look like their typical ratty-assed attack boats. What the hell's going on?"

"I don't know. Maybe since things haven't been going so well of late they're planning to kick it up a notch," Dawson replied. "It doesn't really matter, though; we need to take them all out."

"With what? I agree having them plan something this big is a gift. But we don't have enough explosives for all of those boats."

"Uh, actually we may," Dawson said. "If you recall, we have a set of backup charges back on the inflatable. If we use those, we'll have enough with one to spare."

Quint sighed. "Call Dakota and have him bring them."

A few minutes later, the RIB with Colin and Marcia back aboard idled into the shallow water and the three men swam out to meet the inflatable. "What's the deal, why you needing the backup charges?" Dakota asked.

"Because our pirates have backup boats," Dawson replied, handing him the glasses so he could see.

"Shit," Marcia said. "Rogers' intelligence indicated the most they ever use is eight."

"Evidently his intelligence was wrong. We can't very well ask them not to use the other seven, so we'll have to rig them, too. The good news is that if we can pull it off, we'll catch twice as many pirates in our little trap."

"But now you have twice the number of boats to rig and we've already lost time. Maybe we should wait until tomorrow night," Colin said.

"No," Dawson said firmly glancing at Quint. "We don't know when they're planning their next move but we do know that Jenny only has a few more days. There's no way we're going to miss this chance. I say we go now,"

"He's right, it's not the first time we've been forced to improvise," Quint said. "We'll just have to work fast."

"Since I'm done, I'll go with you. It'll make it go faster," Colin said and Quint nodded.

"I can go too—" Marcia began.

"No," Quint interrupted. "Stay with Dakota to cover us if things go to hell."

The three men stuffed the extra charges into their backpacks and donned their snorkel gear before easing back beneath the dark waters. Stealthily, they swam toward the pirate boats less than a quarter mile away. As they approached the shore, each chose a different boat, starting closest to the sentries who appeared to still be asleep.

After finishing twelve of the boats, Dawson joined Colin on the thirteen and fourteenth while Quint made for the last boat nearest the latrine, where the guard appeared to be most active. As Colin placed and armed his last charge, Dawson peeked over the side of the boat with his M-16 with the MAUL attachment, capable of delivering four nasty twelve-gauge surprises, ready just in case.

He saw no movement and signaled to the others, who raised their snorkel mouthpieces back in place and began to swim back across the lagoon to where Dakota and Marcia were waiting.

"That was smooth," Marcia commented.

"That just means we've used up too much of our good luck," Dawson replied. "Let's get back to our base camp." The team slid back into the RIB and Dakota eased the boat out of the lagoon. Once they were outside, they ran the short way back to their base before slowing to run the inflatable up the small tidal creek where they could camouflage it. They pulled the boat as far as they could into the ravine and then covered the engine and transom with cut bushes. Unless someone was looking for it, anyone chancing by was not likely to spot it.

Marcia opened the cap of the four-inch diameter PVC pipe and withdrew the miniature drone Nigora had brought back from her training school. She folded the wings into place and then retrieved the foam-wrapped control console from the bottom of the tube. She quickly went through the initialization procedure.

"That's pretty neat," Dakota said.

"Yeah, Nigora talked our trainer out of it and thought it might come in useful. We named it Angel— something to watch over us."

Quint smiled. "So how long can it stay up?"

"Barring mechanical problems, pretty much indefinitely. The wings are lined with solar cells so once it reaches altitude, it acts as a glider, and the battery pack has plenty of capacity to power it at night."

A minute later, Marcia started the tiny engine. The hum of the electric motor was barely audible while she held in her hand but once she launched it into the wind, it was impossible to detect.

Angel climbed out over the sea, steadily gaining altitude, though the video screen remained black. With a few strokes on the mini-keypad, Marcia switched on the monitor and the screen showed the terrain on the cliff top above sliding slowly by. The left side of the screen displayed a map with Angel's position appearing as a small red dot.

As the drone banked back toward the cliff in a long sweeping arc, Marcia began to fly it using the small video screen. She worked the joystick and flew a course toward the salt factory ruins. She then changed course and began orbiting over the vessels moored offshore. After completing her initial reconnaissance, she turned to Quint.

"It's easy to fly. I can train each of you in minutes. Then we can take turns and continuously monitor the pirates without leaving our base."

After each of the men had taken a shot at operating the drone, Marcia resumed piloting it. Fifteen minutes later, with Angel circling on autopilot, the team became bored and collapsed for a much-needed rest while Marcia continued monitoring the screen.

Two hours later, Dakota, infatuated with the drone, insisted on taking the first watch to relieve Marcia. Throughout the rest of the day, they each took turns monitoring Angel's video monitor while standing guard.

By early morning, it was Marcia's turn once again. She switched off the autopilot and swung the tiny drone toward the coast to make a pass and confirm the pirate boats remained beached in a row. She then commanded it to resume circling in auto mode.

A half hour later, she noticed a boat appear at the edge of the screen, headed for the freighter anchored farthest from shore. She dropped the tiny drone down to a lower altitude and reduced the size of its orbit to closely monitor the boat.

She could see several men on board as they pulled alongside the freighter, where two disembarked and were handed what appeared to be buckets. She saw the two men climb to the ship's main deck, then continue to the stern, where they climbed several more flights of stairs, disappearing through a doorway one level below the bridge.

Meanwhile, two armed men climbed down to the small boat, which returned to shore. For the next half hour, Marcia saw little activity as Angel continued to orbit.

"Anything interesting?" Quint asked as he approached from the nearest tent.

"Not much. I noticed a few men wearing uniforms near a building to the north of the village that could be barracks. And a boat just made what appeared to be a changing of the guard on that big freighter."

"Could that ship be where the hostages are being held?"

"Possibly. Armed guards and what could have been containers of food and water suggests it might be."

"Keep monitoring. I'll go make us some coffee and then relieve you." A few minutes later, he handed her a steaming cup of coffee. "Anything?" Quint took a sip from his own cup.

"Look." Marcia pointed at the screen, where Quint could see two men standing beside what appeared to be a doorway on the ship's bridge. A moment later a third stepped out and began walking toward the front of the ship with what appeared to be an armed guard trailing.

"Think it's a hostage stretching their legs?"

"Sure looks like it."

"You may have found what we're looking for. Good work," Quint said. "Take a break and I'll watch for a while." Marcia rose to stretch and work the kinks out of her lower back muscles.

CHAPTER 44

When they came for Raoul, he stood with as much dignity as he could muster and walked from the room, head held high. After deciding there was nothing he could do to stop them, he was determined to at least deprive them of the satisfaction of seeing how terrified he was.

They led him back to Ethan's office, where Ghedi stood smiling before the large desk. The chairs had been moved to one side and a sheet of plastic lay on the floor. A small stool with a gleaming machete lying on top was positioned in the middle. An open cooler sat a few feet away labeled "O.D."

"Have we made our decision, left or right?" Ghedi said with a laugh.

"Left, long," Raoul replied, a quiver in his voice despite his best efforts.

"Care to make one last call to convince your boss?" Ethan asked.

Raoul nodded without speaking while Ethan dialed a number. "I have your captain here. He wishes to speak with you."

Raoul took the phone and could hear his boss's voice. "Raoul, I'm so glad to hear from you."

"Have you convinced them to pay our ransom?"

"I've tried, Raoul. They owe it to you to help. But the owner won't budge. He refuses to pay. I've been to speak with the board, but so far they haven't agreed to it. I just need more time. I—"

"I don't have any more time. They're about to cut off my arm if you don't agree to pay the ransom right now."

"Shit! Raoul, I'm sorry. There's nothing I can do. I've tried, you have to believe—" Raoul handed the phone back to Ethan, who hung it up and then gave a nod to Ghedi.

Jenny looked up when the door opened and saw them dragging Raoul into the room, where they tossed him onto the floor like a sack of potatoes. As the door slammed back shut, Jenny sprung up and ran to him.

Raoul was still breathing but was unconscious. "One of you men, give me your shirt. He's lost a lot of blood and will die if we can't stop it."

One of Raoul's crew stripped off their shirt and handed it to her. She wrapped it around the stump and drew it tight. "Now, give me your belt," she said to another crewman standing nearby. Without replying, the man removed his belt and handed it to her. She quickly wrapped it around the already bloodied material and drew it tight.

For the rest of the day, she stood by doing the little that she could to help him, ashamed at the relief she felt that it hadn't been her or Brad.

CHAPTER 45

"What now?" Colin asked.

"We wait until the pirates leave on their next foray," Quint replied.

"What if they don't leave for another week?" Colin asked.

"Then we go to Plan B since we can't just sit here and let them sell Jenny," Dawson replied while tracing circles in the sand with a stick.

"Hopefully, they'll leave soon. And we need to be ready to free the hostages when they do," Quint said.

Marcia volunteered to monitor Angel most of the day, making notes from time to time. As evening approached, each team member broke open an MRE and quietly ate.

"So brief us on what you've seen today," Quint asked Marcia.

"It appears that every six hours, they rotate a fresh crew out to the hostage ship," Marcia began. "I've noted the number of guards and their positions to the extent I could see remotely. We'll be working by the seat of our pants. We have no idea how many hostages are being held or if they're all located together. This won't be easy," Marcia said.

Dawson nodded. "Never thought it would be."

"Plus, most of the pirates are on drugs. Those with money use cocaine or heroin while the poorer chew khat," Quint said. "This means that they may behave like berserkers, so if we intend to go on breathing, we cannot afford to go easy on them."

Tossing his stick aside, Dawson continued. "We'll need to take full advantage of our silenced weapons."

The team continued to lounge around killing time. Throughout the night, they rotated shifts such that all had at least some sleep.

By the time dawn broke, they were drinking coffee when Dakota spoke. "We've got movement," Dakota said with his eyes glued to the monitor. "Looks like our pirate buddies are about to go for a cruise. No, wait a minute, they don't look like the badasses we were expecting." As he continued to watch, he saw a half dozen skiffs head for the pirates' hostage ship, where they came alongside. A minute later, he saw armed men herding what appeared to be a group of hostages down a ladder toward the skiffs. "Shit, they're moving the hostages," Dakota said.

"Where to?" Quint asked.

"Don't know, we'll have to wait and see," he replied while the team gathered around him watching the scene unfold.

"We need a hostage count," Dawson said and began scanning the monitor.

"I count seventeen. It looks like they're taking them to the village," Marcia said. The boats pulled alongside the dock to unload the hostages. Next, they marched them up the beach to a walled compound near the salt factory ruins. "It appears that they're taking them to that large blue building near the middle of the compound."

"I wonder what that's all about," Dawson mused.

"Maybe they figured it's easier to guard them there with so many of the more experienced about to leave in all of those boats," Marcia said.

"Maybe, but now we're forced to go after them on land instead—" Dawson's reply was interrupted by the sound of an electronic alarm. "What's that?"

The sound grew louder when Marcia opened the transponder control unit to find a blinking red light. "Shit. The transponder signal has dropped."

"Maybe the antenna slipped," Dakota said.

"Dakota, run Marcia and Dakota back to the lighthouse so they can deal with the problem," Quint said.

"In broad daylight? Isn't that risky?" Dakota asked.

"Not as risky as having those charges start cooking off. It's still early, not many folks are up yet, so just be stealthy. Think invisible. I'll fly Angel to give you some air reconnaissance."

"Don't mean to add to the stress, but the pirates may be about to saddle up," Dawson said.

The three team members climbed into the inflatable and sat low as Dakota hugged the far edge of the lagoon headed back to the lighthouse. Marcia and Dakota leaped from the inflatable as soon as they were near the beach and ran for the lighthouse. They ducked through the hole in the fence that Dakota had cut earlier. They then climbed the stairs two at a time, arriving at the top out of breath. Marcia wiped the sweat from her eyes and immediately spotted the problem.

"The antenna's down. That explains why the signal got weaker without going completely away."

Dakota nodded. "A bird or the wind must have knocked it down." He withdrew a roll of duct tape from the canvas bag slung over his shoulder and used half the roll wrapping the antenna to the railing.

Marcia raised Quint on the radio. "We got a better signal?"

"Yep, everything's back to normal. Get on back," Quint replied, sounding distracted. "Uh, it looks like we have another problem."

"What?" Dawson asked anxiously.

Quint pointed to Angel's video monitor. "Two large trucks just pulled into that compound. They're filled with soldiers."

CHAPTER 46

Jenny was still unsettled by being moved off the freighter and into the derelict salt factory compound. Though the building where she was imprisoned was somewhat intact, the rest of the hulking old factory was mostly just a shell. It appeared to have been built early in the last century.

The heat was merciless. The sun beat down on them through huge holes in the rotted roof and the building's walls blocked any hint of a breeze. A mixture of desert sand and salt coated everything inside the ramshackle building. Jenny shifted position on the concrete trying to find a way to ease her aching body.

I just hope that if Kira's sending help, it's soon.

Ethan saw the familiar number and answered his ringing cell phone. "Asad, it's good to hear from you so soon." As was Asad's standard protocol, Ethan sent Asad an email outlining his request and what he was willing to pay for the information. If he liked the price, Asad would soon reply with the information. If not, there would be no contact.

"As it is you. How are things going with your operation? I heard you had some... difficulties recently. Wasn't your mother ship attacked and sunk?" Ethan knew Asad made it his business to find out why his customers wanted to use his services and was bound to hear about his financial troubles.

"Yes, we don't yet know who was behind it. But they really didn't do much, other than sink that old scow and kill a few of our gun-toting cowboys. Perhaps it was some competitor looking to get into business on the cheap. When we find them, they'll be out of business—permanently." Ethan thought it best to minimize the effect that it had on their business and make it clear they were prepared to be ruthless. "Can I assume you have good news?"

"That I do. In two days, a ship named the *Saresyn* will be in range. It's carrying a sophisticated missile system and assorted other high-value cargo. Though they went to great lengths to keep it secret, I have confirmed through two different sources that there's a substantial amount of gold bullion onboard. In excess of fifty million dollars, I am told!"

"That's wonderful news, Asad. You've truly earned your fee this time."

"And a small fee it is considering my risk in serving you."

"I understand." Ethan suspected he was worried that the recent mother ship problems might affect Ethan's ability to pay. Desperate to avoid any demand for upfront payment, he made a preemptive offer. "In addition to your normal fee, I'll include a twenty-five percent bonus if all is as you say. I will wire the funds immediately after we take her."

"Spendid! Just make certain to do so," Asad replied.

Ethan had heard stories about the fate of those who used Asad's services but refused to pay his fee afterward. He had no interest in learning firsthand if the stories were true. Asad provided the departure time and suggested coordinates for the intercept before he broke the connection.

Ethan summoned Ghedi and thirty minutes later, they were convened in his office. "While I was skeptical of your idea at first, it would appear it was fortuitous. I have information on the target of our dreams." He went on to tell him about the *Saresyn,* with a cargo including actual gold bullion—every pirate's fantasy.

Ghedi smiled as he poked a wad of khat leaves into his mouth. "Excellent! I will ready my entire fleet of boats filled with the best men."

"Since we know precisely when and where to attack, your plan to go without a mother ship appears feasible. We can assume that such a prize will be armed, so I will back you with the heavy weapons you requested. The ship will arrive in two days. You must be ready to meet it."

"I will have the boats fueled and doubly inspected to ensure they are fully operational," Ghedi launched a green glob of spit into the corner, away from Ethan's desk this time.

"Where are you planning to get the men to mount such an attack?"

"That is not your concern."

"Ah, but I disagree. It is I who have stuck my neck out on this one and am on the hook to pay that bloodsucker Asad. Nothing can go wrong on this trip. Do you hear me, Ghedi? Nothing."

For a moment the two men glared at one another. "Perhaps you have stuck your neck out with Asad but it is I who had my mother ship blown out from beneath me and—"

"How well aware I am of *my ship* being sunk," Ethan interrupted.

Ghedi ignored Ethan's barb. "And now I must square off against what will certainly be a well-guarded ship."

"It still sounds risky. I doubt many of your new men have experience capturing ships."

Ghedi laughed. "How much experience does it take to yell, point a gun, and follow orders?"

Ethan floated another concern rather than answer. "And we don't want to lose our prisoners."

"The same prisoners you were crying about the cost of keeping imprisoned when no one seems interested in ransoming? The same ones you plan on killing soon if the ransom goes unpaid?" When Ethan did not respond, Ghedi continued. "Once we have the *Saresyn*'s rich cargo, you'll forget all about them. But with the prisoners consolidated in one place on shore, it will take only a few guards."

Ghedi paused for a moment to spit, then with a contemptuous smirk looked Ethan in the eye. "Nonetheless, I arranged with a militia friend of mine to have a couple of dozen more guards sent over while we're gone. The trucks just arrived."

CHAPTER 47

The next morning, Ayan was in the kitchen when Jamal entered her modest home. "There's hot water on the stove, make yourself some tea. Your breakfast is nearly ready and thanks to you, we're having canjeero... with ghee. You did well."

Jamal blushed but felt proud that he had been able to help out with groceries. It made him feel like a man. He finished making his cup of tea and sat down deep in thought. "Have you thought any more about leaving?"

Ayan laughed. "Nearly every minute of every day. Why?"

"We really do need to."

Ayan set the plate of breakfast down and stroked Jamal's hair. "Is this about my being... uh... what happened Friday?" Jamal nodded. "Has Korfa been making it tough on you? Because I can speak with Ghedi."

"Please don't, I can handle my own affairs. I don't need a woman to take care of me." Instantly, Jamal regretted the words and hoped Ayan didn't take offense. "I mean, it is I who should be taking care of you."

"I appreciate your concern but I'm used to it."

"Don't you see? That's the problem. One day it may not just be getting roughed up by that asshole." He stopped as he saw her shoot him a look over his language. "You could... uh... you could end up getting killed." His voice broke on the last word and he sat looking down at his hands.

"Jamal, it's not that I don't want to leave. It's that we have no place to go."

"We'll find a place. We have to," he stopped, tears streaming down his face and onto his lap.

She held him against her side and rubbed his head for several minutes. Finally, she let him go. "Eat your breakfast before it gets cold."

Jamal ate slowly. After finishing, he hugged her. "We'll talk more about this later."

He didn't like the new arrangement with the hostages in a single building. Gone was the structure he had enjoyed on the ship. Plus there were more bosses ordering everyone around. The good news was that he had seen less of Korfa. The bad news was that Korfa had taken away Jamal's AK-47, giving him a rusty 9mm pistol in its place, before reassigning him to help with food preparation.

While Jamal had seen Jenny several times, seldom was there a chance to talk like they had done on the ship. He did, however, manage to slip her scraps of food and an occasional bottle of water.

Jenny and her husband were together in the left wing along with a few others. The rest of the prisoners were housed in the opposite end of the building. Every day he would check to see if one of his friends had been assigned to guard her wing. Twice he had been able to visit with her in exchange for taking the rest of his friend's shift.

Jamal spent hours practicing the finger patterns she had shown him on the paper keyboard of his imaginary piano, though he found his thoughts now tended more toward escaping this place. He knew that if Ghedi's next trip was a bust, they might have little choice. *But where to go?* Deep in thought, he chewed on his right thumbnail.

Roble left the meeting with Ethan and headed for the docks, where he found Jamal and Nasir working on one of the engines. "All of the boats must be fueled and working perfectly by the end of tomorrow. We leave before sunrise the following day to capture our biggest prize ever."

"It will be done," Nasir replied. "And I'll have my best man personally attend to your boat," pointing at Jamal's bruised face with his chin.

Jamal beamed. "Yes, and I could go with you... just in case you had a problem... or something."

Ghedi grunted and ran his hand over his slick scalp. "Not on this one. I need you here guarding the hostages. Perhaps next season. What happened to your face?"

"I... uh... fell," Jamal said, deciding it best not to mention Ayan's rape and the fight with Korfa. Ghedi nodded and left without commenting.

"Thanks for doing that, Nasir."

"It was nothing. You work hard for the little that I can pay. You deserved it. Now, we best make certain that these beat-up pieces of shit are running like new or they'll have both our heads on a pike. Go get started on Ghedi's boat."

Jamal scampered down to Ghedi's boat, one of the few with twin engines, where he lavished attention upon it. After he had fueled the boat and changed the oil, he ran the engines. As he went to hop out of the boat, he noticed an odd bulge on the transom near the waterline. He gently pried on the dark mass with a screwdriver, increasing pressure until it separated from the hull. He was about to grasp it with his left hand when the sound of Desta's voice distracted him. His hand slipped as he jerked his head up and the object fell from his grasp to disappear in the waters below.

"Hello, Jamal." Her ebony hair glowed in the sunlight and the curves of her figure excited him as always. He eagerly greeted her, noticing she had deliberately chosen to walk near the boats on her way down the beach.

Her smile nearly broke his heart she was so beautiful. "Too bad you're working on those boats. I'm going to Kobina's to get rice for my mother. It would be nice to have company."

He nearly swooned from the offer to spend time with her. "I just finished... with Ghedi's boat," he said, making certain she knew whose boat he had been trusted to work on, "and I would love to go with you." He fell in beside her like a faithful dog and she took his hand as they walked away. The curious bulge on Ghedi's boat was forgotten as his thoughts turned to one of his own.

CHAPTER 48

Quint and his team were covered with bug bites, sore from sleeping on the ground, and bored waiting for the pirates to make their move. They had continued to fly the miniature drone, hoping it would keep working until no longer needed.

Marcia had just switched off the night vision and was wondering if the pirates would ever leave when she spotted a large group gathering on the beach. "Guys, we've got movement."

The men jumped to their feet and poured out of the tents to join her before the drone monitor. One by one, the skiffs filled with men and pulled away from the beach. "Showtime," Dawson said quietly.

Dakota retrieved the control unit and sent the arming command to the transceiver in the lighthouse. A green light on the control unit confirmed the command had been received and all fifteen charges were now armed. When the charges could no longer receive the transmitter signal, the primary timers would start. In the event of a malfunction, the default timers would trigger the charges within three hours.

Ghedi's boat was already loaded with his heavily armed team. All fifteen boats formed up single file and headed for the harbor mouth with Ghedi in the lead. The throng on the beach stood waving until the skiffs throttled up and headed out of the bay.

A few minutes after leaving their base, Ghedi steered in the direction of the coordinates provided by Asad and pushed the throttles to the stops. As the boats headed away from shore, the transponder signal received by the attached explosive charges weakened. By the time the lighthouse was out of sight, the mines were armed. The timers on the detonators were now counting down, except for Ghedi's, which thanks to Jamal had no mine.

"When do we go in?" Marcia asked once the last of the pirate boats had disappeared from view.

"Midnight," Quint said.

As they ran through the light chop, Ghedi proudly scanned the fleet of small boats behind him. They all appeared to be running perfectly despite their age and condition. With the onset of monsoon season still a few weeks away, the boats skimmed along over the mirror-like seas on their way toward their grandest prize ever.

After running for over two hours at full throttle, a man with binoculars in the front of Ghedi's boat yelled excitedly.

"A ship! There on the horizon. Could it be the *Saresyn*?"

"If so, it's ahead of schedule. Maybe they finished loading early, in which case we shall take them early. Should it prove to be some other ship, we shall have two prizes."

As they closed to within five miles, the timers on the limpet mines which Quint's team had planted reached zero. The effect was impressive when the first boat exploded and burst into flames. The pirates were slung through the air, their visions of riches fading along with their lives.

Ghedi and his crew looked on slack-jawed unable to think of what to do. One by one, the charges blew off the transom of the remaining boats, igniting their fuel tanks to form giant fireballs.

Those pirates not immediately killed in the blast were either burned or blown apart as the munitions they carried began to "cook off" in the heat. Those men lucky enough to remain alive struggled to keep their heads above water despite a variety of serious wounds.

The boats sank leaving only the dead, a few pieces of wreckage, and a handful of men. The dazed survivors treaded water while watching their intended prey cruise past them.

The *Saresyn*'s first mate spotted the explosion in the distance. "Did you see that?" he asked as several more flashes erupted. The captain simply nodded. The mate hesitated, waiting for a further response from the captain before finally asking, "Do you wish us to alter course to search for survivors?"

"Absolutely not. These are pirate waters. Let God show them mercy or speed them to hell as he wishes. Stay the course," he said firmly.

The crew of Ghedi's boat turned to him with a questioning look and one asked, "What should we do?"

"Save the survivors," he finished with a string of curses. In anger, Ghedi slammed the throttles forward and the boat leaped up onto a plane. But after travelling only a few hundred feet, they heard a thud and the engines died as they struck submerged wreckage.

"Damn it all!" Ghedi raised the engines to inspect the damage. The starboard outboard lower unit was severely damaged, barely hanging though its prop appeared to be unscathed. The port unit appeared undamaged but one fluke of its propeller was bent at a crazy angle. He shook his head as he lowered the engines back down.

"One of you get in the water and take the good prop off the starboard engine. We'll swap it for the bent one on the port side." His men stared at the sharks already drawn by the blood and commotion and stood mute. Ghedi whipped out his .357 pistol and waved it at the farthest man. "Get in the water. Or I'll shoot you, then you'll go into the water."

More afraid of Ghedi than the sharks, the man slid over the side of the boat and hugged the transom. They handed him a wrench and he frantically set to work removing the starboard prop, hoping to quickly get back out of the water. He had removed the prop nut on the starboard engine when the first shark struck without warning.

Screaming in pain, the man released his grip on the prop to beat on the shark's head with the wrench. The beast swam off with a large chunk of his thigh, only to be replaced by a second shark which latched onto his other leg. Ghedi's men fired at the shark but it was hopeless. A shot in their colleague's head ended the misery of being eaten alive.

Ghedi glanced back down just in time to see the prop slide easily off of the shaft, which Jamal had coated with a thick layer of grease. In slow motion, it began its journey into the deep. "That's great, now we've lost the good prop," he remarked, seeming more upset at the loss of the prop than the man. His remaining crew breathed a sigh of relief that none of them would now be forced into the shark-infested waters.

While Ghedi's crew rescued the few survivors, they watched in horror as the sharks fed on the bodies of the dead. They fired at a few of the nearer sharks but did little to disrupt their feast.

One by one, the bodies disappeared beneath the surface. It was nearly dark by the time Ghedi turned toward shore and began limping back on their remaining engine with its damaged prop. Only a few bits of wreckage and an oil slick gave witness to what had happened.

CHAPTER 49

Other than the odd explosion that occurred in the water where Ghedi's boat had been docked, things had been quiet since the pirates' departure. Jamal had finished his work preparing the hostages' meal and was seated with his back to the front door of the old salt factory building where he was guarding hostages.

On the small table before him lay his paper piano keyboard. He was focused on practicing when he caught the sound of the door opening. He looked up to find Korfa standing two feet away staring at him.

"What the hell is that?" He sneered at the dog-eared sheets of glued-together paper which lay before him. Jamal looked up wide-eyed without answering.

"I'll be damned, it's a piano keyboard. How fitting that the paper tiger should be playing a paper piano." Korfa's hand darted out to snatch the paper and Jamal reacted a second too slow, just catching the end. With a wide grin on his face, Korfa jerked the paper tearing it from Jamal's grasp. Slowly, he ripped the paper keyboard into small pieces and wadded it up.

Jamal leaned forward as if preparing to fight, his rage barely concealed. Korfa loomed over him with a taunting expression. Finally, as if the air had been let out of him, Jamal backed down, controlling the futile urge to throw himself at the big brute of a man.

"You should be doing your job and learning how to be a man, not playing sissy games." With a sneer, he tossed the balled-up paper into the corner and walked back out.

Once the door had closed, Jamal leaped to retrieve his pretend keyboard. But as he unwrapped the wad, it was clear it could not be salvaged. He flung it back onto the floor and stomped on it, then stood there with the rage burning inside. He was proud that no tears flowed.

When one of his buddies drew night guard duty that night, Jamal offered to stand his shift for the chance to see Jenny. At midnight, he hugged the shadows as he approached the building where the hostages were imprisoned inside the compound. Jamal froze at the sound of voices and melted into the shadows beside the building. With his heart thumping he held his breath, hoping to make his small form even smaller. For an instant, he was glad not to be carrying the bulky AK-47 that Korfa had taken from him.

He saw two guards leaned against the far corner of the building, smoking and chatting. One passed a bottle and he realized they were drinking. Jamal was relieved that neither was Korfa.

Once the men finished smoking, Jamal heard the sound of one relieving himself on the dirt, after which they continued on their patrol around the village. When they were out of sight, Jamal slipped around the side and entered the building through the front door.

He stood for a moment while his eyes adjusted to the even darker blackness inside before easing toward the west end of the building where Jenny was being held. "Hey, I wondered if our deal was still on." His buddy whispered as he saw Jamal approach. "Things are quiet. I'll do a quick bed check of the hostages and then leave you with it. I've got a warm bed with a hot woman waiting for me."

Five minutes later, his buddy was gone and Jamal eased past the doorway to the room where Korfa slept. Using his friend's key, he unlocked the door to the room where Jenny was being held and pushed it partway open. The sound of loud snoring came from more than one bed on the far side of the room, where he saw the hostages lying on their tattered pallets.

He approached Jenny, who sat on the side of her bed with her face turned away. "You ready for me to begin coaching you on the piano scales?" she whispered to keep from waking her husband, who was sleeping soundly.

Jamal shook his head. "Korfa tore up my keyboard."

"Oh. I'm so sorry," Jenny replied, her head still turned away. Curious, Jamal switched on the tiny penlight he carried and looked at her face. One eye was closed with an ugly bruise and her jaw was so swollen she could hardly speak. "What happened to you?"

"It's nothing."

"Was it Korfa?" Her silence answered his question. "That bastard. That rotten bastard. It's time to deal with him."

"No, Jamal," she pleaded in as loud of a whisper as she dared. "You're just a—"

"Boy? Is that what you were going to say?" Jamal leaped to his feet and headed back down to the hall in a blind rage. The image of Ayan being raped and Jenny's beaten face filled his mind. He wiped the sweat from his right palm on his pants leg and withdrew the 9mm pistol from his pocket.

So strong was his hatred for Korfa that he intended to shoot him. At least he wanted to. But fact was, he had never shot a man. *What if I can't do it?* He didn't want to think about that. Maybe he should just leave and go back to his bed. No, he needed to deal with Korfa before he hurt someone else he cared about... or Jamal himself.

Before he could lose his nerve, he swung the door open and entered Korfa's room with his rusted pistol extended in his right arm. Halfway across the room to Korfa's bed, he had a sickening thought. *Is the pistol's safety off?*

As he stopped to check, the form on the bed in front of him moved and a giant hand thrust out to snatch away the pistol. It missed but continued on to strike him a glancing blow, the mighty fist knocking him across the room, where he landed on his back.

Jamal knew the full force of the punch would've killed him. He couldn't survive a second one. Still seeing stars, he shook his head and raised his pistol.

"You little bastard. It's time you learned some respect." Korfa lumbered forward. Jamal knew he had one chance and one chance only. As Korfa loomed over him and raised his fist, Jamal pulled the trigger.

The giant continued forward, landing on top of Jamal and crushing the air from his lungs beneath the mountain of flesh. Warm blood oozed out onto his chest and Korfa's body quivered. With all of his strength, Jamal pushed the dead weight to his left while rolling to his right, managing to wiggle free. He struggled to clear his mind while catching his breath.

With the gun's barrel pressed into Korfa's stomach, all of the force and gases of the cartridge had entered his body, muffling the sound. Jamal listened for footsteps but heard nothing. Perhaps the guards outside had been too drunk or too distracted to notice.

I've got to get out of here. He eased the door open and after checking the hall, tiptoed back to Jenny's room.

"I heard a gunshot. What happened? What did you do?" she asked in a shaky voice.

"He's dead. Korfa is dead."

"Are you okay?"

"I think so." Jamal's whole body was trembling.

"What are we going to do now?"

"I'm afraid I don't know," Jamal replied.

CHAPTER 50

It was 1 a.m. when the inflatable eased toward shore. Quint was confident that the dark hull would not be seen in the moonless night, nor would the low murmur of the engine be heard.

"I only see two guards," He pointed to the two positions at opposite ends of the compound while scanning the shore with night vision glasses. "The one furthest to the left appears not to be moving, probably asleep."

Dawson nodded and donned his scuba gear, preparing to slide over the side.

"I don't like this. We should be going with you," Dakota said, Marcia nodding in agreement.

"You guys need to stand by and be ready to come save our butts." Quint ended the conversation by slipping into the water behind the other two men.

With their regulators in place, the three men slid beneath the surface, where they took a compass bearing and began their swim toward shore. Twice they surfaced to check their bearing, finally reaching a skiff with no engine. The men eased out of their scuba gear and secured it to a piling beside the boat. Quint confirmed that Dawson and Colin were ready before ducking from behind the skiff to snorkel toward shore.

In a case of truly bad luck, the lone alert sentry approached just as Dawson emerged from behind one of the boats with the man on his blind side. "Hey!" the guard challenged as he ran toward the boat.

"Boys, we got company," Quint whispered as he saw Dawson's mistake. "Colin, take him down."

Dawson stood up in the shallow water, boldly waving at the man to create confusion.

Colin raised his silenced machine pistol, brought the laser sight to bear on the man's torso, and squeezed off a shot. The man fell to his knees, crumpling in a heap. Dawson leaped onto the dock and, in a crouching run, made his way to the man and rolled the body into the water. Colin then pushed it out from shore so that it would float out on the outgoing tide.

"Sorry," Dawson said. "I should have seen him."

"He was on your blind side," Colin said to comfort him.

"Yeah, that's just it. My disability is going to get us all killed," Dawson replied.

Seeing no point in arguing, Quint said, "Ready?" Dawson nodded.

"Damn!" Colin cursed. "I can't find my snorkel gear. I must not have secured it to my waist clip."

Quint grimaced. This meant they would be taking the hard way out. "Probably doesn't matter, I doubt we'd be able to risk swimming back out anyhow," he replied, trying to put the best face on it. "Let's head farther up the beach, away from the dock. After we're done, we'll work our way back to the bay entrance and hail Dakota to pick us up there."

"You got it," Dawson agreed as the three men swam a few hundred feet away from the dock and turned toward shore. Once they were reached shore, they ran up the beach.

Pausing beside the latrine Quint scanned the area and saw the second guard, apparently still sleeping undisturbed. Then he spotted another. "There's one more guard, must have come to replace the guy we took out. He's wide awake."

The men donned their comms units and checked to make sure that they were working before following a path through the brush just off the beach to skirt the main part of the village.

"How did we let ourselves get talked into this one?" Dawson whispered as he avoided a large snake lying in the middle of the path.

"Good question. I'm just not sure if it has to do with being gullible, stupid, or just being nice guys," Quint replied.

"I'm going with stupid," Colin replied.

"I hope we don't end up nice dead guys," Dawson added. The three men ducked into the underbrush and froze when they heard voices. Two young boys armed with rifles nearly as big as themselves passed on patrol.

Once they were out of sight, the men continued until they reached the edge of the clearing behind the building where the hostages were being held. The men slid off their backpacks while studying the building. The back had a door and a row of windows just like the front. "Do we go in stealthy or big using our explosive toys?" Quint asked.

"Given that there are only three of us and a bazillion of them, I'm going with stealthy," Dawson replied, with Colin nodding his consent. "Then we go big once we stir up the hornet's nest." Dawson and Colin sighted on the two guards standing on either side of the entrance and took them down within seconds of each other.

With Dawson and Colin providing cover, Quint crept to the back of the building, where he waved the others on. The two men quickly followed, with Quint ready to provide cover should they need it. They dragged the two dead guards up against the side of the building.

Dawson was preparing to breach the door when it abruptly opened. Quint grabbed Dawson's shirt collar and jerked him back into the shadows as a large man stumbled out, appearing drunk. The three men hugged the side of the building.

Dawson slid his wicked-looking KA-BAR knife free, grabbed the man by the neck, and made a slashing motion with the knife. The man slumped without a sound and Dawson pulled him back against the building. "Once again, my one eye almost screwed me. I have to be more careful."

Ignoring his remark, Quint whispered, "I think our boy was a little drunk. Probably headed for that tree line to pee." Quint then swung his night vision goggles into place and peeked inside the building.

"Okay, let's do it." Quint quietly entered the building. He gestured to Dawson to break right as he went to the left, signaling Colin to continue forward.

Quint heard Colin's silenced pistol fire twice and Dawson's three more times. Quint waited until he heard each man click their mics twice indicating they were clear. He then reseated his night vision goggles and raised his foot to kick in the door to the left wing.

CHAPTER 51

"Was that gunfire?" Jamal asked in alarm at an odd muffled noise and the sound of cushioned footsteps.

"Maybe we're being rescued," Jenny said.

Could this be his chance? Jamal had told Jenny how bad things were and how he and Ayan wished to leave. He was still sorting through his confusion when the room door flew open in a shower of splintered wood.

Quint saw a man beside the bed holding a pistol.

"Don't shoot," he heard a woman scream just as he pulled the trigger. "Don't shoot," she screamed again while lunging in front of his gun.

"Here, take his weapon. Jamal's unarmed now. Don't shoot," she yelled repeatedly.

Quint eased forward, smoke curling from the barrel of his M4A1. He jammed the pistol into his pocket and raised his night vision goggles while switching on a powerful flashlight. The light shown on a mere boy clutching a bloody shoulder. Seeing that the bullet had just grazed the boy, Quint panned the room counting nine forms lying in bunks.

"You here to rescue us?" she asked.

"Yes ma'am. You Jenny?"

"Yes," she said excitedly, "and this is my husband." Brad sat up, awakened by the commotion.

"Kira sends her love. What's the deal with the boy?"

"He's been with the pirates without much choice. Is he okay?"

"The bullet just grazed him. I pulled up when you yelled." Quint reached into his lower left cargo pocket for a small first aid kit and a spare flashlight. "Patch him up but make it quick."

Jenny nodded.

"Are any of the others unable to walk?"

"There's a man with the other group who's in bad shape. He'll need help but most of the rest of us can walk... provided it's not too far. We're all weak from hunger." Quint nodded and then turned to Brad. "Rouse the rest of the hostages."

A few minutes later, all the hostages were gathered at the door.

Quint keyed his mic. "We're clear. You guys?"

"We've got the second group," Dawson answered.

"I know you've got at least one who can't walk on his own. Any others?" Quint asked.

"Just the one."

"I've got Jenny. Gather up your group and meet me out front."

A moment later, Quint herded his group toward the front of the building.

Quint found the man who needed help. Given the bloody shirt that he had wrapped around his side, it wasn't hard. "What's your name?"

"Raoul."

"Can you walk?"

"I'll try, but I'm weak."

Quint and Dawson helped him to his feet and out the door. Quint turned to Jenny. "This is everyone?"

She saw Walter and the group she had last seen in the ship bilges. "As far as I know," she replied.

Quint scanned the faces of the rest, each nodding in turn. "We have a short walk to get you out of here. Keep quiet and follow us. Dawson, can you help him?" Quint motioned at Raoul, being held up by two of the hostages. He nodded and lifted the man in a fireman's carry, finding the man's light body easy to bear.

"What about him?" Dawson asked pointing at Jamal.

"Please, take him with us, he's just a boy," Jenny begged. Quint started to object and then nodded.

"I'm not leaving without Ayan," Jamal said.

"Who's Ayan?" Quint asked.

"She's... uh... like my mother... sort of."

Quint shook his head. "Where is she?"

"Not far. I'll go get her and bring her back." Before Quint could reply Jamal took off running.

"We need to go," Dawson said.

"Damn it!" Quint swore. "Colin—follow him. Make sure he doesn't raise an alarm."

"And do what, bring both him *and* Ayan along?" Colin asked.

"Uh... yeah," Quint said in resignation ignoring Dawson smirk. "But be damned quick. Meet us at the rally point." Colin took off after the boy, by now barely still in sight.

"Let's go before things continue to sour," Dawson said and rounded up the rest of the hostages before heading to meet Dakota.

Fully expecting to be in the thick of it by now, Quint was amazed when they were back on the trail without problems. With Quint taking point and Dawson guarding their rear while carrying Raoul, the group continued down the path. When they reached the far end of the village, they were forced to skirt the last guard post closer than Quint preferred.

They were nearly home-free when one of the hostages coughed, waking the sleeping guard. Instinctively, he sounded the alarm even as he brought his rifle up and fired without aiming. The sound was like a cannon.

"Uh-oh, things are about to get ugly." Dawson squeezed off a short burst and brought the guard down.

Quint turned to the hostages. "Head to the beach and then work your way toward the mouth of the bay."

"Give me a gun. I can help," Brad argued, wanting to stay and fight.

"No, you take lead with the hostages. Carry Raoul so Dawson can fight," Quint replied.

"But I—"

"Do it! Now!" Quint yelled back, ending the conversation. Brad gathered the others and broke for the beach, carrying Raoul on his back.

CHAPTER 52

"Ayan, Ayan, we must go." Ayan awoke from a sound sleep rubbing her eyes and started to light a cigarette. "No time." He threw her thin dress to her.

"Where? What?"

"Our chance… to finally leave. Come, I'll show you."

"I need a minute to pack."

"There's no time. We must go now."

"I can't. I'm afraid."

"Afraid of what?"

"I don't know."

"What do we have here?" There was no comment. "Nothing, we have nothing. But I won't leave without you." Ayan nodded and Jamal looked off as she rose to dress.

Colin stepped in. "Ma'am, if you want to come we'll take you. But we have to leave now." She took a single quick glance at her modest home and then walked out the door forever. They made it only a few yards when the sound of gunfire broke the quiet. "You two, meet the hostages at the east end of the beach. I've got to go help Quint." Without waiting for a reply, Colin took off at a run.

Colin joined Quint and Dawson and the three men continued, on alert for more armed pirates. Before they made it past the large barracks building, men began pouring out in response to the gunfire. The first armed man headed directly toward them. Quint stopped the man in his tracks at the price of focusing attention on them. Gunfire erupted from the steady stream of men emptying the building. Colin screamed as a bullet smashed into his leg, dropping him instantly.

The air was alive with bullets, pinning the three men in the brush at the edge of the beach. As Quint dragged Colin into a shallow depression offering at least some cover, a bullet tore into his arm breaking the bone just above his elbow.

Dawson heard his yell of pain. He dug his first aid kit out of his cargo shorts and tossed it to Quint while maintaining cover fire. Placing a large piece of gauze over the bullet hole, Quint wrapped it and then Colin's leg wound using the entire roll of adhesive tape. With their bleeding under control, Quint lifted his gun with his good arm and returned fire, answering each muzzle flash.

Dakota heard the gunfire. Surmising the three men weren't able to make it back to the extraction point, he headed in the direction of the commotion. While he ran the boat, Marcia raised Quint on the radio.

"Marcia, I see you but I'm not sure what you can do. It'd be suicide for you to try to get to us, they'd mow you down halfway across the beach."

"Give us a minute to come up with something. I won't let you down," she said, turning to Dakota. "They've got their butts in a serious crack. We have to help them."

After a moment's silence Marcia burst out, "I've got it! Dakota, veer off to the right and bring us in behind that point of land, away from the action. I'll go when you have us in close. Then you follow behind and bring all the firepower we've got."

When the inflatable reached shore, Marcia leaped from the moving boat. She ran up the beach to the protection of the brush where she stumbled upon the hostages hiding. After beaching the RIB, Dakota joined them, carrying his own AA-12 shotgun.

"Marcia," Colin called on the handheld radio. "We're pinned down just east of the large barracks building at the brush line near the beach. Oh, and there's two more. A boy and a woman should be there any second. Hold your fire and don't shoot them," Colin added. A moment later, Jamal and Ayan came running up the trail.

"Colin, we've got the hostages and are coming to help," Marcia radioed and then turned to the hostages. "Stay hidden. We'll be right back." Marcia continued west with Dakota.

"The guys are pinned down over there." Marcia pointed to her right. "Let's give them a hand." They followed the trail through the high grass, skirting the barracks to approach from the side opposite Quint. Marcia held a fist up to signal a halt as she swapped the standard drum magazine on her AA-12 for one filled with fragmentation grenades. "Quint," Marcia whispered into the radio.

"Marcia, we're shot up, nearly out of ammunition and about to be overrun. Where the hell are you?"

"We've flanked them and are about to rain all manner of hell down. Sit tight. When their firing eases off, head south across that little point."

"Marcia, you get us out of here, I buy the beer," Quint replied, his lighthearted manner doing little to conceal the stress in his voice.

Marcia turned to Dakota and mouthed, "Ready?"

He nodded as he rose from his knees. Marcia headed to the left side while Dakota made straight for the barracks. Once Marcia cleared the barracks corner, she spotted muzzle flashes and began firing grenades from the AA-12. While she methodically blasted away at the remaining pirates, Dakota did the same with his shotgun on the far side of the building.

Dakota paused to lob a satchel-charge explosive into the barracks. "Fire in the hole!" he yelled as they ducked. A moment later, an enormous blast demolished the center portion of the barracks. When the debris finished falling, Marcia rained havoc with the AA-12 to squelch the remaining fire while Dakota cleared the inside of the barracks.

As the firing eased, Dawson carried Colin in a fireman's carry while Quint, holding his carbine with his good arm, provided covering fire. The three men retreated toward the point with Marcia's blizzard of ordnance suppressing the remaining opposition.

After firing all thirty-two grenades, she ducked behind the barracks corner and swapped out the empty magazine for one with standard 12 gauge rounds. She then resumed laying down heavy fire to cover their exit, creating a virtual wall of lead between the beach and the barracks while Dakota returned fire against individual muzzle flashes with his M-16 as he ran for the beach.

By the time Marcia's second magazine was empty, most of the pirates were either dead or unable to mount further opposition. With their ammunition nearly depleted, the pair continued away from the barracks. Marcia caught a glimpse of movement to her left but before she could react, an enormous force slammed into her side, knocking her to the ground. One of the pirates trying to flank them had scored a lucky shot.

Dakota swung his M-16 around and let loose with a round from the MAUL, then saw the man tumble backwards from the explosion. He was reaching for Marcia's arm when a force like a sledgehammer knocked him on top of her. As he fell, his combat harness hooked on Marcia's middle two fingers, bending them back and breaking them with a sickening crunch. Rolling to his side he raised his weapon and fired off the last of the MAUL rounds and then emptied the M16 magazine before the return fire finally ceased. Though their Kevlar vests had protected them, Marcia had badly bruised or maybe even cracked ribs and Dakota's back would be sore for days.

He rose and jerked Marcia to her feet, the gun falling from her ruined hand. He snatched her empty shotgun off the ground, slung it over his shoulder, and then grabbed her around the waist to help her toward the beach.

CHAPTER 53

"Dakota, I'll stay here while you move the first group of hostages across the bay," Marcia said. He nodded and she watched him fight his way toward the inflatable. A few minutes later, he had half the hostages herded into the RIB and was headed across the bay.

A short while later, they saw Dakota return to move the remainder of the hostages to safety. He edged the boat into the shallow water, where Dawson helped load Colin into the boat and then guided the rest of the hostages in.

"Ayan, what are you doing here? I thought you went with Jamal in the first hostage group." Dawson asked.

"She wouldn't go," Dakota replied. "We couldn't get them all in and once Jamal was in the boat along with Raoul and the hostages in the worst shape, she and Jenny refused to get in."

Quint nodded. "Pick us up after you have the rest of the hostages safe."

"That's a really bad idea. You're about out of ammo and we don't know how many pirates are left. I don't want to leave you here."

"The RIB can't handle the weight," Quint replied.

"Get in and we'll see. If it's too much, we'll regroup," Dakota replied. Once everyone was loaded in, the RIB sat low in the water but was still floating. "I'll have to take it slow to keep from submarining, but we can make it."

Ayan was still standing beside the RIB. "Get in," Quint yelled.

"No, please take care of Jamal, but I'm not leaving. This is my home, it's all I have."

"That's crazy, we can help you start a new life. Please just get—" A rifle burst interrupted him and he ducked while forcing Ayan down too. Dawson returned fire and the incoming fire ceased.

"My home is here. I'll make do."

Quint paused to look at her for a moment. "Ayan, we already sunk the mother ship."

"I know, but now they have a whole fleet of smaller boats."

"No, they don't. They're all gone, too. It's over. Come, go with us." Ayan hesitated a moment, seeming confused, but let him guide her into the inflatable.

Dawson pushed the inflatable's bow away from the beach and leaped inside. Dakota eased the throttles forward as far as he could without the RIB taking on water and made for the far side of the small bay as gunfire resumed from the shore.

Dawson rummaged through the duffle bag in the bottom of the boat and found one of the last remaining magazines. After reloading, he returned fire until he was empty, by which time they had moved out of range.

Ghedi was continuing toward shore at his maddeningly slow pace, constantly glancing at his cell phone. When he finally had a signal, he dialed his base. Ethan answered.

"Ghedi, help! We've been attacked; I think they freed the hostages."

"You *think* they freed them?"

"Yeah, I'm hunkered down in my warehouse. I'm not about to get in the middle of what sounds like a hell of

a firefight with automatic weapons and grenades. Get
your ass back here."

"I've got my own problems. We were attacked too,
and only my boat survived. We're barely moving on
one engine with a damaged prop but we're nearly to
the mouth of the harbor."

"Hurry, you may still be able to catch them."

Ghedi slammed the throttle forward until the
vibrations from the bent prop threatened to shake the
boat apart. As he turned into the harbor, the wake of
the team's inflatable was visible three hundred yards
ahead and he steered for it.

"Get your guns ready, we're going to kill these
bastards!" he yelled to his men in the boat.

CHAPTER 54

"While I don't think we'll get high marks for stealth, we got lucky," Quint said cradling his aching arm.

"I sure don't feel so lucky," Colin complained.

"Neither do I." Marcia agreed, nursing her ruined hand.

"Well, at least we're all still breathing," Dawson replied.

Glancing off to their left, Quint saw the phosphorescent wake of an approaching boat. "Uh, folks, we ain't out of the woods... er, waves, yet," pointing at the boat.

Dakota altered course from the approaching boat and bumped the throttle up. As small waves began breaking over the bow, he was forced to back off. A minute later, they were still out of range when gunfire erupted from the boat behind them. The two-boat chase continued in slow motion with the RIB too heavily loaded to run and Ghedi's bent prop slowing him.

Ghedi eased the throttle forward willing to risk ruining the engine to get a little more speed now that he was back in protected waters. Gradually, he gained on the team while his men continued to lay down rifle fire.

"Oh no, it's Ghedi," Ayan said and then hunched down in the RIB. "He's the leader of the pirates. He and his banker, Ethan."

"He planned on selling me and harvesting Brad's organs," Jenny said.

"Nice guy," Dawson said sarcastically.

As Ghedi continued to close on them and bullets struck the water around them. Quint saw Ayan raise up to look back and then suddenly sit bolt upright facing toward the stern, a red spot blossoming on the front of her thin dress.

"Jamal... I love him," she said, a single tear rolling down her cheek. "Please tell him—" The rest of her broken sentence stopped as another bullet struck her in the back of her head and her body toppled into the water.

Marcia, who had just finished taping her broken fingers together, looked up. Without a word, she dug in the spare duffle and brought out another drum magazine filled with grenades for the AA-12.

"You know, I've had just about enough of their shit." She dropped from her seat on the side of the RIB to kneel on the floor, steadying her weapon on the engine cowling.

Carefully, she placed her broken fingers beneath the trigger guard and slid her trigger finger into position. She waited until the boat chasing them was within range before unleashing her first round. Her first shot landed in front and to the right of the boat, sending up an enormous geyser of water as the boat ran through the spray.

Dawson cried out as a round ricocheted off the metal pipe cage protecting the engine and slammed into his chest, knocking him backwards over the side of the boat.

Colin's arm shot out to snag Dawson's combat harness, just missing it as he watched him fall out of their careening boat. Before Dakota could react Quint screamed, "Keep going—we have to draw that boat away. Colin, keep your arm pointed at Dawson and don't you dare take your eyes off him until we can get back to pick him up."

Dakota swung the wheel hard to the right, hoping to draw their pursuer away, with no luck. They watched helplessly as the boat aimed at Dawson and ran over him as he ducked to the side.

Marcia turned her focus back to the pursuing boat and, once they were far enough away from Dawson, launched another grenade. This shot bracketed the boat, exploding well behind it. Dialed in, she let go with three rounds in rapid succession. The first hit right beneath the bow, slamming it up as the following round fell inside the boat in front of Ghedi, shredding him, the boat, and the other men. Immediately, the boat stopped and began to sink as water rushed in through a huge hole in the side. "Bingo!" Marcia yelled. The burning wreck's bow pointed high as its heavy stern sank below the surface.

Dakota spun the wheel and headed the boat back where Colin was pointing to get Dawson. He ignored the black smoke pouring from the outboard, apparently a casualty of all the gunfire.

"There he is," Marcia shouted and without hesitation dove over the side, reaching the limp form in a few strokes. She snatched Dawson's harness and pulled his face from the water. Dakota pulled alongside and, with a mighty heave, swung Dawson completely out of the water and into the boat. Marcia followed close behind and quickly cleared his mouth with her good hand. She began CPR, ignoring the deep prop wounds on his leg for the moment.

It seemed like forever before he finally retched and vomited salt water. Marcia collapsed backwards weak from the adrenaline rush and the relief that Dawson was still alive. He lay on the floor of the RIB semi-conscious while Dakota got them underway.

"His vest stopped the bullet but the pirates' prop cut his leg in a couple places. Luckily, no arteries were severed," Marcia said as she applied temporary patches to his wounds.

While they were underway, Marcia used the satphone to contact the chopper. The hostages were waiting when they reached shore. One of the men saw the bullet holes in the boat and the smoking engine. "Boy, you guys are tough on your toys." He became silent upon seeing all the blood and how badly the team was hurt.

"Yeah, we're pretty tough on ourselves as well," Quint sighed, holding his broken arm.

"No shit," the man replied in a low voice, seeming to regret his outburst.

"You ought to see the other guys... er, corpses," Dakota quipped as he and the hostages unloaded Dawson out of the boat and then helped Colin from the ruined inflatable toward shore.

While they waited, Marcia approached Dakota and after a brief conversation, the two joined Quint, who was in obvious pain from his broken arm.

"What's up?" he asked, seeing the somber expression on their faces.

"We're not done," Marcia replied.

CHAPTER 55

"What do you mean?" Quint asked. "We've killed most of the pirates, sunk their boats, and rescued the hostages."

"Ethan's still alive," Marcia replied.

"Help me out again, who is Ethan?"

"The head hombre," Dakota answered. "We leave him alive and the chances of them regrouping go way up."

"So, what is it you want to do?" Quint asked.

"Kill him," Marcia replied. "Me and Dakota."

Quint looked up. "I don't think that's such a good idea."

"You're right, it's not," Dakota replied. "But it won't get any easier. Marcia and I want to go back and finish this."

"How? They shot out the engine in our boat."

"We just need the chopper to drop us off before they head back with the first load of hostages. They can pick us up when they return."

"Guys, that's a really bad idea," Quint said.

"Quint... we need to do this. I want your blessing, but..." Marcia said.

He could see she was determined and couldn't argue with the value of taking out the leader. Quint would never have asked them to do it but, if not for his broken arm, would have joined them. Finally, he nodded.

Twenty minutes later, the chopper arrived. After a brief conversation with the pilot, Marcia and Dakota boarded and it lifted off. A minute later, they were across the small bay, where they landed a short distance from the warehouse location Jenny had provided. As soon as the two hopped out, the chopper lifted.

Marcia and Dakota ran in a low crouch for the cover of small bushes a short distance away. They scanned the warehouse area with their night vision glasses. By the time they heard the chopper lifting off to ferry out the first group of hostages, they had confirmed the position of the remaining guards.

The pair slowly approached the building where they split up, each holding a silenced pistol with their heavy weapons slung on their backs. Marcia crept close to the guard on her side of the building and fired two shots, dropping him to the ground. She continued around the building where she rejoined Dakota. "Get yours too?" she asked and saw him nod. "Ready?" Again he nodded and they crept toward the main warehouse entrance.

Dakota tried the door and was pleased to find it unlocked. He eased it open and scanned the interior with his night vision glasses before motioning Marcia to follow. Using Jenny's detailed description of the warehouse, the two split up once again, each heading along opposite sides of the building toward the office.

They met in front of the office door where Dakota slowly turned the knob and cracked the door open wide enough to see that the light inside was on. He removed his night vision glasses with Marcia following suit. "Cover me." He kicked open the door while firing a burst from his M-16 on full automatic.

When he stopped firing, the smell of whiskey filled the room from the shattered bottle that lay on the desk, the brown liquid still seeping across the surface. In a blur, Ethan popped up from behind a mound of boxes and fired his pistol into Dakota's chest until it was empty.

"Surprise! Looks like I win," Ethan said and reached for his unbroken tumbler half-filled with whiskey. As he raised it to take a drink, the movement of another person entering the room caught his attention.

"Surprise again!" Marcia yelled, blasting away with her AA-12 filled with 12 gauge rounds. Ethan was blown backward across the desk, landing with half of his head missing.

After a quick check of the room for more pirates, Marcia ran to Dakota's side. One of the rounds had pierced the fleshy part of his thigh but the rest had struck his Kevlar vest. She watched as his eyes fluttered open.

"Damn, that hurts," he said as she helped him to sit up. "You get him?"

"Yep," Marcia said as she helped him to his feet. "We need to get that wound bandaged, but let's get you to the pickup point first." She stopped to snap a photo with her cell cam so that they could later confirm Ethan's identity. With Dakota leaning on her for support, the two headed back to their drop-off point.

An hour later they heard the sound of the returning chopper. It swooped in and in seconds, the two were aboard and headed back across the bay. After loading up the remaining hostages and team members they were airborne once again while the medic bandaged Dakota's thigh.

When the chopper landed at Camp Lemonnier, they headed for the clinic to check on Dawson, Colin, and Quint. After confirming that they were okay, Marcia and Dakota waited their turn to get patched. Two hours later, they were all eating a hot meal chased down with a gallon of hot coffee.

"Marcia, I owe you a big thanks for saving our butts," Quint said.

"More importantly, don't forget the beer you promised."

"After what you did, I'll buy you a whole case of beer," Colin retorted.

"Make that a whole truck," Dawson chimed in.

"Shoot, I'll buy you your own bar if you want," Quint offered with a laugh.

"Nope, a couple of ice cold Kaliks will do fine, but they have to be at Captain Tony's in Key West," Marcia replied.

"You got it," all three responded in a chorus as a man entered the room to tell them that the plane which Rogers had sent was waiting. Declining the offer to bunk down for a few hours, the team chose to head back to the Sanctuary, planning to catch a few winks along the way. The plane had been airborne only a few minutes when Quint tried to raise Kira on the satphone. Due to the late hour, he wasn't alarmed when there was no answer and stretched back to get some sleep.

CHAPTER 56

"Good job," Nigora complimented Mimi as the Predator made a perfect lift-off to the west in the still night air. Mimi banked out over the ocean, then flew back in low over the island's west beach. Using night vision, she targeted "enemy" coconuts, putting a single round into each. "Here, you try," she said handing the controls over to Nigora, who immediately made an approach imitating Mimi's.

"Good eye. Now take it up to sniper altitude and practice some stealth shots. I'm going to get another cup of coffee. Want some?" Nigora nodded and continued to work back and forth on the beach, simulating high-altitude combat.

Leo pushed away the remains of his breakfast as Mimi entered the kitchen for coffee. "Up already? It's early."

He turned to her with a smile. "You know me, up at the crack of dawn. Where's Kira?"

"She joined us for a few minutes but then went to call her doc."

Leo nodded. "I thought you ladies were going to go fly UCAVs this morning?"

"We've already launched the Predator and Nigora is practicing. What's for dinner?" Mimi asked as she poured two steaming cups of Leo's fresh-ground Columbian coffee.

"I hope to snag a few lobsters to grill. Then I'll come up with sides that'll leave you ladies smiling."

"We'll be watching you with our 'Eye in the Sky' so be careful," Mimi said as she left the room.

Leo headed up the stairs to begin his hike down to the dive site he had chosen just off the east beach. He wanted to get started before it got too hot and his enthusiasm waned.

Under curtain of dark, three military-style inflatables swung around the west end of the island, following the coast as they headed back east. Their silenced engines were scarcely audible at a hundred yards, but they stayed well over a mile offshore in the event the wind might carry the sound or their phosphorescent trail might be spotted.

As the lead boat approached the inlet channel, it throttled back, the two trailing boats following suit. By the time they entered the channel, the boats were at idle, their black hulls scarcely visible in the moonless night. They headed for the north shore of the lagoon where, one at a time, they eased slowly toward the sand beach located to the east.

The man crouched in the front of the first boat leapt out, anchor line in hand, and pulled the inflatable onto the beach. A final burst from the engine grounded the boat firmly. He then set the anchor well up in the sand to ensure the boat would still be there upon their return. The other two boats repeated the procedure, the night silence returning as the engines were switched off.

"We'll remain here until you destroy their communications. Once you have them cut off, we'll start our attack," the leader said. "The jammer may still be working, but I don't trust it." Three men broke off and headed toward the communication tower on the high ridge. The remaining group secured the boats, assembled their gear, and then unloaded a pile of equipment.

A short time later, the three men tasked with disabling the communications tower reached their objective. Using a small C-4 charge attached to the base of the comms tower, they blew it and severed the power and data cables. After signaling the main group, they headed for the airstrip. The others were preparing to head west toward the entrance to the concealed harbor when they spotted a man approaching.

Mimi joined Nigora back in the drone control room. "Make a pass around the entire island with your remaining flight time and then we'll take a break," Mimi said.

"Okeydokey. I not got much ammo anyway," Nigora replied. Maintaining altitude, she banked the drone and flew down the south side of the island.

"Leo just left to take his walk. See if you can sneak up on him using the UCAV thermal imaging. It should be a good exercise."

With it still dark, Nigora used the drone's split-screen display with the low-light night vision displayed on one side and the thermal camera view on the other. The women were relaxed watching the Predator's progress on its routine flight east down the island's south side in search of Leo. It took only a few minutes before she spotted a form below. "I think that him," Nigora said.

She banked the drone and her eyes widened as she spotted three long shapes on the east beach inside the inlet, not far east of Leo. "Look."

"What the...?" Mimi blurted out, pointing to the bottom of the thermal side of the video screen.

The two women sat with eyes riveted to the screen as the drone drew closer. "They're boats," Mimi exclaimed, "and I'm guessing that's not two dozen tourists gathered on the beach."

"Big trouble," Nigora nodded. On the beach below, the Predator's high altitude approach was undetected. "What they do?" she asked.

"I don't know. But the only reason I can think of for them being here is to attack our base. Go tell Kira." Mimi took over the controls as Nigora dashed out and a minute later returned, Kira trailing close behind.

"Are you okay?" Mimi asked.

"I'm afraid that the doctor was right. I have pre-eclampsia. I scheduled an emergency seaplane pick up. They promised to be here in a couple of hours, although given this, maybe not."

Kira studied the display and saw the men gathered beside the inflatables. "Shit! If they scatter, we're screwed. We've got to do something while they're still gathered in a nice neat group."

"But what if they're here peacefully?" Mimi said.

"What if they're not?" Kira asked. "They could be standing right here beside us in less than an hour. You willing to bet on not getting raped or killed? I'm not."

"So what, you want me to just shoot them? I can't do that." Mimi looked at Nigora, who cast her eyes down like she was studying something on her shoe. "Maybe one of us should go and talk to them."

"You want to go do it?" Kira asked.

"No," Mimi replied.

"What if you make a pass and strafe them," Kira said. "Maybe we can scare them into leav—"

"Look, Leo see them!" Nigora shouted as Kira slid into the seat next to Mimi. They could see Leo's form emerge from the tree line and head directly toward the men gathered by the three boats.

"It's light enough now, Mimi, switch to regular video," Kira said.

The three women watched the screen in silence. They could make out Leo and one of the men break from the group and walk to meet him. The man carried a rifle in his hands and as he neared Leo, without breaking step, swung the butt of the weapon, striking Leo in the head and knocking him to the ground. Two more men dragged Leo back to the closest inflatable, tied him up, and then dumped him inside.

"I think that answers the question as to their intentions," Kira said, breaking the silence.

"What do we do?" Mimi asked, her voice shaky with fear.

"We shoot them!" Kira replied. "Look, try to imagine that it's simply a video game."

"I... uh... can't do it, Kira. I just can't."

"Okay, you send an SOS to the guys, I'll fly the Predator." Kira sat down at the controls.

Mimi lifted the receiver on the satphone to call Quint, only to find it dead. She then turned to the single side band radio and found it too was dead. Next, she tried to log onto the Internet and found it down as well. "Damn, we're cut off. They must've already hit the communications tower."

"I'll swing the UCAV around and check it out." Kira swung the drone toward the center of the island and saw the crumpled tower. "Yep, they took down the tower. Now where are they... there!" Kira exclaimed pointing to three dots moving along the ridge away from the tower toward the airstrip. In seconds, they disappeared beneath heavy foliage.

"It would appear that our newly practiced drone combat skills are going to be put to the test. Whether we like it or not, we're about to square off against two dozen troops, who we can assume are well armed and trained or they wouldn't be here. Let's go hunting," Kira said, attempting to sound a lot more optimistic than she felt.

Mimi coughed and then spoke up. "Uh ... that's a great idea, Kira, except the Predator's only got a few rounds of ammo remaining and it's running on fumes."

"Damn." Kira swore.

"Fumes? What you mean?" Nigora asked.

"We're down to fifteen minutes of fuel reserves."

"*Really* big problem. But you sick, maybe you go lie down." Nigora placed her hand on Kira's shoulder.

"I appreciate your concern, Nigora, but if those guys get in here, pre-eclampsia will be the least of my worries. Mimi, break out some weapons."

Mimi headed for the armory returning a few minutes later with an armload. All three women donned combat harnesses outfitted with a knife and extra ammunition clips and then each strapped a pistol to their thighs. Mimi gave each of the women a handheld radio.

"What happen when seaplane come?" Nigora asked.

"Good question," Kira replied.

"How about if Nigora and I go ready the other two UCAVs?" Mimi finished buckling her combat harness. "You can fly the Predator and guard the hangar, keep those guys from getting too close."

"Okay, but are you up for that?" Kira asked Mimi.

"Does it matter? No problem, I've got it." After doing a radio check, Mimi patted Kira on the shoulder and headed for the door, with Nigora trailing close behind.

"Keep in touch and be careful." Kira struggled to mask her pain... and her concern.

CHAPTER 57

Kira was scared. She knew that the other two women needed her to be strong. But she also knew that the chance of three women holding off the two dozen trained men attacking their base were long odds. For a moment she considered just grabbing Mimi and Nigora, jumping in one of the boats, and making a run for it. At least then they might have a decent chance.

But even if she could convince herself to cut and run, leaving the Sanctuary undefended, she was too sick. *Besides, if we try to run and get caught, we certainly would have no chance.*

Being shot and killed was one thing. Being brutally raped and tortured to death was quite another. *Then there's the baby.*

Kira's sweaty palms kept slipping off the controls, making the UCAV fly erratically as she struggled to calm herself. She forced herself to focus on flying the drone and banked in a long circle to keep the camera panned at the airstrip where she expected the three men might appear.

Kira picked up the radio. "Mimi, I spotted those three on the ridge line along the edge of the tree line."

"Can you... deal with them?" Mimi asked.

"Yes, once they're out in the open headed for the hangar." Kira needed to get all three before they could scatter back beneath the cover or make it to the camouflaged hangar where Mimi and Nigora were working. Though she had practiced shooting at inanimate targets with the UCAVs, she had never fired at anything living, much less a human. Yet if she didn't, there was a very good chance they all might end up dead. The lead man was squarely inside the firing reticule as the Predator approached. *Could she do it?*

Mimi's hands were slick with perspiration too as she wiped them on her shirt and readied herself. She didn't have the experience to be in this. *But it's up to me.* Without Kira's words of encouragement, her doubts went unchecked. But when Nigora looked up at her, Mimi smiled, refusing to let her fear show.

The squad leader lay on the ground dressed in combat fatigues, studying the area surrounding the airstrip with his binoculars. At the far end, he spotted a dark shape.

Looks like a building, maybe a hangar as Preston suspected. Switching to thermal vision, he scanned the area and, seeing no threats, rose and motioned for his other two men to advance with him. Though he was uncomfortable out in the open, they didn't have time to work their way around the airstrip through the thick jungle, so he elected to risk a direct advance.

"After we enter the hangar, begin searching to capture one of them so we can extract information on their base facilities and defenses," the squad leader said. They were a third of the way down the airstrip when one of his men stumbled and fell.

"Get up, you clumsy ass, and be quiet." He chastised the man who remained lying still. As the leader moved toward the fallen man, his other man dropped to the ground. Instantly realizing the danger, the squad leader sprinted toward cover at the hangar side of the strip.

He heard the sound of a bullet striking the pavement a few feet away and ran harder. He was almost to the tree line when an enormous blow struck his left upper arm, sending him sprawling a few feet from the cover of the brush, his weapon falling to the pavement behind him.

Blood poured from a wide gash in his arm where a huge chunk of meat was missing. Fortunately, the massive .50 caliber slug had penetrated only the fleshy part of his left arm, or he would have joined his two comrades lying back in the middle of the airstrip.

He still wasn't sure who was shooting at him but he did know one thing—to remain lying there was certain death. Fighting the excruciating pain, he pushed himself back to his feet. With his left arm hanging limp at his side, he left his weapon behind and sought the cover of the dense foliage beside what now was clearly a hangar.

"We don't have time to completely fuel the UCAVs. We'll just get enough in them to buy us an hour or so of flight time." Mimi helped Nigora slide a fuel drum into place and, once they had the pump transferring fuel, began loading ordnance. They were just finishing prepping the second UCAV when they heard Kira's voice on the radio.

"Damn! Mimi, I took two down and I'm pretty sure I hit the third. But before I could make another pass, he made it to cover in the trees. Sorry."

"Hey, at least you got two and a half," Mimi replied.

Kira cast her eyes down to check on her fuel. "Crap, I'm nearly out of fuel. The Hawk and Reaper about ready?"

"Just finishing."

"I'll have to land the Predator before it crashes," Kira said.

"Kill the engine and glide in. No point drawing attention," Mimi said. "We'll taxi it into the hangar once the Hawk is clear. I'm opening the main hangar door so we can have the Hawk ready for you to command. Let me know when the Predator is on the ground. We'll launch the Reaper last."

"Can do," Kira replied. She watched the monitor screen and, once the drone was lined up on the airstrip, cut the engine. She waited until she was past the bodies on the strip before gliding in for a landing.

Mimi punched a mushroom-shaped button and the hangar door began to open. Using the handheld control, she started the drone's engine. She waited with the pistol held ready in her hand and peeked out to check for threats. As soon as she had the doors opened far enough to give her sufficient clearance, Mimi taxied the Hawk out the door, with Nigora following behind.

"Predator's on the ground, Mimi," Kira's voice burst over the radio.

"Roger," Mimi replied in a low voice. "The Hawk's in position. It's yours."

In response, Kira rotated the nozzles while applying full thrust and the Hawk lifted from the strip, then gained forward speed. In seconds, it was out of sight.

Mimi taxied the Reaper out and radioed when it was in position. Kira placed the Hawk into a long circle pattern before engaging the autopilot. She then slid over to the Reaper console and took control of it. A minute later, it was airborne as well.

Glancing nervously about for any sign of the third man that Kira had wounded, Nigora walked a hundred feet toward the Predator to get in range for the low-power handheld remote to assume command of the UCAV. Firing up its engine, she guided it inside the hangar and a minute later punched the button to close the hangar doors.

"Looks like maybe we got lucky," Mimi said, placing her pistol back in her holster and buttoning the flap.

"Go down and help Kira fly the drones. I'll pre-flight the Predator, just in case." Nigora nodded and headed below.

The hangar doors were nearly closed when Mimi thought she saw movement, but she saw nothing when she stopped to look. *I'm getting the jitters.*

She went to the back of the hangar and, using the pallet jack, moved a fuel drum beside the UCAV. She opened the drum and connected a pump to begin fueling the plane. While it was fueling, she unpacked a full belt of .50 caliber ammunition and readied it to load. When the UCAV tank was full of fuel, she switched off the pump.

Draping the belt of ammo over her shoulder, she positioned the ladder and climbed up to load the cannon. With the belt in place, she closed and latched the gun compartment.

Two steps from the floor, her foot was jerked off the ladder and before she could steady herself, she fell backward. Her hands shot out to break her fall as she twisted her body. But instead of concrete, she fell against the black uniform of a large man, knocking both of them to the ground. Her hand landed on his wet left sleeve and the man yelled out in pain.

Mimi struggled back to her feet and took a step back toward the door down to the Sanctuary when his arm caught her foot and tripped her again. Before she could get back up, he threw himself on top of her and snaked his right arm around her neck.

She felt his grip tighten, only his wounded left arm keeping him from snapping her neck. With both hands, she grabbed his heavily muscled arm and pulled with all her strength to break his grip, but he was far too strong. Already her vision was narrowing.

Mimi forced away the panic. She felt for the butt of the knife on her combat harness and snatched it from its sheath. With her remaining strength, she plunged it into the man's right thigh. When his grip eased for an instant, she broke away, leaving the knife stuck in his leg.

As Mimi ran away across the hangar, he pulled the knife from his thigh and threw it. Her scream pierced the air when the knife found her upper left arm. She ducked behind an empty fuel drum, her shaking legs barely able to support her. Leaning to one side, she vomited twice, then wiped her mouth on the sleeve of her bloodied shirt. Her whole body ached and her mouth was so dry she could barely swallow as she steeled herself, no time to deal with the knife.

Her hands frantically searched for her pistol and her fingers found it, unclipped the flap, and drew it in one motion. She peeked around the barrel and saw the man still lay bleeding where she had stabbed him. He reached for his own pistol at that same instant he saw her.

Mimi swung her gun up and took aim at his torso even as she saw his pistol clear its holster. Having her safety already off bought her the instant she needed and she pulled the trigger, sending a round into his chest. The man fell backwards as his own gun went off, firing a round which struck the concrete inches from her face, showering her with fragments.

She cleared the dust from her eyes with the back of her hand, finding it wet from cuts on her face. She searched for the man, afraid that he might be wearing body armor, and when she spotted him still lying a few feet away, she fired once again.

The second round struck his right arm and the third his groin, but the next two hit him square in the face, ending the conflict. She dropped the pistol to clatter on the concrete floor of the hangar as Mimi wrapped her right hand around the knife. With a grunt, she pulled it from her left arm and tossed it on the floor then lay there, catching her breath. Finally, she summoned her reserves and slowly pulled herself up by the ladder.

"Mimi, you okay? Mimi?"

She heard Kira's voice on her radio and found it lying beside the drone. "I just got to meet your third bad guy. You did wing him but he was still very much alive. But now, not so much."

"But are you okay?"

"He put a knife through my left arm, hurts like a bitch. Did Nigora make it back?"

"Yeah, she's here flying the Reaper."

"I'm going to finish readying the Predator, then head back to control."

"You okay to do that?"

"I'll manage." Mimi clipped the radio back on her belt and went back to finish. A few minutes later, she came walking into the UCAV control center.

Kira was shocked to see Mimi's arm wound and bloodied face. "You look really bad."

"You should see the other guy." Mimi gave a thin laugh. "A round hit the floor in front of me. Luckily, I got sprayed with concrete fragments not lead."

"I fix arm." Nigora tried to lead Mimi toward the team's small clinic.

"No, you keep flying the Reaper. I'll take care of it." Nigora nodded and eased back into the seat alongside Kira.

"We reconned the island," Kira told Mimi. "They split into two groups. The larger group, maybe a dozen, is headed for the harbor entrance. A smaller group is heading for the ridge. I didn't engage them. Figured we might pick off a few stragglers but we'd play hell getting the rest if they scattered."

"Good job," Mimi said and headed off to doctor herself. She wiped the wicked-looking knife wound in her arm with an alcohol-saturated gauze pad and bandaged it before going to work on her face. She quickly cleaned her facial wounds and slapped on several small bandages. A minute later, she rejoined the other women in the UCAV control center.

Kira moved the Hawk into position above the main group to the east. "Nigora, position the Reaper over the group headed for the ridge."

"You want I launch?" Nigora asked.

"We'll wait a bit. Maybe they'll form up tighter and provide a better target for one of the Reaper's missiles," Kira replied.

"I'm afraid you don't have much longer. If they make it to the hangar, we could end up fighting them inside the Sanctuary," Mimi said, the tension thick in her voice.

"I'm going after my group. Maybe the sound of their return fire will draw Nigora's group together to discuss a response. If so, you can nail them."

The Hawk flew stable in the calm air as she trained the firing reticule on the rear-most targets. Kira squeezed off a burst from the Hawk's .30 caliber gun and dropped four men instantly.

"Eight," she called out, referring to the number of remaining enemies. Before the rest of the group could react, she fired again. "Seven—six," she yelled in quick succession. "Damn! My luck ran out," she said as the six remaining forms below scattered and began returning fire at the Hawk even as Kira banked the UCAV tightly and moved away. As soon as Kira's men began returning fire, the men in Nigora's main group drew together.

"Looks like your strategy is working," Mimi yelled.

"Fire now!" Kira yelled. Nigora fired a missile from the Reaper.

"Cha-ching," Kira yelled as the missile hit. "I count six still standing," she said as she swooped in with the Hawk and lined up the sighting reticule, firing three times in succession. "Five left," she said as return fire forced her to pull away.

"We got them," Nigora squealed.

"We got some but we're still outnumbered nearly four to one," Kira replied.

"My guys go in woods. I no can see," Nigora said.

"I'm betting they fall back to their boats," Kira replied. "If so, it's going to take a while. Nigora, double-team my guys."

"What means double-team?"

"Both of us shoot at the same bad guys."

"I coming." Nigora flew the Reaper to join Kira's Global Hawk.

"I see one." Nigora banked the Reaper hard to line up a shot. Kira spotted ground fire and began sweeping her cannon over the area.

"Crap, I miss," Nigora yelled.

"Uh-oh," Mimi said as an explosion marked the access door beside the main hangar door being blown. "Some of them are about to be in the hangar and then down here with us. We'll have to go face them," she said hesitantly.

"Mimi, you can't go. Those guys are trained mercenaries," Kira replied.

"I don't see where we have a lot of choice. Either we wait for them to join us here or we try to head them off. And my going makes a lot more sense, with you being sick and pregnant." Kira didn't argue.

"I place Reaper in auto-orbit, like Lt. Lewis teach us. You and me, we go together, no?"

"Nigora, I don't know about that," Mimi said, with genuine concern.

"Uzbek women, we tough," Nigora said and followed Mimi to the armory. They loaded up with rifles and a couple of flash-bang grenades. Mimi was thankful for Dawson's obsession with having a wide array of heavy-duty weaponry and his insistence on training.

"You as scared as me?" Mimi asked Nigora.

"No," Nigora replied, "more." The two women headed for the stairwell leading to the hangar above. Mimi stopped to flip the breaker for the stairwell lights. They eased up the stairs to the first landing, carefully peeked around the corner and, seeing nothing, sat down on the steps to wait.

CHAPTER 58

While Mimi and Nigora lay in wait for the men to attack from above, Kira circled the Reaper over the hangar area in case the two women needed her to provide cover. She then maneuvered the Hawk to search for the remaining men on the beach. As she feared, there was no sign of them.

She made a quick swing to the west in hopes that they might have continued toward the concealed harbor entrance. Seeing nothing, she swung the drone around and headed it back toward their inflatable boats on the beach.

As she approached the boats, she saw three figures working along the tree line at the top of the beach, headed toward the boats. "Bingo," she said and put the Hawk in a climb. She would give them time to get to the boats, where it would be easier to target them.

The men broke cover and ran down to the middle boat, leaving Leo still inside the inflatable to the left. One of the men jumped in and fired up the engine as the other two pushed the boat off the beach.

Kira unsafed her last missile, waiting patiently for the men to board the inflatable. Once they had the boat running, it would be difficult to target them as they bobbed and weaved in the choppy seas outside the inlet. As soon as they had moved away from Leo, she swung the Hawk into position, willing the target reticule to move faster. When the missile's heat sensor was locked on to the outboard's heat signature, she fired and the missile leapt away.

The driver was still backing off the beach, about to swing the bow around when he spotted the incoming missile. He yelled a warning and the two men in front dove overboard hoping to escape the missile's impact. The driver threw the engine into forward and slammed the throttles to the stops in a desperate move to escape. But the incoming missile was locked onto the hot engine and moving too fast. It struck, blowing the engine off the boat, instantly killing the driver. The wreckage of the boat continued moving forward back onto the beach, where the remaining tubes deflated as the boat burned.

"All right!" Kira yelled. "Ooops, spoke too soon," she muttered through clenched teeth as she saw two men climb from the water into the farthest boat. *At least they didn't pick the one with Leo lying inside.*

Once again she bided her time, giving them time to get into the second boat and off the beach. *Looks like I'm about to get a second shot.*

When the men were once again clear of the beach, Kira sent the Hawk into a dive, aiming at the driver and engine. Flipping off the safety as soon as the reticule was on target, she pressed the trigger of the .30 caliber cannon and held it down as she swooped over.

Banking tightly, she saw that the boat had moved far enough back for the bullets to strike between the two men, chewing up the inflatable's floor but injuring neither. Cursing, she swung tightly around while the boat picked up speed. Again she sighted on the two men and opened up. A stream of bullets walked across the bow and struck the man in front, sending him sprawling over the side. The boat's starboard side was sagging noticeably and it no longer seemed to be gaining speed.

Glancing down, her stomach knotted as she noticed she'd forgotten to ease off the trigger in the excitement. *Damn! I'm empty.*

Kira glanced at the monitor and saw no activity outside of the hangar. *The Reaper's not doing anybody much good there.* She put the Hawk into a circle and switched it to autopilot. She then banked the Reaper toward the inflatable. She wasn't sure exactly how many rounds the Reaper had left but knew it couldn't be many.

What she did know was that it was getting dangerously low on fuel. Whatever she was going to do, she would have to do quickly.

The boat had managed to gain speed by the time Kira got the Reaper into position, and was already headed down the inlet toward the open ocean. She brought the Reaper down low and slowed, trying to match the speed of the boat. As the reticule was lined up on the driver, she held her breath and slowly squeezed the trigger twice. Just as she fired, the boat made it out of the inlet and struck a three foot wave, forcing it to lurch to one side.

Missed, she swore to herself as two more times she lined up the reticule and two more times missed the erratic target.

The boat was now through the steeper waves near the beach and was running smoothly over the offshore swell, the remaining air chambers providing all the buoyancy needed for the light load it now carried. Kira closed in tighter and lined up again, praying beneath her breath as she pulled the trigger again.

Damn! She missed the driver but hit the engine, as evidenced by a trail of black smoke. Immediately, she lined up one more time and fired again. The driver fell forward as the boat suddenly swung into a tight turn. She saw he was injured but still alive, struggling to sit back up and gain control.

Kira lined up again and pulled the trigger as soon as the reticule was on the driver. Nothing. A voice in the console announced the gun was now empty. She watched helplessly as the boat continued away, the wounded driver back in control.

What do I do now? I sure can't let them escape with firsthand knowledge of our base. Kira's mind raced and then she knew what she had to do—she would sacrifice a UCAV in a kamikaze attempt to take out the boat and driver.

She swung the Reaper up to gain altitude. A few seconds later, she brought the nose back down and pushed the throttles to full power. The drone gained speed and she kept it aimed directly at the plume of thick black smoke trail, preparing to crash into the boat.

As the Reaper plunged down, she could see the wounded driver seated in front of the dying engine. Seconds away from impact, a bright orange flash marked the explosion of the boat's fuel tank erupting below.

Kira pulled up on the controls as she banked away from the cloud of orange flames, desperately trying to avoid needlessly sacrificing the Reaper. The UCAV's nose slowly began to ease up as it approached the heavy swells in the ocean below, but as spray covered the camera lens, it appeared she was too late. Inches away from smashing into the ocean, the Reaper begin to climb.

Kira let out a long sigh and flew the drone back over the burning wreckage. Through the salt-covered lens, she could barely make out the driver floating face down in the midst of the debris field beside the sinking boat. "And then there were none," Kira spoke softly. "Glad I didn't have to sacrifice the Reaper, though it would have been better than letting them get away." She turned the drone back towards the strip, managing to land it before she was completely out of fuel.

She then moved to the Hawk console to find the Hawk's fuel tank nearing empty, too. *Must have taken a hit in one of the wing tanks.* She took it out of autopilot and had it lined up for a landing when the low fuel alarm sounded and its engines stalled.

Holding the controls in a death grip, she kept the Hawk lined up and a moment later had it on the ground. She took a deep breath and reached for the radio. "Nigora, Mimi," she called, but there was no answer.

CHAPTER 59

When Quint awoke, they were still in the air, halfway back to Miami. He glanced up and saw Colin trying to reach Kira on the satphone "No answer at the Sanctuary?" Quint asked.

"Nope. Yeah, I've tried several times since we took off, but no banana. Quint, I think it means trouble."

"I'm afraid you're right. I'll have another plane ready for us as soon as we land." A minute later, he had Rogers on the phone. "We've been trying to raise our base for hours with no luck. I think we have a problem. We need a ride waiting to take us back to the Sanctuary when we land."

"You want the Osprey again?"

"If you can swing it."

"Hang on, let me check," Rogers said and placed a call on his desk phone. A few seconds later, he was back on his cell. "They've got one in Okeechobee for some sort of training exercise. I'll have it in Miami and waiting when you land."

"Great. Can you also arrange to have somebody deal with the hostages? They are scheduled to leave tomorrow. Some were in need of medical care... and then... there's Jamal."

"Who?"

"One of the pirates, but really only a boy."

"You brought one of the pirates with you? Have you lost your mind?"

"Had to."

"Last time it was Nigora. This time it's... who did you say?"

"Jamal—he's only a child."

"True, but he's not a puppy. You can't keep him."

"We need to help him."

Rogers paused and took a deep breath. "Quint, you can't bring the rest of the world back to the U.S. with you. You're making a habit out of this and it needs to stop."

"The boy needs a break. He can provide you with some useful information." Quint hung up before Rogers could comment. Quint briefed the rest of the team and they immediately began taking inventory of their remaining equipment.

"We're low on ammo but we've got plenty of weapons. I wish we could get in touch with Kira for an update so we'd know what we're facing when we arrive," Dawson said with a worried look.

CHAPTER 60

Nigora and Mimi sat listening to the sound of the men breaking through the hangar door above. "I wish I could stop shaking," Mimi whispered.

"Me too, but my father, he brave man. He say focus on what must do next, not fear," Nigora said and then fell silent.

"We have to make the most while we have the advantage of surprise," Mimi whispered and went on to share her thoughts with Nigora. Mimi saw the light blink on her radio with Kira calling, but couldn't risk breaking their silence

The sound of AK-47 automatic weapons fire from above announced that the door above was being breached. The two women rose to their feet and stood ready.

Mimi heard them kick open the door and spray bullets through the doorway into the darkened stairwell.

"Lights," a man whispered before the beam of a flashlight waved back and forth down the stairwell.

When the men began descending, Mimi nodded to Nigora, pulled the pin on a flash-bang grenade, and tossed it around the corner of the landing.

The sound of it striking the metal stairs triggered a burst of gunfire from above, nearly striking Mimi as the two women scrambled back down the stairs. She raised her M4A1 and pressed the trigger just before they rounded the door at the foot of the stairs. There the two women waited with their eyes closed, mouths open, and hands over their ears.

They heard one of the men start to yell, "Grena..." but before he could get the entire word out, the stairway turned white as the flash bang erupted with a deafening explosion.

Both women switched on the flashlights attached to their weapons and ran back up the stairs with the explosion still dissipating, raking the area in front of them with bullets as they went. Mimi fired a burst at a figure that, though not moving, might not be dead and then joined Nigora in firing at two more men standing disoriented at the top of the stairs, blood pouring out of their ears from the force of the grenade. The women kept firing until their guns were empty and they were certain that the bloody mess lying on the top landing would do them no harm.

The women paused to reload their weapons and eased through the door into the hangar but saw no movement. Mimi inspected the outer door and found the broken deadbolt where the door was breached. She found a length of chain and ran one end through the door handle several times before wrapping the remaining chain around the leg of a nearby workbench to secure the door.

The radio's LED blinked on Mimi's belt. When she slid it out of the nylon holder and turned up the volume, she heard Kira's voice. "... you okay?"

Mimi keyed the radio to reply. "Uh... actually, I think we are."

"I kept calling and couldn't get you. I thought you were dead," Kira replied with obvious relief. "You headed back?"

"Yep," Mimi replied wearily. Still shaking from the adrenaline rush and her relief at having kept out the invaders, she entered the UCAV control room with Nigora. She briefed Kira on what had happened, Nigora talking over her in the process.

"You guys did great!" Kira hugged Mimi and then started to do the same to Nigora when a man's voice boomed out from behind.

"Yes, it was most impressive." The women whirled around to find Preston standing in the doorway at the far side of the room.

CHAPTER 61

"Preston! What are you doing here? You're a little late if you came to save us," Mimi said.

Preston wore an odd smile on his face as he stepped inside.

A second man, his automatic rifle raised before him, followed close behind and spoke next. "But it would have been even more impressive if it hadn't simply been a diversion. Ladies, please step back and face the wall."

"What... what do you mean? Preston, stop him," Mimi said, staring confused at the man holding the rifle aimed at them.

"Preston, stop him," the man said in a high voice, mocking Mimi. "That's rich. I'm afraid Preston will be helping, not stopping me," he added with a laugh as he jabbed her in the chest with the barrel of his gun, forcing her against the wall with the other two women.

"I loved you," Mimi said as tears filled her eyes. "And I thought you cared for me too." Preston looked back at her, his face a cold mask of indifference.

"Lady, I'm afraid you're what we call collateral damage," the other man said with a laugh.

"Is that true, Preston? I'm collateral damage? That's what I am?" Mimi sobbed.

"We do what we have to do," Preston replied in a low voice, devoid of expression or the slightest hint of regret. Mimi shook her head and then vomited into a trash can.

"Nice place you have here," he said. "I see no reason why it couldn't serve our needs equally well, after we... uh... finish dealing with you and the rest of your team."

"How did you get in here?" Kira asked.

"That little side door at ground level beside the main harbor entrance. How else?" the second man asked. "The hangar entrance was reserved for our diversion. But enough chitchat."

"Look, I'm really sick. If I don't get to a hospital right away, I could die. There's a seaplane headed here right now to pick me up and—" Kira stopped at the muted sound of a distant explosion that rocked the Sanctuary. A moment later, Preston's radio erupted with someone calling him. He stepped into the next room and after a brief conversation returned.

"Uh... that was your ride. Our boys got a little trigger happy and one of them, an ex-sniper as it were, managed to nail the pilot. Quite a mess on the side of the ridge, I'm told. So you'll be staying here. But don't worry, we'll take good care of you." Preston laughed, seemingly enjoying Mimi's look of pain at his betrayal.

CHAPTER 62

"Sanctuary, this is Quint. You copy?" Kira glanced at her VHF radio lying on the console and heard Quint call once more.

"Do as I say or I'll put a bullet clean through your tummy," Preston said to Kira. "Tell him everything is hunky-dory and you have everything under control. You're busy now but you'll fill him in when he gets down here." Kira hesitated while staring at the gun trained on her.

"If you value your life and that of your baby..." He emphasized his point by poking her in the stomach with the gun barrel. She nodded and snatched the radio off the desk.

"Quint, this is Kira. Go ahead."

"Why are all the UCAVs out of the hangar?"

"Uh... we've been doing practice flights."

"I just wond—what the hell is that?" Quint said, interrupting himself as he spotted the third inflatable and the remains of another.

"What?" she asked.

"Those inflatables," Quint replied. "One is burning and another appears to be beached with a man lying in it. And there are bodies lying on the airstrip and more on the beach beside the inflatables."

"Well, that's why we've been a little too busy to get the UCAVs back in the hangar. I'm down in control and can fill you in when you get down here," she replied and slammed the radio into the Preston's waiting hand.

"Excellent! If I had my box of gold stars, I'd put one right on your forehead."

A few minutes later, Quint and the rest of the team landed. With Dakota helping Colin, Quint led the way toward the hangar while Dawson remained on the airstrip examining the drones. Though he was limping, his leg wounds appeared to be more painful than serious.

The lock had been shot out on the hangar side door. With the handle chained to a workbench, it took a minute to break in.

Quint entered the stairwell to find the remains of a couple of men who had been shot repeatedly. "It looks like the aftermath of World War III," he said upon entering the control room. "What's the—" He stopped as he saw a man standing on the far side of the room, an automatic rifle held ready.

"Welcome, we've been waiting for you," the man said.

Quint turned to dive behind the console when the man fired a burst from the rifle. "Not a good idea. If I miss you, I'll shoot the ladies." Confident the man wasn't bluffing, Quint stopped in midstride and remained with the rest of his team.

Quint spotted Mimi's bloody arm, filthy clothes, and bandaged face. "No offense, Mimi, but you look like shit."

Mimi rolled her eyes, "Yeah, I've been getting that a lot lately. Of course, you don't look so hot, either," she said, nodding at his arm in the sling. Quint peppered her with questions, as she filled him in on the situation.

When she was finally finished, Quint whistled, "You did one hell of a job."

"Yes, but not quite good enough," Preston said, reappearing from the next room. "Good of you to join us. Please have a seat against the wall where we can keep an eye on you."

"Bastard!" Quint spat.

"Preston has been called worse. Just ask Willy. Oh, that's right, he's no longer with us." Preston chuckled. "I see everyone's here except for Dawson. Where might he be?"

"Last time I saw him, he was drinking tequila down in Matamoros," Quint replied, earning him a whack on the head with the other man's AK-47.

CHAPTER 63

Dawson knew there was trouble when he heard automatic weapons fire. Since the team had taken all the weapons down to the Sanctuary, Dawson was unarmed. Deciding that following the stairs down the same path would prove unwise, he limped out of the hangar to climb down and approach the Sanctuary through the harbor area.

He arrived outside of the main harbor entrance and saw another black inflatable tied to the concrete dock outside. Before he could open the small side door, he heard a boat engine. Coming down the inlet were two more black inflatables filled with more men. In a couple of minutes they would be close enough to see him.

"Uh-oh," he muttered.

Dawson slipped through the side door into the harbor area. At least for the moment, it appeared he was alone. He wracked his brain to develop a plan and an idea began to form. He made his way to the dive locker and grabbed a set of gear along with mask, fins, and a light. He checked the wounds on his aching leg and found them seeping blood but otherwise okay. Before he could disconnect one of the filled tanks from the air bank, he heard footsteps on the metal stairs above.

Out of time, he grabbed a nearby tank that had not yet been refilled and scampered across the dock, where he slid into the water. He slipped the mask in place, took a deep breath, and sank below the surface just as two men stepped from the stairwell.

With his light off, the waters of the darkened harbor concealed him. Ignoring the throbbing from the cold water on his wounds, he connected the regulator to the tank by feel. His lungs were burning and he was fighting the urge to burst from the water to get a breath of air when he cracked the tank valve and air flowed from the regulator. He thrust it into his mouth and, while inhaling deeply, slid the tank into the buoyancy compensator and slung it over his back.

After a few seconds, his breathing had returned to normal and his eyes were adjusted to the dim light. Ahead of him, he noticed the dark opening he had spotted last time he dove in the harbor. While he was still trying to decide what to do, the main harbor doors swung open. The two inflatables he had spotted earlier idled in, docking a few feet away.

A quick glance at the air gauge showed he had less than seven hundred pounds remaining. *Not much, but it's probably all I'll live long enough to need.* Edging along the wall, he worked his way to a spot near the bow of the closest inflatable where his bubbles could rise without being seen.

Cautiously, he rose between the boat and the dock, hoping to get a count on how many men there were. He eased his head above water where he immediately heard shouting and the sound of gunfire. Bullets began striking the water around him. He had been spotted; it was time to run.

He headed toward the dark opening at the end of the dock, hoping it might offer refuge. He swam hard along the base of the dock, hugging the bottom.

The four-foot-wide recess led to a narrow tunnel which continued on into the inky black. He rose to the surface and found an air pocket where he could remove the regulator and breathe. The pain in his leg had eased and he was relieved that the wounds were not bleeding again.

He could still see the dim light of the harbor in the distance and hear voices as they continued searching for him. He switched on his light and continued down the passage, keeping on the surface to conserve air. He rounded a bend and saw that the ceiling sloped down toward the water's surface. *Great!*

Checking his air he found he was down to five hundred pounds.

With his regulator back in his mouth, he sank to the bottom. Ahead, the ceiling continued to slant down further, narrowing the tunnel. Continuing forward, the stone scraped against his stomach and then his back and then both. He could barely move as the tunnel opening grew tighter and his tank pressed him hard against the rock floor. If the tunnel got much smaller, it would be a dead end—literally.

He swung his light in front of his mask and saw that the tunnel remained about the same size as it disappeared straight ahead into the blackness. Calmly, he continued working his way forward, taking shallow breaths and sucking in his stomach and chest when he heard a "clank" and could no longer move forward.

Deciding to ease back and slide to one side, he came to the sick realization that the bottom of his tank had popped into a slight indentation in the cave roof. He was unable to move forward or backward. He was stuck—wedged tightly between the cave ceiling and floor. Alone, nearly out of air, deep inside a cave that none of the team realized even existed—there would be no rescue party.

CHAPTER 64

Quint saw a man approach Preston and whisper. Preston nodded and then the man left. "It would appear that someone, my guess is Dawson, is still roaming around like a loose cannon. I apologize for the brief intermission while we search for and either capture or kill him."

"He's your brother," Quint said.

Preston laughed. "And you think that's important because...?" Quint stared back without speaking as Mimi was seized with another bout of nausea.

"What do you want?"

"Me? Money, what else? But Syndy, now she wants your entire team dead. Except for you and Dawson, that is. She plans to finish what she started on her yacht before your lady-friend there"—he pointed his gun at Marcia—"interrupted her. I intend to honor Syndy's wishes."

"Well, you better hope she finishes with me before I get my hands on you," Quint said in a steely voice. Preston laughed and then, without pause, pulled the trigger and shot Nigora four times in the chest. The team stood open-mouthed as she slumped to the floor, eyes still open. "Best not to piss Preston off," Preston added and turned casually away as a second man stood with his gun ready and aimed at the team.

Dawson had no idea where the passage before him led. One thing was clear—the opening before him was too small to make it through with his tank on.

He swept aside a layer of loose rock and pieces of what looked like broken pottery. But it did little to open the small space. With no other choice, he worked his hand beneath his chest, found the harness release buckles, and unstrapped his tank.

With his left knee and fin pressed against the cave wall, he reached over his left shoulder to grab the tank valve. Grunting from the effort, he slid the tank to his left while inching his body to the right. He bit down hard on the regulator's mouthpiece, partly from the pain as he scraped chunks of skin from his chest and right shoulder, and partly from the pain from the wounds in his leg. With a final violent jerk, the tank popped free.

He took a deep breath. Resistance signaled that the tank was nearly empty. Dropping the regulator, he worked the tank around until the bottom was in front and the valve by his face. With the mouthpiece stuffed back between his teeth, he exhaled while fingering the purge valve to clear the second stage and greedily sucked in a lungful of air. He longed to just lie there for a minute while taking deep breaths to give his heart rate the chance to slow. But he knew there was not enough time... or more precisely, enough air.

Despite his racing pulse, he forced himself to breathe slowly, desperate to stretch his remaining air.

After a few more feet, the tunnel gradually widened. The choke point was caused by the partial collapse of the rock ceiling. He slid the tank back on, securing the harness straps as he swam.

The tunnel floor appeared worn smooth. Perhaps it had once been above water and occupied by humans. Some two hundred feet later he came to a fork. Lacking the slightest idea which was the right direction, he was certain he would not live long enough to explore both.

With little else to go on, he chose the one with the worn floor and began kicking, ignoring his aching leg. As he raced toward the bend ahead, a glance at his air gauge showed the needle buried on empty.

Frantically, he swung the beam of his light back and forth but could see nothing but rock walls extending on to another bend in the distance—one he wasn't sure he could reach. Kicking with all his might, he continued. It was nearly impossible to breathe now; only a few lungfuls of air remained in the tank. He fought the sense of panic at the sensation of being smothered.

Halfway to the bend, able only to draw half breaths from the drained tank, the image of his long-dead wife and daughter appeared before him. Suddenly, things didn't seem so bad; he would be joining them shortly. A few bubbles escaped from the corners of his mouth as a smile broke the seal with his regulator mouthpiece. A moment later, he released the regulator and it floated away.

Still, Dawson continued kicking but as he neared the bend, he was now swimming to his family. They were quite close now. He could almost touch them. But as he approached they continued to ease away. He kicked harder, but still they pulled farther from him.

Darling, don't leave! Baby, I'm right here! Don't go!

"Look, you've got me and will probably soon have Dawson. At least let the women go—the ones still alive," Quint said in a steely voice.

Preston grinned. "And pray tell, why would I want to do that?"

"They've done nothing to Syndy. She'll never know."

"Sure, that is until she gets her hands on you and you start blabbing."

"No, I won't," Quint said.

"Quint, please quit," Preston said with a chuckle. "That's not going to happen so you can stop with the groveling."

"So can I assume that you're not really dying from cancer as you claimed?"

"You really have to ask?"

CHAPTER 65

Dawson was disoriented. He felt weight on his chest and his own voice echoing in his ears. Snatching off his mask, he realized that he was halfway out of the water and... breathing in the pitch black.

His felt his dive light trapped under him, a dull glow illuminating the lanyard still wrapped tightly around his right wrist.

Swinging the beam in an arc, he could see he was lying on a rock slope in a few inches of water. After popping the straps loose, he rolled the empty tank off his back and climbed to his knees while sucking great gulps of air. As his head cleared, he saw that just beyond the last bend the tunnel dead-ended into a larger cave. He had swum its length along the bottom, becoming beached on the far side as the bottom rose above the water.

"Thank you, Lord," he repeated several times. The cave was maybe a hundred feet in diameter and nearly as high. Along the ledges on the far side sat a number of clay animal figures and several pots. Above them, the wall was covered with crude paintings of animals, trees, and human figures.

Awestruck, Dawson admired the ancient art and artifacts before finally returning to reality—he was stuck in a cave somewhere beneath the Sanctuary.

He stacked his fins beside his mask and tank and headed for the far end, where the floor seemed more worn. As he neared the far side, he found an opening concealed behind a large rock jutting out from his left.

He entered the opening and saw the worn floor had steps cut into it. Twice he slipped on the steep, slippery stairs, skinning both knees in the process and causing one of his leg wounds to begin seeping blood. A hundred yards farther was a second cave festooned with more wall art. But what drew his attention from the smooth cave walls was a mound of rubble on the far side, at the top of which he saw a shadowy spot. *An opening?*

Scrambling up the mound, he shone his light into the large room beyond, filled with stacked crates. He eased through the opening, where he dropped onto one of the stacks and climbed down onto the rock floor. As he swung the beam around he noticed that the crates were stenciled with German writing. Below the lettering was a symbol—an eagle with spread wings atop a swastika marking the property of the Third Reich.

It was the same insignia he had seen on the scrap of wood he had found on the harbor bottom after he'd first arrived on the island. Dawson shivered, uncertain if it was from the cold or the sight of what lay before him.

He walked through a shallow pool of salt water and unlatched one of the crates, sucking in his breath as the light shone on a row of bright gold ingots. He examined one and found the same eagle-swastika symbol imprinted on its face. A long row of identical crates were stacked three high. "Damn! There must be hundreds of these bars, maybe thousands," he muttered in a low voice.

Continuing past the crates of gold bars, he found stores of German World War II weapons, ammunition, rations, and uniforms. Shaking from the cold air, he draped a uniform coat over his shoulders and then opened one of the rations. He went through three more, finding that none were still edible. He was hungry and it would have been good to get something in his stomach, but the rations were far too old. He managed to find a tin of fresh water which appeared to be potable and opened it with a bayonet.

After draining it, he removed the bandages that had not already fallen off while he was in the water. He found a shirt in one of the crates and tore off strips to wrap his leg. Once he was warm and had regained his strength, he explored the room.

On the far side, he spotted a wooden door and cautiously approached. He could see what appeared to be a thin line of white plaster between the edges of the door and the frame.

The door barely moved when he pulled on the handle. Returning to the pile of equipment crates, he found a bayonet which he worked down the seam, tapping on the butt with one of the gold ingots. *Hell of a hammer.*

After working around the entire door, he set down his "hammer" and pulled on the handle once again. He could feel it flex as he worked the door back and forth. Finally, he braced his feet and gave it all he had, and the door popped open. There behind the door was— nothing, a blank wall.

Dawson tapped on it with his knuckles. It sounded like either more plaster or maybe drywall. Using the bayonet, he cut a six-inch square in the middle. A final tap with the ingot and the piece popped out. He shown his light through it and realized he was looking into the Sanctuary's warehouse.

The Germans must've plastered over the door to keep it hidden. Without realizing it was even here, the Russians had then later added the wallboard over it as part of the warehouse construction.

For the next few minutes, he worked to cut a hole large enough to fit through. After stepping through the opening, he looked back to see the rectangular dark stain he had spotted earlier on the warehouse wall.

Well, that solves one mystery. I guess that was mold from the cave's moisture growing over the old opening. He went back to the Nazis' stash, where he collected some guns and loaded several magazines with bullets. Armed and with a bag full of spare ammunition, he returned to the warehouse, where he made his way toward the door on the far side.

Dawson eased the door open and saw that it led to the harbor. He could hear the muffled sound of someone speaking outside. Two men in black combat fatigues were carrying AK-47s on the dock beside the harbor.

Wincing from the pain in his leg, he eased the door closed. He slung the bag of loaded magazines over one shoulder and the German machine gun over the other. He wasn't exactly certain how it worked and hoped he had the safety off. He jammed two Lugers in the pockets of his shorts and, with one more held in each hand, swung the door fully open with his foot.

Silently, he stepped through the door and slipped behind a stack of wooden pallets. Peeking over the top, he reconfirmed the position of the two men. Then, with pistols held outstretched, he rounded the corner.

He felt for the safety when his stomach knotted. *Which way is off?* For a moment he panicked imagining himself bringing the weapon to bear as one of those men did the same, only to find his gun wouldn't fire.

He was relieved to find the safety was, indeed, off as he fired three shots at each man. Both men collapsed without firing back. He then took the machine gun off his shoulder and pressed the trigger with it pointed at the closest man—nothing happened. Luckily, he hadn't had to use it. He flipped the safety lever, more confident now that the gun would fire when needed.

After pulling the bodies behind the stack of pallets, he stripped the fatigues off the man closest to his size and donned them along with the man's hat. He reloaded the first two Lugers and took both guards' silenced guns. *These might come in handy.*

With the hat pulled down low over his face, he eased up to the main door leading to the Sanctuary above.

"Okay, everyone up, we're going down to the harbor," he heard a voice say.

Preston?

"You traitorous asshole," he heard Mimi say.

"Sticks and stones..." he replied with a smile. "Now, get moving. Otherwise, I'll just shoot you right now, though I'd prefer not to have to lug your fat ass out of here. Then again, I might not shoot to kill. I may choose to shoot you in the stomach or groin so that you spend your last few minutes in agony. Now move!"

Dawson heard the sound of feet shuffling and footsteps on the stairs. He ducked back behind the pallets and a minute later saw several armed men march the team into the harbor area, where they were forced to stand at the edge of the dock facing the water.

"Take a few minutes to think of any last words you'd like to say. The fun will begin in a few minutes, once my men find Dawson. Oh, and when you're shot, please try to fall into the water so that we don't have to deal with you." Two more men appeared carrying Nigora's body and tossed it into the harbor.

Those bastards. Dawson clenched his teeth. *I'm about to have some last words for you, Preston.*

CHAPTER 66

Through the windows of the conference area on the second floor, Dawson could see Quint and Colin handcuffed and guarded by a couple of armed men. He emerged from behind the pallets and boldly strode across the dock behind the group to the stairs leading to the conference room.

No one paid any attention due to his confident manner. Dawson climbed the steps, pausing twice to rest his aching leg. When he reached the conference room, he pushed the unlatched door open with his foot and walked in. Seeing his black fatigues, the two guards assumed he was with them—until he took them both down using the silenced weapons.

"About time. You take time out for lunch?" Quint asked.

"Yeah, and then a short nap." Dawson walked over to the glass holding his weapon up in plain view and waved at one of the armed men on the dock. "You keep trying to be a comedian, and I may just leave you handcuffed."

Rifling through the dead guard's pockets, he found a knife and cut off their flex cuffs. Quint grimaced from the pain in his broken arm. "Why didn't they take you two down on the dock with the rest of the team?"

"They were saving me, and hopefully you, for Syndy. As for Colin here, I'm guessing with his injured leg, they left him intending to carry him down to the dock later," Quint said. "They planned to kill the rest of the team once you were found. Then the two of us were going back to face Syndy."

"Well, I for one, don't much care for that particular plan but I have one of my own. It goes sort of like this—we kill all of them and feed their bodies to the sharks."

"Simple... but effective. I like it," Quint replied with a laugh.

Quint donned one of the guards' uniforms, pulling the shirt on over his sling. They handed Colin a rifle and the two men left the conference room. Dawson returned the way he had come and Quint took the overhead catwalk with a rifle slung over his shoulder. One of the men below noticed him and he waved with his good arm while continuing on to the far end where he stopped to wait.

When he was certain that no one was looking, he slid awkwardly down onto his stomach. Once in position, he waited until Dawson appeared below, at which time Quint began firing at the armed black-suited figures below.

Six fell before they realized what was happening. When those remaining turned to take cover, Dawson opened up at point-blank range, killing all of the men on the dock except for Preston. Mimi snatched his weapon away and then pointed it directly at Preston's head. "Please, do something stupid so I have the excuse I need to put you down," she said through her teeth.

"See, that's the difference between us. I wouldn't need a reason," Preston smirked.

Dawson glanced up at Quint, who pointed at their ship docked at the end of the harbor where Preston's men had been loading crates of supplies and equipment they were planning to steal along with the team's ship. While the rest of the team scrambled to retrieve weapons from the dead men, Dawson ran toward the ship, boarded at the stern, and quickly climbed to the higher deck.

He eased down the outside companionway and spotted a man crouched near the end shooting at Quint. Without breaking stride, Dawson leveled his pistol and fired twice, hitting the man in the back of the head and between his shoulders.

When Dawson reached the man's position, he spotted two more of Preston's men crouched on the bow. He fired two shots at the closest and two more at the second man. They both went down but he still fired two more shots into each.

Marcia picked up a gun and approached the forward end of the ship along the starboard side where she took down two more while Dakota got three more on his side, ducking to avoid fire from the top of the ship.

Dawson met Dakota at the front of the ship. "We still have one in the wheelhouse. I'm headed for the bridge. You check out the engine room." Dakota nodded and walked away.

Dawson limped around the backside of the ship and then up to the bridge, where he slowly opened the door. Hearing him enter, the man studying the controls responded without looking up, "I got the engines fired up. We'll be ready to get underway as soon as Preston gives the word."

With the AK-47 pointed at the back of the man's head, Dawson replied, "I don't think so. Not unless you want the last thing you see in this world to be your brains splattered over that console. Now step back and get on the floor on your stomach. Do it now!" he yelled as the man nearly fell where he stood.

Dawson quickly frisked him, then ordered him to get up. With the man's shirt collar bunched in his left fist, he jammed the AK-47's barrel into his lower back and marched him out of the ship and onto the dock.

A few minutes later, Dakota emerged from the engine room prodding the last of the attackers along before him. He noticed Quint beside Kira, who was lying on the concrete dock with her head cushioned in his lap.

"You don't look so good," Quint said.

"I might have pre-eclampsia. They wanted me to fly back this morning, but Preston's thugs shot down the sea plane."

"Let's get you upstairs and we'll get another plane on the way," Quint replied.

"Okay, I need to take my blood pressure," Kira said.

Dakota scooped her up and carried her up the stairs. "Follow me. She wants to go to her pod," he said when he saw Colin saw hobbling toward them.

CHAPTER 67

The team returned to the Sanctuary from the harbor, with Mimi prodding Preston before her. While she stood guard, the men took Kira to her pod.

Dakota set Kira down on the bed where Colin fussed over her and helped take her blood pressure. She then dragged herself into the bathroom to do another urine-protein test.

"What's the verdict?" Colin asked when she returned a minute later.

"Not good. Both are high. Much higher than the last time I checked. I think that maybe I—" Kira stopped and Colin saw her start to collapse. Dakota lunged forward, catching her before she fell. As he gently lowered her to the floor, she began convulsing.

"Shit!" Colin grabbed her head and opened her mouth. "Help," he yelled as he rolled her onto her left side and cushioned her head, checking to make sure she wasn't biting her tongue. "Hand me a blanket or towel." Quint came running into the room, ripped the blanket off the bed, and handed it to him. Colin folded it and placed it gently beneath her head.

"She needs medical help. Grab the satphone and get another seaplane headed here—now!" Quint yelled. Dakota bolted from the room and returned a moment later holding the phone. "What should I tell them is the problem?" Quint asked.

"Pre-eclampsia, maybe eclampsia by now. Both she and the baby are in danger." Quint nodded and left the room to make the call. When he returned a few minutes later, Kira was no longer convulsing and appeared to be conscious but disoriented. "You get us a plane?" Colin asked when he saw Quint back off of the phone.

"Be here as fast as they can, maybe an hour but could be two."

"We need get her doctor on the line," Colin said. "Check Kira's cell phone in the drawer by our bed for the number."

Quint handed Kira's cell phone along with the satphone to Colin before heading for the door. "I'll be back in a few minutes."

When Quint entered the dining hall where the rest of the team were now gathered, Mimi had Preston backed into a corner, the gun pointed in his face. Quint turned to Marcia and whispered, "I think we're seeing the full fury of a woman scorned. While I don't blame her one bit, make sure that her emotions don't lead her to doing something stupid." Marcia nodded and continued to keep an eye on the two.

"I loved you, how could you do this?"

"You meant nothing to me," Preston replied. "You were just a tool."

As Mimi raised her rifle to strike Preston, he lunged forward and jerked it from her grasp. Preston fired off a wild shot at Marcia, who ducked behind one of the tables just as Dawson entered the room with his own gun pointed directly at Preston.

"Don't move," Dawson said in a steely, calm voice. Preston froze and looked up as he heard his name.

Ignoring the command, Preston turned toward Dawson while lowering his weapon. "Brother, glad you're here. There's been a misunderstanding. Syndy forced me to work with them. She would have killed

me if I didn't pretend to help. Thank God it's over,"
Preston gushed.

"Preston, don't even—"

"Don't even what? Thank my brother, my own flesh
and blood I—"

"Drop the gun, Preston," Dawson ordered as he saw
his brother's arm slowly rising.

Mimi had moved slightly to the right and was now
partially blocking Dawson's shot. "You can't think that
I, Preston, your very own brother would—" Preston
paused as he jerked his arm up, but Dawson was
ready.

"Drop," he yelled. Mimi fell to her knees, clearing
the path between the two brothers, and Dawson sent a
bullet into Preston's stomach. He stood upright with a
look of disbelief on his face before slumping to the
floor, the rifle falling away from him.

"We may have had the same mother, but you're not
my brother. Never were," Dawson said. Mimi rose to
her feet and walked, slowly at first, and then more
quickly toward Preston. She was staring into his face
as she saw his right hand reach toward a pistol lying a
few feet away. Without pause, Mimi stooped and
retrieved the weapon and looked straight at Preston
while raising it.

Marcia walked up beside Mimi and put her hand on
the gun barrel, keeping her from raising it far enough
to fire. "Mimi, don't do this. He's gut shot. This far
from any serious medical help, he's a dead man." Mimi
didn't resist when Marcia gently took the gun away.

"I'm shot! I can't believe it. My own brother shot me.
I'm dying." Preston lay on the floor clutching his
stomach, his hands drenched in blood, more pouring
from the gunshot wound. His face was white as he lay
there writhing in pain and moaning.

"You bastard! All this time, you played me for a fool.
You betrayed the team, your own brother, and used
me. It was all a sham. I can't believe I fell for it, that I

actually believed you. And I even tried to get you on the team," Mimi said, the tears flowing down her face. "You're every bit as bad as Dawson said, and then some. I just wish I'd had the honor of sending you to hell. I hope that there's a special place there for scum like you, Preston, where you can burn for all eternity."

"Mimi, I'm sorry... for everything. I'm so sorry," Preston said, his voice nearly a whisper. "Help me, please help me. I don't want to die. God, I'll change if you just let me live."

Dawson walked over to him. "It's a little late."

"Don't say that. God, don't let me die now. I don't know why I was the way I was, but please forgive me, brother."

Dawson stood beside Mimi in silence for a while before Dawson spoke. "I forgive you, Preston. I forgive you and hope God grants you the mercy you don't deserve."

"It hurts so bad," Preston moaned, his voice barely loud enough to hear. "And you, Mimi, can you forgive me?"

"Yes," she replied, a stream of tears sliding down her cheeks. For several more minutes, he lay there, a certain calmness descending on him.

"Then I'm ready. I'm so sleepy but I think I'm ready." Preston spoke his final words and his body went limp.

CHAPTER 68

An hour later, Kira lay on a stretcher as the men carried her down to the harbor dock where the seaplane awaited them. Once Kira and Colin were on their way to Miami, the team headed back to the dining room.

"Where's Leo?" Quint asked.

"Preston's buddies tied him up and tossed him into that inflatable. I guess he's still on the beach," Mimi said.

"Then he's probably ready to be rescued and certainly hungry by now. Dakota, would you mind checking on him? In case there's still more of Preston's buddies roaming around, go armed. Call if you need help." Dakota grabbed a rifle and a radio before heading out the door. Quint headed toward the coffee pot, where the rest of the team was gathered.

"Hell of a mess, partner." Dawson handed Quint an empty cup.

"That it is." Quint poured himself some coffee and stirred in vanilla creamer while he thought. "Item one is the pile of bodies lying all over the place. What are your thoughts on dealing with them?"

"Stick to my plan. Load 'em up on the trawler, steam a few miles south, and feed 'em to the sharks, just like I said," Dawson replied.

Quint laughed. "You were serious."

"Better believe," Dawson replied in a flat voice.

"What about Preston?" Quint asked.

"What about him? He's gone. I think a burial at sea is fitting."

"I'm just glad it's over." Marcia dropped into a chair, cradling her hand with the two broken fingers.

"But it's not," Quint replied.

"Huh?"

"We still have to deal with Syndy and any of her men who are still on the island. It's well past time to put an end to her nonsense," Quint said.

The doctor spoke to the nurse who had just finished taking Kira's vitals. "Her blood pressure is one sixty-five over one fifteen. Between that, the elevated protein level in her urine, the convulsion, swelling of her extremities, and other symptoms, she's in eclampsia."

"What do we do?"

"No choice—we'll have to induce labor."

"But won't that put the baby at risk?"

"At week thirty-five, the baby's got a better than ninety-five percent chance of survival. Actually, after week thirty-four, its chances are about as good as a full-term baby."

"Isn't there some other choice?"

"I wish there were. Do I have your permission?"

Colin paused for a moment, perspiration forming on his forehead as he looked at Kira. "You're the boss."

Kira's face was drawn tight both from the pain and fear for her unborn child. "If you say that's what we have to do, then do it," she quietly replied.

The doctor placed his hand on Kira's shoulder. "It's going to be all right. I promise to do everything humanly possible to help you... and the baby."

CHAPTER 69

"If any of Preston's boys survived, they're still on the island," Quint said.

"We got a good head count before things got ugly. We're pretty sure there were twenty-four, but I saved the UCAV video so you can play it back to confirm our count," Mimi said. "With the one I nailed offshore, the two dead in the water with the inflatables, and the two prisoners, there should be twenty-one more lying around the island."

Quint just shook his head and laughed, "Well, it's pretty obvious you didn't need us. Since you ladies did the heavy stuff, we'll go recon and get a body count so we know if we have any survivors."

"I'm afraid it's not quite that simple," Dawson said. Quint looked up at him. "Two more boatloads of men arrived when I was playing commando down in the harbor."

"But we took care of them here in the sanctuary or down in the harbor," Marcia said.

"Maybe, but we'll still need to sweep the entire island to make sure," Quint said. "Mimi, launch one of the drones and fly surveillance while we do a sweep. You can radio us if you spot anything."

"Can't I just shoot them?" she asked.

Quint shot her a surprised look but she wasn't smiling and made no reply.

"Dawson, your leg wound has to be killing you so you stay here." Quint was surprised when he didn't argue. "Marcia, come with me. We'll find Dakota and Leo and do a sweep of the island."

Marcia led the way to the armory, where she grabbed an AA-12 shotgun and Quint loaded an M-4 carbine and a pistol. He then picked up two more rifles and a bag of spare ammo. "Could you carry these?" Marcia nodded. "Give me a second," Quint said and stepped into the kitchen, where he filled a bag with snacks and a couple of bottles of water. The two then headed for the stairs.

They found Mimi in the hangar readying the Predator. "Once you get the drone in the air, help us find Dakota and Leo." Mimi nodded. "Then we'll search the island."

They spotted Leo and Dakota before they reached the end of the air strip. Quint handed over the bag of food and Leo tore into it. "Any problems?"

"We ran into two more and took care of them," Dakota replied while Leo stuffed his face. Quint went on to explain the plan to sweep the island.

Two hours later, they had located three more of Preston's men. When they refused to surrender, Quint radioed Mimi, who took care of them with the drone. After completing a cursory sweep of the island, Quint and the rest of the ground team returned to the base while Mimi continued patrolling with the drone.

The team was sprawled in the dining room, some eating, the rest recovering from their exhaustion. Dakota entered with Leo hobbling in behind. Dawson greeted them, "Hey, guys. There's more sandwiches over on the counter." Leo bolted for the food. Armed with a plate full of sandwiches and bottles of water, they found Mimi in the drone control room.

"Sandwich?" Quint offered.

"No thanks. I managed to choke one down earlier to steady my queasy stomach. Guess I'm still feeling the adrenaline rush. How did it go?" Mimi asked.

"Well, we found pieces of what we judged to be the men a missile hit. Then we found some on the stairway, the airstrip, and the beach. With those that you just shot and the ones Kira killed in the inflatables, we count twenty-two."

Quint turned to Mimi. "We jury-rigged a temporary door for the one they blew in the hangar to give us time to regroup. You did a hell of a job." Then noticing her face, he asked, "Mimi, you okay?"

Mimi looked beat, "Yeah, Quint, but it was tough. I wouldn't have believed we could have done it. I guess in a situation like that you don't think or have time to worry—you just react. But now that it's over, I'm drained. That ... and sick about Nigora. That bastard."

"Look, you've done plenty. Land your drone and then go get some rest. We'll take it from here."

"No, I have to stay and help," Mimi protested.

Quint sighed. "You're being ridiculous. Go! Now! That's an order."

Reluctantly, Mimi taxied the drone to the hangar and then headed toward her pod. Just before she exited the mess hall she heard Dawson's voice. "I just finished reviewing the UCAV video. Their headcount was right. Looks like we still got two more unaccounted for."

Mimi stopped and started back. Seeing her, Quint yelled, "You-go-now!" She hesitated for a moment and then left the room.

Mimi returned as it was nearly dusk.

"Okay, which drone you want to use?"

"You pick."

"I guess I'll go with the Reaper."

"Okay, we'll help you taxi it out." Quint and Dakota grabbed their weapons and followed Mimi back up to the hangar. As they ascended the stairway, each stepped over a body lying sprawled across the landing.

Dakota headed to open the door to stand guard once they entered the hangar.

Quint helped Mimi prep the UCAV and taxi it out onto the strip. "We'll lock things up and stand guard until you have it in the air."

"Thanks," Mimi said and headed back down to the control center while Quint and Dakota headed outside, where they stood guard patiently. Finally, they heard the sound of the engines starting and a minute later, the drone was airborne. Dakota punched the button to close the hangar and they headed back down to the control center to join Mimi.

CHAPTER 70

Before midnight, Mimi spotted the remaining men and engaged them in a one-sided firefight. It was the first time that Quint had seen her in action with the drone. "I'm impressed," Quint said. A few minutes later, Dakota had it back inside the hangar.

The next morning, they all gathered for breakfast. With Quint's broken arm, Marcia's broken fingers, and Dawson's wounded leg, they were hurting but had survived. Quint refilled his coffee cup and decided it was time to address the team.

"I want to congratulate all of you for a job well done." Quint paused as everyone followed him with a round of applause.

"I would like to ask for a moment of silence as we remember Nigora." The room remained silent, with some sporadic weeping, until Quint finally continued speaking.

"Mimi managed to find what we believe to be the rest of Preston's crew. However, since we can't be certain, we will need to be cautious for the next few days."

Dawson caught his attention by tapping on the side of his coffee cup with a spoon. "With all that's been going on, I haven't had time to tell you about my little discovery. When Preston and his goons were hot on my butt, I grabbed some scuba gear and jumped into the harbor. When they spotted me and sent a wave of lead into the water, I was in a bind. I found a tunnel that led out of the harbor. Turns out that it led me all the way to a cave which adjoins our warehouse."

"Fascinating," Leo said sarcastically.

"No, what's fascinating is why I risked my life and nearly drowned to save your fat ass." Dawson paused to glare at him for a moment before continuing. "But what's even more fascinating is what I found inside that cave. A stash of Nazi gear along with a whole bunch of wooden crates filled with... gold bars."

A collective gasp filled the room. "You're shitting me," Leo said in astonishment.

"No, I'm not and if you'll follow me, I'll be happy to show you." The entire team jumped to their feet and followed Dawson as he hobbled down the stairs to the warehouse and showed them the hole he had cut into the warehouse wall. As the team filed into the cave, one by one, there just as Dawson had described was a row of crates with one open and the gleam of gold illuminated by their flashlights. Another collective gasp rose from the team.

When they were finished oohing and aahing, everyone had had the chance to hold one of the gold bars in their hands, and Dawson had grown weary of the accolades, Quint herded them all back to finish their meeting.

"Many thanks to you, Dawson, for saving our butts as well as finding a truly impressive treasure. I guess one thing on our future agenda will be what to do with it."

"I have a good friend who works at the Ferrari dealership in Miami. I'm sure he can help."

Marcia shook her head. "Leo, I know you're joking because not only is that gold not ours, it's Nazi gold. It was most certainly stolen, perhaps even from the mouths of those poor Jews slaughtered in the holocaust."

Quint was amazed when Leo actually blushed, a first to the best of Quint's knowledge, and actually seemed to agree. "Well, we don't have to decide now, so everyone give some thought to what to do with it," Quint said. "That leaves one remaining item... Syndy."

Quint continued, his eyes narrow and his voice firm. "It's clear that she's determined to get revenge and is simply not going away. I'm tired of letting her choose the battlefield—it's time for us to go on the offensive. Problem is, we don't know where she is."

"You leave it to me. I'll find out where that bitch is," Dawson said and left the room. He entered the empty storage room, which had been pressed into service as the "brig." Seated in the room were the two remaining prisoners from the attack party, their arms and legs tied to those of the chair. Leaving the door open, he walked over and took a seat before them without speaking.

From outside the two prisoners could hear what they believed to be one of their comrades being questioned. Each time Dakota would ask a question, Leo would answer, "I'm not telling you assholes anything." Then Dakota would deliver a hard punch to one of their dead comrades tied to a chair as Leo grunted. This continued until Dakota finally fired several rounds into the lifeless body. "Next," he yelled.

Dawson smiled at the two prisoners and then began, "Eeny, meeny, miny, moe." He picked the man on his right and wheeled his chair outside.

A half hour later, he was back in the dining room with the rest of the team. He poured himself a fresh cup of coffee and sat down at the table.

"Dakota and Leo, good acting job. They told us what we need to know. As we suspected, the attack force was launched from the *Syntillate*. They were operating as a bunch of tourists on a dive trip. The plan was for her to stand by for forty-eight hours in the event that her goons were unable to communicate with her, so she can't be too far away."

"Good work," Quint said. "Since Mimi saw the inflatables approach from the west and according to Kira, the ones that she engaged were trying to escape in that same direction, it's safe to assume that's where we should start our search. Of course, Cuba is a big island and it could take quite a while to find her sh—"

"Maybe not," Dawson interrupted and outlined his plan. When he was finished, Quint spoke.

"Excellent. I think that's the perfect solution. Mimi, can you ready the Hawk?"

"Happy to," she replied.

"Dawson, it's your plan so you should take charge of putting the rest of it together," Quint said.

Dawson nodded. "Dakota, dig us up a couple of bricks of C-4 while I round up the rest of what we'll need. Then bring Marcia and meet me down in the harbor workshop." Dawson limped out of the room headed for the warehouse to gather the supplies.

Dakota arrived in the workshop to find Dawson soldering. Once he had put the finishing touches on the wiring harness and circuit board, he looked up and said, "Perfect timing. Let's go down to the dock where their remaining inflatables are. Marcia, bring our prisoners and meet us down there in ten minutes. Leave them cuffed and hooded. Oh, and bring a knife along."

Dawson backed out from beneath the inflatable console holding the remains of a roll of duct tape. "Everything's ready and I see our main players are about to arrive." Marcia was prodding men along, barking orders as they stumbled along the dock, unable to see. As they approached, Dawson removed their hoods. Marcia handed Dakota the knife and he cut the plastic cuffs from their hands.

"You told us that you knew how to find your way back to Syndy's ship. Is that true?"

The prisoners nodded as if one. "Okay, then it's your lucky day. We're feeling generous today, so we're going

to let you go. All I expect in return is for you to take
Syndy a message." The men glanced at one another,
relieved that the death they had assumed was at hand
wasn't.

"Uh... sure. What do you want us to tell her?" the
larger of the men asked.

Dawson looked at Quint who then spoke up. "Tell
her we're coming. It ends now."

"That's it?"

"Yep," Quint replied. "Now you best get on your way
before we change our minds. Go!" The men scrambled
into the inflatable and a minute later had made it
down the channel and were out in the open sea headed
west. "Care to join me back in UCAV control?" Dawson
asked.

"By all means," Quint replied as they all headed
back inside.

They found Mimi at the control station monitoring
the drone. The video screen before her displayed a
bird's eye view of the inflatable as it ran down the
channel. The team pulled up chairs and sat watching.
"How far away do you think the ship is from here?"
Mimi asked.

"I'm guessing no more than twenty miles," Dawson
replied. "With those calm seas, they should be there
soon."

Sure enough, forty minutes later, they saw
Syntillate in the distance. A short time later, the black
inflatable approached the ship, which slowed and
opened a door at its stern. A ramp was then deployed
and the inflatable ran halfway up before it stopped
and the ramp was retracted. A minute later, the door
closed.

"Showtime," Dawson said. "Care to do the honors?"

Quint shook his head. "Nope, it's your idea. You get
to be the master of ceremonies. Just make sure you
give the guys in the inflatables a chance to get above
decks to at least give them a fighting chance."

Dawson picked up the radio mic for the drone communication module. "*Syntillate, Syntillate*, this is Sanctuary control. Do you copy?"

"Uh... this is *Syntillate*. With whom am I speaking?"

"An old friend of Syndy's. Have her come to the bridge. I need to tell her something that she's dying to hear. But in the meantime, I suggest you order your crew to abandon ship...now."

A few minutes later, the ship's captain handed Syndy a portable VHF radio and her mechanical voice erupted from the radio speaker in a demanding tone. "Who is this?"

"Syndy, is that any way to speak with an old friend?" Dawson said, a wide grin on his face.

"What old friend?"

"You don't know? It can't be that hard as I don't believe you have many now that your old buddy Hester has gone to the great beyond. Why, it's Dawson."

There was a long pause before she replied. "Dawson? I thought... I mean..."

"You thought I was dead. Nope, I'm afraid your boys just weren't up to the job. I can only imagine how disappointed you must be."

"I doubt that. And Quint?"

"Right here beside me."

"Where is here?" Syndy said in her mechanical voice.

"Roll your ugly charred ass out on the port side of the bridge and I'll show you. I promise not to shoot you."

Dawson turned to Mimi, "Bring the Hawk down and do a flyby down the port side of the ship. Keep the video locked on the ship's bridge." Mimi nodded and put the drone into a steep descent. On the monitor, they could see the door open below and Syndy emerge. A moment later, the drone flew by a few feet away.

"Cute drone. What's the point?"

Dawson handed Quint the mic. "The point is, do you remember what I told you the last time we were together?"

"Quint?"

"Very good. Now answer my question." He smiled as he noticed the crew emerge from below decks, seeming to be checking life rafts.

"I honestly don't recall anything you've had to say any more than I can recall the color of the last insect I smashed."

"Well, Syndy, I'm hurt, I really thought you'd remember. But since you don't, allow me to repeat it for you. I told you to crawl back into your hole... that the next time I saw your ugly evil-assed face would be the last. I promised to kill you on sight. Well, I count this as our third and final meeting."

"And what do you plan to do, talk me to death or annoy me with your remote-controlled toy? I didn't notice any armament on it."

"Don't need any. I sent it with your boys. You always liked to play with fire. I'm about to arrange for you to play with it for eternity. Hope you enjoy our little surprise." Quint nodded to Mimi, who keyed a series of commands into the drone control unit. Seconds later, the drone transmitted a command to the unit Dawson had attached to two bricks of C-4 and placed beneath the console of the inflatable.

The explosion blew out the upper decks of the yacht. Miraculously the hull remained intact, preventing the sea from pouring in. The yacht slowed and then came to a complete stop as the stern settled lower in the water. The panicked crew began tossing over the life rafts and jumping off the decks into the warm waters of the Caribbean.

Quint keyed the mic again. "Like our surprise?"

"Not as much as the one I've got in store for you."

Uncertain what she meant, Quint chose not to pursue it. "Goodbye, Syndy. Say hello to Hester when you get to hell."

"We'll see about that."

Mimi made another pass with the drone alongside the yacht. As it approached, Syndy lifted the blackened claw of her right hand and used the bones of her remaining fingers to pluck away the mask, which fell to the deck and shattered.

On the monitor, the team could see the horrific face which had been concealed by the porcelain mask. As the drone continued to circle they could see Syndy refuse the efforts of the crew to lower her into a life raft.

Syndy wheeled herself back inside, refusing to admit that her ship was sinking. She made it into her stateroom and closed the door. Through the expanse of windows and billowing smoke, she could see the crew loading into the life rafts below while the drone continued to buzz overhead.

"Damn you, Quint! Damn you to hell, Dawson," she screamed.

An explosion rocked the boat. In an odd quirk of fate, far below in the bowels of the ship, the enormous fuel tank containing thousands of gallons of fuel had created a raging furnace. A burning hell floating upon the sea.

One by one, the decks above melted and collapsed. Syndy could feel the ship shudder in its death throes.

Very much alive, Syndy plummeted into the sea of angry orange flames to land in the burning fuel tank. Her mouth opened and an unearthly, moaning scream burst forth, continuing through her dying breath.

Though she lived only seconds before the flames consumed her, it seemed an eternity. Long enough to experience the totality of the pain that she had caused to so many. Long enough to see their faces as the life ebbed from her body. Long enough to see a black hole open in the fiery cauldron and see hell an instant before plummeting into its very depths.

The drone continued to circle in the sky overhead. Quint saw the upper decks when they collapsed and thought he caught a glimpse of Syndy's blackened face before she tumbled from her wheelchair into the raging inferno below.

An enormous cloud of steam erupted as the yacht settled lower in the water and the sea was finally unleashed to quench the burning hulk. A half-hour later, only the bow section remained above water.

Mimi made a low pass with the drone and, at Dawson's suggestion, wiggled the wings as a parting gesture to her. A few minutes later, the ship was gone and only a handful of the crew remained, flailing about in the water trying to understand what had just happened and watching the drone disappear in the distance.

"What do you reckon she meant about a 'surprise in store for us?'" Quint asked Dawson.

"Probably just screwing with you."

EPILOGUE

An hour before sunset, the team gathered back at the Sanctuary in an open space on the far side of the air strip. A simple cross stood at the head of the grave that Dakota and Leo had dug. Later they planned to add a small engraved granite marker at the foot.

Quint was standing in front of the gathered team. "Since Nigora has no immediate family, it made the most sense to bury her here, where her life ended. I'll now begin our memorial service." He went on to read a scripture and then Dawson led a short prayer.

Once the sun had set, they all made their way back to the Sanctuary to gather once again. "Though we don't have to decide right now, we will need to address the issue of the Nazi gold which Dawson stumbled across."

"I think we might as well discuss it right now," Leo said. "Why don't we just divide it up amongst the entire team?"

Mimi gave him a sour look. "Leo, sometimes you can really be a jerk. That's not our gold. We should give it back."

"To who, Ms. High-and-Mighty?" Leo shot back.

"As much as it pains me to admit it, he raises a good point," Quint said. "All of the original owners are no doubt dead. And even if not, how do we find out who originally owned the gold that was melted down into all that bullion."

"Yeah, and finding their heirs, at least legitimate ones, would be virtually impossible," Leo eagerly added.

After a brief silence, Mimi rose to speak. "I've given this a great deal of thought. I agree we shouldn't keep it. I also agree that finding the original owners is impossible. But I would hate to see the government—be it ours, the Cubans, or the Europeans—end up taking a big portion if not all of it to squander away on pork or siphon off into their own pockets. So, I propose that we set up a foundation in the name of those who have died helping us."

"You mean Nigora and Boris?" Dawson asked.

"And Willy," Mimi added.

"I assume we'll be excluding Preston," Leo asked with a straight face but then broke into a smile as Mimi made a rude gesture.

"How would this foundation work?" Quint asked.

"We keep the gold's existence a secret. Then we set up a board to select individuals who have suffered oppression and are deserving of a new start and help them. With all that gold, we could do this for many years to come. I was thinking that one possible project could be in Somalia."

"I like that idea," Dawson said. "It fits perfectly with our philosophy in establishing the Sanctuary."

"I agree," Dakota added, "and propose that Mimi be the point person charged with setting up the foundation and selecting its board." He made a motion and after a quick vote, it passed unanimously.

"Okay, Mimi, your idea is approved. In a couple of weeks, we'll meet to discuss the details of how it will work. After our war with Syndy's goons and dealing with the shambles the place is in, we should all take some time off to decompress.

"Evie has given me strict instructions that I'm to be back in Key West by the end of the week and—"

"And you're not man enough to disobey," Dawson said with a grin.

The sun was barely up the next morning when the seaplane pulled inside the hangar. Dakota helped Dawson up the steps with his stiff leg. Quint and Marcia followed close behind. "You guys be okay?" Quint asked the three remaining team members.

"No, Dad. We got it covered," Dakota said with a wink to Leo and Mimi. "We can't all fit on this trip anyhow but there's a few things that need to be finished. You and Dawson go lick your wounds and we'll finish up in time to fly back on the plane tomorrow."

"Say hi to Kira and Colin," Mimi said as Dakota closed the door.

They watched the plane taxi out of the harbor before closing the door and filing back inside. "If you two can take care of the odds and ends, I'll cook us up a royal meal."

"But nothing weird," Mimi said without a smile as Leo laughed over his shoulder on his way to the kitchen.

"It's hard to believe that less than twenty-four hours ago, we were fighting for our lives," Mimi said. "I'm glad we've finally seen the last of Syndy."

Dakota nodded. "That was a close one. I hope that—" His last words were lost in the blinding light and deafening roar of a massive explosion. He looked up in time to see the entire roof of the cavern come crashing down.

Colin walked into Kira's room to find her nursing their baby. He kissed her on the forehead first and then the baby. "Well, you look fully recovered."

"I am. Isn't she beautiful?" Colin nodded his reply and then turned as he heard a voice behind him.

"Okay to come in?"

Kira looked up to see Jenny standing there alongside a dark-skinned boy. "Jenny!" Kira yelled without thinking and started the baby crying. Jenny came to her bedside while she calmed it.

"She's beautiful. What's her name?"

"Ava Nigora," Kira replied.

"Who's your friend, Jenny?"

"That's Jamal, from Somalia," Colin said. "But a better question is, how is it that he's here?"

Jenny placed her hand on Jamal's head and stroked his hair. "Brad and I are adopting him. Rogers pulled some strings so that he could stay with us while we jump through all the hurdles."

"So I take it that you and Brad—"

"Things are fine. Our little kidnapping episode helped bring things into focus. Once we were free from the pirates, the first meal, the first shower, the first set of clean clothes, everything felt extraordinary. I felt like I'd been reborn.

"We met Jamal while being held captive. Since he had no family, Quint agreed to let him come back with us. Brad and I invited him to become part of our family."

Throughout the exchange, Jamal had been toeing the carpet with his left foot. "So, Jamal, what do you plan to do in your new life?"

Jamal looked up. "Play the piano."

Kira laughed. "So when is the rest of the team heading back?"

"The seaplane should have already picked them up and returned by now. In fact, this might be them calling now," Quint said as he answered his ringing phone.

Dawson started to say something but stopped when he heard the tone of Quint's voice.

"When? Are you sure? Any chance that some of them might have... I see. Thanks," Quint finished and hung up the phone in silence, a look of horror on his face.

"What... did something happen?" Dawson asked.

"That was the seaplane pilot. He just got back and—"

"Are they alright?"

"No, they're not. As he approached, he saw a massive explosion in the Sanctuary."

"Did Leo, Mimi, and Dakota make it out okay?"

"He didn't land. The entire place was demolished. All that was left was a big hole. They're all gone. They're dead."

The End

NOTE FROM FRANK

"Thanks so much for reading my fourth novel, *Tears of Coral*. I know that you have many choices of what to read and I truly appreciate your investment of time. If you did enjoy my book, please take a minute to place a review on **www.GoodReads.com,** the retailer's website, or on my own **www.FrankWilem.com**. Oh, and please tell your friends."

AUTHOR'S NOTES

The lighthouse referred to in *Tears of Coral* is actually the *Cape Guardafui (Ra's Asir) Light.*

During the final days of the Second World War, while Hitler's empire was crumbling, Nazi submarines smuggled millions of dollars worth of gold across the Atlantic to Argentina. This gold was for the express purpose of financing numerous high-placed Nazi officials in their post-war lives. An Argentine documentary, *Oro Nazi en Argentina (Nazi Gold in Argentina)* provides chilling details.
LINK:
http://www.independent.co.uk/news/world/americas/nazi-gold-shipped-by-uboat-to-argentina-532304.html

Though not widely publicized, it appears that toxic waste was indeed dumped off of the Somalia Coast. After the Indian Ocean tsunami of 1994, barrels of nuclear and toxic waste ended up on the beach, sickening and killing many of the local villagers.
LINKS:
http://www.aljazeera.com/news/africa/2008/10/2008109174223218644.html

http://www.infowars.com/is-toxic-waste-behind-somali-piracy/

According to Tom Oertling, a Texas A&M professor, "a notable pirate attack involved Julius Caesar. At age 25 and years before he became emperor of Rome, Caesar was captured by pirates and held for ransom. The pirates wanted 20 talents of silver (more than $500,000 in today's dollars) to be paid for his safe release.

"Caesar was deeply insulted and told them so – he said he was worth far more than that, at least 50 talents," Oertling explains. "He managed to escape and later had the pirates captured and eventually crucified."

LINK:
http://tamutimes.tamu.edu/2012/07/24/modern-day-pirates-here-to-stay/#.VACWbmd0x9A

ABOUT THE AUTHOR

Frank J. Wilem, Jr., is an entrepreneur living in Gulfport, Mississippi with his wife, Dee Dee, and daughter, Brittany. Frank's love for the sea blossomed during his high school years at West High in Torrance, California when a friend convinced him to snorkel off Lunada Bay in Palos Verde. When it was his turn to use the mask, one look beneath the chilly Pacific waters and he was hooked.

After graduating from Texas A&M with a Bachelor of Science in Electrical Engineering, the call of the ocean led him to the University of Miami where he earned a Masters degree in Ocean Engineering. Frank worked in the R&D departments for two Fortune 500 companies before his love of the ocean led him to join Computer Sciences Corporation at NASA's Stennis Space Center.

He left there to become a founder of Triton Systems, Inc., which he and his partners grew into a $100 million company and the nation's largest manufacturer of automatic teller machines. With the sale of Triton, Frank purchased his sportfish boat Vixen and pursued his passion for bluewater fishing. Most days he and Captain Eric Gill can be found in the northern waters of the Gulf of Mexico or the Bahamas, chasing billfish, tuna, wahoo and dolphin.

Tears of Coral is Frank's fourth book.